KHAN'S LEGACY

A novel in the History Detective Trilogy

by

David J Andrews

Also by the same author

Lobster Calypso

Endeavour's Legacy

History Detective Trilogy

Chasing Columbus

Bahamian Rhapsody

Dedication

To

My son Christopher
You will always be with us.

'Study the past if you would define the future'

Confucius

'In Xanadu did Kublai Khan
A stately pleasure home decree
Where Alph the sacred river ran
Through caverns measureless to man
Down to a sunless sea'

Samuel Taylor Coleridge

Prelude

Part One

East Africa Coastline
Malindi
The year 1294

Marco Polo was headed home; he'd been away over seventeen years serving his Asian Master, the Great Kublai Khan. He had left a boy and would return a man to tell of things no one from his world could imagine in their wildest dreams. He was incredibly proud of his homeland and couldn't wait to tell the world of his adventures in Asia. In doing so, his name would become synonymous with travel. Before sailing for Venice he had promised the Khan he would complete a secret task his master would entrust only to him.

The task had taken him from Asia across the Indian Ocean to Zanzibar and from there north to the great Kenyan estuary where he made landfall. Here, in a new and strange continent, he would complete his mission which was to ensure the Khan left a legacy that would underpin his Empire. He had given Marco two metal boxes; they were beyond value and required every possible measure to preserve what they contained for future generations.

He journeyed upstream, the jungle closing in on all sides. Eventually he found a suitable place to bury half of the Khan's legacy and having completed that task he headed back to the ocean. He intended to hide the remaining half of it on a tiny island in the Indian Ocean. After three days' hard sailing, he landed on a small beach covered by undergrowth right down to the shore and only visible at very close quarters.

This was the only voyage he wouldn't be able to talk about in his subsequent tales. His tasks now completed, he could return to his beloved Venice to help build its stature and prominence in the world.

Admiral Zheng He could hardly believe what he was seeing. The noonday sun was disappearing, night was replacing day. The crews of his armada looked to him for guidance. Trying to keep calm he ordered the sailors to their stations to furl all sails, and fasten themselves to anything fixed to the deck. In total darkness the ships rocked violently and the more daring men lit torches. Slowly they regained confidence, the world wasn't coming to an end but Zheng hadn't experienced anything like this before.

He was a pupil of the Mongol dynasty and had been chosen to educate the barbarian countries beyond the Mongolian borders by his Emperor, Zhu Di, the first to recognize the need to understand other countries' cultures. He regarded it as his first duty to the greatest Mongol ruler, Kublai Khan. To carry out the programme, he had assembled the world's largest ever fleet. It was to be an undertaking to exceed all his other achievements. Unfortunately, Zhu Di's rule ended in 1424 and his death put an end to the idea of a maritime expedition. The new Emperor, Zhu Zhanji, revived the project but on a smaller scale and Zheng He was again given command of it.

The Admiral looked apprehensively at the darkening sky; he was concerned for the safety of the legacy entrusted to him. The sky gradually lightened, illuminating the dark clouds with an ethereal glow; he wondered if this was God's final strike. He hadn't failed the Emperor totally, he had already deposited two of the three Artefacts entrusted to him, but what of the one he still had on board? His mind whirled as he thought of his own personal legacy - something he had done of his own volition that would be just as important to him as the Emperor's task.

During a voyage the previous year he'd established a group of trusted leaders in a monastery on a remote island called 'La Gomera' and named them, 'The Elders.' No one knew of his secret plan to engineer a world that would honour those who, like him, from humble birth had fought their way upwards to become powerful and revered. He hadn't left the Emperor's Artefacts with the new community; they needed to prove they understood his plans and find them from pointers left by certain historical leaders. He had still to deposit the remaining Artefact but that final task was in dire jeopardy.

Zheng sensed something more frightening was imminent. The eye of the storm had passed but worst was yet to come. They made slow progress towards land before the world exploded again. Zheng's eyes were seared by a flash of light and felt as though they were on fire. A comet twenty-six times brighter than the sun, screaming and blowing out the eardrums of the sailors had fallen near them and the howling wind ripped their main mast off. The world went black again.

Zheng regained consciousness in semi-darkness and staggered up the gangway to see that Zhang Li, an experienced captain, had managed to regain control of the terrified crew who were now trying to work the oars. The ship was moving towards land, but struck something hard and grounded. He realized he would have to act fast to salvage the Artefact before the vessel broke up. It took eight men to move the crate from his cabin, slowly they maneuvered it onto the deck and heaved it over the side attached by a rope to a small boat that towed it ashore; the Emperor's legacy was intact.

Prelude

Part Two

New Zealand
Poverty Bay
October 9ᵗʰ 1769

Captain James Cook, selected by the Admiralty for his exceptional navigational skills, thought Poverty Bay, off the North Island of New Zealand, a most suitable name for the harbour. It lacked any form of vegetation and had an inhospitable air about it. They were critically low on drinking water after the long voyage from Tahiti on *HMS Endeavour.*

His Mission was to map the entire coastline and prove that New Zealand was not the Southern Continent, to observe the transit of Venus, and claim the vast lands in that hemisphere for His Majesty the King. So far he had succeeded. On his first attempt to land, natives had attacked the landing party, four had been killed and three more captured. The Marines returned later to get the critical water supplies, this time there was no resistance.

Cook and his chief botanist, Joseph Banks, explored the terrain. On the top of a small hill Cook found a uniform pile of rocks, their sides interlinked with straight edges; no natural rock formation could ever look like that. He ordered marines to investigate and they began digging. They found a large iron casket, so heavy they needed to use lifting gear to get it out. There were Chinese characters on it and the date 1423. He ordered the casket to be put aboard *Endeavour.* He later established, from the Chinese script, that the casket had been put there by Admiral Zheng He and it required the finder to regard the casket as a legacy and re-bury it in nominated positions in different parts of the world. Cook accepted the responsibility to carry out the request.

Australia 1770

Three months later after his successful circumnavigation of New Zealand, Cook sailed to Botany Bay, so discovering Australia. He mapped its eastern coastline with its verdant and healthy looking topography and sailed steadily eastwards. The plan was to identify where the land ended, then head northwest. They made good progress and he noted the waves breaking further out to sea; he ordered a reduction in speed. The depth remained consistent so he decided to sail on through the night passing control of the ship to Lieutenant Molyneaux. In the early hours of the morning, on June 11th he was thrown from his cot by a violent Craaaack! The ship was held fast on a coral reef and settling down hard onto the sharp organisms, the ship's timbers splitting as they did so; there was little that could be done until the tide changed.

Land was at least eight leagues away and the odds on their survival weren't good. Cook ordered everything moveable be thrown overboard even the cannons. The casket he had taken from New Zealand he treated differently, he and his cabin boy Svente made the box watertight, then threw it overboard with the rest of the ballast. He wrote the precise coordinates into his diary. Cook despaired at what threatened to be an inglorious end to an otherwise successful exploration.

Through the great efforts of the crew, the ship was lifted from the coral reef with the rising tide. It was taking on too much water and clear they would sink long before they reached land. Cook resorted to fothering the ship, a process of pushing a spare sail under the damaged area of a broken hull to act as a huge bandage. Coated with wool and oakum it was fastened into place and, to their great relief, stabilized the ship. Eventually they made landfall in a river delta. He was amazed they hadn't sunk when he saw the bow had been ripped clean away revealing a gaping hole which would require major repair work.

Joseph Banks was delighted to find a tropical rain forest to explore. He'd never seen such flora and fauna. Cook gloomily calculated what would need to be done to set the *Endeavour* afloat. Cook regarded it as a matter of honour to carry out the wishes of a fellow explorer but he and Svente set to work to ensure the safety of his own legacy too.

Alaska January 1778

Cook's third and final voyage on *HMS Discovery* took him to the frozen wastelands of northern Alaska. He was commissioned to find the North Western Passage, said to connect the Pacific Ocean with the Atlantic. He shouldn't have agreed to undertake it. Everything he did seemed harder and he found himself constantly dreaming of his London home and beloved Yorkshire Moors. Only his commitment to leave his legacy as instructed kept him going. They had surveyed the harsh Alaskan landscape without finding an entry route to the Atlantic and now he headed west into Russian waters.

Wearily he went ashore with two trusted marines and Svente. In the most westerly point he could find they located a suitably flat, sheltered surface and cut into hard tundra. The work finished, he stood back and saluted, honour between the explorers was complete; his mission was accomplished. He made copious notes in his diary before passing it to Svente. To everyone's relief, he gave orders to set sail southwards, back to warmer climes. Cook had honoured a man he regarded as one of the world's most daring sailors. Instinctively he knew what he had done would be of value long after his death. The following February in 1779, after again sailing around the Pacific, he lay dead on the shores of Hawaii.

Chapter 1

Soufriere St Lucia
Present Day

The gentle breeze rustling the sails did little to cool the heat of the day as Guy Tresanton carefully navigated his yacht, *Hidalgo*, between rocky outcrops under the Twin Pitons on the south-western coast of St Lucia. He, his business partner Rose Lin, and their clients, an Australian couple, had been sailing around the more southerly Caribbean. After visiting twelve of the thirty Grenadine Islands in the past ten days, and fished for marlin and swordfish, they had steadily made their way back north. The return voyage had been exhilarating but he was glad to be heading home.

They made an unlikely looking team. Guy was just over six feet tall and had a mop of unruly sandy hair that obscured his wind-bronzed features. Rose, a petit Chinese girl, was shorter, much younger, and had long black hair secured at the nape of her neck with a crimson silk scarf. Having given up the rat-race to establish his own business here, Guy was determined to make a success of their venture. Rose came from a different background. Before meeting Guy, she had intended to be a detective but had become involved with him in a maelstrom of tumultuous events that had almost killed them. Despite these obvious differences, they had a wide range of skills that complimented each other perfectly, and contributed towards the progress of a moderately successful charter business. The company now owned two yachts, the *Hidalgo* and a smaller vessel currently undergoing engine repairs, called *Yellow Dragon*.

They had been drawn together initially after discovering their fathers were in the same field of psychiatry. Subsequent events served to bind them even closer. It was a comforting first for Guy to have a female friend without the spectre of sex and relationships becoming involved. They had gradually melded into an easy-going partnership that led, over time, into them using affectionate nick-names. Rose called him Bear and he called her Viper. There wasn't much Guy couldn't share with his partner, instinctively trusting her vision and instincts, whilst Rose saw

Guy as a rock in an increasingly fraught world. Their partnership also enabled them to fight a common enemy.

Six months had passed since their exhausting battle with a ruthless Chinese criminal named Zheng Wan, known to both friends and enemies as *The Teacher*. They had survived numerous brushes with death during a struggle with him for possession of a priceless Artefact called Drake's Shield. It was a conflict they had lost. His success meant he was now in possession of two of the four priceless Artefacts they both sought; the Columbus Cross and Drake's Shield. In addition he had earlier captured the iconic Sword of Islam, originally discovered by the English explorer William Dampier. Supported by a network of devoted followers and meticulous in his planning, he was always two steps ahead of them and well on his way to gaining the remaining Artefacts and thereby succeeding in his ambitions.

Though he never understood how it was possible, Guy found he was often able to access The Teacher's innermost thoughts; the information told him what the man was planning. Zheng Wan knew of the connection and regarded it as intolerable; it made Guy a marked man who must be destroyed. Guy and Rose had increasingly become exposed to The Teacher's growing strength and, following their frustrated efforts to secure Drake's Drum, had gratefully taken a sabbatical, glad of the time to recover from their bitter disappointment. They had their own lives to lead and this was what Guy really enjoyed, detached from the world's problems with only nature to contend with in the shape of wind and sea, and of course the occasional mechanical breakdown.

There were other problems. The Teacher was now President of the Elders; an organisation set up centuries before by the explorer Zheng He and dedicated to overseeing and guiding human affairs. From this powerful position, he fully intended to further his own ends by using their power and influence. The Members had recently realised his real motives and were beginning to fight back, but their retaliation had been compromised by a painful schism that had ruptured their unity and threatened to destroy them. The second problem was more personal. The fathers of both Guy and Rose were in the power of Zheng so anything they did needed to take that into account. A further worry was the mysterious disappearance of their policeman friend, Brian Montcalm, known to everyone as 'Monty', the Chief Inspector of Police in Bermuda.

The *Hidalgo*, a Southerly 135RS, forty-five feet long and custom-built, had been totally refitted after incurring significant damage in previous exchanges with The Teacher, and now sailed like a dream. Guy was already looking forward to the next charter even though he knew he would never escape his enemy's attention that was like an itch that wouldn't go away. He relaxed in an easy chair on the deck basking in the warmth of the sun and waiting for their guests to appear.

The itch returned with a vengeance from the most unlikely quarter, Rose. She emerged onto the deck wearing her standard uniform, torn denim shorts with a rumpled red tee shirt and crimson silk scarf in her hair. Her face wore a worried frown as she strode towards him. "Guy, we can't hide forever, our fathers need us," she said, the frown deepening. He was somewhat taken aback by her opening remark and wasn't so sure. "Don't you think they're safer if we aren't visible; you know how The Teacher reacts when he sees me? Besides someone would have contacted us from the Elders if we were needed, that was the deal."

"You're kidding yourself; you know our fathers are likely to be deep inside The Teacher's organisation. We have to find them… and besides what of Monty."

"He too told us to disappear. We said a year, Rose, it's been only eight months and if we get involved again it may make things worse. Our fathers must have The Teacher's trust to have survived this long, that is if they've survived at all. For all we know they could be dead."

"I can't believe you are saying that. Has the sea air gone to your head? We must do something," she said crossly.

"Do what, exactly, Viper?"

"Don't call me that it makes me even madder. We know his base is in Vietnam. We should strike there, catch him by surprise; he'll never expect it." Guy shook his head. "Even if we could find his headquarters, which I very much doubt; we'd be dead before we got within a hundred miles of it. Besides we only have it on second-hand information that he is based there. The Elders insist we maintain a low profile after Aruba, until they judge the time's right. They haven't let us down before. I had a personal message from Emerald, she was very insistent that we should keep away."

"Yes well, she isn't personally involved," replied Rose with feeling, "for all we know she could be working for the damned Teacher."

"Rubbish, she's done a lot for us Rose; you know that, she is also a link to The Whistler."

"You still believe that such a person exists?" replied Rose incredulously. "That's never made sense to me, why does he only whistle to you and not actually talk? If he's gone to the huge trouble of finding you, then why doesn't he give you detailed advice rather than just whistling at you for God's sake?"

"Rose, I've told you before, I don't know, but I do know what I hear. I sense it during the night, you know that. I know it sounds crazy but I've heard it a number of times, the whistle cadences wake me and there's no one there. It always delivers a warning. I just know the sounds exist. God! You're in a feisty mood today Viper, how about an early morning swim to cool off?" His suggestion was swept aside, she waved her hand in the air and her face became more animated. "And you are being impossible," she retorted. "We can't go on hiding like this after all we have put into the fight. Can't you see that, or has this lazy environment got to you? People's lives are at risk and it's too serious to believe in whistlers or ghosts who choose not to make themselves known to you." She was becoming ever more agitated and Guy again tried to calm her down. He took hold of her hand and drew her closer to him. "The risks are huge if he is a spy in The Teacher's circle," he said quietly. "We wouldn't want to lose his help, would we? I think we should wait a little longer."

"Very well, so assuming that is the case, why aren't the Elders helping us more directly?" asked Rose, her chin held high in a challenging attitude.

"Jade, the Chair, can't be seen to be taking sides, The Teacher is their President so she has to appear neutral. Perhaps that's why they utilize The Whistler. Maybe he's unable to speak, a mute, perhaps. I do know that on La Gomera there is an ancient tradition of Silbo which is men communicating over vast distances through networks of whistlers. They say whistling carries much farther than the human voice." Rose was unimpressed. "So you think this is their way of communicating with us in this high tech age?" Guy pulled a face and looked defensive. "Sometimes the old ways are the most effective. I am quite sure he will let me know if there's a problem."

"So we just sit here doing nothing until something happens? For God's sake, Guy, we've both lost track of our fathers, your mother has vanished too and you just sit there as if nothing can be done. Well I'm sorry but it's not in my nature to do that. I accept I should have told you earlier but I've already taken some action."

Guy sat bolt upright, suddenly alarmed. "What!" She met his gaze calmly. "I made some enquiries last month when we stopped off in St Lucia," she told him. "I met with Aunt Beatrice and Blackie."

"I didn't know you'd been to see Blackie, you should have told me; he might know where my mother has gone."

"I doubt it, they hate each other's guts, I know I should have told you but it was only a brief visit when you were busy refurbishing the *Hidalgo*. They're both pretty senile now so you wouldn't have enjoyed it anyway, and I know you don't like my aunt."

"So what was the old battleaxe's advice?" Guy asked.

"To try and find out more about my father by talking to The Teacher's people; they might give something away." Guy shook his head and gripped her hand harder. "I can't believe you did all this without talking to me, Rose, we're supposed to be a team, remember?"

"You didn't want to talk about it, so Beatrice advised me to call them."

"I bet she did, who did you contact?"

"I made the call and before I knew it I was speaking to Sabine. When I realised it was her I hung up pretty fast." Guy leaped to his feet, all thoughts of comfortably sunbathing gone from his mind; now he was worried, really worried. "You did what?" he snapped. "We promised Jade that we'd make contact only through the Elders. You must know that Sabine is The Teacher's most ruthless killer. What the hell did you tell her? "

"Only that I want to know where my father is." Rose was beginning to share his concern.

"For God's sake, Rose, it's a wonder we haven't had The Teacher's hordes after us here already; she will almost certainly have tracked down your location."

"I told you I hung up." Rose protested weakly.

"It doesn't matter; you've put us in great danger." Guy began to pace the deck, concentrating on what might happen as a result of Rose's action. She still seemed unaware of the possibilities.

"Perhaps but it's better than just waiting for others to suffer; we have to do something," she said defiantly.

"I care as much as you do; only I'm trying to be sensible," snapped Guy. Rose turned away and stormed below, dismissing Guy and his comments with a toss of her head. Women! He would never understand them. It was so unlike Rose to do this; she was normally so stable and sensible.

As Rose vanished below deck, Duncan, a large ruddy faced man, came through the hatch and made his way across to the stern rail where Guy was gazing thoughtfully at the horizon.

"Bit of trouble with the domestics, mate?" he grinned, "She seemed a bit upset."

"Nothing to worry about," Guy replied; but he wished the man hadn't witnessed his spat with Rose. He strode across the deck, dropped into the swivel chair in front of the control panel and pressed the button to start the engine. After raising both anchors, he carefully edged *Hidalgo* into the south eastern shoreline, an uninhabited area of cliffs fringed by rainforest. "I was going to ask if the two of us could go ashore today, I need some female-free time if you know what I mean… and I'd guess you do too," said Duncan taking a drink of water. "The forest over there looks interesting."

"Well, you're the client; we could go fishing, there's fresh water fish." Guy said. Suddenly he realised that what Duncan had said was true, he did need a change of scene and company.

"Are the fish good there?" asked Duncan, his weather-beaten features accentuated by the sun's heat and his considerable stomach flowing over his shorts. "Good enough," replied Guy, "up there on the hillside there's a fast flowing stream." He pointed with his right index finger. "I was chased by a mad Spaniard along its ridge last year, hell of an experience. I saw the river then. I'll move closer inshore and re-anchor."

"Male bonding time, sounds good and looks like you need some space," smiled Duncan. "Freshwater fish it is. Ailsa's a bit off colour today so she'll be happy to stay aboard and read." Rose had locked herself in her room; Guy wished they hadn't argued;

they so seldom fell out. It constituted a strong defence when encountering constant threats to their very existence. He cursed silently and resolved to make it up immediately on their return. He'd been naive to think he could get away from it all for a year. Rose had taught him before, you had to stand up and be counted; you can't always just run.

"Right, let's go now then," he said brusquely.

Though he regretted arguing with Rose, he was still angry she could have put them all in danger. He could see the need to push things along, as Rose had so forcibly pointed out, but it had been a grave mistake to make that call two weeks ago; there was no telling what could have happened since. He was surprised they hadn't had a visit already. Deep within him he knew it was time to re-enter the fray and just recently had begun to think more and more about Lorna, the only surviving daughter of the evil Stig Oleson. She had left him to work in her father's old base up in the Arctic Circle with her step-mother Diane. He couldn't understand why she had gone; they had been lovers and for a short time she had been the girl of his dreams, dreams that were tinged with sadness. His previous girlfriend had been Lorna's sister, Leila, who had died in tragic circumstances at the hands of The Teacher's men. Perhaps Lorna hadn't been able to live with that and left rather than tell him the brutal truth. Either way he needed to find out. The obstreperous Aussie and his shrewish wife, Alisa, would be gone tomorrow and they would be free to make plans to re-engage on their terms before The Teacher found them. His day-dream was shattered by a loud call from Duncan. "C'mon mate, don't hang about, it's our last day, let's make it a good 'un."

"We will," Guy assured him. He had long since tired of the Aussie's strong but shallow opinions formed by a weak intellect. It was the only downside of the yacht charter business; you didn't get to choose your customers. They climbed into the dinghy at the stern of *Hildago* and headed for the shore a couple of hundred yards away.

Duncan stepped out of the dinghy and set off up the beach, his legs wobbling slightly after so long at sea. He turned to Guy and said. "I've brought my binoculars; hope there's something worth seeing."

"You only need the rods for fish," mumbled Guy sarcastically as he passed them over.

"What's the deal with Rose and you?" Duncan asked during a rest they had taken for a breather. Guy had no intention of discussing personal matters with his client.

"What do you mean?" he asked.

"Well… you're not an item are you?" Duncan gave a suggestive wink.

"That's none of your business." The response came so sharply that for a moment Duncan said nothing then he said. "She seems a nice girl; I quite fancy a quiet evening with her."

"You're a married man," Guy reminded him.

"Never stopped me before," replied Duncan, grinning mischievously.

"She's off-limits as far as you're concerned. Don't go near her or you'll regret it." The menace in Guy's voice was unmistakable, but the Aussie either ignored the threat or failed to note it. "Only wondering if she came with the deal; I'm happy to pay extra if you know what I mean." He gave a lop-sided grin and a wink to show he was used to doing this sort of deal. Guy felt his temper rising. "I'll ignore that remark, just this once," he snapped and strode ahead, wondering why he was getting so defensive about Rose. She could look after herself. Duncan was unrepentant. "Only asked," he said, "no offence meant, mate." He waddled up the bank puffing heavily. Guy watched him, he realised that he really didn't like this man. "Hope you fall and break your damned neck," he whispered. Rose was right, they had work to do, and this wasn't it.

They climbed higher into thick, tranquil forest, the sun shining brightly through the trees. Guy scanned the scene, looking for the freshwater stream and at the same time trying to keep the two rods from snagging on the low undergrowth. "It's nothing like as impressive as Oz, though it does remind me a bit of Danetree. That's a real tropical jungle, full of snakes," said Duncan. "It's a damn sight more dangerous too; we've got seven of the eight deadliest snakes in the world for a start."

"There's only one deadly snake here and it's got a fat arse," murmured Guy to himself. He spotted the stream he had been searching for. "Over there," he gestured, hoping they would catch something quickly so he could get back to Rose. He cursed as he saw his mobile's signal had gone so he couldn't call her.

"There's a narrow gully in the trees ahead, and the fish will be waiting, so keep quiet," he said softly.

"Right behind you," whispered Duncan and they crept forward, the big man wheezing heavily.

Guy gently pushed his way through the thick undergrowth and finally emerged into the gully he was looking for. "We're here," he said, noticing his mobile now had a signal; he pressed the call button, relieved to hear the familiar dialling noise. He lifted the unit to his ear and as he did so the world exploded around him, blackness enveloped him as he fell headlong forward into a world of nothingness.

He was travelling down a long black tunnel feeling at first absolute peace, then suddenly he felt intense pain as reality returned with a vengeance. What had happened to him? He cursed as he felt a painful throb on the back of his head. He reached up and pushed wet ferns out of his face and looked around him. He had landed on a large boulder at the edge of the stream, just inches from a long drop. He staggered to his feet and saw the sun was sinking beyond the hill to the west. God! He must have been laid there for at least six hours. What the hell had happened and where was Duncan? He felt dried blood on his neck and leaning carefully over the edge of the boulder fell forward into the stream, ducking his head into the freezing cold water. He drank a little and slowly his head cleared though he felt matted blood and a huge bruise under his hairline. He'd fallen some forty feet and could see the large boulder that had stopped him from going right over the edge to certain death. He had to get back to *Hidalgo*; Duncan, the bastard, had clearly knocked him out with the binoculars and then pushed him over the edge hoping he would be killed. It couldn't have been anyone else but the Aussie who had planned all this, but for what reason? Rose was in grave danger; that damned call to Sabine had sent Duncan here working for The Teacher.

His head buzzed and ached at the same time. For a while he wandered around the same hills he had traversed a year earlier. He shook his head in despair, his mobile was gone, and so were the fishing rods. He staggered down towards the beach relieved to see *Hidalgo* in the distance peacefully at anchor exactly where he'd left her. He reached the shore twenty minutes later and cursed, the inflatable dinghy had gone, the cove was deserted. He shouted across to *Hidalgo* but there was no response. There was nothing else for it; he would have to swim the two hundred yards. Gathering his strength he plunged into the sea, gasping as the cold penetrated his light clothes, and ten minutes later reached the yacht, grateful that the ladder had been left down at the stern. He clambered aboard tired, cold and very worried. The whole thing had been a charade, the charter trip, the whole damned lot and he had played straight into their hands. "Rose where are you?" he yelled.

He ran below looking for any clues, but found nothing. He groaned as he noticed the smashed communications system. They had a second mobile phone for emergencies and to his relief it was still in its hiding place under the navigation table, it was flashing with a text message, his eyes widened in surprise as he saw the familiar name, Monty. Its battery slowly died as he held it, leaving him staring at a blank screen, then ran to Rose's room hoping to find her mobile. He found it hidden under the mattress on her bunk. The very fact she'd left it meant she was in big trouble. She never went anywhere without it. His stomach lurched as he grabbed it and checked the messages…nothing. He tried to make a call out but the damned thing wasn't working, he was well and truly alone.

He shivered, he needed a shower to warm him get rid of the aches and pains of the last hour. As he towelled himself dry he looked around; everything was in perfect order as if nothing had happened, a modern day Marie Celeste apart from Rose's clothes; they were strewn around haphazardly; she obviously hadn't gone of her own volition. He sat down heavily and carefully scanned the horizon with binoculars, but saw nothing of interest. Turning on the yacht's emergency radio, he surfed the shipping channels but nothing had been reported in the area. How the hell had they got away? He examined the decks and found some long marks on the main deck area, a bloody helicopter, he should have realized. He took stock, at least they hadn't taken *Hidalgo* and as far as he could tell nothing was missing from the boat and the engine worked; this was more sinister than piracy or stealing.

He mechanically started the engine feeling guilty about Rose, who could be dead now or in Duncan's clutches. He recalled how the man had talked salaciously about her; he had been a fool. He went over to the bridge to set the direction. As he raised the sails and took a bearing from the old, much treasured brass compass he had restored and spent hours bringing into working order; he saw some words scribbled on the floor. The instrument was his prized possession and underneath it in a false bottom he kept important documents. He bent low to read the words and found a scrawled note in lipstick that made his blood go cold - *Teacher*.

Chapter 2

The fierce wind carrying icy sleet cut like sharp knives through the man's heavy clothes as he strode from the land-cruiser into Valgrind, his base and refuge in the frozen north. A powerful man in both stature and countenance he automatically attracted attention as he entered the building. Born a Russian he was used to the cold so the location didn't faze him; in fact he preferred it; it helped him think more clearly. His cold, feral eyes gave the impression of a wolf ready to pounce, but this predator had become the prey. He had been a graduate of The Teacher's academy, where the most fanatical and loyal supporters were indoctrinated. None of the other students had questioned their tasks, however outlandish or extreme, but he'd realised they were being brain-washed and had rebelled. It was an act of bravery, or idiocy, that no one but he, Jochi, had ever attempted. It was a precedent The Teacher would not allow to become established. He was now regarded as a traitor to the cause who must be eradicated and as a result he needed to be constantly on his guard.

His master had seen his exceptional potential, had re-named him after Genghis Khan's first son and promoted him. The name had not been endowed lightly and Jochi had at first considered it a great honour and later a great irony; his namesake had also rebelled against his father. However, unlike the original Jochi, who had been hunted down and ruthlessly murdered by his father, he had so far survived. His opportunity to act effectively had come when The Teacher ordered him into active duty. He had used money and influence with three senior Elders who thought he would be a safe alternative to The Teacher. They were convinced they had bought his services, but he was beholden to no one.

He had succeeded in orchestrating a split in The Teacher's ranks and at the same time a schism in the Elders' organization. This had seriously damaged The Teacher's power with the group and for that there would be no forgiveness. Both the Elders and

The Teacher's organisations were now in some disarray. It was a schism they could ill afford and The Teacher was struggling to stay in control of each. In another direction, he had subsidized Diane Oleson and become a partner in the business she had established at the site of Stig Olsen's notorious experiment with breeding control, known as *The Huldra Twelve*. That had involved twelve girls selected to receive the gift of eternal life and, using stem cells, create a new master race. The project had been swiftly discredited and defeated. Still the base provided ideal cover. It was the last place his enemy would look for him while he planned the next stage of his activities. He was his own master now and had chosen his course carefully; all part of his break from the strict Islamic teachings that The Teacher was focused upon. Most importantly, he had the second Artefact, Drake's Shield, safely stored at the base and a strong lead to the whereabouts of the next one. Literally from the roof of the world, he would launch his plan to acquire more Artefacts. He had declined the opportunity to steal the Sword of Islam and left it in its hiding place. It wasn't part of the set of four Artefacts with Chinese script detailing directions, he believed, to finding the Khan's Prophecy.

His major breakthrough had been when The Teacher's trusted associate, Sabine, had confided to him that a piece of paper had been discovered that would lead to a diary written by a cabin boy on Captain Cook's journey, that was the next Artefact. She had inadvertently told him it was located in an old antiques shop down by the waterfront in Gothenburg. For his partner, Stefan, it had been relatively easy to acquire the paper and it did indeed give a clue to the diary's location. Unfortunately the damned piece of paper had gone missing; it was intolerable. There must be a traitor operating in Valgrind who had to be found and dealt with, which was why he was here now. He took off his coat and shouted for his attendant. He would find the damn thing if it meant turning the place inside out.

———————————

Despite her age of fifty years, Diane Oleson had a striking figure which helped run her ex-husband's health and beauty resort. The spa was marketed not only as being able to heal the body but, with the bracing air of the Arctic, healing the mind too. Her motivation was partly a fierce determination to succeed and emerge from her husband's shadow, and part philanthropic to help the survivors of its unsavoury past as a Nazi-style breeding camp. She had provided employment to some of the unfortunate victims of her husband's horrendous experiments in Aryan purity. However, finances were a constant problem due to low numbers and the remote location. After much soul-searching, she had accepted Jochi's offer of help, help he had assured her would be in the form of a partnership and was purely to help the girls. It was an offer that having accepted, she was now bitterly regretting. It had put her under his control and the effects of it felt like a vice clamping ever tighter as he exerted greater domination.

The product of a violent childhood herself, she was determined not to give up; she knew the girls were psychologically damaged and would not find it easy to reacclimatize to the modern world, so she employed them at the spa, giving them the chance to restart their lives. After nearly a year, she felt they were reaching a tipping point that made her think about her own future. She had advertised the spa as being the ultimate in providing relaxing, luxury breaks that featured the spectacular Northern Lights. Initially demand had been good, but recently it had fallen away dramatically, forcing her to re-assess the business and conclude she had no chance of survival. She had been supported in her venture by Lorna, her stepdaughter; they had formed a strong bond through suffering mutual tribulations. Fortunately they had a solution in the form of an offer she had received from the most unlikely of places. Together it would take them away from Jochi and his bullying ways; all they needed was a little time and a considerable amount of money. That remained a problem since her dead husband's estate had been impounded to pay his victims. She received Jochi's call to meet him in his office with some trepidation.

Her fears were confirmed when she saw his face. She stood and stared back at him across the wide desk. "The page, where is it?" he demanded, seeking to intimidate her from the beginning. Diane spread her hands. "We've looked everywhere; with all these workmen on site it's impossible to know who has it."

"I won't tolerate this Diane, you are responsible for security." He leaned across the desk and fixed her with a hard stare. Diane was unmoved and stared back at him. "We are doing what we can." she said firmly.

"Seal the base. You have until tomorrow to find it or I will take action." He leaned back in his chair, his face a mask of fury.

"What sort of action?" she asked and felt full of foreboding at his reply.

"You'll find out, now send me one of the girls."

"I don't approve of that," replied Diane coldly," "besides there's only Lorna and Soraya here."

"I want a massage, that's what they do isn't it?" he snapped.

He rose from his desk and stormed off to his private rooms slamming the door of the office behind him. Diane groaned to herself; the man was a monster and her only male support was a retired police officer called Rochembach who physically would not last five minutes against this man.

"The girls hate him," her friend Soraya told her angrily when Diane recounted what had happened. "He scares them." One of the survivors of Oleson's experiment, she had stayed on to help with the administration. "Not for long," Diane assured her, "we'll soon be out of this mess, besides you know how to cope with him, get him drunk and he'll fall asleep before he can touch you."

"It's very dangerous for Soraya," Lorna said as she entered the room. "We need to get rid of him; hopefully this Stefan can moderate his behaviour a little."

"First time here, came from Germany," replied Diane, "but he's probably just as bad."

"Probably," snapped Lorna in disgust, "they're after only one thing; Jochi has been after it from me ever since he came here, and to think he saved me from rape in Prague last year, what a change in him!" A tall slim and striking Nordic blond with piercing cold blue eyes, Lorna dominated any situation she was in. Her father's death had been a Nirvana moment for her as she came to terms with what he had done. She had been spoiled by him as a child and later by awestruck male admirers. Her mother and father had parted; her mother Jacqui going off to live abroad with Leila, her sister, she had chosen to remain with her father.

She had eventually seen through him and had been about to join her mother and Leila when they both suffered a horrible death, her mother Jacqui drowned, her sister was murdered. The subsequent violent death of her father and realization of what he had done made her determined to make up for his misdemeanours. The girls were under her care and she was fiercely protective of them. She was here despite the appealing attentions of Guy Tresanton; it was chance to make good her past, was her own cleansing ritual and the reason she'd come back to this freezing, remote part of the world. Until now she hadn't regretted her decision but she had a deep sense of foreboding at the behaviour of Jochi.

"He needs controlling." she said firmly.

"I can't do that," Diane confessed.

"I can, and I will." Lorna scowled, brushed back her blonde hair and stared defiantly across at Diane. "Then we move on, Stephy." She used the pet name for her stepmother when she was trying to make a point and smiled.

"How is the next batch of bookings?" asked Diane.

"Mostly Russians, which means fat old ladies where it's hard to tell where the flesh ends and the body starts," smiled Soraya. She'd shared many experiences with Lorna on Oleson's other project, a floating health farm, and their bond was exceptionally strong, another reason Lorna had come back to help.

"Are there any new ones?" asked Diane.

"Only a couple; it's time to move on Diane, the cruiser idea will work. I did a rough market survey and it's clear there is a strong demand for the concept of a floating health farm. I have total ownership of it and from what I'm told it is now seaworthy, albeit not fully fitted out for work yet."

"How long is it to completion?"

"About two months to be totally ready but possibly earlier if I can find the money. As I said it's seaworthy but you know what my father did to it so the money is very tight. As you know it's a significant size and had six diesel engines that have been refurbished plus a gas turbine. It's an impressive sight when ready to sail."

"Exactly why we have Jochi," replied Diane. "We need to generate some cash while we wait for the ultimate in floating health clinics to be made ready. The possibilities are huge, and will be our tickets to the big time so please stick with him for now."

"If he tries to attack me, it will be all over. It's a good job Soraya knows how to handle him; one day one of the other girls will get badly hurt."

"How much more money do we need?" asked Diane.

"A million euros," replied Lorna quietly. "It's taking all the money I was left plus maxing out on my credit limits against this place; we have to face facts, we will need help. They're going to take it on a major sea trial and look for a commission whilst they slow down the refit. I'm told there is the possibility of a big cargo commission on the horizon which would give us the necessary time and money."

"We'll find a way," agreed Diane, "but now we need to find that damned sheet of paper."

"Diane, I hate to tell you but Rochembach was the last to see it; he said he would check that it was authentic for Stefan."

"Then we do have a problem," said Diane in horror. As she turned, her old friend entered the room, his sad eyes confirming the worst. "I'm so sorry Diane, I did take it but I have a reason, a very good reason but I must keep it to myself."

"Keep it to yourself?" Diane exploded. "Have you any idea what trouble this is causing? I must be told where it is, who has it and why you gave it to him." Stefan spread his hands and shook his head. "I can see all that but I can't tell you until tomorrow. I promise I'll tell you then."

The base was deathly quiet as a hooded man surreptitiously left the compound at three o'clock the following morning, taking great care to keep to the shadows. He made his way across to the vehicle compound, the overnight blizzard had eased enough to enable him to get a snow mobile moving. He wasn't used to the biting cold and had taken a big risk by taking the assignment from his superior at Interpol. It meant he was unable to tell anyone, even Guy and Rose or his beloved niece, Jemina, all so he could get ahead of The Teacher and find the third Artefact. Bringing him to justice was now his life's major task and he couldn't have picked a harder quarry, one where extraordinary nerve and determination were necessary.

Chief Inspector Brian Montcalm had been nearing retirement when his world had been turned upside down by the arrival of Guy and Rose. Not that he was bothered by that, on the contrary they had given him a new lease of life, a sense of purpose that had become a personal journey for him. He had taken extended leave of absence from his posting to work in secret for Interpol and an Inspector Jakeman had taken his place. But his recent efforts had been a strain on his constitution and he realised he was getting too old for this sort of activity.

He had by chance listened in to a conversation in Aruba between Sabine and Jochi. They had revealed the clue and the need to act quickly. His superior at Interpol had immediately agreed they should take precipitate action in what was a growing crisis. He had approached his old colleague, Kurt Rochembach, on his arrival who had arranged for him to enter the complex in the guise of a contractor and had given him the precious piece of paper sought by Jochi. Now, with the net closing rapidly, sparked by Jochi's unexpected arrival, he had to get out whilst there was a break in the weather. Thanks to Rochembach's trust in him, he had remained under the radar screen for two days before grabbing the chance to escape. During his time at the base he had discovered, to his dismay, the local police were on Jochi's payroll, so what should have been a straightforward run to police headquarters had become impossible.

He gritted his teeth against the cutting wind and accelerated the snow mobile, heading out into the dark night anxiously hoping he hadn't been seen. He drove north to Tromso because there was nowhere else to go and as he drove he reflected on his assignment. The International Community was faced with a challenge that needed precipitate action. He had to take the fight to The Teacher or they would be beaten. It was an intricate game of chess where the defensive player was making a daring raid to the opponents' back line. Rochembach had been reluctant to give him the piece of paper but had eventually done so. He hoped the man wouldn't be persecuted but wasn't in a position to help even if he was. He was now himself a hunted man, a novel experience for a copper made worse by not being able to call on the local police for help. He took a final look back and slammed the accelerator down hard just as a bright beam of light suddenly sliced through the darkness. He ducked down and veered off northwards into the night, praying they wouldn't catch him. Something whistled through the air and the snow sprayed up to his right; bullets! He ducked instinctively as all hell broke loose.

Chapter 3

Fortaleza Hidalgo
La Gomera

It was with some trepidation councillors made their way to the old monastery in the centre of the island, the ideal location for the Elders' secret headquarters. They arrived, as always, with the greatest secrecy, usually at night to preserve their anonymity, their helicopters dropping out of the sky like visitors from another planet. They were a secret organisation comprising benefactors and rich industrialists whose mission was the same as it had been for the last six hundred years; to form a supporting body, designed to help all and any government around the world. They operated without any of the constraints faced by the United Nations, regarding themselves as a safety valve to mankind's affairs; unfortunately that safety valve had ruptured. A schism within a schism had occurred. It was a nightmare scenario for those who had devoted years of their lives to the movement, though some had opted to publically declare themselves to be backing the emerging new forces, creating further tension.

The Chair of the Elders, Jade, was now in her late eighties and increasingly feeling her age as she tried to hold her beloved institution together. She had ruled wisely and been saddened as The Teacher slowly usurped her power from his role as President. Her life's work was here as it had been for her mother and her grandmother, Victoria Silver, who was the woman credited with transforming the Elders a hundred years earlier. Her mother had taken the reins after her death and led them to a powerful position in the previous generation. Now Jade was the leader and it was her responsibility to wrestle with the increasing demands of her office. In her weaker moments she wished she could retire and had actually identified a successor, but first she must ensure the organisation's survival.

They were a philanthropic entity and had been since Admiral Zheng He established them in the fifteenth century. They kept a very low public profile refusing all requests for interviews from the media. Being so secretive, it was often misunderstood and frequently thought of as subversive, like the Freemasons. Still, they had prospered and were the recipient of wealthy foundations, always seeking to manage the vagaries of human nature. Now for the first time they had to face internal conflict. With the challenge written into their constitution to find the great Artefacts, Jade had decided to act robustly.

A senior Elder, Dr Oboto, had informed her of the rebellion, and without his intervention she would never have known of the plot. Acting decisively she had confronted the three members who had broken the rules by meeting Jochi clandestinely, pointing out that small groups of Elders were forbidden to take the rules into their own hands.

The pressures of the modern world were creating great obstacles to the achievement of the objectives set by Zheng He. Within the last hundred years there had been two Asian breakaway movements both from Zheng Wan's family. The Teacher was carrying on the disruptive work begun by his father; they were a family who saw the Elders and the Artefacts as power to be used for personal advancement, rather than for philanthropy. The ticking time-bomb was coming to fruition eight hundred years after the rule of Genghis Khan. The time of revelation was fast approaching; all involved intimately with the Elders knew what that meant. The Artefacts were the key; they had to be found and quickly brought under the Elders' protection and control.

The last helicopter arrived and the final delegates made their way to the conference hall. Jade braced herself; Jochi would not be here as he wasn't on the council and wouldn't want to risk being near The Teacher. The meeting began in its customary darkened environment, only Jade, her secretaries Emerald and Amethyst, plus the President were visible to all delegates to ensure everyone could speak their minds freely. Her longtime aide, Indigo, had recently retired leaving Amethyst as her day-to-day support. Jade reflected on how much she depended on her two faithful aides. Emerald had always been her strong right arm, ready to go into a fight and with a significant role outside the Elders; she had advocated action against The Teacher time and time again. Amethyst was far more reflective and had always been the one to advise caution. She could see, and would consider, all perspectives. She, too, though had finally come to the conclusion that action was now inevitable. Both were what kept her sane, her female warriors, ready to fight to the end. The code names were another part of the Elders' tradition, only Jade knew their real names. For Emerald it was a necessity, she had to preserve her anonymity from her day job at all costs.

Jade rose to her feet looking around the darkened room, a room full of memories, and delivered her opening words redefining the Elders' true values she held so dear. Confronting Zheng needed direct action if they were to stop him using the Presidency as a means to his own ends, and leading to their ruin. "My friends, we have existed as a noble and benevolent body for many centuries, a conduit for humanity, ensuring its affairs are well managed. We have often steered politicians from conflict unless it's irretrievable as it was in the case of the last two World Wars. We have managed to stay independent from all nations and creeds during this time, a fact I am particularly proud of. If we ever lose that independence, we lose everything. Riches and political power are strong temptations to deviate from our path, and have to be handled with great care as we manage our affairs below the world's sight line. We have succeeded until now, but we are in danger of falling victim to the most repugnant of conflicts, a civil war that turns friends against each other and leaves all wondering who is to be trusted. All this is happening when we must be the sole guardians of the symbolic Artefacts. Our mission was laid down by our Founding Father when he landed on these shores centuries ago. It is to find those Artefacts when the time is right, and to ensure that the Khan's Prophecy is found and made safe. Grave responsibilities that affect us all and can only be achieved through harmony; this is a most critical time."

Zheng Wan rose to his feet. He had been named by his father, Zhou Wang, after the great explorer Zheng He. Zhou had instilled his own ambitions into his son's mind and Zheng had forcefully carried them forward, though defiantly dropping the 'g' from his surname as a sign of independence. He also insisted on been called The Teacher by all those who deferred to him to demonstrate who was in control. It was only with the Elders that he had to accept the use of his real name.

"It's clear to me," he began, his voice clear and commanding, "That our mission is straightforward. Philanthropy is all well and good but we have to take direct action as a body and be ruthless.

My philosophy has always been to lead with purpose and direction; I see precious little of that here at the moment. Indeed fiddling whilst Rome burns comes to mind. It is clear that what we have is a renegade who should be expelled. The Artefacts must be found and where I differ from our Chair is that I believe that must be done aggressively. We cannot sit back and wait for due process, listening to the ramblings of an old lady."

Jade was stung into a sharp response. "I may be old but I understand better than you what this institution stands for," she snapped, "we must remain neutral, if we get directly involved we are no better than those who wish to use violence. We have followed Zheng He's principle of enlightenment for six hundred years, now Zheng Wan here seeks to damage that with his dangerous ideas. Yes! For the first time on our history a schism has been created in the movement, one that I must act to heal."

"Forgive me, I am new to this august body," said the Italian Fabrizio, a new entrant to the Elders. "As a robust body shouldn't we embrace differences of opinion?"

"Absolutely, but not at the expense of our over-riding principles," Jade stated firmly.

"So what do you propose to do to solve the problem of a fundamental difference between you and Zheng?" rasped an American billionaire called Stanton.

"My position is clear and cannot be compromised. We are bound together by our oaths of philanthropy; all other considerations should be secondary."

"But we have a schism do we not, I see little sign of leadership either from our President or the Chair?" replied Stanton harshly.

"You are entitled to your views," Jade conceded. Stanton was voicing her private thoughts about Zheng, now she had to persuade the majority to a course of action favoured by her and her supporters. She continued. "I will be frank. The schism does represent a failure of leadership. Fortunately, on this occasion I have been able to repair the damage. It was created by the actions of Zheng Wan. You all have the details of his misdemeanours. They are made more serious by the fact that he has deliberately kept the recovered Artefacts under his personal control. I therefore propose a formal vote of no confidence in Zheng Wan's leadership as President,"

"Seconded," came the voice of Dr Oboto.

"The proposition, duly seconded is before you. So please vote now," she said, and Jade smiled with relief as six green lights came on. Her voice reached every corner of the room. "The Chair can report that the proposal is carried. Six members voted for the motion and this automatically triggers a vote on whether the current President can remain in office."

"This is preposterous," snarled Zheng standing up indignantly. "I was voted President for a full four year term."

"If you check the rules," Jade said calmly, "you'll see such a vote is perfectly in order."

"This is a crisis caused by your poor leadership not mine,"

"No sir, it is you who has misused the terms of your office by appropriating two of the Artefacts and not returning them," observed Stanton.

"They are being stored safely for the Elders," replied Zheng uncomfortably, conscious that Jochi had stolen the Shield from under his very nose.

"I for one believe Zheng's motives are honourable," intoned the voice of Fabrizio. "Why have a vote of no confidence at such a difficult time, I fail to see why the current President has acted incorrectly."

"The evidence is clear," opined Stanton, "we have not seen the Artefacts despite repeated attempts and requests to get them here."

"I have it on good authority," interjected Dr Oboto, "that not only has our President no intention of returning the Artefacts but has apparently lost one of them, which I would describe at best as being very careless."

"That's a damned lie," retorted Zheng. "I have the Sword of Islam."

"But that's not classified as an Artefact. And why does the one called Jochi claim to have Drake's Shield?" asked Oboto. It was a question Zheng couldn't or wouldn't answer. He tried to bluff his way out of trouble. "They will soon be back under my control," he rasped.

"Really? I too am convinced our President isn't fit to lead us, and decisive action must be taken before he ruins us all with his naked ambition. I for one did not dedicate my years here to go in such a direction."

"I strongly object," began Zheng angrily, but was interrupted by Jade. "Above all we must preserve the integrity of this institution," she said. "Now a formal vote of no confidence please."

"You need a two thirds vote to support a no confidence motion … eight people which you will never get," snapped Zheng.

"Not so!" The voice of Amethyst joined the discussion. Issues of Governance were her area of expertise. "The rules state that in an emergency, as defined by the Chair, a simple majority will suffice. We are directly in danger, so six votes is sufficient from the twelve."

"I warn you all it is a very dangerous move to allow this woman and her lackeys to bend the rules like this," snapped Zheng looking around. "I have served this body for many years."

"The Artefacts," Stanton pursued his attack. "Do you deny the accusation?"

"I am merely their guardian, looking after them for the Elders. Do you think it wise to keep them in this decrepit place?" snapped Zheng.

Jade decided it was time to take the heat out of the discussion. "We will take a short recess," she announced, "When we return you all will have had the opportunity to consider the implications of what you are voting for. There must be no mistakes; our future is at stake."

"If you follow this woman then you will all fail," cried Zheng getting to his feet and stalking to the back of the room. "Before you is a choice between success with me or back into the dark ages."

"That's pretty clear," Amethyst whispered to Jade. "The die is cast now, either to self-destruction with Zheng or survival with you. It all hinges on the next thirty minutes."

The vote of no confidence by secret ballot organized by Amethyst was duly held. As she looked at the result of the ballot, Jade smiled and breathed a long sigh of relief; she had won. She addressed the assembly again.

"Members of the Council, the vote of 'No Confidence in the President' is carried by a majority vote of seven to five."

She looked across to Amethyst raising her eyes and smiling. "So, Zheng Wan I formally declare you dismissed as President and call for a new election to be held immediately." She was elated; the intensive lobbying had paid off, that, plus her threats to expose the pro-Jochi faction. Now she could move to the second stage of her plan. "I now move to…..."

"This is intolerable," roared Zheng angrily banging his fist on his table.

"Only because you make it so Zheng," retorted Jade, then moving swiftly on added. "The Chair proposes Dr Oboto from Nigeria be our new President. He is a long term member of the Elders, a philanthropist to whom we owe a great deal, and someone I believe can put us back on our original course. If you recall Zheng, I did nominate him as your mentor last year but you didn't accept the help."

"I am delighted to second Dr Oboto's nomination," said Stanton.

"Are there any other nominations?" asked Jade. She looked around the darkened hall quickly. "No other nominations? Can I have a formal vote please?" Jade smiled as this time ten lights came on. "I do believe Dr Oboto that congratulations are in order," she said, above the applause from the members.

"Thank you, Madam Chair and the council," smiled Dr Oboto a rotund looking medical doctor from sub Saharan Africa who had made his personal fortune through medical vaccines in the field of leprosy.

"I'll have no part of this travesty," snapped Zheng.

"You orchestrated an undemocratic vote."

"Are you resigning from the Elders?" asked Jade innocently.

"No! Certainly not! I won't give you that pleasure."

"Very well, you will take your place with the others. Dr Oboto the floor is yours." All heads turned to the sixty-year-old African as a light snapped on above his head.

"Thank you Councillors," said the Doctor looking slowly around the room. He was unaccustomed to the light on his face. "We must move now to heal ourselves and, as Madam Chair has stated, avoid civil conflict at all costs. History shows us that is always the worst kind. I have given many years of my life to this cause and am proud to take the helm, though it will only be for a short while until the crisis is over and our historical objective is achieved. Then I will retire in peace and with a fulfilled mind," He smiled broadly as he spoke. "I will deal dispassionately with this situation," he continued. "I have always believed in being direct and forthright, it is the only way to succeed in my country so I will now say what Jade has not said. She is a true disciple of our founding father, Zheng He, and indeed what is known as the 'Medici Inheritance'.... Stanton interrupted him. "Sorry," he said, "I know nothing of this 'Medici Inheritance' what's that all about?" The Doctor smiled at his fellow Elder. "It is the principle that rich benefactors can control and run a state from behind the scenes; Cosimo Medici did this in Venice centuries back. Our founder Zheng He went there before forming the Elders and enshrined that principle in our constitution."

"First I've heard of it, especially the bit about the Medici link," said Stanton peevishly. Doctor Oboto acknowledged the comment with a brief smile and continued. "Paternal rule is always preferable to that of violence. Far too often the rule of force has dominated. That is my greatest burden and the reason I am here. Millions have died so that selfish tin-pot rulers could enrich themselves at the expense of their people. From Bokasa in the Congo, Mugabe, Charles Taylor in Liberia, Bashir in Sudan, I could go on. I will not allow this institution to fail because of similar behaviour. We will ultimately succeed despite the efforts of men like Zheng Wan."

His remarks provoked a wild outburst from Zheng. "Don't lecture me when you're from a bankrupt continent," he shouted. "Success comes through strength of purpose not through paternalism."

"You would break this institution, if allowed to do so," said Oboto firmly. "Fortunately wisdom and good sense have won the day."

"Madam Chair there is one other item," said Zheng slyly holding up a manual for all to see. "I'm sure you will know this as a stickler for governance and regulations; I believe any outgoing leader has three months to hand over power unless fraud or murder has been committed. It's called the period of grace."

"He is right," confirmed Amethyst frowning. "Technically you have the leadership, but it has no power, it is therefore meaningless."

"I'll be the judge of that," snapped Zheng. "So, I invoke the three months clause." he rose from his seat and strode to the door. In that time he would make damned sure he got what he needed, after all Jade was right, this was all only a means to an end for him.

Later in the quiet of the old monastery's atrium Jade sat sipping Earl Grey tea with Dr Oboto, sharing a peaceful moment after the tense meeting. "Well we've declared our hand now, it's going to be tough to move forward when we have to second guess the damage Zheng can cause in the next three months," pondered Oboto. "We have worked together too closely on this to fail now."

"I should have expected something sneaky from him but it doesn't matter, you are the officially elected leader," replied Jade quietly. "Besides what can he do in three months?"

"Try to subvert the Elders before the next meeting without a doubt, and maybe use the authority of the Elders the wrong way." Oboto wasn't inclined to under-rate Zheng.

"How can he do that with a secret organisation?" queried Jade.

"You've seen how devious he is and unquestionably he has huge influence; a breakaway movement is possible."

"Unlikely, his authority here is limited now and I can veto anything he seeks to do, though we do need to take pre-emptive actions. I have found an interesting lead for us in the archives."

"And you the passive philanthropist," smiled Dr Oboto.

"I have my moments," smiled Jade, "Needs must, and besides he has an Achilles heel."

"Which is?"

"He believes there is someone who can interpret his actions, almost as though he is reading his mind. We can use that person without compromising our own position. Frankly, without him and his partner we would be in a much worse position than we are. Now we must actively help them; they have already suffered a great deal but they also have some personal involvement."

"What sort of involvement?"

"Their respective fathers have disappeared into Zheng's organisation."

"It is unfair to ask so much, particularly now we have raised the stakes," said Oboto quietly. Jade replaced her tea-cup onto its saucer and put them down onto the table, a thoughtful frown on her face. "Guy Tresanton and his partner, Rose, have proved themselves immensely resilient so far," she said.

"Perhaps, but it's a different battle now, a real war, one where we need professionals. This lead you mentioned. What is it?"

"Something I read in my grandmother's diary. I retrieved it from the vaults the other day or at least Amethyst did. She seems to know where everything is stored. She has been such an asset since she came here full time. Ironically the diary points us to Africa"

"The location is ideal for the person I have in mind."

"This person must work with our friends; as I said they are Zheng's Achilles heel."

"Understood. I think there will be a good fit; this person is someone who knows how to fight a dirty war."

"Who are they to link up with?" Jade knew of no group active in Africa.

"A scary lady called Tapiwa; she's an African uncut diamond with a reputation for ruthlessness and an attitude to match," replied Oboto smiling ruefully. "She grew up in the jungle and is lethal at unarmed combat; a professional killer. I saved her brother's life once; we can trust her implicitly."

Zheng Wan's private jet slowly descended into Abu Dhabi. He had just two months to find the Prophecy before the Elders turned on him. He'd bought himself a little time but was in no doubt the stakes had changed; they would fight him all the way. The Elders were purely a vehicle to him but one that was slowly coming out of a deep sleep. He might have to make a pre-emptive strike at the head of the institution before it became a threat to his plans, particularly if they started to expose his connections at the monastery. His helper within the organisation had given him a lead that could be invaluable. As always, they had met deep in the recesses of the old building when all were engaged elsewhere and this time it had paid dividends.

He had underestimated Jade, though that alone didn't worry him unduly. Success was his for the taking. Just a little annoyance to get out of the way in the North first then he would finish the Elders once and for all. He would destroy the place just as his father, Zhou Wang, had recommended all those years ago, he, Zheng, would finish off that work. As soon as they landed, Sabine, his greatest asset, came aboard; he was pleased to see her.

She was his most loyal foot soldier, someone who would use whatever means were necessary to ensure success. Above all she knew Jochi intimately and therefore knew what had to be done. She dropped into the seat opposite her master, her lithe figure clad in tight leathers, her green eyes sparkling, complementing her red hair.

"This page that Jochi has found, is it genuine?" he asked her after the briefest of greetings.

"Yes, the information comes from one of my most reliable sources," she replied. "Jochi misused our relationship back in Aruba and will pay dearly for that."

"You have learned a most important thing; now we need to strike fast," Zheng advised her. "Time to show our traitor what happens to those who rebel. The Corporation ZTW is gearing up; the bases are nearing fruition so there is a small time window, the timing is critical."

"I'll take that as an order to proceed as we discussed," observed Sabine unzipping her leather suit and revealing the tops of her breasts. Zheng knew she had pierced nipples and it never failed to excite him. "I do so like a man with a plan and power," she murmured. She got a sexual thrill out of killing people, her own personal turn on was when she saw naked terror on her victim's face. "Have no fear Teacher we will succeed."

Chapter 4

Kenya
Tsavo East National Park

The jungle air was humid, the undergrowth wet and dense as the two men hacked their way through the trees cursing as they went. Bankrolled by a huge amount of money and the promise of more to come if successful, they had been given a rough-looking map and had set out four days earlier. They had little idea what they were looking for, only that it had great significance and must be found urgently. The phone call had come to the older of the two men, Helmut Krupp, through his usual conduit. He had no idea who the end client was, but that wasn't unusual.

The timing had been ideal as he and his partner were both currently down on their luck. They had flown north the next day from their homeland in South Africa where they had been narrowly ahead of the law. His partner was a fat Greek called Georgiou who helped him earn so called dirty money, but, for now, they needed to make themselves scarce; this time after a nasty gambling incident in Lesotho. So they were in this God-forsaken jungle at Tsavo East, full of dangerous animals and with Somali pirates just up the road for good measure. Hardened as they were, this was difficult terrain and a tough challenge to find something in such a remote place. The proverbial needle in the haystack with only rough map coordinates to guide them. They were seeking some form of casket. It defied belief how it could have got here unless through a plane crash, but if someone wanted to pay out thousands on a fool's errand that was their business. They had been told that someone else could also be searching for the same thing so they needed to move fast. Both veterans of the Rhodesian war and tough grizzled South African Boers, they relished the chance of a fight providing it was on their terms.

"Stop Georgiou," snapped Helmut suddenly. "My instincts tell me something's wrong."

"What could be wrong here?" Georgiou asked with a lop-sided grin.

"I heard something, away to your right, now shut up."

"OK, you're the boss," grumbled Georgiou. He was perspiring badly in the fierce heat and glad to flop down on the rough ground not caring what was there.

"I am and don't you forget it," growled Helmut. He squatted down and listened hard to the jungle sounds. The light was fading fast and the rain turning from a drizzle to a more persistent downpour. "Time for one of our specials," he gestured as the rain became heavier.

"Really?" groaned Georgiou. He felt a griping stomach pain as they set to work. They quickly completed their task and found somewhere to hide on the jungle floor, then settled down and waited.

Twenty minutes later Helmut hissed. "Don't move an inch." Georgiou groaned, wondering what the hell was clambering up his leg, it didn't bear thinking about and he opened his mouth just as Helmut slammed a hand over it. "I said don't move a muscle," he whispered.

"Shit!" The profanity was loud and Helmut smiled at the startled cry. It was followed by a whoosh and the loud rustle of trees. Jumping up he ran forward to the target area where a figure was thrashing about in a net suspended from the bent tree sapling that had whipped back to its natural form when the trap had been sprung; he lifted his machete and advanced slowly.

"Looks like we've caught ourselves an unusual animal," he sneered, looking at a writhing figure in the netting. "The old net trick always works."

"My God," hissed Georgiou leering at the figure. "Are we going to have some fun, prime meat for the taking, Helmut you've netted us great after dinner entertainment; he peered closer and whistled. "What a backside on her, can't wait to get her clothes off and…." The rest of his words never came as something hard rammed into his face knocking him backwards. Helmut cursed and swung the machete as he looked past the prone body of his colleague. Somehow the girl had cut his net. He moved in fast and caught a blur of movement before instinctively blocking the swinging arm with his own, grimacing as he slammed his fist into her head. "That should soften you up my beauty," he snarled.

"What happened?" asked Georgiou groggily sitting up, "did you get the bitch?"

"Yes, she's a real beauty," smiled Helmut gesturing across to the rope trussed figure, "a regular spitfire and don't get any more ideas, she'll eat you for breakfast, the bitch split my best net and only that rope is holding her."

"At least let's strip her and have a better look."

"For God's sake get sex off your mind and don't go near her," snapped Helmut angrily.

Taking in the scene around her Tapiwa cursed herself for being stupid enough to get caught by these two idiots. She had been tired after walking through the jungle all day and the heavy rain had made her careless, a stupid mistake that she must rectify quickly if she was to get out of this mess alive.

"She's something else," breathed Georgiou lustily. "Look at those curves and the legs." Tapiwa cursed again to herself again for wearing the figure hugging black tee shirt and army fatigues. She thought fast, the tall one was the problem; he didn't let his crudity rule his thinking like the smaller one. Over six feet in height with a muscular, slim figure she prided herself on being able to tackle any man in unarmed combat, unfortunately this wasn't the case here.

"Be a shame to kill her without a bit of fun first," Georgiou rubbed his hands in anticipation.

"Don't even think it!" Helmut knew she wasn't to be taken lightly. "She's dangerous."

He walked over to the trap and regarded Tapiwa with interest. "Now, bitch how about you tell old Helmut your name and why you are here. Don't bother to make up some stupid story. There can only be one reason and it's the same as ours so get talking before I start carving. My old buddy here would love to do something nasty to you and maybe I'll let him later after taking a few pieces of flesh."

"Go to hell," snapped Tapiwa cursing herself again at how like a novice she'd allowed them to catch her. Her mentor, Dr Oboto, had called her two days ago to come here to find a lost casket. He'd told her it was a task of the utmost importance, something that could make a significant difference to a lot of people. She had been given a map reference on a piece of old parchment. He knew that in the jungle, her natural habitat, she would have a good chance of finding it. The Doctor hadn't told her others were also looking for it; still that was no excuse for her carelessness. She felt the ropes trying to sense even the slightest movement in them working her supple hands carefully over the knots without showing any signs to her captor. She always carried a small ceramic knife which she had used to cut the net earlier, but in the ensuing struggle she had lost it. "I have really nasty ways of making you talk," Helmut told her lifting his machete. "Pity to spoil such nice features but frankly I have no time or patience, now, one last chance."

"I was minding my own business as a forest warden; my superiors will hear of this," said Tapiwa, her face glistening as the machete came closer to her face.

"Oh really?" smiled Helmut running the machete along her arm drawing blood.

"You will die in hell for this."

"Most probably but you'll be there before me. Forget the forest warden crap and tell me why would a nice girl like you be out here in the jungle all on your own unless you were searching for something special? Perhaps you were following us ready to strike when we weren't looking; maybe you've already found something?"

"I am travelling to the local villages as a tree specialist," lied Tapiwa, still working the ropes hard. She gasped in alarm as Helmut thrust down with the machete slicing open her tee-shirt. He smiled greedily at the exposed flesh. "Georgiou you were right she has a nice figure," he grunted, pulling the ripped shirt away. Tapiwa wore no bra and grunted with disgust as her breasts were fondled by the tall South African. "Great pity to disfigure these beauties," he murmured as he raised the machete again, but work is work."

"Bastard," spat Tapiwa squirming back from the wicked looking machete and trying desperately to free herself. Putting all her strength into her hands she detected enough movement and noticed the ceramic knife in the wet grass, she could just reach it, her only hope.

The machete nicked her right breast as she slammed it aside with the loosened rope and sprang forwards like a cat. Her years of bush training for moments like this took control of her movements; this was quite simply kill or be killed. Helmut dropped the machete in shock as she smacked into him and he fell backwards.

Tapiwa had him off balance and grabbed at the machete, she missed it but used her knife to slash away at the rope remnants until she was completely free and scrambled to her feet. Coldly and rationally she weighed up the options as she advanced, both men were caught off guard. Her brain went into overdrive, her senses alert to every danger, she kicked out hard at Helmut's groin and he fell backwards to the ground in great agony. Seeing that he was out of action for the time being she deftly swung her knife towards the threat from the fat man. Recovering from the initial surprise, Georgiou was stung into action, he grabbed for his gun, then stiffened with shock and looked down at his chest, the ceramic knife was embedded between his ribs. He gasped and fell backwards, eyes glassy and disbelieving. Helmut struggled up bellowing crazily and trying to find his gun. He found it but was unable to evade the vicious swing from Tapiwa as she stepped forwards to kick out again, this time at his gut. He fell back with a thud and she rammed her boot down onto his neck, snapping it like a twig.

Slowly getting her breath back Tapiwa impassively retrieved her knife cleaned it on the wet grass and pulled a spare shirt out of her bag. Bloody amateurs should have finished her off when they'd had the chance; they deserved to die because of their sheer ineptitude. She examined their meagre possessions, there was no clue to their employer's name, but an identical map told her everything she needed to know and intriguingly gave a few more details than those she already had. With the opposition eliminated, her chance of success had improved, assuming there weren't more out there. By her own calculations she was no more than a day's walk from the position indicated on the map. She decided to get down to the river as soon as possible and out of the jungle; it was impeding her progress. Using what was left of the daylight and wanting to put space between her and the bodies that would attract dangerous animals, she tracked south for about half an hour and then wedged herself high up in a tree for the night, casting her mind back to her childhood as she dozed.

This land had made her; she had been brought up by guerrillas that had killed her parents and kidnapped her and her brother when they were just ten years old. They had lived in a camp in northern Nigeria; both had shown great promise as fighters, which had probably saved her from rape and him from a quick death. She had been forced to kill to survive. Then a raid had failed and her brother had suffered a badly injured leg. She had gone to find help and stumbled into Dr Oboto. He had saved her brother's life though he lost his leg in the process. The Doctor had enough influence to arrange their release from the guerrillas and had taken them south to Botswana where, in Garonne, she had come to know peace for the first time. Oboto had paid for her schooling in a country relatively rich and stable, thanks to the diamond fields, and a benign ruler that valued education. She performed well at school and had been ready for a good career but her home was the bush, she was a fighter at heart and had returned to combat training as a volunteer in the army. She had found her calling in life, but then it all went wrong when her Captain had attacked and tried to rape her. She had killed him but his family connections meant she had to leave the country in a hurry. Doctor Oboto had stood by her and founded a martial arts school for her in Kenya where she could teach and also provided the odd lucrative assignment. It gave her purpose in life, to use her fighting skills for worthwhile causes rather than tribal warfare. The good Doctor had looked after her like a father and used her in the way she wanted to be used, she knew no other way.

The next day she made her way to the river and found the place she identified on the new map. She diligently followed the instructions on it, retracing her steps into the jungle measuring each step to ensure she was accurate. After half an hour she found what she was looking for, a small glade with a pile of stones and breathed a sigh of relief; this had to be the place. Kneeling down she removed the stones carefully and saw a larger rock underneath. Triumphantly she lifted the bigger rock straining with the effort. It was all in vain, underneath was a large empty space. She cursed in disappointment as she scanned the hole and something on the bottom caught her eye. She reached down and extracted a worn looking business card for a man called Joseph Cain, Purchasing Manager for the Government of Malawi. It looked as if it had accidently fallen there and was partly hidden by a small rock. It must have fallen out as the man lifted the box out. From its appearance she judged it had been there no more than a couple of years or it would have rotted. She replaced the rocks thinking furiously. She had to talk to Oboto.

Chapter 5

Australia
Port Douglas

Eagle's Nest was an ideal location for Jack Hogarth. Set on the eastern edge of the oldest rainforest in the world, ten miles north of Port Douglas, it towered majestically, and incongruously over the landscape, its steel structure and glass windows shimmered in the sunlight. The white marble finish ensured it could be seen from miles away in any direction and its ornate swimming pool was envied by all who saw it. Built on a prominent hill high above Captain Cook Highway, the long coast road stretching down Queensland's eastern coastline and parallel to the Great Barrier Reef, there was no other building like it in the entire area.

It had been designed to be an impenetrable fortress and its single harbour carved into the rocky shoreline deterred all but the most curious, especially as the seawater surging around the estuary was home to the world's largest and most deadly crocodiles. That suited Hogarth who was paranoid about his privacy. His main transport was a helicopter, located on a small pad on top of the building's main tower. The estate was protected by a small entourage of minders, though the warning signs about two rogue male crocodiles nicknamed Scarface and Fat Albert were usually enough to deter unwelcome visitors. Both were over fifty years old and continually fought for dominance of their respective stretches of river. Fat Albert had recently attacked a tourist boat taking a chunk out of the guard rail which made state news headlines and suited the owner of Eagle's Nest admirably.

Hogg, as he was known to his friends, was a man who had made his money from drugs, gambling, and prostitution. He'd invested his ill-gotten gains carefully to give him financial security for life, or so he'd thought as he poured money into local conservation projects and bought patronage and influence by corrupting politicians in local, state and national political parties. He felt confident all his largesse would make it difficult for officialdom to ask questions about the sources of his wealth. All had been rosy until the world financial crash. Jack lost a huge sum in the Madoff scandal in America, so, left with little more than Eagle's Nest and his old contacts, he sought a new way of earning money, not least because he wished to maintain a string of expensive mistresses and an extremely spoilt daughter called Sandy.

A heavily built, jowly man with a shock of silver hair, he had the weather-beaten features common to his family. He went to America vowing revenge on Madoff but was diverted by an intense Chinese man who had offered him his most lucrative venture ever, one he was sure would restore his business fortunes. The price was risk, secrecy and the need to kowtow, but the rewards would be immense. The first assignment from his new partner had been a job in New Zealand. He'd completed the job flawlessly and at the same time made a little extra over and above their agreement. He sensed the Chinaman intended to pay more attention to business in Australia but that didn't concern him at this stage

Jack turned to his latest conquest, Lucinda, one of his many expensive consorts from a succession of high class prostitutes. She was a body builder with artificially enhanced breasts, well past her sell-by date and in urgent need of an upgrade. From another direction came the familiar voice of his daughter, Sandy, a vivacious twenty-five year old blonde. Her hair gleamed in the afternoon sunlight streaming in through the large picture window. She pointed towards the beautiful scene outside. "Nice views Dad and I don't mean the tart," she said sarcastically and grinned.

Directly below them, in a separately fenced pool were three tame crocodiles raised in freshwater.

"You wanted to talk to me?" her father asked, ignoring her remark and before waiting for a reply added, "I have something I want you to do for me, an errand."

"A job you mean?" she knew her father well and was immediately suspicious.

"If you like, fact is our finances are not good thanks to bloody Madoff so I've a little job I want you to handle for me; it'll be very lucrative."

"Not dangerous, I assume?" said Sandy brushing her hair back.

"Just need you to oversee a delivery for me, that's all, nothing to it really. You can get some sailing in too; I'll even send Ailsa with you."

"There has to be more you're not telling me."

"There is but I'll tell you when the timing is right."

"The timing is right now."

"The crocs are getting hungry." He tried to change the subject.

"They can go for a month without eating so don't bullshit me, what's happening? You forget that I know everything, even who your latest piece of skirt will be before you do."

"It's none of your business," growled Jack.

"Bet you've told that old fart Duncan." He again ignored her remark.

"Cash flow is a problem and I have found a lucrative overseas partner."

"Doing what?" Her suspicions were now really aroused.

"A delivery business basically, plus some exploration, it's a chance to get into the big time." Jack wondered if involving Sandy would be more of a liability than an asset. Still he had to trust someone with the last of his cash and surely his own daughter was trustworthy. The DNA results had proved her lineage; there had been too many one night affairs for him to argue once the test results were proven. Since then, in a strange way he had grown to like her.

"I need more," she insisted.

"I have to find something for my new partner. In the meantime he's sending a team across to help with a delivery, I can't trust anyone else."

"Exploration you said and delivery?" In spite of her suspicions, she couldn't help being intrigued.

"Yeah, Duncan will lead the exploration; it's more risky?"

"He's a liability plus he's a letch always eyeing me up even in front of his wife."

"He may have a roving eye but he's no liability; he's just proved himself with a difficult assignment, and he can dive."

"Dive? Dive where?"

"Out on the Barrier Reef, beyond Agincourt and into the Endeavour fields.

"That's a protected area," she reminded him.

"I've got special permission."

"I'm a conservationist, Dad, remember? We have to protect

the outer reefs, too many damned tourists wearing them down. The fish are leaving so are the turtles. People shouldn't be diving on that reef." Jack's temper began to show, he stood up and walked towards her. "I won't damage it," he said aggressively. "I've bought a large block of shares in Siversonic and we are adapting one of their vehicles to get on the reef, so your bloody conservationists will have nothing to bleat about."

"One of their vehicles? That's even worse, what are you looking for down there anyway?"

"Best you don't know for now." Jack wasn't going to be drawn further on the subject and moved swiftly on.

"Now to your part. You are to be a rich and lucrative diversion to bring in the dough."

"What sort of diversion?"

"The sort that matches your unique talents. A nice trip to sunny Auckland."

"Auckland? It's beginning to sound more like a tour of Oz."

"Yeah, it's the land of sheep, hidden inlets and remote coves, more boats per head than any other country in the world and great for smuggling."

"So I take the risks and you become the corporate citizen?"

"It's safe, I've good contacts down there and a great distribution route from Latin America, and you know I would never put you at risk."

"It has to be drugs and they're bloody dangerous, particularly getting them into Oz. If I get caught I'll spend the rest of my days inside."

"There's no fear of that. It's a foolproof route over the Tasman Sea, by yacht it takes about six days. They're delivering to our diving platform; it's the perfect hiding place. It's even protected by the government."

"I hate the sea, you know that."

"Others will be doing the hard work. A full sailing team is coming over; all you need to do is watch them and top up your tan. I don't trust anyone else and Ailsa will be there to keep you company."

"If, and I say if I do it, I shall want a twenty percent cut."

"Twenty percent? That's outrageous!"

"Then there's no deal."

"You drive a hard bargain."

"It's in the blood Daddy dear," she smiled sweetly. She had no intention of doing just as he wished. She would make a killing on the side. She was bored with her current life and needed a challenge; perhaps at last this would be it. She turned and flung the red meat down from the balcony and watched in amusement as Fat Albert and Scarface tore at it.

Chapter 6

Vietnam
Tay Ninh Compound

Doctor Jack Tresanton and his closest friend, Doctor Zichu Ling, had been kidnapped by The Teacher in Hong Kong. Renowned psychologists, they worked on advanced forms of mind control and their prominence had brought them to the attention of their kidnapper who, after spiriting them away to his lair in Tay Ninh, had forced them to use their skills on what he called mind programming, but which was really an advanced form of brainwashing. They had been responsible for preparing sleepers based in Spain and Aruba. At first they had been regarded as non-believers in their captor's vision, and as such had been isolated in a separate part of the compound but, after the sleepers had worked well, they had been finally been accepted.

What they discovered profoundly shocked them. It was no less than the systematic abuse of starry-eyed teenagers, unaware of what they had let themselves in for. The camp was run by Zie Lao, a despicable little man who, behind the façade of the Caodaists, spent his time indoctrinating and terrorising everyone. Jack and Zichu, like all the other followers in their green and yellow uniforms, had no access to outside news. Both felt they had little choice but to co-operate and compromise their values in the work. Threats against their respective offspring, Guy and Rose, were constantly made and they thought them to be in great danger. Survival was their main driver but at the same time they attempted to derail The Teacher's schemes from the inside.

In the deepest recesses of his mind, Jack had to confess he enjoyed operating at the edge of science. He wrestled daily with his conscience; breaking ethical standards of practice but comforted by the thought that if he didn't someone far more ruthless than he would do it. There was an unending stream of disciples willing to act as human guinea pigs and take part in the use of mind-bending drugs; fortunately the results had been very gratifying despite the dubious ethics. They were making real progress in understanding the human brain.

Sabine too was based at the complex. She was nearing thirty-five years old and beginning to wonder where her future lay. Her striking figure, long red hair and green eyes ensured she always stood out in a crowd. From a very poor background in Texas she had risen through the ranks in The Teacher's organisation by using her intelligence and, when necessary, her body which contained many interesting piercings. All her efforts had been met with approval but she didn't yet feel part of his inner circle. The affair with Jochi had hurt her badly; he'd been someone she'd trusted completely and he had betrayed her. She knew The Teacher blamed her partly for Jochi's defection; now she had a chance through an opportune discovery to regain his confidence.

She had for some time been puzzled by Guy Tresanton's apparent advance knowledge of her master's moves. His father was employed at the camp which struck her as dangerous so she'd investigated further. She discovered that whilst the older Tresanton's skills had certainly worked with Nasrid in Spain and Karuku in Aruba, Jochi's defection was suspect and made her wonder. Why, if Tresanton's skills were so good, hadn't he been able to stop Jochi from defecting? The two doctors appeared to be cleaner than clean and they had no way of meeting or contacting anyone outside the complex. Yet they were up to something, she just knew it. She struck gold one evening whilst enjoying herself with one of the camp girls. She had seen a movement out in the shadows. Leaving the girl, she had watched a fleeting figure move through the trees and enter the small hut that Doctors Tresanton and Ling shared. Creeping across to the window she had seen a small deaf mute man communicating with them by a mixture of signs and whistling. She smiled to herself in triumph at the scene; her future had just taken an upward turn. She quickly returned to her room and made a call on her mobile.

The vibrant City State of Singapore gleamed in the early evening darkness. After arriving from Changi airport by helicopter, Zheng Wan took in the view from the window of his luxury apartment on the new waterfront development just under the Singapore Flyer, the world's largest Ferris wheel. He had reached it through numerous security doors. It amused him to know that the world research centre for Interpol was based literally next door to him. If only they knew what was happening on their very doorstep! It was one of his homes few knew about, a place where he could relax secure in the knowledge that he was anonymous. He had thought long and hard about the Elders and their quest for the ancient Artefacts. He had no intention of surrendering them to a group he considered ineffectual. In reality his loss of the Presidency would have little impact on his plans. Tresanton's father and his fellow psychologist, Zichu Ling, were monitored day and night. Still the extra insurance would come in handy which was why he had authorised the kidnapping of the latter's daughter, Rose.

His mobile rang insistently; he answered it and listened intently to what Sabine had to say. "Thank you," he said, "I'll be there as soon as my business here is completed." Singapore suited his purposes ideally as the privacy and its geography were ideal for Vietnam and his new venture in Australia, his two developing areas. He looked at the Singapore Flyer and permitted himself a sardonic smile, he had as many balls in the air as there were pods on the ride. The archaic Elders didn't matter in the bigger scheme of things. The Contagion Project, his master plan to release a virus that would cause the rapid spread of sickness, was approaching readiness and would be active long before the new President, Dr Oboto, could interfere with his plans. The Elders' connection had served its purpose; all he needed now were the secrets that lurked in the basement of their monastery.

He had never been allowed down there but his spy ring on the inside had produced an ancient map of Kenya. His main concern was much more testing and needed to be addressed before it was too late. ZTW (Zheng Technologies Worldwide), who bankrolled his activities, was no longer content to play the sleeping partner role. Their Chief Executive wanted to make decisions in matters that until now had been his domain. He drank his gin and tonic mulling over the many possibilities open to him. He would need to find a way to take care of this development, keeping one step ahead was his mantra. He wished his father, Zhou Wang, was still alive to advise him. He completed the areas of business he had come to oversee and boarded his private plane back to Vietnam.

The sun rose over the horizon heralding a new day as his jet touched down at the small local airport north west of Ho Chi Minh City. It had been a military airstrip but was now in private hands. As Sabine greeted him, he was again struck by her flame red hair and athletic figure that reminded him of her animal magnetism. He knew she was without morals or inhibitions and fiercely ambitious. It was time to elevate her, his most valuable, effective and loyal servant.

"You're supposed to be in the north," he commented after exchanging the briefest of greetings. "I had to make a diversion," she replied as she slid into the back seat of the Mercedes beside him and was driven to the compound at Tay Ninh, some forty miles from the Cambodian border. It was to the outside world a religious retreat founded to enable the practice of Caodaism, a fusion of Buddhism and Confucianism. In reality it was a cover for his organization; a centre of training where the disciples learnt to be good servants of his empire, willing, impressionable and able. Now more than ever they would have a role to play as the Contagion Project approached.

"So what's so important about Tresanton?" asked Zheng as they entered his office.

"I have found the leak from here." said Sabine judging the timing carefully, her stomach muscles tightening. She hoped she knew Zheng well enough to be able to gauge his temperament for receiving bad news. "I've found the traitor in our camp." She went on to explain what she had found. He listened with a growing fury; carefully laid plans could be compromised by such treachery. His decision to kidnap doctors Tresanton and Zichu Ling were crucial to his plans and had, he thought, proved to be all he'd hoped for. To lose their involvement at this stage of the project would cause severe problems.

"Have you taken care of whoever it is?" he asked. "I am about to," she said, "I thought you might like to see how I deal with it?" she gave a satisfied smile and assured him, "there will be no more leaks from this site."

They left the office and strode across the compound into a conference room in which the doctors were lecturing some of the students. "Leave us," Sabine ordered the small audience, "I want to speak privately to the doctors." Jack looked at her coldly. "How can we help you?" he asked. "Oh it's beyond that," snapped Sabine, "you aren't fooling me, Tresanton."

"Fooling you? What are you talking about? " he replied. He knew she hated them with a passion; and glanced across at Zichu in alarm.

"So why did Jochi fail? She asked, staring at each of them in turn.

"The tests are inconclusive," replied Zichu.

"I find that hard to believe," rasped The Teacher. "I think it is time our good doctors had a new mission and a few home truths. Incidentally, Ling, your daughter Rose is also an honoured guest of ours, she joined us yesterday."

"Rose? She's here?" Zichu was horrified.

"No, she's not here; she's being looked after in Australia, courtesy of my new partner who is helping me expand our business interests there. I'm sure she can count on your strong co-operation, as for you, Tresanton your son is about to be arrested."

"He's still alive then?" commented Jack proudly.

"Not for long. Now, if that's not enough, as a further incentive perhaps you'd like to look out of the window, there's something that'll interest you."

"Oh my God," Jack shuddered, and felt himself sway as he saw the familiar face of his little friend, the man who had been his sole communication with the wider world, the Whistler. The body was hanging there with the wind blowing him in grotesque circles.

"Why on earth have you killed him? He was a mute and could not have harmed anyone; his help was invaluable to me."

"He was alerting your damned son. I don't understand how he did it and I really don't care but you've cost him his life."

"You murdered him, a harmless little man."

"A traitor and I don't suppose you knew he was sending coded messages out of the camp?"

"He couldn't do that," whispered Jack, a cold feeling of dread spreading through his guts. The Whistler, his sole contact with the Elders and to Guy, was dead; his world was collapsing around him. He sagged and held the bench to stop himself from falling as Zichu reached out. "Put extra guards on them both and make damned sure they do as they're told. I trust you both will not end up the same way," Zheng warned them and turned to leave.

"Yen Lui you have done well," he said to the site's second in command, a sadistic Vietnamese woman, as he made to leave the room.

"All in a good day's work," she smiled.

"Sabine, my office if you please," said Zheng and she followed him across the compound oblivious to fearful glances.

"We must have the logistics ready for the Contagion Project; this place gives me the creeps with all these religious zealots, I'll be glad when we move to the new location," he told her irritably.

"Contagion is nearly ready and guaranteed to succeed but I don't share your trust in the Doctors, let me kill them now."

"They'll die when the time is right, but for now they have their uses and you have work to do, time to find the third Artefact; any news from the north?"

"It's confirmed, the Artefact is an axe called the Dragon Slayer; the source inside Jochi's camp has confirmed it."

"Good, you've done well Sabine; I'll appoint you my senior advisor with immediate effect. You will share richly in the rewards coming our way."

Sabine, delighted with her new status, left the camp and took Zheng's private plane to Singapore. Death always energized her as if she was absorbing the dead person's energy into her own. She smiled knowingly at the pretty stewardess, either sex suited her when she was in this sort of mood and she beckoned the girl over. It was a long way north and she needed company; she was sure the girl would be sold on her piercings.

Chapter 7

La Gomera
Fortaleza Hidalgo

Jade surveyed the familiar corridors of Fortaleza Hidalgo, her noble fortress and home, a place she had come to love despite the persistent cold and dampness in its walls. She knew the familiar sights without looking, the winding steep valley and the mountain peaks across to the sea that long ago had spelled the western edge of the known world. It was the very reason why their founder had chosen this island, a perfect place to build an organisation of the future. Her private apartment was at the top of the building with a fantastic view through the Valley of Hermigua and in the background the peak of Mount Garanjonay. She turned from the window, dropped into her favourite chair and cast her mind again over the recent meeting. They had faced the greatest crisis that had ever threatened their existence and this was precisely the reason why she had abandoned convention in inviting Doctor Oboto to stand as President. Extreme times called for drastic measures and despite Zheng's manoeuvre she felt more confident. Oboto had pledged to stay on and help her take the strain of the leadership; surely even Zheng wouldn't attempt anything too dramatic now.

She recalled her grandmother Victoria's written recollections of the last century when the monastery had buzzed with excitement. A happy time that had ceased abruptly when first her daughter, Veronique, and her husband, Vincent, had drowned on the Lusitania, followed soon after by her mother who had died of cancer. Victoria had met a rogue called Jack Silver and together they had ensured the Elders growth and relevance as they sought the Artefacts. She had dedicated her life to the organisation after her mother's premature death and had since known great joy but also some pain.

Her spirits had been lifted by the arrival of Doctor Oboto; he had brought a fresh approach, urging her to examine the mountain of archived records particularly relating to Zheng Wan right back to Zhou Wang. She had started to do so, revealing facts that made her wonder about Zheng Wan. He had sought to corrupt the Elders and she feared greatly for anyone in contact with the man. Particularly worrying was the report from Africa of the missing Artefact and the loss of contact with the Whistler. She looked up and smiled as the door opened.

"Lovely place, my dear, just what the Doctor ordered." Oboto came across the room to greet her. She was pleased to see him.

"Walter, you must find it dreadfully cold after Africa," she said.

"Not at all, it's lovely, a great place to relax and think, steeped in history."

"Have you had any more thoughts?" she asked him. She was anxious to press on with their plans.

"My time in the academic world taught me to look for solutions to problems where you least expect to find them. The clues are often right under your nose, so close to us that we don't see them. I'm convinced that what we are looking for lies right here in the vaults below us; that map of Kenya proved it. That's why Zheng wants to stay connected to the Elders."

"But we've searched and searched. I've spent hours poring over records of previous Elders' meetings going back hundreds of years."

"There has to be something more."

"There are more rooms further below that haven't been opened for decades, mainly religious storerooms and records," she told him thoughtfully.

"Then perhaps that's where the answer lies."

"Very well, we'll start looking there today," Jade promised him. She looked wistfully down the valley as the sunlight reflected off the stream. "This is such a beautiful place, I shall be sad to leave it at the end."

"All very logical and proper and a testament to the hard work of Emerald, by the way why do you all use code names?"

"It's decreed under the original rules, it protects anyone working here."

"What's your real name?" he asked her. She paused for moment before replying then said.

"Marie Victoria Silver." She answered slowly, being unused to saying them. I'm the granddaughter of Victoria and Jack Silver who are credited with the restoration of the Elders."

"Restoration? Perhaps the religious archives have the

answers," said Walter, "there is no more likely place to start. Your grandmother found the first Artefact, the Cross, right?"

"Yes, you're right. Perhaps my dear grandmother has the answers after all. She was very religious towards the end of her life."

"Could well be, that's where I'd put my money, who exactly are Emerald and Amethyst?"

"Emerald works in a very influential position outside La Gomera but even you can only be told if you work here."

"And Amethyst?"

"She joined me recently, she lives here and replaced Indigo who retired; she is my cousin."

"You can usually trust family more, have you had any life outside of here?"

"Before my mother died, I met someone, an islander I wanted to marry."

"And what happened?"

"He belonged to one of the oldest families on the island and wanted to come to live here but they had strict rules about who they married. He vowed to break those rules but his father was too powerful. He learned the whistling language, the silbo to communicate to me across the valley but we were very young."

"What happened?"

"He married someone else, they had a son, a mute who learned the silbo, and we call him the Whistler."

"The Whistler?"

"Yes he's a very talented man. I am very worried about him, I've just been informed by his family that he's disappeared; they don't know any more details but he was invaluable with his communications to Guy and Rose."

"I am sorry to hear that," said Walter sympathetically.

"It's a war now," replied Jade grimly, "we have skilled and talented people running an organisation dedicated to making sense out of the chaos of human existence; it's worth fighting for isn't it?"

"Of course it is," said Walter. "Now, is there anything else you can think of, anything that doesn't quite fit into your grandmother's story?" Jade's brow furrowed in thought. Then she said. "There's only one thing I can think of, a football challenge match here on the island with a notorious battle afterwards. Why it was held here never made sense to me?"

"That's the sort of thing I mean. It must be worth investigating," said Walter, "We'll look in the religious vaults."

It was a working monastery with monks located at the front of the building so they went through their archives past the sign pointing downwards to the cellar. "This is it," said Jade brushing cobwebs hanging from the ceiling in front of her face, "the only part of the monastery I've never explored."

"My guess is this is where we will strike gold," replied Walter. They entered the room and were confronted by rows of shelving. "I think I know where we might strike lucky," said Jade and went to the left hand side. An hour later she unearthed the story of The Columbus Cross, the first Artefact to be found. "Where did you find the information on Kenya?" asked Walter.

"A note left under my door, one of the monks warned me," replied Jade.

"I thought you had been given a tip off by one of the Elders?"

"No it was a note talking about a man called Steppenhof," replied Jade her pulse suddenly quickening.

"I bet the note was from the same person who tipped off Zheng. I'm afraid we have a spy in the camp. Who else has access to this area?"

"Just my two secretaries and a couple of the monks and nuns."

"A couple of monks and nuns?" echoed Walter.

"Yes, they look after the archives."

"You need to check them out, Jade. This other man, you say his name was *Steppenhof?*"

"Yes it was on the note."

"Then it does link to the football match. The journal you've just found here says that a Klaus Von Steppenhof was part of the German team and left with the battleship Dresden which was subsequently involved in a fracas with Jack Silver."

"I just knew there had to be something here," said Jade. "Why had so many participated in such an odd challenge with the game only just becoming popular?"

She picked up the journal Walter was reading and scanned the neat handwriting. "A man called Salazar conducted a long-running feud with my grandfather, Jack Silver, their mutual animosity sparked a great deal of antagonism which spiralled into a challenge match," she read. "The puzzle is that Germans and Asians competed in the challenge also," her brow furrowed. "Ah look at this!" she exclaimed and turned to show Walter what she had found. Instead she saw Amethyst who had just arrived in the vault with concern showing on her face. "You need to rest," she told Jade and shivered in the damp, cold air. "It's cold down here."

"There is no time; we have to act fast before Zheng Wan out-manoeuvres us. I am convinced the answer lies here; it's no accident that the hunt for the Artefact kicked off here on the island. It's this damned challenge match, our ancestors were part of it as were the Germans, but why?"

"It certainly is odd," said Walter. "Almost as if the Cross was the magnet, but how did they hear about it?"

"Steppenhof is the answer; he must have known about the other Artefact hidden in Africa and came to get the Cross for himself."

"You may be right," said Walter doubtfully, "but it needs more research. You also have to talk to the monks. We must catch the spy and stop the leak of information to Zheng."

"Emerald will take care of it," replied Amethyst, "she knows them best."

"Someone came here and it's sparked the hunt for the Prophecy," said Walter. "At last we have an advantage if we can use it, keep searching. Look through those blueprints over there, they are of several buildings."

Chapter 8

The road was deserted as Monty alternately ran and walked briskly, desperately trying to keep warm. He saw the snow-covered signs to the Knutsenskagen district and headed in that direction. The gunfire had been wild and no one had followed him out into the cold, probably reckoning that he would die anyway. His initial elation at escaping from the complex had turned to exhaustion and now feared he was in great danger. The open spaces exacerbated that feeling as he looked up to the sky seeing the dramatic green tinges of the northern lights. He wished he could see them properly if only for their company. A confirmed bachelor and something of a loner he had never felt a need for others, but now he felt lonelier than ever. It was if he was the only person left on the vast expanse of an ephemeral white earth, his bones creaked in the harsh cold as he hurried onwards. He had ditched the snow mobile two miles back when the fuel had run out; in any case it was too conspicuous.

His watch said two-fifteen as he pulled the heavy coat tighter around his neck and shivered involuntarily as he looked ahead down the road to Tromso, his only way out of this God-forsaken place. Twice he'd dashed for cover as cars sped past him, he assumed they were from the complex. The only other drivers on the road were the slow lumbering articulated trucks which occasionally roared past with a fearsome noise. For the umpteenth time he silently gave thanks for his heavy coat, and tried to lessen the stinging his breath caused as he exhaled. He thought of the cause of his flight, the single page nestling in his pocket. It was written in a language he didn't understand but he was convinced it contained information on the next Artefact. He comforted himself with the warming fact that he had struck a heavy blow against superior forces; for the first time in a proactive act against both Jochi and The Teacher. He hurried on feeling colder than ever. He heard the approaching growl of an engine and moved cautiously to the side of the road. It was decision time, he must risk asking for a lift or freeze to death. He stepped out onto the road breathing a sigh of relief as he saw it was a long haul truck. "Car broke down," he yelled as the massive vehicle towered over him. "You should have stayed inside it," said the man in broken English; it's twenty degrees below."

"It was overheating and smoking so I thought it a fire risk and best to walk."

"Jump in," He wasn't interested in Monty's problems; he turned his eyes back to the road and engaged the gears.

The sun was rising as Monty, tired and cold trudged through the Tromso back streets to a small bed and breakfast house. The town itself was a fishing port with identikit wooden houses that ran along its sea front and then up into various avenues. It was innocuous and large enough to get lost in which suited his purposes admirably. First he needed to sleep. He was so tired he wasn't thinking clearly, then he'd have to move fast to get out of here before they found him. After eight hours sleep he took a roundabout route to the small airport where he'd seen something that disturbed him greatly. On the way he purchased a cheap mobile phone on a pay as you go tariff and made the call.

"I thought you were dead, where on earth are you Uncle?" Jem answered his call and sounded very anxious.

"I'll explain later Jem, please just listen," said Monty. "I was hoping to get out of here through the airport but there's a problem, The Teacher has just arrived in town."

"What the hell are you doing there?" Jem, the daughter of his younger sister was now a Detective Sergeant. She was his only living relative and they had formed a strong bond when he had taken under his wing at the Bermudan police academy. She was the apple of his eye, someone he'd do anything for. "Please Jem just listen," he replied and tried to explain the situation. "The good news is that we have a small advantage; we need to keep it."

"What I see is that you need help," replied Jem. "I've been worried sick about you. You're nearly at retirement age for God's sake, why haven't you involved the local police?"

"Corrupt as hell and in the pay of Jochi," whispered Monty. "That's the problem. I signed on as a contractor and saw the Police Chief taking a back-hander. I can't trust them Jem, believe me the stakes are too high. I suspect that Jochi bankrolls half the police force here."

"I'll get you some help," replied Jem, thinking furiously.

"Leave it with me but tell me exactly where you are."

"Tromso."

"My God! At his bloody headquarters, I assume this is all sanctioned?"

"Of course, that's why I went off the radar. I'm sorry but it was necessary, their tentacles spread a long way." He rang off and made his way back to the run-down bed and breakfast house and settled down for a long wait.

Barbados

The small airport was noisy and looked chaotic as Guy tried to walk inconspicuously through the terminal. Still dazed by the events in St Lucia, he had been delighted when Jem called him and arranged a private plane to a remote island airfield. He wouldn't have been able to leave St Lucia under his own steam as the police had already questioned him about Rose and were becoming increasingly suspicious, particularly after the run in he'd had with the previous police chief, a madman long since buried, called Grasshopper. It had sparked an ongoing feud with the island police that was still in evidence judging by the furore over his recent activity. He looked around for the exit heartened by Jem's news that Monty was alive and well, the first good news he'd had since Rose's disappearance. He knew her well from their previous meetings on Aruba. She was a born fighter against the innate prejudices of being both a woman and the niece of the Island's Chief Inspector of Police. If you were a friend of her Uncle's, then she would help you no matter what the situation.

Guy kept his head down as he went through Customs relieved to get through without being questioned. If there was an international alert out for him, Jem had managed to suppress it. He was using the second passport Monty had obtained for him over a year ago. Jem was now his only hope of getting out of the Caribbean; he switched on his mobile and saw the text words *'Harrison Caves-J'*. Checking the name against the map at the car hire counter he noted they were tourist caves in the centre of the island. He quickly hired and, with great relief, drove a small Fiat Uno northwards. Taking little notice of the scenery, he drove inland past the old racecourse and white colonial buildings and headed into the hills. There were no signposts on the island so he had to stop twice to check his directions before seeing a ramshackle sign to Harrison Caves. Jem met him at the elevator, her petite frame and blonde hair belying a tough interior. "Good to see you again Guy," she welcomed him with a smile, then said grimly. "I'm afraid the situation has got worse. There's been an accusation against you of kidnapping; a general police alert has been issued so we need to get you out of sight quickly. I've made some arrangements to help you; this lift takes us down the valley where we can find you a better disguise."

"I've been set up," explained Guy.

"Of course you have, that's why I'm putting my career on the line, that and the fact my Uncle trusts you implicitly. I don't understand why there's been such an extreme reaction to you though."

"My old adversary, Grasshopper," replied Guy. "Dead and gone yet his malign influence lives on. It's his old cronies out for revenge."

"I see, well, I guess that would explain it. I can only ignore the alert for so long, you need to leave the Caribbean quickly." Jem knew the people Guy was talking about and could easily believe their desire for revenge.

"I owe you for this." Guy said thankfully.

"Quid pro quo. As I said, Monty needs help badly; he's had a breakthrough but needs reinforcements up in the Arctic."

"I can hardly believe he's gone back up there but you've got a deal," Guy said grimly.

"It's too bloody hot here in more ways than one so the cold will be a nice change."

"The old fool has tried a crazy stunt and doesn't stand a chance of getting away with it without your help. Come on into the cave; there's someone here who can disguise you."

"What about you?"

"I intend to disappear a while until this blows over. I'm due some leave, out of sight, out of mind as they say."

"Smart move Jem, I'll repay you I promise."

"Damned right you will."

They joined the tail end of a tourist tractor pulling six carriages heading into the caves. Guy relaxed as the cool air hit him; the lower temperature and the permanence of the rocks making him feel more secure. Ruefully he realised that any chance of keeping out of The Teacher's affairs had been a total pipe dream. Rose had been right; this was a fight to the end. Even old Monty had shown him the way; it was time to re-engage.

"Did Monty mention Lorna or Diane?" Guy asked her.

"No it was a very quick call. He was afraid of being tracked; apparently the local police there are corrupt."

"Par for the course then, present company excepted," retorted Guy as they went ever deeper into the caves.

They were in further than Guy had imagined and travelled slowly downwards. It was well organized with numerous other tractor trailers passing them on the concrete tracks. Jem nudged him gesturing to a dark corner area next to a small pool. "It's time to part company, no one is looking, come on, hide in the corner of the cave." They alighted quickly as the trailer slowed to turn the corner.

"Here?" queried Guy looking around the small cave.

"Yes!" replied Jem following behind him. Guy found it eerie with the sudden quiet and almost total darkness.

"You're one hundred and sixty feet under the island," Jem told him and shone her flashlight ahead of them as if searching for someone. "Ah there you are, my old friend," she said and Guy shuddered involuntarily as a ghostly lumbering figure emerged from the shadows. Jem shone her small torch forwards, the beam bouncing off the stalagmites and stalactites. They added to the ghostly atmosphere of the cavern, then gestured for Guy to follow her into a small hidden recess. "Roland will help you with your disguise." She shook the hand of the small hunched man who had appeared out of the gloom.

"I need to check the police channels, there's heightened activity at the moment." she told them. The newcomer reached into his bag, drew out a sandy coloured beard and fixed it to Guy's face. "This will stay attached to your face for about three days," he murmured and turned away from him. "Hush someone is coming," whispered Jem. "Come on we need to get out of here fast, someone must have reported seeing you, we'll use the emergency exit over there."

"Where exactly are we?" panted Guy as he ran up the stairs and emerged through a large doorway out into the sunlight. He shielded his eyes and looked around him.

"Well away from the tourist hordes," replied Jem pointing towards the cliffs and the passenger lift, the police are searching over there. You were spotted, don't know how but we have to move fast." A door to their right jerked open and a shout pierced the air as two policemen appeared. "Run for it Guy and keep your head down, I'll delay them," hissed Jem. "Good luck, there are tickets in your coat pocket and the flight leaves in two hours. Find my uncle he's very dear to me, I'll try and put matters straight here."

"Thanks Jem, I owe you big time for this."

"It's nothing; I'm going on a well-earned vacation to keep my head down, some remote island far from anywhere because with my mad uncle and you I've a feeling it's a good time to lie low.

"You're probably right and you deserve it. I can't thank you enough."

"Just look after Monty."

"Do my best." Guy turned and ran to the open lift, the doors closing as he jumped in ignoring the startled look of the other passengers.

The lift was glass on three sides and Guy turned his head away feeling very exposed despite the disguise. The lift slowly rose into the air alongside the cliff walls. He imagined the entire island's police force watching as he saw Jem gesturing angrily to two policemen. Just when he thought he'd made it without been seen they both pointed up in his direction and started to run. Guy cursed inwardly and prayed for the lift to speed up. With agonizing slowness it finally reached the top and he ran to his car as fast as he dared. Keeping as calm as he could he drove slowly heading north, away from the area thronged by police cars and up into the remote hills. He reckoned they would expect him to head south to the airport so he drove in a circuitous direction and slowly relaxed as the roads became more and more remote. Finally he found a faster road and headed along the west coast road past sumptuous properties before finding the road to the airport. As he entered the terminal he looked around nervously but security guards paid him no attention as he strode to the passport areas and breathed a sigh of relief as he was waved through by a bored looking guard. The disguise had worked and he hoped Jem would be able to talk her way out of the situation. He double checked the ticket and made his way to the British Airways gate; for the first time since losing Rose he felt energized. I'm on my way he thought grimly; time to renew old acquaintances.

The room was cold and dark, the streets crawling with thugs he assumed worked for either Jochi or The Teacher; either way he was in trouble. Could it get any worse? Monty grimaced to himself; he was miserable and unsure what to do next; the hunter had indeed become the hunted. Everywhere he went he felt as if someone was watching him. The little town gave the impression of being under siege, the more so because in effect it was an island serviced by the large Bruvegen Bridge that dominated the town. The cold felt even more intense in the slowly emerging Norwegian spring as he completed his second day of aimless wandering around the town. He'd kept a low profile, reading in his bedroom and trying to translate the diary page without success. It was a language he hadn't seen before. There was no doubt he must leave town before the noose tightened further. There was only one viable solution, a sea passage. He had enough cash on him to buy a berth on one of the many fishing vessels heading south for Oslo and Gothenburg. His initial enquiries had yielded a couple of possible berths to be confirmed today.

Stepping out into the cold air he wore the long old coat he'd purchased in a local charity shop. The precious piece of paper was well hidden in the newly hollowed out heel of his boot. It was nearing three o'clock and the light was fading; he reflected that at least it wasn't dark half the time as it was in winter. He made his way past the Polar Museum onto the familiar pier adjacent to the Bruvegen Bridge and groaned as he saw a group of men heading towards him from the pier head. They didn't look like locals or Jochi's men. As they came within range he saw they were Asians, The Teacher's men. The leading man locked eyes and Monty stared back. He desperately looked around wondering whether he should try to bluff it out with his police badge and quickly concluded that it was too risky.

"You, old man, what's your name?" scowled the leading Asian,

"Joe Smart from Boston New England."

"You don't sound American."

"No? My mother was English."

"What you doing here?"

"I'm a sailor," explained Monty patiently. "Waiting for a ship home, my berth left without me."

"Show me your passport"

"You're not the police, you have no right to ask for my passport," protested Monty. The other man was squinting hard at his mobile gadget. "I'm already late for an appointment so if you don't mind."

"When I'm ready," he said and turning to his companion said, "what you got Xi?"

"Grab him," snapped Xi.

Monty reacted instantly. He grabbed the man's mobile phone and flung it out into the water then pushed the man down, falling with him and at the same time grabbing the gun he'd seen half out of his pocket. The leader, Wang, looked on in astonishment as he found himself staring down the business end of a very dangerous gun barrel. "On the ground both of you," snapped Monty looking around for the best way of escape.

"You won't get far," snarled Wang slowly lying down, "there are many more of us. You have no chance, so just give up old man otherwise you will never leave here alive."

"I'll take my chance," retorted Monty taking Wang's gun as well. He groaned as he saw another Asian at the other end of the pier looking at them closely. Shoving one pistol into his coat pocket he flung Wang's weapon into the sea and set off at a steady canter toward the houses. The newcomer came running towards him. When he was twenty yards or so away from him Monty pointed his gun at his head. "Drop your gun now," he yelled. The gun convinced him to act quickly and he did as Monty instructed. "Who are you?" He asked with a puzzled look on his face. He clearly didn't know what had happened before Monty had turned the tables on his attackers. "Ask your mates," snapped Monty, as he kicked the dropped gun into the sea and then gestured to the floor. The man dropped to the ground and clasped his hands over his head as if expecting to be shot. Monty left him there and ran from the pier into town, desperately looking around the wooden-faced houses for somewhere to hide. He didn't have much time; they wouldn't be far behind him. That damned paper was going to be his undoing; he couldn't see how he was going to get out of this mess. He spotted an alleyway and darted into it as he heard shouts from behind and another from somewhere up ahead. He closed his eyes and bent double trying to slow his breathing as he looked anxiously around. He was beginning to think he was getting too old for this sort of adventure.

The shout came again, nearer this time and out of the gloom came Wang followed by a motor car. Monty groaned; he was cornered. Wang walked slowly towards him smiling coldly, exposing rotting teeth as he did so. Monty desperately looked around him; he was certain he'd heard a different voice. Wang and his followers approached him warily, remembering he had a gun and knew how to use it. Monty backed away trying each door he passed. "In here," someone whispered and he saw a door swing open close to his right hand. He had no choice; he stepped inside and slammed and bolted the door behind him. He stumbled into a quieter, saner world. "This way," said the voice again, and what seemed to be an old man brushed past him to take the lead down a flight of stairs into the cellars. "Great smuggling area this, used it a lot during the war to run food past the Germans; the passages are all interlinked as a labyrinth," he told Monty and ran on along half-lit corridors. Monty estimated they must have covered over four hundred metres before they finally came to a halt. "You've just covered about half the floor area of Tromso and are about five meters from the sea; it's another world down here."

"Who are you friend?" asked Monty seeing the old man's face for the first time.

"Name is Tocsin, I have been watching you for some time. I was waiting for the best moment to step in. The bastards are strolling around as if they own the place, bloody Asians. The folk here just hide but not me, it's time we stood up and fought back like we did in the war." Monty had no idea why the man was helping him but was very grateful that he was.

"Thanks for your help," he said, "It was desperate out there; you're a resistance leader then?"

"I was, sixty years ago, yes," said Tocsin smiling. Monty realised the man must be over ninety. "They don't realise that they are taking on people like me who will fight back. You're not alone." Tocsin assured him.

"You knew I was here?" asked Monty looking around.

"I guess you could say that. I have weapons and supplies here, a great hiding place and my old contacts, which is how I knew about you."

"Who exactly are your contacts?"

"The Elders; I used to be linked to them as an observer in the War, we watched and reported; don't think they ever did anything active but I was only young, kept the link ever since, I got a call to look after special guests."

"Guests?" Monty was intrigued to know who else could be wandering around these frozen wastes.

"Let me introduce my other recent acquisition," smiled Tocsin opening a thick door. Monty was dumbstruck for a moment when he saw who was on the other side. "For God's sake is that you under the beard?" he said only half-believing what he saw.

"Good to see you, Monty," smiled Guy and clasped his old friend to him. "Tocsin has been a fantastic help getting me out of the airport under the very eyes of The Teacher's men."

"The Airport was built over one of my labyrinths so it was easy," smiled Tocsin. Guy released Monty from his hug and said, "I was going to come up and help you but Tocsin had a safer plan."

"It's bloody dangerous, that's for sure," replied Monty, "thought I was a goner back there, by the way. I don't think much of the beard." Guy grinned. "Your niece's idea, she saved me, Monty. I owe her, anyway the beard has done its job," Guy smiled and, wincing as he did so ripped it off his face. "You've no idea how great it is to see you again." he said to Monty.

"We need to move further down into the labyrinth," interjected Tocsin. "They may be able to find this place so we must go deeper; a safe place provisioned for a nuclear attack," he said proudly. You can rest there and recover whilst I check things out."

"Won't they find the tunnels" asked Monty

"We have a way to disguise and then booby-trap them," smiled the old man who was clearly enjoying himself. Monty and Guy settled down with copious amounts of food and drink, able for now to relax and re-gather their strength.

"What the hell were you thinking of Monty?"

"I've wondered that myself many times in the last couple of days."

"So why?"

"After the horrors of Aruba, Interpol agreed that there had to be a more proactive stance against The Teacher's conspiracy. It was threatening to hit the media with negative publicity so I was called in to go undercover."

"It's not your fight, Monty."

"I'm in this as deeply as you."

"But why the secrecy? We could have done this together?"

"I told you I had my official orders from the Secretary General himself in Lyon, France. They were very specific that this operation had unprecedented levels of security so I could not involve you in an official operation; anyway I've had a breakthrough."

"What is it exactly?"

"Here," said Monty producing the paper from his boot. "Belonged to a cabin boy called Svente who served Cook on his voyages. It's genuine and contains clues to the location of a diary apparently leading to the next Artefact."

"How do you know all that?"

"Because we got a lead in Aruba inadvertently from Sabine. She was talking to Jochi at the time which was picked up by our surveillance cameras. Jochi decided to turn on The Teacher and got his henchman Stefan to track down the clue. I managed to appropriate it at the camp. He's been ripping the place up trying to find it ever since and I overheard Stefan saying it was the clue to the Axe Artefact."

"So what does it say?"

"That's the problem; it's in a strange language though I can figure out that the diagram shows directions to a schoolroom in Helsinki."

"A schoolroom?"

"The school symbol here look, and the word Helsinki."

"That Svente was on Cook's final voyage fits with the two previous Artefacts being linked to explorers. Columbus and Drake," said Guy thoughtfully. "No doubt The Teacher is here to find it; how on earth did you get it?"

"I was at the Valgrind camp undercover and heard Stefan talking on his mobile about the Cook voyages. God knows who he was talking to but he didn't hear me; a name was mentioned."

"What name?"

"A Chinese man called Zheng He."

"Zheng He, I assume the explorer and not Zheng Wan The Teacher."

"As you say, there is a pattern involving Columbus and Drake and finding them in remote locations thought reachable only by explorers. Perhaps Zheng He engineered the whole thing to ensure that only explorers could find the Artefacts."

"The Teacher knows all this too?"

"Yes, he's ahead of the game as always, which is why we forced the issue. I tried to be clever and look what happened? Still you're aware that there has been a falling out between Jochi and The Teacher; it should work to our advantage."

"All very interesting stuff but what do you suggest we do?" said Guy.

"Retreat, this stuff is way out of our league," replied Monty.

"Hmmm. It's gone beyond that, I'm afraid, this is now personal," said Guy and explained Rose's disappearance. "My life will never be normal until all these plots are finished once and for all; besides the Elders are now directly involved. I haven't heard from the Whistler, though, he seems to have disappeared."

"But the Elders don't get directly involved; it's not their style."

"Not without breaking their own rules of practice, but times are changing."

"So Rose has disappeared? You two should be an item."

"She's my business partner Monty; it's Lorna I care about, which reminds me have you seen her?"

"Yes, she's OK but obsessed with a new venture, don't know where or what it's about."

"So at last we have something The Teacher wants; that's a start, plus he's out for revenge on Jochi. Is he here?"

"Don't know for sure but his men most definitely are and have occupied the top hotel in town. The entire top floor. Worst thing is I can't trust the police so I suggest we take advantage of Tocsin's tunnel and escape."

"I'm not going to run again Monty, I'm done with that. In any case I have to get Lorna. I have another option."

"Which is?"

"Get the Artefact; we have Tocsin's inside knowledge and your paper, plus they don't know I'm here if indeed they think I'm still alive at all."

"Tocsin is an old man for God's sake, this lot are trained killers. I should know I've crossed swords with them often enough recently."

"Sorry Monty, I told you, I'm through with running; I'd rather die fighting."

"I was talking of a strategic retreat not running. Finland holds the clue we should go there directly."

"It's too vague Monty. All you have is a page with a few directions; for all we know it may be incomplete, and Jochi holds the rest of it. I'm going to Valgrind," replied Guy grimly. "She is in huge danger if The Teacher is planning to attack Jochi, I'll do it alone if necessary." The expression on his face told Monty that there was no point in trying stop him mounting a rescue attempt. He shrugged his shoulders. "You're mad, the conditions there are dire but you need someone to look after you and I guess that's me, so I'll no doubt finish my life in that God-forsaken place." Guy grinned, the urgency and excitement of the situation was beginning to energise him. "You said the complex is being refurbished," he said thoughtfully.

"Yes, that was my cover there, as an electrical contractor."

"Could that work for us both?"

"Maybe…we'd need a different cover story though; they won't fall for it again."

"We need a reason to go in late at night, then we stand a chance of catching them by surprise. An emergency problem that needs fixing, something like that."

"It'll have to be electricity or water then."

"Water this time, how do they get it supplied?"

"Piped in from Tromso; it could work if we can find a way to shut it off," replied Monty thoughtfully.

"Your police contacts?"

"I told you I can't trust them, not when their leader is in the pay of Jochi."

"Then Tocsin can help us prepare for a night entrance. From what he tells me, there seem to be few limits to what he can do. I bet he knows someone at the water plant."

Tocsin not only knew someone at the Nordling Water Company, he was able to arrange a fake explosion to register on their website causing them to announce a temporary shutdown of supply. He also fixed it for them to be employed as contractors, complete with uniforms. It took a full day to get things arranged, so Guy and Monty took the opportunity to get some rest. The following night they left the warmth of the tunnels and went out into temperatures over twenty degrees below freezing as they made their way across the frozen wastes to the main entrance of Valgrind.

Nestled between two snow covered ranges, the complex sat on a plateau designed to ensure no one could approach unseen; it was certainly effective. The scene was just as Guy remembered it from his previous fraught visit over a year ago and shone like a ghostly presence in the night air. They knew Nordling's snow mobile would be spotted on Valgrind's sophisticated surveillance system, so made no attempt to disguise their approach. Their plan, such as it was, involved using Monty's knowledge of the layout to reach the maintenance room where Guy had previously been incarcerated. They could then access the central computer control systems and cause enough chaos to allow the time to search for Diane and Lorna, and hopefully more clues to the whereabouts of the Axe. They parked the snow mobile and made their way to the rear of the building with some trepidation.

The door opened and a surly guard gestured them inside. "Get the damned thing working," he mumbled, "the boss is moaning like hell about his bath, main contacts are over there." He pointed with a finger to a corridor along which an array of fuse and control boxes were lined.

"We'll fix it as soon as we can, but there are process checks we need to make," Guy murmured, keeping his head down and walking confidently along the corridor. He was grateful for the warmth and quickly found the maintenance room. They carried out what they hoped was a convincing inspection of the installation and promised to call the guard when they had finished restoring connections. Guy sent a prearranged signal to Tocsin, knowing the water would start to flow again in ten minutes. Monty used his old security pass on an adjoining door which led through to a small console unit with a battery of television screens and keyboards.

"This is the control centre, I'll try and shut the computer system down. That will give us a chance to find the girls whilst they are distracted." He sat down at the terminal and began tapping the keys.

Guy looked around, too late, he heard a bang and the door slammed open, lights blazed on and all hell broke loose. "You've got a nerve, I'll give you that," roared a voice and Jochi emerged surrounded by guards. "Take them both to the guard room and get the diary paper off him." The guards surrounded them and grabbed hold of them before they could move. Jochi called to them as they were dragged out of the room. "I thought you would come for the girls, a fatal error but no doubt one you think chivalrous. Ingenious to stop the water but not clever enough, I'm afraid, and I'm so glad you brought the elusive Tresanton with you."

"You don't think I would have been so stupid as to have brought the page with me do you?" retorted Monty.

"Don't play games old man, Tresanton will do anything to save his girl," replied Jochi. "I must tell you she does a good massage," he grinned. "Now hand it over."

"The Teacher is coming for you," replied Guy.

"He won't come until he's sure he can win, that's his way. He doesn't know what defences I have here so he will bide his time unless he senses a weakness. He wants the Artefact, that's all that interests him. He also knows you have the diary page so you have helped me by diverting his attention."

"He's getting ready to strike tonight, I saw it with my own eyes," replied Monty coldly. "If I were you I would get out of here fast."

"And you both came here under this charade just to warn me, how touching."

"As you said I'm old fashioned and chivalrous, we came to save the girls," snapped Guy.

"Give me the page," demanded Jochi.

"Assuming I have it," replied Monty.

"I could have you both killed here and now."

"It's been translated already and copied, the exact location of the Artefact is no secret now," replied Monty watching Jochi's face. "Clear directions copied and sent to Interpol. Anything happens to me and they open it."

"Well, something is about to happen to you. Are you offering a deal?"

"Yes! The girls leave with us and you'll get it all; you have the second Artefact, you get the third."

"That's enough," snapped Jochi and turned to one of the guards. "Take it from him, and bring the girls to my room." Looking back at Monty he said, "You'll talk soon enough after I torture the girls and then hand them over to my men." Monty and Guy exchanged glances.

"Very well," said Monty wearily, He bent down to extract the paper as Jochi gestured to the guard. "Bring the girls here," he ordered. "I want to talk to them."

Fifteen minutes later the guards returned with the girls.

"Lorna it's so good to see you again," smiled Guy when Lorna entered with Diane and Soraya.

"Guy what on earth are you doing here?" said Lorna in astonishment.

"Just passing by," smiled Guy.

"What's the meaning of this, Jochi?" snapped Diane. These are friends of mine, why the guns?"

"Don't treat me as an idiot." Jochi brandished the recovered paper. "You passed this to the old man and so have forfeited any rights; our partnership is over."

"Really? Then leave my premises immediately."

"I will when you repay me the money I invested," he said knowing she wasn't able to do so. He looked again to the guard.

"Take Lorna to my room, her torture should loosen some reluctant tongues." Another guard entered the room and attracted his attention. "What is it," he snapped."

"Intruders about half an hour away from here and approaching fast."

"How many are there?"

"Well over twenty."

"Right, lock this lot up and get the contingency plan ready." The guards again surrounded them and marched them all off to a strong room at the other end of the corridor. The door slammed shut and they heard bolts sliding into position.

"I think I might have some news for you," said Diane as the footsteps of then guards receded. "Jochi mentioned some intelligence that he picked up when he arrived back here yesterday."

"What sort of intelligence?"

"He has a spy in The Teacher's camp, there were rumours a girl was kidnapped on his orders; it's probably Rose."

"Did he say where she was?" asked Guy, he was delighted to have some news of her at last.

"Yes he did. She's in Australia."

Chapter 9

Queensland
Eagles Nest

Balancing his glass on the bar, Jack balefully surveyed the room. Sitting comfortably waiting for him to speak were his cousin Duncan, his wife Ailsa and his Aussie bodyguard, a bruiser from the seedier streets of Brisbane called Marc. "This deal isn't for shrinking violets so listen close, it's our ticket to the big time," he began.

"How's it any different from past jobs?" asked Marc, his blue eyes alert and his uncombed blonde hair half covering a hardened face. Jack had bought his loyalty years ago and there was nothing he wouldn't do for the boss.

"Chalk and Cheese. This is bigger than anything you've ever dreamed about, so do exactly as I tell you," Jack told him. "The stakes are too high to fail; you are now part of a multi-national operation."

"Fine by me," said Duncan, "it's time we moved upwards from the petty stuff.

"The petty stuff was doing okay," said Marc who was beginning to feel out of his depth.

"No it wasn't; this place is costing me a fortune and the bloody politicians are so corrupt they make me look like Mother Theresa. I've had enough of that crap; think of this as an investment for your pension fund, a retirement plan."

"I assumed that's why you wanted the insurance policy," replied Duncan, "It's always a good idea when times are tough."

"That was a specific request from my new partner but one that we'll turn to our advantage; it wasn't cheap bringing her all the way here. Still it sent a clear message and shows we are competent to carry out difficult international assignments. You did well."

"It was relatively straight forward in the end, the wonders of drugs kept her quiet."

"Have they arrested Tresanton yet?"

"No, but they will. He's disappeared, but the police are confident they'll find him and lock him up. I dropped enough hints with them; do you want me to rough the girl up a little?"

"No! I told you, this is big league stuff; we don't rough people up now, particularly not this one. She's too valuable and will have a role to play when the time is right. A little mental conditioning might help though, soften her up," Jack replied thoughtfully.

"Isn't that risky?" said Ailsa. "She's a spitfire and might escape to damage us all; I suggest you leave her alone."

"Not if we handle it carefully," replied Jack taking a sip of his drink and staring out of the window. "Before we get into detailed plans it's time you all understood a little of the background to our venture and how I am positioning us with our new colleagues. They see Australia as a major investment opportunity and I've convinced them we are the main players here. They like our track record so we've gotta live up to it and show them we're their equals.

"So who are these partners," asked Ailsa.

"I'm coming to that," Jack said, the woman irritated him; a plan for her future was forming in his mind.

"Well, I for one am up for it; it's time to think big. We won't get anywhere without scaling up our operations." Duncan gave his opinion in his usual direct manner.

"This will take intricate planning but I am convinced it will work," continued Jack and went on to give details of what was needed. "The company is ZTW, a mining conglomerate; that's why they are interested in Oz, I'll be their head here," he said proudly.

"Wow that's big," conceded Duncan as Jack finished detailing the plans. "I'm really impressed."

Jack smiled and relaxed a little and took another drink. It was coming together nicely and he felt good as the whisky warmed his throat and lips. "The history of this place particularly impressed my partner; he said it was a good omen for his plans and very pertinent with the Mongol connection."

"Mongol connection? What's that all about? Asked Ailsa, puzzled.

"The original Eagle's Nest was the stronghold of a group called *The Assassins*, Adolf Hitler just borrowed the name."

"The Assassins?" queried Ailsa.

"They ruled a kingdom in the Himalayas. In 1090, Hasan Ibn al-Sabbah set them up in a mountain outpost at Alamut south of the Caspian Sea. They called it the Eagle's Nest. Their real name was the Nizaris."

"And the Mongol connection?" asked Duncan.

"The word 'assassin' derives from an Arabic phrase meaning 'those who eat Hashish'. The Mongol leader, Heulegu, dislodged them from their nest after a three-year siege. They made a vow to hunt down and kill the aggressors and quickly struck in China. An assassin murdered Heulegu's brother, the new Mongol Khan, Mongke, in broad daylight. His throat was cut by a fake Yam rider, that's their name for the courier service. Kublai became the next Khan and my new partner said it was fate and the Mongols have a significant part to play in his plans. What that part is I don't yet know."

"Now Duncan," he looked at his Rolex watch, "it's time to check on our insurance policy".

Rose was in no mood to be 'checked on', she was furious at her kidnapping and subsequent treatment.

"Tell the gorilla to let me go," she spat as soon they entered the room.

"Don't push your luck lady," snapped Duncan, but gestured to Marc to leave.

"Go to hell."

"I gave her double the tranquilizer dose," replied Duncan looking at her with anticipation. "She'll soon be more malleable."

"What the hell is this all about and where am I?" snapped Rose.

"You are my honoured guest," Jack told her with a smile. "So please make yourself comfortable. I'm sorry these men upset you, maybe they've been over zealous."

"If you mean have they been trying to grope me at every opportunity like dirty old men, then yes, they have. Your other gorilla there attacked us in the Caribbean. Where's Guy?"

"I'm asking the questions."

"So where the hell am I?"

"Land of Oz, a long way to walk back I'm afraid."

"You brought me half the way around the world for what?" demanded Rose.

"You really ought to be grateful, if it wasn't for me who knows what could have happened to you. Treat me nice and I'll see you alright," purred Jack looking appreciably at Rose's slim body. Not much meat but enough to make an agreeable experience, perhaps she could substitute for the pneumatic blonde he had just kicked out.

"And what would treating you nice constitute?" Rose asked, looking at him angrily, though she already knew the answer.

"You're an attractive girl, you work it out."

"I'd rather die."

"That too can be arranged," smiled Jack opening the door. "Think about it. All I will say is you've got some powerful enemies, people who murder for pleasure so you need friends like me whether you like it or not."

"So you're one of The Teacher's lackeys; scares you does he?" snapped Rose. Jack called Marc back into the room and told him to take her to the dungeon and lock her up.

"We'll take a look later when she's calmed down," he said with a leer.

Rose groaned as she was manhandled down the stairs, the days since her last clear recollection on the deck of the *Hidalgo* were one long blur. She recalled the gun that Ailsa had held on her and Duncan returning. First he told her there'd been an accident then grabbed her and plunged a syringe into her. She had scribbled a note on Guy's compass before they had bundled her half-unconscious onto a helicopter. The rest had been like a bad dream.

She fell to the dungeon floor and the door slammed behind her. She cursed as she lay in the pitch darkness. She was alone and God alone knew where Guy was, assuming he was still alive. She had always been a plucky fighter and they had been in many rough scrapes before, but she wished she hadn't yelled at Guy before they had been separated. She didn't believe he was dead; not for a minute, but she bitterly regretted fighting with him and having contacted Sabine. Patience was a virtue she had not displayed. The long flight, when she had been conscious, had given her time to reflect on her life. Aside from fighting The Teacher she was fighting herself as she determined what she really wanted. Being with Guy was exciting and at times exhilarating but it was not the future. They worked together, but she doubted it would ever be more than that; would either of them want more? She suspected any lead in that department, if it came, would come from her. Anyway at the moment it was totally irrelevant; they were both in grave danger.

Her captors had other matters to attend to and, as they hurried back to Jack's lounge, they discussed her capture.

"You reckon you took care of Tresanton with the police?" queried Jack.

"Stitched him up real fine," replied Duncan. "If he survived my blow, he'll struggle to get out of the country; what's it all about with those two?"

"The new partner wanted them taken care of, very specific over that, They were particularly insistent on the man being incarcerated. The girl is added insurance for us in case the new partner doesn't play ball; our own variation on the order if you like."

"So she stays here."

"For now, yes, until I understand the lay of the land, I like to cover all angles. He seemed all right with that providing he gets her in the next few weeks, which will depend on how we stand with him on our insurance policy," he smiled. "Now to work, we start operations immediately; no time to lose I want you out on the reef."

"No one can go onto the Endeavour Reef; it's restricted territory."

"Bribes can achieve anything in Brisbane. I need you out there fast, fling some cash around, and we need the best divers."

"What exactly are we looking for?" asked Duncan. Since returning from the Caribbean he'd developed a taste for action. He'd enjoyed outwitting Tresanton and spending a week with Rose had whetted his appetite for her; he'd seen enough to want more and he'd have the opportunity too. Jack had told him he had something he wanted Ailsa to do for him in New Zealand it had also seemed a great chance to get to know Rose better.

"Why the Endeavour Reef?" he asked his boss.

"There's something very special out there. An old casket covered in barnacles and extremely valuable I am told. Just got to make sure we get there first."

"Ahead of whom?" he wondered if there was to be a fight for the old casket.

"Others who will be ruthless. Now, get to it."

"What's my wife going to be doing in New Zealand?"

"Some merchandising; it's a run to create a distraction to the authorities and provide some hard cash for us."

"Isn't it dangerous?"

"No more than your last assignment. My own dear daughter will be with her; have faith, after all omelettes require the breaking of eggs." Duncan nodded, as Jack said this was his chance for the big time and he would be well rewarded. He licked his lips at the thought of Rose. Jack regarded him with disdain, wondering to himself how he came to be related to such a man. He was an amateur, but time was of the essence and the Chinese man was in a hurry.

Chapter 10

Valgrind

The room was well lit and had comfortable armchairs into which they each sank gratefully. When they had all recovered from the rough handling by the brutish guards, Diane said. "Looks like you were right Guy; The Teacher is moving in tonight, how did you know?" Monty answered for him.

"Tocsin tipped him off. The Shield was going to be moved tonight; we counted on their mutual antagonism doing the rest; looks like it worked."

"Where's Rose, Guy?" asked Lorna.

"She was kidnapped, a couple of weeks ago. I have no idea where she is or if she is even still alive." His face showed his concern.

"You care for her don't you?"

"Yes…We've been business partners for some time. I just wish I knew where she was."

"Jochi told me The Teacher had ordered her kidnap to support a new business adventure. He wasn't totally sure of the details as it came here in an unusual way," continued Diane.

"What do you mean unusual?" asked Guy.

"It was in Morse Code. He said it sounded like a new venture for The Teacher."

"My God," groaned Guy. "She couldn't be further away. And Morse Code, can you believe that?"

"Indeed who uses that these days?" said Diane.

"It could be the Whistler," said Guy quietly. Then, hoping again that Rose was safe he forced his mind to focus on their current predicament. "I wonder what Jochi's contingency plan is?" he mused half aloud.

"He has vehicles on standby at the back. This place is shut for maintenance so I'm not sure how fast he can get out," said Diane. "Incidentally I recall you came here last in the guise of electrical contractors. It's becoming a habit." They all smiled at the comment.

"How many people here?" asked Monty?

"Rochembach and Kirstin are here in addition to us two;

Jochi has half a dozen thugs."

"Sorry I had to steal the page," said Monty to Diane.

"I thought I recognized you, your disguise was crap," smiled Diane. "Anyway the project here is finished; Lorna and I have an alternative plan B."

"Plan B?" queried Guy.

"Yes, a floating health spa," replied Lorna. "My father's old cruiser is being revamped, needs a bit of money though."

"We need to get out of here first." said Guy. "The two tigers have fallen out and there will be a hell of a scrap. Is the Shield here?"

"I've seen it, why is the paper so valuable?" asked Diane.

"It leads to the next Artefact, The Teacher's Holy Grail," replied Monty casting his eyes around the room in the hope of finding a way out.

"And Jochi now has it?"

"I gave him a worthless sheet," smiled Monty. As he spoke the door opened. "Get ready we need to catch them off guard, it's our only chance," he said. But his hope faded as he recognised the two newcomers who had also been roughed up by the guards. "Ah my policeman friend!" he exclaimed as Kurt Rochembach and Soraya stepped into the room. The door slammed shut behind them. As Monty and Kurt shook hands the policeman whispered in Monty's ear. "Jochi is listening, the room is wired. We must find a way out of here they're setting charges to the place."

"Charges? Oh my God," exclaimed Diane. "We'll have no chance if the place explodes and the rooms lock down."

"Can't understand why you came back here Diane," said Monty. "So many memories it must be painful for you."

"It was my home for many years and I had a duty to look after the damaged girls; a means to an end; something different before the long term plan."

"There may be a way out, the way I used on my last visit," said Guy looking upwards. "The ventilation system," he whispered to Monty. "I need to get up there." He stood on a chair and began trying to lift each panel in the ceiling, eventually he found one that moved. "Ah here it is," he said, and lifted the panel to the air vents. As he did so the door starting opening again. "Very touching," snapped Jochi appearing at the door with

Stefan, "I want the real paper, old man, before I shoot you just for the fun of it. Did you really think you would get away with such a stupid ruse?" He pointed to Lorna and Soraya "You two follow me," he ordered.

"No," shouted Lorna in anguish, as she was dragged away by the guards.

"Let the bitch and her copper out but I warn you, lady, don't get in my way," snapped Jochi. "This place will blow in ten minutes so goodbye for good Tresanton."

"You're a fool! Your greed has put everything at risk." shouted Diane.

"Auf wiedersehn," said Stefan pushing Diane and Lorna ahead of him through the door, once more slamming it shut, with Monty and Guy inside.

"What now?" asked Monty?

"The ventilation shaft," Guy told him. "It's our only chance. I could see it was open; come on there's no reason why it won't work again, give me a lift." Monty helped him up onto the tallest chair and took his weight as he clambered into the space leading to the ventilation shaft.

Working quickly he loosened the screws with his keys and looked into the familiar space. With some difficulty Monty struggled behind him and they shuffled their way along to the next room, "I recall this shaft is about ten metres long," said Guy. "There's a light up ahead and I recognize the room. Hopefully the screws will still be loose from the last time. No reason why they would have tightened them." He breathed a sigh of relief as the panel gave way and they both lowered themselves down into the room. Its door was open and Guy felt a glimmer of hope as they ran through it. "We need to get to the outside fast, God knows when it will blow," he said. The moonlight gleamed off the white snow as they stumbled through the reception hall, relieved to get out of the building though they were still far from safe. "We need to get some transport," said Monty as the night was lit by flashes of brilliant light followed by the sound of explosions. "Too late Monty, The Teacher has arrived," said Guy. He cast a searching glance around and ran back into the reception hall to retrieve some heavy coats he'd seen just inside the door. He grabbed two of them, handed one to Monty and they replaced their overalls with the coats.

Ahead shadowy figures were illuminated on the horizon as two armoured trucks appeared, their headlights blazing through the gloom their guns swivelling slowly towards the camp. "Bloody hell, this is getting dangerous," said Monty and prepared to run. There was a sudden movement away to their right and they could just see two vehicles preparing to leave. "Jochi's taken the only ground transport."

"Never mind that, we must get away from the building; the charges are going to blow any minute." Guy reminded him. "The snow mobile is our only chance."

"What about Diane and Rochembach?"

"They said they knew a way out, we have enough problems of our own." Guy insisted. A gun fired. They ran out into the night air as a huge explosion rocked the ground; a shockwave followed and what felt like an invisible hand flung them into the snow. They lay there gasping with shock and the sudden intake of cold air. They saw figures moving and the two escape vehicles driving slowly away from the building partially hidden from the attackers. "We are going to struggle to get to the snowmobile," gasped Monty, "it's too far away and exposed."

"We've got to get behind the building, over there, come on," yelled Guy as the ground shook violently with another heavy explosion from the front of the building. "Jochi is in the lead vehicle over there," Guy could see Jochi and his men struggling with a large object that had worked loose. The Shield! There was another huge explosion and as if in slow motion the wheels lifted off the second truck and it toppled slowly onto its side. Guy groaned as he saw Lorna struggling in Jochi's grip; he pushed her into the first truck next to Soraya.

Guy broke into a run and soon felt as if his lungs were bursting, but the vehicle was too fast. They staggered across to the snowmobile and started the engine. Monty grabbed the accelerator and edged forward cursing as it stalled. He looked around; the shooting had stopped as The Teacher's vehicles closed in. Guy lifted his head and saw the lead vehicle turn towards them a grinning man raising his gun. Guy prepared for the worst and braced himself. To his intense relief the gun swivelled away towards something else. "There's a truck coming… bloody hell it's Tocsin," shouted Monty. Sure enough the old man from Tromso drove straight at the lead vehicle hitting it violently from the side. The impact was thunderous as a huge fireball enveloped the two vehicles. Monty and Guy flung themselves to the snow in horror as waves of energy passed over them. "My God," said Monty stumbling to his feet and seeing the other attack vehicle halting "He gave his life to save us."

"He wouldn't have it any other way," said Guy as he slowed down to a halt and looked around. Back in the distance he saw the camp lit up and The Teacher's men lifting the Shield. "That's what they came for but they missed Jochi," he said.

"He's gone to Finland," grunted Monty.

"Guess so," agreed Guy, ducking instinctively as there was another boom and the camp became enveloped in smoke.

"Yep, and best of all they will have done for the police chief, I saw him going in there," replied Monty in satisfaction. "Valgrind is no more, there won't be much left when the fires die down. It's the end of a dream for Diane."

"Oh I don't think so," replied Guy. "She said she has other plans, but we need to get to Finland to catch Jochi; we can get to the airport through Tocsin's tunnel while The Teacher is distracted."

"You know, I'm supposed to keep the peace not disturb it," grumbled Monty as they climbed back onto the snowmobile.

"Perhaps but, as they say, needs must," replied Guy grimly. "It's our fight, not just because that bastard has taken Lorna, the Artefacts are more than mere icons."

"There's something far bigger going on and if I've learnt anything about The Teacher there's more surprises in store, we must hurry."

"First we are going back to Tromso to ensure dear old Tocsin gets the recognition he deserves," replied Monty wearily, "then we go after The Teacher."

Chapter 11

Gothenburg

The cruise liner that at its launch had been hailed as an engineering masterpiece had been in dry dock for nearly eight months. It had become a hulk of rusting steel and lost dreams after its previous life as a hospital ship to rejuvenate the aged. It was a big vessel, over 300 metres long, in excess of 150,000 tonnes and built to accommodate over five hundred passengers. Its previous owner, Stig Oleson, had died after being convicted of a string of felonies, and the ownership had passed to his daughter, Lorna. It stood now, impounded, a huge drain on her financial resources as she set about turning what looked a wreck inside, into a floating spa that could cater to rich clientele. It was a natural development from the Valgrind project or had been until Lorna's kidnapping. Some progress had been made and life was returning to the hulk.

Whatever its condition, it looked like heaven to the occupants of the taxi that drew up alongside the ship. After a long and arduous journey across Norway and down Sweden's east coast, Diane and Kurt Rochembach had finally made it to their destination. They had hidden in a small hut Diane often used on the side of the mountain before returning to the ruins of the complex to salvage what they could after the attackers left. Their escape route had been planned for some time; Soraya and Lorna were meant to have been with them too. "We must find a way to help poor Lorna," said Kurt as they made their way up the gangway to the deck. "Of course we must, but tell me how?" Sighed Diane. Kurt shook his head, "Not in good shape are we, that damned piece of shrapnel has hurt my leg badly?"

"We'll think of a way," Diane assured him looking fondly at the wounded soldier.

The Valgrind dream was over, money was tight and the refurbishment of the cruiser incomplete; the only ray of light was the arrival of a lucrative commission to sail the cruiser to the Indian Ocean for a rich African ruler who wished to hire it for his anniversary celebrations. It was a ray of light that had brought them here to get the vessel on its way. As they approached the bridge they were met by the Captain. "Good day Ma'am," he greeted them courteously. "Good day to you, Captain Jenner," she replied, "Is she seaworthy?"

"Just about ma'am though the infrastructure isn't ready yet," replied the Captain, a grizzled Australian.

"So she can sail?"

"Yes. The Portmaster's lifted the impounding order. We can leave as soon as you are ready to board; she's fuelled up and ready to go. She even has a new temporary name painted on the side, *Lucky Star*. I know the owner has another name in mind, but she hasn't told me what it is. It's bad luck not to have a name on a ship so I chose one myself."

"Lorna wants to choose a new name for her and have a proper ceremony, so don't get upset if she changes it. How long will the voyage take?"

"Three weeks to get around Africa and into Tanzania so we need to get underway tomorrow."

"You have recruited a crew?"

"Enough and their wages will be covered I take it?"

"All of your wages will be covered. We'll board tonight."

"It's a skeleton crew ma'am, and an empty ship, so she will bounce about on the ocean."

"After what we've been through I think we can manage," she said acidly. Then turning to Rochembach she said. "Kurt get hold of Monty and see if he made it away from the camp. He may know something about Lorna; she's a plucky girl and if anyone can survive she can. She's an Oleson and they are a tough breed."

Helsinki - Finland

The wind was fierce and bitingly cold as Jochi drove from the station in their hired Audi. Stefan occasionally checked on the two girls, his insurance policy, with a quick glance in the rear mirror; they were drugged and unconscious. As they drove past the Parliament Building he pointed to a huge wooden ship, a floating restaurant, frozen to the ice. "It's colder here than in Valgrind, bloody winds straight off the Baltic," said Jochi. He pointed to a strange looking church literally built into rock as he drove through the town centre. "Soulless place, doesn't make you feel welcome at all," he observed. He stopped the car next to a large covered indoor market, but left the engine running. "Get us some hot food and drink. I'll watch the girls, they're still drugged but we won't take any chances." he said to Stefan. He'd recruited the German in Prague; he was a natural linguist and had translated the paper so they now knew the exact location of the diary. It was a schoolhouse in a small hamlet outside Helsinki. Jochi had researched Captain Cook's voyages and that of the Finnish cabin boy, Svente, who had travelled with Cook on his final voyages to Alaska and Hawaii. Instinct told him the Alaska visit was fundamental though he was intrigued at the distance Cook had sailed west from Alaska. He was sure the explorer had been directly involved in hiding the Axe so all they needed to do was find Svente's diary to reveal its precise location.

He looked again at the inert figures on the back seat and wondered what he should do with them; to lift them had seemed a good idea at the time, now he wasn't so sure. The explanation he had ready for anyone interested was that they were suffering from a fever. The sleeper train from Sweden had given them time to rest and sleep and he'd reflected on what to do next, losing the shield had been a blow but at least they were ahead with the search for the Axe. It would be theirs soon and The Teacher would have to negotiate.

Stefan returned with some bread and hot soup; Jochi took it gratefully. "Need to get to a motel near this school house, then we rest," he said. Despite being dog tired his adrenaline and will power kept him going. There was little time to lose, The Teacher wouldn't be far behind. He doubted he'd been in Tromso personally, but his tentacles seemed to spread everywhere and, not for the first time, he found himself trying to second guess the man whose team had acted faster than he'd thought possible at Valgrind. The loss of the complex was not a concern. He'd intended to destroy it anyway and hopefully a few loose ends had been taken care of with Tresanton and the others. He wondered why they hadn't been followed, perhaps it was because they would use him to do the hard work and then come in for the prize. He spotted a motel further along the road. At the same time a movement on the back seat caught his eye. Lorna was making a determined effort to open her eyes. He grimaced, the girls were a liability and he ruminated again over the downside; they slowed him down; maybe he should dump them after all.

The night porter in the Novotel Hotel showed no interest in

them as they staggered past with the girls propped between them and Stefan indicating they were drunk. Two adjoining rooms suited their purposes and the girls were laid on the single beds still unconscious. Jochi and Stefan studied the directions on the tattered paper they had recovered from Monty. Jochi knew that when he had learned of the paper's existence from Sabine his betrayal would inevitably end in a showdown with her. He poured over the details again until his eyes closed with fatigue.

It had been difficult to persuade three members of the Elders to back his plans but they had turned when they realised he was ahead of The Teacher. It had been an interesting development but it hadn't lasted; he knew he had now lost their support. It didn't matter to him anymore. He was beginning to snore when he was jerked awake by Stefan. "Found it! I'll stake my life on it, the descriptions match."

"You sure?" mumbled Jochi opening his eyes.

"An old school house twenty kilometres ahead on the lakeside. It's built to the same design as the museum I stole the paper from in Gothenburg, with the same architect. It has to be the place, see how the symbols fit!" he said excitedly, and pointed to them on the scrap of paper.

"We'll go at first light," said Jochi. Then, hearing a noise asked. "What was that?" First a window and then a door slammed. Stefan rushed from the room and returned a few minutes later. "We have a problem," he reported, "the younger one has disappeared."

"Dammit, didn't you tie them up? We'll never find her out there; it's a bloody forest everywhere we look."

"Sorry, Jochi."

"She won't last long in this cold; we don't need her now anyway. Go and get the other one and we'll leave now," ordered Jochi.

Stephan grabbed Lorna roughly, hoisted her over his shoulder and headed back to the room where Jochi waited impatiently. "I'm not just a piece of baggage," Lorna protested loudly as he dumped her on the floor. Stefan ignored her and instead said. "Where has she gone?"

"I have no idea and if I did I wouldn't tell you," replied Lorna, her eyes widening as Jochi advanced on her.

"They don't know anything," said Stefan as Jochi raised his

fist. Jochi changed his mind.

"You and I have unfinished business," he growled. Then to Stefan he said. "Get the car. We go now, the bitch may have gone to the damned police."

Lorna smiled in satisfaction as she was hustled to the car; they had planned the breakout carefully. Soraya was to go for help while she tried to delay the men. Unfortunately they had reacted too quickly and she hadn't had time to disable the car, so now she would get the brunt of their vengeance. She hoped to God Soraya was all right. Rebellion was welling up in her, anything was better than doing nothing, and she hated herself for succumbing to the cocktail of drugs they were feeding into her.

It was cold and pitch black as Soraya ran out into the freezing night, desperate to find help. She was free and intended to remain that way. Leaving the motel behind she soon started to shiver even in her heavy coat, and could see nothing ahead except far in the distance a sole house. There was little choice so she kept moving as fast as she could. She knocked on the door and was greeted by an old woman. They couldn't understand each other so she used sign language to point to the phone to call the police. The woman frowned at something moving behind her and she swung round to see what had attracted her attention. A car suddenly skidded to halt in front of her. "Clever girl," snapped a voice from the car's dark interior. "Come on, I can help you." Soraya had just escaped from one prison she wasn't about to enter another lightly. She wanted to know who she was talking to. "Who are you?" she demanded.

"Get in before you die of cold, the old crone won't help you," the voice said reassuringly, thinking she recognised the voice, she did so, "Thank you," she said and the car accelerated away. The owner of the voice sat in the back with her. "Tell me everything you know Soraya, and you will come to no harm, but don't waste my time, they kidnapped you for a reason, where are they going and why take you?" Soraya became alarmed, had she made a mistake and jumped from the frying pan into the fire? "Who are you?" she asked again, but got no response except an irritated, "I'll ask the questions." She made a grab for the door handle. "Let me out." she screamed.

"Too late, now answer."

"I can't remember, I was drugged," Soraya screamed as something hit her arm; she went dizzy and fell forwards.

She awoke some time later to find herself tied to chair; it seemed to be the only furniture in the room. "I assume you might remember better now," purred a female voice.

"These ropes are hurting me," she complained.

"Where are they going?" The question was repeated.

"I don't know anything, I keep telling you," cried Soraya.

"Listen I specialise in delivering pain; the men you have been travelling with have stolen something from me. I want to know where it is." The woman's voice was full of menace and Soraya began to feel frightened.

"I was drugged from the moment we left Norway," she cried. The woman hit her in the stomach.

"I told you I like dishing out pain," smiled Sabine, "now there is an easy way or a painful way and I'm sure you value your pretty features."

"I have told you I don't know anything," cried Soraya groaning as she was hit hard again; she slumped forwards into blissful unconsciousness.

"Shit! The bitch has fainted on me." She turned to her aide, a German woman called Greta.

"Wake the bitch up, I've no time to mess about." She considered her options, by now Jochi would know that one of the girls had escaped and be on the move. The bastard had made a fool of her and he was going to pay. Soraya groaned as Sabine grabbed her hair. "Does this help your memory, my dear."

"Don't hurt me anymore, please," cried Soraya. "If I tell you, you must guarantee that Lorna will not be hurt."

"That's better, to hell with Lorna. I only want the two men," snapped Sabine. "Now speak." She turned her attention to Heidi and said "Go get the truck ready."

———————————

A watery sun was casting its early light as Jochi and Stefan drove in silence north-eastwards. "Where are you taking me?" asked Lorna.

"Keep quiet," snapped Jochi and stuck a strip of masking tape over her mouth. "We need to concentrate." They passed through the outskirts of a small village with a lake in the background and saw an old school building by the side of the road. "There it is," Stefan pointed in triumph. They pulled off the road and parked outside the front door. The place looked deserted and leaving Lorna locked in the Audi the two men strode towards it. Stefan examined the lock and using a simple lock-pick, opened the door. It creaked as he pushed it wide and they were greeted by an overpowering smell of antiseptic. "The diary page has a floor diagram with old desks," said Stefan. Layers of dust made him sneeze as they walked from room to room. "There aren't any desks now but look at the marks on the floor; the stains are from original fixings, see the slightly different shade of wood colour."

"You're right," replied Jochi excitedly.

"Ah! What have we over here," exclaimed Stefan as he spotted something near the old chimney. "See the Chinese characters carved ornately into the back of the hearth on the lintel, look."

"They're the same figures as those on the Shield," said Jochi his tiredness fading as he looked closer. Stefan agreed. "I'll need to get in there with a knife; this may take a little while so stand back."

Lorna watched from the car and wondered how on earth she was going to get out of this mess. Jochi had had murder in his eyes since Soraya had escaped. She felt unwell and grubby after irregular eating and constant travel. It had made her dizzy and sick. Ever since they had left Valgrind her arms had been tied and injected with some form of sleeping drug. There had to be something she could do to escape but she could only watch helplessly her body fighting the alien substances.

Stefan sweated and grunted in triumph as the lintel finally shifted and he felt around behind in the black soot for anything uneven, Jochi kept watch for any activity outside. He gave a final grunt and felt something different in the soot; he hacked away at it with a small hammer then finally with a cry of success saw a metal box. Clearing the area around it he finally pulled the box clear and broke the aged clasp with his knife to reveal a small bundle wrapped in oilskins.

"We've got it," exclaimed Jochi in triumph as the diary was unveiled and he quickly scanned the pages. "Written in English and Finnish, come on let's get out of here and ditch the girl."

"You mean kill her?" Stefan didn't like the idea of cold-blooded murder.

"No, just make sure that no one finds her for a while; we can lock her in here."

"But it's deserted."

"So what! Someone will hear her eventually. This diary tells me all I need to know. There's no need for insurance policies now."

"We should take her Jochi; she is of interest to him."

"How do you know that?"

"I heard his men up in Valgrind say that the Oleson girl must be taken because she has value to The Teacher."

"Well, why didn't you tell me earlier?"

"It didn't mean anything until now."

"OK, OK, she stays as insurance. Ah look at this, the Dragon Slayer is the name of the Axe. It's described here in the diagram," he said, his excitement mounting with every passing minute. He was flicking through the diary trying to translate from the Finnish. "So it was Captain Cook who took it," he muttered. Then to Stefan, "Come on Stefan, it's time to go. I'll drive, you translate. I want to know where that Axe is." Jochi slid into the driver's seat, ignoring Lorna's angry stare.

"Where does this cabin boy, Svente, fit into all this then?" queried Stefan. Jochi glanced sideways; there was no harm in telling the German, he thought.

"When Cook was killed in Hawaii, a Captain Clark assumed the captaincy of the ship. Svente was told to serve Clark as he had served Cook and he did so. In his diary he mentions a casket in Clarke's cabin described as being covered in Chinese script. So when you translate it we'll know where to go to find it." He knew the next steps he needed to take. "So where is this Axe hidden?" he asked as he started the engine. "Russia," muttered Stefan. "He was a resourceful bugger; he took it from Australia up through the Bering straits to Russia, the diagram looks like the coast north of Vladivostok."

"It bothers me that The Teacher could be using us as a stalking horse," snapped Jochi. "You drive. I'll read the rest," They stopped the car and changed seats. "The Axe must have been taken by Cook northwards on his voyage to look for the North West passage," he read. He turned in his seat and stared at

Lorna. "What did Tresanton say to you about his partner?" he snapped ripping the tape from Lorna's mouth. Lorna was in no mood to co-operate. "Go to hell." she said.

"Answer the question or I'll dump you here on the freezing road. What is The Teacher up to in Australia?"

"I have absolutely no idea," she said.

"Try harder," snapped Jochi sliding his knife from its sheath and threatening her with it.

"The inspector implied she may have been taken to Australia."

"So he's down there already," thought Jochi thinking furiously. "He knows Cook took the damned Axe to Oz but the diary says Russia, either Cook split the thing in two or The Teacher is looking in the wrong place."

"Could be either or both," conceded Stefan, "But the Svente diary is quite specific. I think we're on the right track and he is wrong."

"More likely the devious bastard split it," snapped Jochi. Was he seeing ghosts where there were none?

Stefan stared ahead noticing in the passenger's mirror that Lorna was struggling silently with the ropes that bound her; she was wasting her time. He concentrated on the road ahead as it stretched out west of the city towards Helsinki airport. There was still little traffic as they sped along and his mind went into neutral as he idly watched Lorna.

"What the hell!" he cursed as a large truck suddenly swerved past him having come from nowhere. "Bloody idiot, they're supposed to have speed suppressors," he cursed again as it swerved directly across his path and he fought with the steering wheel. There came a sickening crunch. Lorna screamed as she was slammed against the side of the car, Stefan fought to regain control watching the truck trying to hit them again.

"What the hell is happening?" yelled Jochi grabbing his gun.

"The bastard is trying to kill us, that's what happening" shouted Stefan angrily slowing the car.

"Don't stop, that's what they want," ordered Jochi as Stefan fought desperately to avoid the menacing shape.

He accelerated and thought he was able to overtake when at the last minute the truck swerved violently and hit them hard again. This time Stefan was unable to keep on the road and cursed as they hit the curb hard followed by a bang as one of his front tyres blew out. They spun around in the road facing the way they had come. Stefan was still wrestling with the increasingly erratic steering, finally the car slowed to a halt. "I told you not to stop," yelled Jochi lifting his gun and looking around him.

"Drop it," came a harsh voice as the passenger window splintered and they were showered with glass. Out of nowhere a motor bike had appeared. "Hello Jochi, snapped Sabine holding a machine gun, "did you really think you would get away? Now I believe you have something for me that you stole in Aruba."

"For Christ's sake, Sabine, you could have had us all killed with that stupid stunt."

"Mad truck driver; they need better regulation," smiled Sabine, "Worth it to see you squirm though now the diary." Jochi cursed to himself desperately trying to raise his gun then yelping as a hand chopped down. "Go ahead I know you want to kill me." The invitation was almost too good to refuse but Sabine did so. "Oh no, that's far too easy, your death is going to be a slow and painful one; now the diary, if you please."

"It's not here." He said sulkily. Sabine was unimpressed. "The first shot is to your manhood then the gut, slow and painful." Jochi had second thoughts.

"Very well," he said, throwing the diary out of the shattered window onto the road. Sabine reached down to retrieve it and Jochi acted swiftly. He grabbed the handle of the car door and slammed it open. It caught her off balance and sent her headlong onto the road only her biking leathers saving her from serious injury. She rolled over fast as Jochi leapt out of the car and came towards her and caught him with a kick to the stomach followed by a vicious blow with her right arm. Jochi doubled over in agony as the intense pain from the blow made him realise she had used a knife. Blood seeped down his shirt as another woman appeared at the other side of the car covering Stefan with a pistol. Jochi felt blood pouring from his wound; he gritted his teeth and kicked out again at Sabine as she tried to stand. "Bad mistake," screeched Sabine rolling away and grabbing the diary. She was annoyed at falling for Jochi's car door trick. "You're only still alive because I want you to suffer a slow death the next time," she spat. "After her," yelled Jochi scrambling across to the car as Sabine ran for her bike. "She has the damned diary."

Stefan saw his chance and rammed his fist into the other assailant's neck as Jochi staggered to the car. "Shoot them Stefan," roared Jochi trying to find his own gun. But Stefan was more concerned with the movement of the truck. "The bloody truck's coming," he said. "We have to get out of here; we're dead if we stay a moment longer," he grabbed the ignition key.

"Shit," groaned Jochi feeling the blood seeping from his wound as Stefan turned the car around. "Get down," yelled Stefan seeing the truck driver raise a gun. Lorna had seen a familiar figure beside the truck driver, "Soraya," she shouted.

"Your bloody friend and probably the reason they knew where we were," groaned Jochi as Stefan accelerated away with shots peppering the back of the car.

Chapter 12

Guy and Monty were exhausted by the time they arrived at Helsinki Airport. They met the local Inspector of Police, a man called Larsson. Monty was determined to go by the book here; the police were not corrupt. He was relieved that Interpol had assumed responsibility for the investigation in the region after the corruption in Tromso. They were driven into the city at speed bypassing the remaining commuter traffic.

"From now on we use the official route, no more maverick stuff; it's a damned sight easier," he said to Guy.

"Providing it gets results," retorted Guy. It was an unusual experience to be on the right side of the law.

"There's a search call out, we'll soon find them." Larsson assured them.

"You know they're here?"

"Oh yes, I've been told that they were tracked entering Finland and haven't yet left unless they have gone out under false passports."

"That's more than possible," Guy commented. He felt dispirited, after all their hard work they were still chasing events.

"Have faith," smiled Monty. His mobile interrupted them and he answered the call. He listened carefully for a few minutes then said. "Great we have a breakthrough; there's been an incident up ahead, a truck and a car, shots have been fired and there was some fighting, come on," The police car accelerated with sirens blaring and fifteen minutes later they arrived at the scene.

As they approached the scene they saw the forlorn figure of a woman standing by the roadside. "Soraya?" said Guy. He approached her slowly; she was obviously distraught and likely to panic at the approach of the police car. A few feet from her he again called her name. She looked through him as if he didn't exist. "Soraya, are you OK, where's Lorna?" he asked her gently. "Red haired woman with green eyes, she's evil." said Soraya vacantly.

"She's in shock Guy," said Monty coming over and recognising the symptoms, 'trauma.'"

"The red haired woman must be Sabine," guessed Guy. "She's riding a motor bike judging by the skid marks. A car was forced off the road over there also," said Monty.

"Where could have they gone?" asked Guy.

"No idea yet," replied Larsson. "Ah wait a minute, we've got something, the car has been reported arriving at the main train station, two men and a girl were seen, one of the men staggering badly."

"Is there time to catch them?" asked Guy.

"We'll give it a go," said Larsson and they all jumped into the car and sped off with sirens making enough noise to wake the entire Arctic Circle.

Helsinki station was teaming with the last of the commuters.

"Which train?" shouted Guy desperately.

"Don't know; they haven't been seen since the original report," gasped Monty struggling to keep up as they ran across the station concourse. He scanned the departure board. "I'd take a long distance train if I were them; put as much distance as possible from their assailants."

"Over there, Monty."

"Russia, that would make a lot of sense," observed Monty. Moscow was showing on the departure board. The train was moving as Guy ran down the platform in an effort to catch it. "There," he yelled at the familiar figure of Stefan leaning out of the train. Stefan cursed and ducked back into the carriage, grabbed his gun secure in the knowledge that Lorna and Jochi were already in a private compartment. He leaned out of the window again and fired a shot at Guy, but the shot went wide. "Lorna," yelled Guy, certain he'd seen her frightened face in the departing window. In the snow-filled morning light it was like a scene from Doctor Zhivago. "We have to stop the train," he yelled back to Monty,

"We can't just stop the train."

"Well, I can't just stand and wait," snapped Guy.

"Russia's a big place, they could be going anywhere. We need to get Larsson's support to stop the train and I can tell you he won't agree."

"So what do we do?"

"Some good old-fashioned police work."

"In the meantime Lorna is in great danger," said Guy, his concern overtaking his caution.

He was feeling more frustrated than ever, again his whole

world was being controlled for him and he was convinced they only succeeded against The Teacher when they were dictating events. Without the Whistler and Rose he was finding it increasingly difficult to judge what would happen next despite Monty's best intentions. "She must be valuable to them, they'd have dumped her by now if she wasn't; we'll find out where they are heading and intercept them," he said.

"No," Monty answered. "This must be tackled carefully. "We'll go and have words with the local police and see what they recommend. Hopefully they will be able to make some arrangements to enable us to follow Jochi or suggest another way of finding out where they have gone." Guy could see the sense of Monty's thinking; reluctantly he nodded his head in agreement. "OK," he said "Let's go and see what they have to say."

They made their way to the city's Central Police Station on Kaisaniemenrauta Street beside the Botanical gardens. Guy was feeling disconsolate at having lost Lorna again. They had been frustratingly close and the next train to Moscow wouldn't be until six in the evening. Monty insisted on seeing a superior officer and eventually they were ushered into Captain Larsson's office. He gestured to the seats in front of his desk inviting them to sit down and re-assured them that, although Soraya had hardly spoken, she was fine and being very well looked after. "The suspects are heading into deepest Russia so don't expect miracles; it's a difficult country to work with," he said pointing to a large map on the wall. He leaned across his desk and spoke quietly to Monty. "A private word if you please, Inspector, police business." He gestured to Guy to wait outside and Guy left the room wondering what was going to happen now.

"Do you trust Tresanton?" he said as soon as Guy closed the door.

"Of course, why do you ask?" asked Monty.

"There's an international arrest warrant for him right here on my desk, so give me a good reason why I shouldn't apprehend him." Larsson held up an official looking piece of paper.

"Trust me on this inspector," replied Monty and hastened to explain what had happened.

"Very well on your head be it, but be careful Inspector, there are those who like to see any copper fail when he puts his head above the parapet; it's the nature of the profession."

"I'll take my chances," grinned Monty.

"The girl has said a few words to one of our female officers, which is another reason I wanted to speak to you," said Larsson his short cropped hair gleaming in the strong lights.

"She's talking?"

"Yes, she told us about the police chief in Tromso, shocking and a disgrace to the profession. I'm almost glad he died in the explosion," said Larsson. "She also told us a lot about the Huldra Twelve and her treatment at the hands of Stig Oleson. Good job the bastard is dead or I would have thrown the book at him. What a way to treat young girls."

"I'd like your help to get this Tromso business sorted with Oslo," said Monty.

"Consider it done, I may disagree with you about Tresanton but bent coppers are out of order." Monty breathed a sigh of relief; at last he'd found an officer who was as straight as himself. "Do you know where the suspects are heading?" he asked.

"They have through tickets on the Trans-Siberian to Vladivostok. Jochi is a Russian citizen so you can imagine the response from Moscow to my request. Niet, you've lost them I'm afraid."

"The Bering Sea and Cook's Alaska journey," mused Monty. "Going to where he landed as we suspected. Thank you Captain for your support."

"Just so you understand my position," replied Larsson stiffly. "I've got a break-in reported at a school house in the north and this incident on the road plus a traumatized girl all add up to enough to hold Tresanton."

"If you must, but first talk to my boss at Interpol, he'll put you straight. Now, please, can we leave?"

"Very well but be careful, Inspector."

They made their way back to the hotel next to the station and rented a room for the day, not sure of their next move. "We have to do something," snapped Guy. Monty agreed but didn't want to rush off in the wrong direction. "I know it's difficult but we have to think logically. I'm going to call Doctor Oboto," he said.

"Yeah, OK. If you must," said Guy miserably. He stared out of the window and heard Monty lift the phone and ask for a number. He felt he'd again failed Lorna when she most needed him. Rose was still missing and his parents too; the damned

Teacher was always one step ahead. He turned as Monty replaced the receiver and said, "Monty, we have to find a way to stop him; we can't keep playing catch up." Monty nodded his head in agreement. "We may have a way to do just that," he said with a smile. "It means putting your concerns about Lorna on ice for the time being though. You must know that Jochi can't afford to hurt her. Oboto has just told me he thinks we've found a way to turn the tables."

"Great! What does it involve?"

"Some warm weather for which I for one will be eternally grateful. Come on we need to leave here before the officious Larsson changes his mind and arrests us both."

***

Sabine boarded the private jet cursing herself for underestimating Jochi. She had nearly been killed because she hadn't acted professionally and finished off her enemy when he was down. Past feelings had clouded her judgment; it would not happen again, he would die fast next time. Still she now had the diary so her mission had been accomplished. As her jet rose into the morning sky, she reflected on the events and Jochi's ingenuity. He was a stronger foe than she had believed, but next time she would have her revenge.

Chapter 13

The Hilton Hotel in the very centre of Hanoi is surrounded by traditional Vietnamese buildings. Set amongst crowded streets from the bygone age of colonial Vietnam, it creates a fusion of the old and new. Inside the hotel the very latest gadgets are there for all to see and use, and yet, in the old streets, busy vendors ply the same trades as their forefathers. Zheng had flown in for a meeting from his base near Ho Chi Minh City and was greeted at the door by Jacques Savior the European President of ZTW, a suave Frenchman who had effectively transformed the company into a respected trading entity.

The meeting of ZTW's Board of Directors had just ended, Zheng hadn't been involved; he just pulled strings from behind the scenes. A metals mining and trading corporation, it used shadow companies around the world to control many of the world's semi-precious metals. The market was getting ever more crowded and competition fierce, particularly now that China was operating in the market, but they preserved a niche. Headquarters located in Bermuda, it was on the face of it run by Jacques and the Chinese controller Else Tan, a Chinese businesswoman who had shouldered her way to the top. Zheng had worked with them both for a number of years now and nodded his head curtly as they entered his room, adjacent to the boardroom, and sat down, effectively an extraordinary meeting outside the official board meeting.

"Else, what's going on?" asked Zheng.

"We have a problem," replied the fierce looking woman.

"Which is?"

"Our share price is plummeting; there has been intense selling around the world."

"But our profits are solid, Else, you told me yourself that trade with the Chinese government is at record levels." Zheng was puzzled; it was unlike her to give inaccurate information.

"It is. There's someone out there spooking our shareholders," interjected Jacques, "A coordinated attack."

"Well find them and deal with it. I don't see why I need to be involved."

"I've tried to stop it but they cover themselves too well." The President looked as worried as Else.

"So what do you suggest," asked Zheng.

"Get the big pension schemes to invest," replied Jacques. "We are too exposed." The suggestion was met with a shake of the head from Zheng.

"We are exposed but we will do something different," said Zheng, "I shall move the company out of the world markets. I am arranging some secret deals I don't want open to public scrutiny, particularly by pension funds. The public listing gave us credibility when we needed it but now…we head off in a new direction."

"It's not the best way forward," frowned Jacques.

"I agree with Zheng," replied Else, "It increases our flexibility and we don't need the money any more. If we can't reverse this slide quickly, we should start buying our own stock."

"Good, then we are in agreement, the company will be reformed." Zheng gave a nod of satisfaction. His European President wasn't so happy. "You've left me in charge for years, Zheng, why this change now," asked Jacques coldly. Zheng stood up to indicate the meeting was over. "You have made yourself a fortune while you have worked for me, so get us out of this mess the way I have ordered, see to it."

"It doesn't make sense," Jacques repeated, also getting to his feet.

"This meeting is over," said Zheng walking to the door and opening it. His aides Zie Lao and Yen Liu from Tay Ninh entered. In desperation Jacques turned to Else. "Else, we've being colleagues for a long time. This is wrong, you know it is," pleaded Jacques. She was unmoved. As far as she was concerned Zheng was the boss and whatever he said she would do. "Sorry Jacques but it's for the greater good," she said quietly and strode across to stand with Zheng. "So Else are you fully behind me on this?" Zheng asked her as he led her outside the room away from a fuming Jacques. "You know I am, Zheng," she assured him.

"Jacques will need to be watched as he handles this, make sure he doesn't do anything underhand. I trust you but he needs close attention and is expendable. Do I make myself clear?"

"I'll take care of Jacques."

"Manage him but make sure he does as he's told. Now I want to introduce you to someone." The Teacher activated his speaker mobile phone system. "This is a man who is about to play a very important part in the future of our enterprises in Mongolia."

A voice she didn't recognise came onto the line. "Teacher, it's good to hear from you." said Shaka. The Teacher smiled. "I have Else here to go over the details of the mining rights with you. We don't want any confusion," he looked at Else. "Shaka is to appoint ZTW the sole concessionary for the north eastern mining rights for all precious metals."

"For all metals once I am President," confirmed Shaka.

"I will leave you two to iron out the fine detail. Else has my full confidence, so see to it that she gets all that she needs." Zheng left the room as Zie Lao approached him. "You have an urgent call waiting, Teacher," he said quietly.

"Who is it?"

"Just said he was a fellow academic and it was urgent."

"Academic?" Zheng's blood ran cold, the word meant only one thing to him. "See that no one disturbs me." He picked up the phone and before he could say anything a voice said. "The Artefacts, where are they?" He paused a second or so before replying. "Being prepared for shipment to you as we speak," he said.

"You retrieved the Shield recently and yet there are no messages, what am I to make of that?"

"The shipment is planned and they will be with you soon. Why this sudden interest? You have the Cross." The voice seemed disinclined to enter into any discussion. "The next two?" he asked.

"Within our grasp?"

"But not actually in your control. We are at a critical point and timing is essential."

"Some at the Elders are flexing their muscles, nothing more; trust me as you have to do this my way. Plans are well advanced; you have no need to get involved as we both agreed."

"The Elders are mobilizing against you Zheng, it seems to me they are out of your control."

"I can manage them; there's a meeting in two days where I will bring them under control."

"See that you do and get the share price sorted out; it's gone through the floor."

"Trust me," snapped Zheng cursing as the line went dead; the bloody Elders had just upped the stakes and would pay for this.

Tay Ninh Camp

The small man was treated indulgently by the camp followers; he was non-threatening and would always help with the chores. Often he disappeared for weeks on end but no one asked where he had gone. It was assumed that he went out into the countryside and wandered around, gifted with the magic powers of a mute. Only two people at the camp could communicate with him, the two doctors with whom he spent most of his time. He was a man of the islands, specifically La Gomera, and felt very sad as he now knew with certainty that he would never see his beloved homeland again. That made it all the more important that this last task was completed successfully. Jose Parte, one of the native silbo speakers of La Gomera looked around the camp smiling at some of the memories.

He'd travelled a long way on this assignment, his most difficult yet. He had served his various masters at the big monastery all his life and no one could fault him for effort. In his own little world he had lived a thousand lives; each had its own story because he could never talk to others directly. It was a silent world that he loved because he loved his boss. She had been his only inspiration, his own saint when he had been born without the power of speech. He knew she would never know the real truth about him, but didn't care, to have served was enough. Hopefully he had done his own small part in keeping his beloved organization, the Elders, successful. His last wish was to have the opportunity of casting his eyes over his beloved homeland one last time, but he knew in his heart it was not possible. Now he had one last job to do. It would not be his usual signature event but would assist those he sought to help.

Eastern Russia

It had been a gruelling four days as the Trans-Siberian express wound its way across the frozen and seemingly endless plains of Russia headed towards Vladivostok. To relieve the tedium Jochi had locked himself away to finalise his plans. The Teacher's non-appearance troubled him and so did the news that his enemy was now concentrating on Australia. He wondered if he was being used or if even The Teacher was being driven by someone else.

The wounds inflicted by Sabine's knife had been attended to by a doctor on the train and he was feeling stronger the further east they went. Another day and they would reach the outpost of the Russian Empire, a place he had never visited. They came to a halt after completing four fifths of their journey and booked into the only hotel in town. Jochi went straight to his room and took a long bath, luxuriating in the warmth. The loss of the diary in Finland wasn't disastrous; he had taken the precaution of copying the key pages on a mobile app at the hotel in Helsinki. Better still he had removed from the original diary the key direction page; he smiled as he pictured Sabine's face when she found out. He climbed out of the bath feeling much better and on impulse he went to check on Lorna's room opening the door to find her half undressed by the window.

"What the hell are you doing?" he asked her.

"Damn you! Don't you knock before entering someone else's room?" she snapped stepping back in alarm.

"Not when you are my prisoner and trying to escape," Jochi said, staring at her naked back as she struggled to pull the bath towel around her.

"I wouldn't be trying to escape naked in this freezing weather would I," she retorted.

"Perhaps it's time you showed me a bit of respect after I saved your life at the camp?"

"That's a perverted way of looking at it," replied Lorna angrily. "Don't expect me to thank you after all you've done to me."

"There are other ways of thanking me," said Jochi. He was finding it difficult to tear his eyes from the parts of her body not covered by the towel. "It's been a long boring few days with no exercise, it would be good if you demonstrated a little friendliness, after all I did save you from being raped in Prague last year." As he spoke he moved swiftly towards her and snatched the towel away from her. Lorna screamed as he pushed her onto the bed. "In this part of the world you take what you want," he gasped and dropped on top of her, fumbling with his clothes. "You Bastard!" screamed Lorna writhing to get away from under him, but with increasing hopelessness realised he was too heavy for her to move. "I always wondered what the high and mighty boss's daughter would be like in the sack; you never came to give me a massage, too good for me eh? Bitch. Well now we are all equals only I'm more equal than you," he snarled. Lorna lay still trying to decide what to do next. Fate made the decision for her. The door to her room opened and Stefan entered. Jochi, furious at the interruption shouted, "What the hell do you want, Stefan; can't you see I'm busy?"

"I can see that you intend to do something that makes us worse than animals," Stefan answered, a look of disgust on his face.

"Who the hell are you to judge?" snapped Jochi, but Stefan's entrance had broken the rush of excitement. He stood up and said furiously, "OK have it your way…for now. Lock the bitch up and I'll get a real woman." He went out and slammed the door. Lorna covered herself with the bedclothes and smiled gratefully at her rescuer.

"Thank you, Stefan," she said quietly. "He's under a lot of stress," said the German brusquely and left the room, locking the door after him.

My God, how the hell am I going to get out of this? Lorna thought despairingly as she stared out the window and across the snowy wastes. She slept fitfully with a chair jammed under the door handle, dreading the sound of someone trying to get in. Next morning no one spoke as they made their way back to what she called her mobile prison. She had considered trying to escape, but there was nowhere for her to go. A feeling of relief washed over all three as they completed the last leg of the journey and saw the Pacific Ocean.

Jochi had decided to forget the Elders; they had served their purpose of distracting The Teacher and his sources there had been turned anyway. His goal now was to beat The Teacher to the remaining Artefacts then bring his whole edifice crumbling down. He had discovered the man's Achilles heel; first though there was the Axe. He had read and re-read the diary a dozen times in addition to accessing many websites to learn more about the voyages of Captain Cook. He compared official ships' logs with Svente's diary and the information he found in the official journals verified his notes.

The suspicion grew stronger that the Axe he was searching for might only be half the Artefact. Cook had split it after floundering on the reef. He also wondered why the explorers Drake, Columbus and Cook were inextricably linked to the Artefacts, and why had they all gone to the tremendous trouble of re-hiding them. Perhaps it was personal financial gain, and they had intended to return at some point to collect their booty but had died before they could do so. Cook had been savagely murdered in Hawaii a month after depositing the Axe in the north. He recalled that Russians still thought of Cook as one of their own due to the news of his death being carried across Russia back to England from the *Endeavour;* there was even a popular Russian folk song about the event in Vladivostok.

He tried to put his reservations aside; only he knew the exact location of the Artefact. Even if the Axe was split he would have part of it. He extracted the piece of paper ripped from the diary, noting that Cook had been meticulous with his map references. He recalled that modern satellite images of New Zealand were almost identical to the contours Cook had plotted with no more than a sextant and a ruler; an impressive man.

They stayed overnight at the Aquilonis Hotel in the centre of town, where Jochi made arrangements for the next stage. From the co-ordinates he had identified the town of Anadyr as their destination. Lorna was surprised when Stefan took her alone to the docks area; he led her into a huge glass shrouded building and left her in the waiting room whist he engaged in a heated discussion with a stranger. They then returned to the hotel. She made a mental note to try and use the information in the future.

The next day they chartered a private helicopter to take them fifty kilometres north to Anadyr, overlooking the Bearing Straits, a cold bleak and forbidding place that had only been inhabited by the Russians since 1830; its name meant river. According to Jochi's records it was the place Cook had made landfall. They registered at the hamlet's only hotel and slept soundly with Lorna locked in a separate room. Jochi reckoned it was safe to give her a little more leeway as she couldn't speak the language; in fact, even he with his native Russian struggled to understand the locals, besides; she appeared to have formed a bond with Stefan.

At first light they hired a car and made their way down to the Anadyr museum. The ripped page was quite explicit, an unusual rock formation on the coastline to the exact grid reference on the page. It took him two and a half hours to find what he was seeking, an unmistakable outcrop of rock on the seashore. The exact location according to the co-ordinates was fifty metres directly inland. He carefully measured the distance and with a nasty shock came up against the back wall of a large mansion. According to the guide book, the site had been developed by a White Russian who had fled for his life as the Bolsheviks closed in. It had stood neglected until a local commune arranged for children from eastern Russia to use it as an orphanage. It was now a shambling, run-down affair in the middle of nowhere; it was the only obstacle to success; they had found the right place.

As they approached the building, Jochi and Stefan agreed subterfuge was needed, Lorna just trudged behind; after the attempted rape she had changed her behaviour towards Stefan. He was taciturn but friendly and she had found herself listening with interest to his stories about his childhood. They resonated with her own and she resolved for the time being to make the best of things. As they entered the orphanage they were greeted by the proprietor, an old ex-fisherman called Stoikov and a group of poor children. "Leave me to handle this," said Jochi. He couldn't believe the building was almost above the hidden Artefact's location. Cook's diary recorded they had been able to dig soft earth in only one place, no doubt the orphanage had been built there for the same reason. "We need to gain their trust and get a look at that old garage building over there, next to the rock, that's where the Artefact is buried," he told Stefan, who nodded his agreement.

They exchanged greetings with Stoikov but before they could give any reason for being there the man growled. "What do you want?" he clearly didn't trust any visitors least of all strangers. Jochi began to explain the reason for their visit. "We are inspectors checking out ground contamination." Stoikov glared at them suspiciously; the news they were from the government didn't please him at all. His small weather-beaten face grimaced at the information. "So, why are you here?" he asked. Jochi hastened to reassure him "The garage over there, we need to check it out for possible subsidence, there's been reports of geological disturbances so we need to dig down to check for sensitivity. We're just carrying out orders; you know what the bureaucrats are like in Moscow. Anyway, the deal is we get the samples then you get the inconvenience money. Oh one other thing, we need to work in total privacy, there may be radioactivity."

Stoikov's face took on a worried frown. "Radioactivity, that's dangerous isn't it? I need you lot like a hole in the head; some food and money for the children would be more useful." Jochi nodded sympathetically. "I understand, you needn't worry, it's only dangerous at high levels. Once we have completed the checks you'll be paid," Jochi had no compunction about lying, he was anxious to get started. "Can I help you with the children while my colleagues do the checks?" asked Lorna smiling sweetly as Jochi translated for her. "Sounds good to me," said Stoikov opening the door to the building and ushering Lorna in. He smiled for the first time. To someone who had known little but opulence all her life the scene that met her eyes horrified her. Ill-dressed, starving children with faces without hope sat disconsolately around the room. She smiled as a little girl came to her and tentatively held out her hand, their hands touched and she reached for some chewing gum. Using sign language she started to arrange games and gave the female teacher some loose change from her pocket to get some decent food.

It took a day and night of hard digging into the permafrost before they managed to make real progress under the house foundations. "See how the ground here has been disturbed and is a different colour," said Stefan sweating despite the extreme cold. "It's a good thing they did build the house, it's protected the site. Cook's men must have gone in here. In fact if you look carefully you can see where they tried to get access with a pickaxe, look at the marks on the rock."

"Just dig," snapped Jochi impatiently. It was Stefan who struck pay dirt. "There's something here," he grunted. His spade bounced off something very hard. He dug deeper and felt the spade hit metal. Half an hour later he pulled out a metal box half a metre square. They soon removed the old lock; it was almost falling to pieces anyway. Jochi opened the box and lifted out the Axe Head. It was made from the same metal as the Shield. "Bingo," he shouted joyfully. "Well done Stefan, so he did split it, the crafty bugger, I bet the other half is on the reef and The Teacher has figured that out. See the Chinese characters on the side and the intricate diagram." They quickly collected Lorna from the orphanage, again promised to send money to them from the Government and beat a hasty retreat back to their hotel. They caught the next train out of Anadyr.

Chapter 14

Fortaleza Hidalgo

Jade had a bad feeling about the emergency meeting Zheng had used the last of his leadership powers to convene. It had been called with the minimum amount of notice so she expected trouble. It was also the first Elders' meeting for two new members of whom she had little knowledge. Under their constitution all significant resolutions required a majority vote so she needed at least six votes and the two new members a Spaniard and Italian businessman were unknown quantities. The Spaniard appeared friendly enough, a traditionalist and therefore wary of new ideas. The Italian was known only as Fabrizio and was harder to read; a tall powerful- looking man who exuded authority.

Her musings were interrupted by a knock at the door. "A monk to see you," said Emerald. "Show him in," she answered. There were a small number of monks and nuns on the ground floor of the monastery; they were given free lodgings and good quality accommodation in return for providing a legitimate front for the Elders and some occasional help. She had asked a young monk called Francisco who had taken a specific interest, to start cataloguing their vast library of documents. It was a real treasure trove of knowledge going all the way back to their inception. "Hello Francisco," she greeted him with a warm smile. The young man appeared nervous. He swallowed hard then said. "I have something of interest for you, ma'am, something you need to see. I found it down in the old altar area."

"Sit down and take a drink, Francisco, I don't believe I ever told you it was your grandfather, also called Francisco, who in the days of my grandmother, played a prominent part in managing the monastery. He was actually the Chair for a while, particularly when Zhou Wan, the current President's grandfather, first came here."

"Really? I didn't know that," replied the monk. He seemed genuinely moved. "It helps me give you the information I have found." Jade listened to him for the next hour making copious notes. Later, as she made her way to the meeting she felt very much better. Francisco had buoyed her spirits and helped her get ready for the ordeal that lay ahead. Unfortunately the young monk had given her some rather disturbing news too.

Zheng Wan looked around the chamber grimly, wondering who had instigated the covert actions against ZTW. Well now he would find out and they would pay when he took full control from the Chair. Jade opened the meeting. "The floor is yours, Zheng, though I must formally register that it's highly irregular to call such a meeting in a transition period, particularly as a new President has been appointed." Jade looked around the darkened recesses wondering what the others were thinking. It was one of those days when retirement seemed appealing.

"I am within the rules and there is a quorum," Zheng responded. "As you all know I was asked to relinquish the Presidency by the Chair but I exercised my right to a period of transition and have taken the time to look into the health of our august body. I have to report that there has been a gross miscarriage of justice and I call for a vote of no confidence in the Chair. I propose myself as her successor."

"On what grounds is the vote of no confidence?" asked Jade calmly.

"Firstly you have been hiding data on the Artefact called the Confucius Staff; you have exact details of its location," announced Zheng. "It would have been proper to turn them over to us all."

"That's exactly what I am doing here and now," smiled Jade, offering silent thanks to Francisco. She knew now for certain they had a mole in the monastery.

"They are in everyone's papers and the next item on the agenda." Zheng paused for a moment. He hadn't expected that response, but he pressed on. "Very well but the second reason is more serious, the Chair has pursued activities contrary to the Elders' interests and to our central ethics."

"I have never done anything that could be construed as such." Jade said firmly.

"Do you deny privately engaging a man named Guy Tresanton, currently wanted by the police for kidnapping and on the run in the Caribbean?"

"The man you refer to has complained to us about your threats to kill him and is I believe aided by the same policeman you mention, one Brian Montcalm from the Bermudan police to be precise. I would also add that I have learned you are holding his father a prisoner in your compound in Vietnam very much against his will," Jade angrily rejected his assertion..

"Tresanton senior is a respected member of my community," admitted Zheng. "The original charge has not been answered, namely that you are pursuing acts to the detriment of the Elders, and I call for a vote of no confidence."

"Such a vote is your right," acknowledged Jade, and having obtained a seconder for the motion who she thought was Fabrizio, instructed Emerald to proceed with the count. She watched in silence as the lights went on and smiled with delight as she saw only two votes for Zheng.

"There is no support for your motion Zheng." Jade announced. Zheng was furious. "You have all made your views clear to me and I am fully aware that some of you have taken covert actions against my company. Do not consider yourselves above the full force of my retribution," snapped Zheng. He rose from his seat and strode from the chamber.

"I invite Doctor Oboto to take his rightful place," said Jade, quietly elated now it was finally over. "Our new President is now formally in charge and will advise us on our next steps." After four miserable years she had finally lanced the boil and smiled broadly as Walter Oboto made his way to the President's Chair. He addressed the members. "Ladies and gentlemen, you've heard Zheng's threats; it seems we are at war and have to now be ready for anything. It's time for the fight back to begin and for the Elders to take a different stance, though we must not deviate one iota from our original goals. I believe it is the duty of the President to point the direction we must take to achieve those goals and that's what I intend to do."

Later Jade met the new President in her private chambers. "My congratulations to you again, Walter," she said. Walter too was pleased with the outcome of the meeting but knew that the battle had only just begun. "There is much work to be done and little time to do it," he told her. "Zheng will make life difficult, we have to move fast."

"We need to get the Artefacts, after all that is our core mission," Jade said, a worried frown creasing her forehead. Walter agreed. "Zheng and Jochi are well down that particular road; all we have is the lead from the archives we gave to Tapiwa, We must concentrate on that area."

"Are we strong enough Walter?"

"Yes, already Tapiwa has managed to fend off Zheng's thugs."

"The monk Francisco advised me that we have a mole here, he gave me this. It's a well-known name," said Jade handing Oboto an aged scrap of paper. *"Doctor Livingstone's demise,"* It meant nothing to Oboto, he handed it back to Jade. She continued. "Francisco also drew my attention to a name that keeps appearing, a Count Von Steppenhof. His name is symbolic with our past when his grandfather and my grandmother were here."

"Where does hit fit into all this?"

"Von Steppenhof was a German industrialist at the turn of the century. He came here, met my mother and developed some form of connection to the place. He was the German Ambassador to Zanzibar but spent an inordinate time in Malawi. It was called Nyasaland then. It starts to fit together as Malawi was where Livingstone ended his days."

Hanoi

Zheng was tired by his long flight back from Fortaleza and in reflective mood after the Elders' meeting, but he summoned Else to his room at the second complex in Vietnam and demanded a report on what had happened while he had been away. She had been busy and ended her report by saying. "You were right about Savior. He is not to be trusted, he talked to others about our plans."

"He must be taken care of when the time is right." Zheng told her. Else agreed and said she would make arrangements for him to disappear. She concluded by saying, "Thank you for showing trust in me, Zheng, I will make sure we deliver." He believed her; her ambition was obvious. "Good," he replied. "The rest of the Board are in favour of our actions so the company changes are proceeding; we will be in private ownership soon; it will take a couple of weeks to formalize then it's all in your hands." She smiled with satisfaction.

"Are the rest of your family involved with this project Zheng? You never talk about them," she asked.

"No, my father Zhou was a founder member of the Elders and helped establish the monastery in the Garonjay mountains; now they have no time for us but we don't need them. Keep Savior under observation for now; we may have a useful role for him before he leaves us."

"What will happen with Tay Ninh?"

"That's not your problem, you just concentrate on matters here and watch Shaka; you are the CEO designate of a privately owned company that will become the richest company on earth in the near future. We will succeed beyond your wildest dreams."

Chapter 15

Lilongwe - Malawi

As the South African Airlines flight passed over Lake Malawi, Tapiwa dispassionately surveyed the other travellers on the aircraft. She was back in a war zone her antennae on full alert; kill or be killed was her mantra. The two mercenaries she had already met were proof that others were on her trail. She knew Malawi was a very poor country; the ramshackle nature of the airport and the largely agrarian economy she had seen on the landing approach confirmed it. The current leader had been the victim of an assassination plot when she had served the previous President. It seemed to symbolize all that was wrong with African leadership.

Her report of her visit to Kenya had intrigued Doctor Oboto. He agreed the business card was a potential breakthrough and had asked her to try calling its owner, Joseph Caine. She had done so several times but, so far, without success. Oboto had then traced the number and found a connection to a Doctor Red, identified as a close friend of Joseph Caine and a former senior minister in Idi Amin's government. It was the lead that had brought her here to Malawi where Red had last been seen. He also told her they had found other signs in the Monastery at La Gomera, that Malawi held key clues.

She passed through immigration, her ceramic knife avoiding detection, and left the small airport for the short taxi journey into Lilongwe where she checked in at what looked like the only decent hotel in town. As soon as she settled into her room she dialled the number Oboto had given her. The number buzzed for a minute or so before a very cagey and non-committal voice answered. "Hello. Who is this?"

"A friend of Joseph Caine, we need to talk about what happened in Kenya," gambled Tapiwa.

"You must have the wrong number," the voice answered. "I don't know any Caine," Tapiwa persevered. "I have information that can help you; all I ask is for ten minutes of your time." There was silence for a moment then the voice said. "The Café Horizon in downtown Lilongwe, one hour exactly, any later I won't be there." She slipped her ceramic knife into the special pouch in her jeans and walked into the town, moving quickly and taking every precaution she could think of, grateful for a sudden cool shower of rain. The Horizon coffee shop wasn't hard to find. She took a seat at the rear where she could see the whole room mindful of Wild Bill Hickok's philosophy of always facing the entrance. She looked around absorbing details of the other people drinking coffee and eating cakes. An older man who kept glancing over his shoulder as if checking to make sure no one was following him shuffled into the café. He took the chair opposite her and said. "You're alone?"

"Yes of course, Doctor Red I presume."

"You have ten minutes, lady," said the old man.

"Would you like some coffee?" She tried to set him at his ease; he seemed very jumpy.

"Very well, you're sure you are alone."

"Check it out if you don't believe me." The man did just that, he cast a critical look all around before saying anything else.

Tapiwa pressed her advantage. "You knew Idi Amin?"

"Yes, he thought I was a communist, saw me reading Chairman Mao's red book one day and labelled me," replied the Doctor. "A sobriquet I was given by a madman doing crazy things. I couldn't even sit in a coffee shop like this without someone informing on me. I survived by trusting no one and taking no chances." She believed him; his jumpy attitude confirmed it.

"The risk is on both sides," replied Tapiwa. "Do you mind if I ask you what doctorate you hold?"

"Not at all," he replied "I was a Minister under Amin. He officially titled all those in his close circle as Doctors; said it made him feel better. The title stuck."

"You left in a rush?"

"Yes, I fell out of favour, though in my case it was self-induced."

"You stole the Artefact," guessed Tapiwa. The Doctor grinned and held up his hands.

"You know, they say Uganda has the strongest economic growth of any of the sub Saharan Africa countries? Well now they've found oil and that's bound to bring corruption." he commented, trying to change the subject, but Tapiwa wouldn't be diverted. "Weak leaders are our disease," she observed, "The corruption of power and tribal loyalties replace common sense. I grew up with such behaviour, but as a friend of Joseph Caine you have information I need," she said.

Doctor Red became edgy again and avoided her eyes. "I don't know how you found me, but everything comes at a price, that's the way it is. You are playing a very dangerous game, my dear, one that could hurt you badly." Tapiwa bridled at the remark.

"I have lived with danger all my life," she told him, "so don't patronize me."

"How did you know Joseph?"

"I didn't, I found his business card in a hole in Kenya."

"Very careless of someone, that has cost him dearly."

"Or it was deliberate; you stole something valuable."

"If I did then it's worth something to you." Now he held her eyes defiantly.

"'So, tell me, what have you got that's worth buying?"

"I told the Chinese man all this, has he not told you?"

"The deal has changed," replied Tapiwa carefully wondering how the hell The Teacher had got ahead of her. She decided it would be best to let Red believe she was working with him."

"It's a Staff," he said. They call it the Confucius Staff, surely you know that, your Chinese friend did?" She thought quickly and answered. "I just wanted to be sure we were talking about the same thing." Red seemed to accept her explanation and continued. "I worked at the top of Amin's regime; did you know the madman had a statue of Adolf Hitler in his lounge? He was totally insane; couldn't handle the pressure and trusted no one, totally paranoid. He particularly hated the British after the army snubbed him and was determined to get revenge, told everyone he was the *Conqueror of the British Empire*. We were sent on one crazy hunt after the other. Amin sent dear old Joseph Caine and me all around East Africa looking for it. We found it, then stole it; we hid it well, too well. In the end we had to flee." He sighed and leaned back in his chair.

"It's an ancient Artefact and quite valuable." she said.

"Yes, he was an idiot to leave his card," repeated Red. "We took what we thought were suitable precautions with what we saw as our life's insurance. Now Joseph is dead and it's my headache."

"Or opportunity, depending on what you do next. People will kill for this Staff. There are others after this, far less scrupulous than me who would kill you without warning."

"Perhaps, but I'm old, my family have grown up, my wife's dead so it's for sale to the highest bidder. You are competing with the Chinese man aren't you?" He'd sussed her out and she had to revise her attitude quickly.

"In exchange for the money, what do I get?"

"A map showing the Staff's location. Amin searched long and hard for it but never found it. He even held my family captive to try to force me to reveal the hiding place; that's when I realised we had to get out." Tapiwa was intrigued, escaping from Amin was no mean feat. "How did you get them out?" she asked.

"I gave Amin part of the secret, there was a parchment with the Staff, I exchanged it for my wife and then ran."

"A parchment?"

"Yes, old with lots of diagrams and in a foreign language," he said.

"Could it be the Prophecy?" murmured Tapiwa to herself, aloud she said. "Was there anyone else who knew about this?"

"Only Amin's closest confident; the doctor who looked after him, a Scottish man, bloody devious individual but guess you had to be to get to that level."

"And where is he?"

"You ask too many questions young lady. I can sell you a map to the Artefact that's all. I reckon it's worth fifty thousand American dollars, bring it to the lake tonight in cash."

"That's a lot of cash; I can't get it that fast." But she made up her mind instantly that she'd find the money somehow.

"It's your choice. Now I suggest that you leave about ten minutes after me and watch your back. Whilst Malawi is fairly safe, I trust no one and nor should you. Call my number when you get to the lake."

She spent the rest of the day relaxing and, as darkness fell, hired a taxi to take her to the lake. She watched the driver negotiate the dark roads as they made their way along the S122 towards Lake Malawi, passing through a town called Salima. She had managed to acquire the necessary cash through a wire transfer from Oboto and Red had texted the exact location for their meeting. Suddenly the taxi driver cursed as a policeman stepped into the road and shone a torch at them motioning them to the side. "Shit!" exclaimed the taxi driver. "What is it?" She asked anxiously.

"Police spot check, they'll want cash," snapped the man. "They're as corrupt as hell."

"Here take fifty dollars," said Tapiwa and showed her passport to the policeman who then waved them through. She tried to calm down; the police check had spooked her and she didn't feel comfortable in Malawi the self-proclaimed *warm heart of Africa.*

She brought her nerves back under control and breathed deeply as the driver motioned to a dilapidated café standing alone by the lakeside near a small hamlet called Senga. "That's the address you gave me," he said pulling into a space at the side of the road. She thanked him and asked him to wait for her. The state of the building made her feel apprehensive. She had her small haversack with her and from it extracted a powerful flashlight before climbing out of the taxi some twenty meters from the building. She preferred to arrive in her own way and approached carefully from the rear. It appeared to be deserted. "You came alone?" asked a familiar voice.

"Yes, as you asked."

"You have the cash?"

"First the map."

"Very well, here it is," said Doctor Red. He came from behind the dilapidated door, held out a document and dropped it on the ground in front of her. She looked down at it carefully, but detected a movement out of the corner of her eye. Spinning around she cursed as two men emerged from the rear of the building holding knives. "You think you can cheat me?" she snarled, grabbing her knife.

"You're part of them, you're all the same, I had no choice," he replied. "I did warn you, I'm sorry." He limped away and looked back sadly, such a naive girl and she would suffer, oh God would she suffer. "I don't mean you any harm, but I have to protect myself."

"Funny way of showing it" snapped Tapiwa. "She snatched up the map and whirled around as the two men advanced on her. She swung at one of them and felt her knife bite into his flesh, the man yelped. She spun round to tackle the next man and groaned as something hit her hard in the stomach; she bent double with the pain. A second blow hit her head and drove her to her knees and someone else kicked the knife away. Then they were upon her pushing her down into the dirt and ripping at her clothes. She groaned and let her body go still. She tried to look around to where the old man had been but could see nothing. She had little doubt that they were going to hurt her badly and she steeled herself for rape; it wouldn't be the first time!

She came back to consciousness in a dark wooden hut about two metres square. Gingerly running her hands over her body she realised she was naked and her body felt as if she had been hit by an express train, but mercifully she could find no real damage. She also discovered to her great relief she wasn't tied up or restricted in any way. She flexed her arms and each muscle in turn. As far as she could tell, she hadn't been beaten or sexually abused. She stood up stiffly and began to explore her surroundings. She found her way to the corner of what appeared to be a wooden shack, at the same time hearing the sound of swirling water coming from below her. Seconds later the water was about her feet and slowly rising. She began to work her way around each wall hoping to find a way out of her prison.

She reflected on her position as she inched along the walls. Isolated in the middle of Malawi, such choices as she had all seemed to have a violent ending. Still she had been born into violence and had learned how to deal with it. She shivered and held her arms across her chest, the water had reached her ankles now and it was still rising. She saw a small chink in the wooden slats of the walls and peered through it at what she assumed was Lake Malawi. With a start she realised that the water wasn't rising, she was held in a wooden cage that was gradually sinking beneath the surface of the lake! It was a weird and disconcerting sensation.

She grabbed at what looked like the outline of a wooden door but it was locked from the outside. She started to try removing the wooden slats as the water level reached her knees; she reckoned she had about an hour at most. The slat wouldn't move and she cursed as she tried another ramming her heels outwards to no avail. Then she heard a movement and the door opened, a stream of bright light bringing excruciating pain to her eyes. "Ready to talk my black beauty?" came a surly voice. She recognised it as one of the two men who had hit her. She kept quiet and moved to the furthest corner. A torch light blinded her again as the man stepped in. "Water not loosened your tongue yet? We reckoned a slow death would work better with you, tough girl that you are."

"What do you want," she asked, knowing full well what they wanted.

"You killed our colleagues; we want the Staff's location. Simple as that."

"Red has it, and he's one of you, you've taken the map he gave me."

"It's a dummy, useless; he says you know where the real one is."

"Then you're an idiot. He has duped you, why do you think I came to this Godforsaken country? It was to get the map from Red."

"Looks like I will have to do some carving after all," the man said with a degree of anticipated pleasure that made her nerves tingle.

"The Doctor has the map you idiot."

"No, his friend had it but he died when we asked him nicely for it in this very hut, a bad case of drinking too much water."

"You killed him, don't you see Red's lying through his nose?" snapped Tapiwa angrily.

"I am a man of little patience," said the man coldly coming forwards and holding a large wicked looking knife. Tapiwa squirmed in revulsion as wet clammy hands grabbed at her breasts. She tried to move but her legs were pinned by his weight and the water. "Just a little blood and there's a particularly nasty little water snake that will do the rest of the damage like it did with Caine." Tapiwa cursed as she saw the large knife moving towards her breasts and squirmed to one side nearly destabilizing the man, but his grip was too strong. The blade swung and narrowly missed her; he cursed and tried to raise it again pushing her back hard against the wooden wall. Tapiwa groaned; she could see no escape; she couldn't get enough purchase to fight back. The shadow loomed larger then suddenly tensed before falling back slowly into the water, a knife between his shoulder blades. His mouth opened in a silent scream and then he went beneath the water. She struggled across to the door and saw another figure emerge as she scrambled for the fallen knife to fight her way out.

"Tapiwa, wait," called a voice she recognised.

"Who the hell is that?" she shouted.

"It's me, Guy Tresanton. Doctor Oboto told me to come, looks like I made it just in time."

"You could say that," gasped Tapiwa struggling across to the entrance and blinking in the beams of the floodlights mounted on the back of a lorry. She saw a sandy haired man staring at her. "What's the matter never seen a naked female before?"

"Err, yes," stammered Guy turning and feeling oddly elated at his courage in killing the assailant. "Here take my coat and come out slowly, it's a rickety contraption."

Tapiwa stepped out of her wooden prison and saw with astonishment that she had been in a wooden box held over the lakeside, a crude wooden box suspended on chains that had been slowly winding down. "How did you find me?"

"Oboto told me about Doctor Red so I called him and he helped me find you. He said that you needed help badly and knew where they had taken you,"

"It was Red who got me into this mess."

"Well, he's had a change of heart. Didn't like what they were going to do to you. He's ready to help us find the map, said that he judged you wrongly, thought you worked for the Chinaman who I presume is The Teacher."

"There was another man here."

"I've met him. He will have a huge headache on the morning but'll live; I have a policeman friend here who will take care of the body."

"Where's Red?" She wanted to know.

"Up there in the car with my colleague," Guy told her.

As soon as she entered the car, Doctor Red began to apologise. "I'm so sorry." he said, and really looked as if he meant it. "You could have handled it differently," snapped Tapiwa glaring at him as he sat cowering on the back seat beside Monty. "You don't know where the damned map is, do you?"

"I'm sorry," he said again.

"If Caine was your friend surely he told you?" She pressed him.

"We agreed it would be safer if he hid the Staff in Uganda,

and the map here. Then he suddenly disappeared; I was really worried."

"He died in that damned box over there, the one you condemned me to," she told him acidly.

"Oh my God did he? All I know is that he kept it near his work in a government building."

"Which building?" she asked. Red seemed not to hear her, he was still trying to apologise for his actions the previous evening. "I'm sorry I left you, they threatened to kill me. I'm sure Joseph hid the map in the government building, but the problem is I can't into get it."

"Let's be positive," said Monty, "I can get access to most government buildings."

"Really?" said Guy. "I suggest Doctor that you tell us the whole story."

"Well, as I told the young lady yesterday, Joseph and I both worked for President Idi Amin. We were tasked with getting the Staff from Kenya; we found and hid it in Uganda, bringing the map to its location back here. Joseph hid it in the government building for safety."

"That must have been years ago."

"It was, Joseph would never tell me where the map was hidden. He said it was for my own good. I've been searching for it for six months but not had any success. Joseph's relatives are all dead and I can't get near the building."

"His business card says he was Procurement Manager for the government, so perhaps what we seek is in his department," said Tapiwa.

"I didn't know he worked there; he was always very secretive," said Red. "The only reason he came to Uganda was because he married a Ugandan. Amin had her killed when he didn't get what he wanted."

"There is something else on the card," said Tapiwa producing it. "A rough drawing of a circle but it also looks like a knight on horseback."

"A knight?" queried Guy looking closely at the tattered card, "seems like your friend was laying a trail of clues."

"Perhaps," replied Red sadly. "We'll never know, but I can't find the Artefact in Uganda without the map. We went into the deepest of forests up there quite deliberately."

"Probably doubted the two of you would survive and couldn't see Uganda getting any better, so left it vague," said Guy.

"Could be a meeting table, I guess," said Red looking again at the tattered card. "We were lucky the card survived the hole."

"We need to get into that government building tonight; you can bet our adversaries will be also on to this. Fortunately my Interpol card will come in useful, surprising how far the police tentacles can spread." Monty started the car and they headed back to Lilongwe.

It took them two hours to get to the Four Seasons Hotel on Presidential Way. They settled Tapiwa into a comfortable room to rest and recover after her ordeal, then went on to their real destination. This was the huge Presidential Government Building. Despite it still being dark when they arrived, there were a number of people working in the offices, their windows adding shafts of light to an area that was already well lit. They approached the security point and Monty showed his Interpol badge. After a short exchange with the security guard, the iron gate swung open. Guy drove the car into the parking area in front of the building.

"What did you say to him Monty?" asked Guy as they got out of the car.

"I told him we were visitors from Interpol Europe and had been asked to carry out a security check on the building. My Interpol badge convinced them for now but I doubt we have long."

"I didn't know you had the badge with you," said Guy.

"It does come in useful occasionally." Monty grinned.

They made their way through to the administration building and up some stairs; Guy pointed to a sign indicating the way to the Procurement Department. "Up there on the third floor," he said excitedly. They used the stairs rather than the lifts; they were less likely to meet anyone that way. Though it appeared a nondescript department it was, interestingly enough, next door to the President's own office. Guy thought he could hear men shouting somewhere in the distance. "There, off to the right, the main conference room," said Doctor Red excitedly. "Joseph told me about this fantastic room on the front of the building overlooking the compound. He always felt very important in there and said his ambition was to have a round table like this one."

"Round table, that's it, don't you see," said Guy excitedly, "Knights of the Round Table, the drawing and circle on the card. It's got to be here, the map will be in the table." They scrambled underneath looking hurriedly as the shouting came closer. "I've got it," shouted Red excitedly pulling a plastic document holder from behind a fake wooden carving. "Great let's see," said Guy more conscious than ever of noises approaching fast. He opened the map and looked at some figures and a drawing with the name Kampala. "Bingo! Come on we need to get out of here."

"The back way," hissed Monty and they moved quickly, "the guards have seen us. We need to get out of here." There was a shout and a group of men appeared at the top of the stairs above them. "What are you doing in here?" one of them called out.

"A security check for Interpol," Monty shouted back as they headed for a door at the opposite end of the corridor. His explanation didn't seem to convince him. "Stop," ordered the leader of the group.

"Keep running," advised Monty. There was no bluffing any more and they slammed through door after door running down empty corridors. They ran into what appeared to be changing rooms for the janitors and service staff; around the walls hung their official uniforms. "Put them on," yelled Monty. Five minutes later they strode across the lawns towards their car, past a couple of guards who stared at them suspiciously. "We made it," said Monty exultantly when they were safely back in their car. He engaged the gears and started to drive, cursing as he saw the iron gates begin to close. "Sod it," he said viciously, and jammed his foot down onto the accelerator. The car shot forward like startled a stag and hurtled between the gates with only inches to spare and roared away into the night.

They disposed of the car in a back street and made their way on foot to the hotel. The number plate would be all over police screens by now. Tapiwa, now showered and rested was almost her old self when they met in her room an hour later. "It looks genuine," she said after examining the folder's contents. "There's no doubt it's the one," confirmed Red. "I remember now, we went well north of Kampala in a forested region."

"Then we need to get there fast," said Tapiwa.

"Absolutely," agreed Monty. His mobile rang. "Excuse me," he said courteously, "it's Jade." He put the phone to his ear and walked away into the bathroom. He returned ten minutes later grinning broadly and for once looking excited. "We have a real breakthrough," he announced. "What's happened?" asked Guy?

"Rose has been sighted in Australia."

"How does Jade know that?"

"The Whistler, your old friend told them in his communique and he was never wrong. Three words '*Viper Cooks Reef*' in code."

"My pet name for her, only he would know that, worrying thing is that he's broken his golden rule to never send actual messages," said Guy. "Where is he now?"

"Traced to The Teacher's camp in Vietnam, according to Jade," said Monty.

"Then he's in mortal danger; he would never normally do such a thing."

"Still, Cook's Reef is interesting," said Monty.

"The Barrier Reef, that's where Cook came to grief," Guy mused thoughtfully.

"So we now have two solid leads; we need to prioritize," said Monty.

"Leave the Uganda Artefact with me," said Tapiwa. "I can handle the Doctor."

"Can we trust you, Red?" asked Guy coldly.

"I will help Tapiwa, you have my word. I also need to check out the details on that Parchment of how to find the Prophecy."

"I thought you gave it to Amin."

"No, he got the tablet; we took the parchment that gives the details of how to find the tablet, one without the other is useless," smiled the Doctor, "you must find this Prophecy; it's far more important than the Artefact."

"First things first, I get the Artefact," said Tapiwa."

"It's agreed then but before we go our separate ways I think a little celebration is in order for the night's activities," said Guy, he rang room service and ordered Champagne.

Chapter 16

Austria
Igls Tyrol

Identical twins Kitzhul and Katherine, known locally as Kit and Kat, lived next to the Panorama restaurant in an isolated house on the very mountain where local hero Franz Klammer had won gold for the Austrians in the Winter Olympics. They grew up untamed and notorious for terrorizing their neighbourhood. In the valley, the peaceful town of Igls had been subjected to their antics from an early age. Their parents had died in a tragic skiing accident when they were in their early twenties. It was an accident in which they were rumoured to have had a hand. By their mid-twenties they had succeeded in building a major extortion ring across the Tyrol but the local police had never managed to pin anything on either of them.

They were now a well-bred killing machine, often using their identical features to confuse their victims and evade capture. They were also involved in international operations, particularly in Northern Italy. From there, under the protection of an indulgent local Mafia Baron, they had gone from strength to strength, each raid more daring than the last. They concentrated on targets for which the public had little sympathy, banks and insurance companies being their favourites; it underlined their Robin Hood attitude. Igls however was home allowing them to hide in the mountains when things became too hot. They often stayed there for months well away from the latest furore they had created. They knew every part of the mountains and often lost the more determined pursuers by hiding in one of the many caves and forests. As their reputation grew, they became restless for greater challenges, one of which had recently been thrown down by a mysterious and reclusive Italian who made them a huge financial offer to work for his organisation. They had accepted it, and the one that followed, completing both assignments to their benefactor's complete satisfaction. The financial rewards were substantial but since both had proved far more dangerous than they had expected; they had called for a summit meeting with their paymaster before considering any more commissions.

Alfonso Rossi shuddered as the old cable car clattered its way up the mountain. He suffered badly from vertigo. Surrounded by excited skiers, he made his way to the centre of the car to avoid looking down and was relieved when twenty minutes later they reached the end of their ride and he stepped onto firm land. Away to his right he saw his destination, a house adjacent to the Panorama restaurant. He crunched his way across the snow to the front door and knocked loudly. Kat opened the door and invited him in. "You made it," he said, "Come in you're welcome." Alphonse wrinkled his nose as he walked along a short hallway to a large shadowy room; the musty smell told him the windows weren't opened very often. "I don't like heights and this meeting is highly irregular, completely against my boss's rules," he grumbled. "He doesn't like variations to his rules."

"It's our lives at risk here;" retorted Kit the more aggressive of the two, "And the assignments are increasingly dangerous. We at least deserve to know who we work for."

"Be careful what you wish for," replied Alfonse.

"So tell us, who is this mysterious boss," asked Kat. "It's not an unreasonable request."

"He's a man who has great plans for the future, someone who in time will be famous and amongst the richest on the planet; but don't try his patience, he values trust above all. Now to business, I have your next lucrative assignment in Asia."

"We won't take a new assignment without knowing his name," Kat persisted.

"A code name is all you get."

"OK that'll do. Go on."

"You should refer to him as the Professor and, believe me, you would not want to make an enemy of him. Have you ever heard of the Medici family?"

"Yes of course, they were around when Venice was top dog," said Kat.

"They controlled both Florence and the City of Venice, overseeing the Doge or Head of State. The Professor works the same way; he too controls events from the shadows. He's a man of power so ask no more questions, do what you are told to do and you will be well rewarded."

"And if we don't accept this new assignment?"

"Having met me, your lives will be forfeit, simple as that."

"So you are threatening us," snapped Kit.

"No, I'm warning you, this is high risk, high reward, so don't pull this trick again. There will be no second chance. It's the biggest opportunity you will ever have; the details are in this envelope," he concluded, throwing the document onto the table and rising to make his way out.

Ten minutes later he made his way onto the gondolier glad to be leaving; he tried to relax as the car slowly made its way down. They were bloody amateurs and yet a scary couple; there was something unhinged about them. The lift shuddered to a halt and the only other passengers, an elderly couple became agitated. He looked around wondering if there was a fault when to his horror the glass shattered and the woman screamed falling to the floor holding her arm, his mobile rang. "Don't ever threaten us again, old man. We will work for this Professor but not because of you. We are the best and we make our own rules. Tell your man that we will let you live as a sign of our commitment to the cause."

"You could have killed the woman." Alphonse said, appalled at what he saw as a totally irresponsible action.

"Why attract the attention of the police unnecessarily?

"We never miss our targets; all three of you would be dead if we had chosen. I can see you don't believe me so let me give you a demonstration."

"W…w…what do you mean?" stuttered Alfonso looking round nervously.

"I hope you are right-handed."

"My God no," Alfonso screamed in agony as his left hand erupted in a mash of blood and sinew the mobile shattered to pieces. He fell down to the bottom of the gondolier as it started to move again.

"I think he got the message Kat," smiled Kit looking through his powerful binoculars.

"This Professor should be impressed," replied Kat smiling. "It always pays to set the boundaries. Wouldn't want them taking liberties would we?"

Chapter 17

Auckland Harbour

Sandy was pleased as Ailsa helped her load the last of the heroin packs aboard the *Starlighter*, a fifty foot sailing yacht that was more engine than sail. Despite the suddenness of the assignment, she was glad to be active again. As Jack's daughter she lived in luxury, yet had little money of her own; she was counting on this venture to make a difference. Her fortune would be made when they landed the cargo in Queensland as she had taken the precaution of secretly diverting a few packages to her own locker. She just had to handle the six day sail which she hoped wouldn't be too arduous, and she was free to do as she wished. She was tired of the macho culture and parochial attitudes to women in Australia. Jack would never agree of course, so she needed her own wealth. The only problem was the crew. They were a hardened bunch of Latinos who had sailed across the vast expanse of the Pacific all the way from Panama.

She shuddered as she thought of them; four hard men and a teenager who made her feel very uncomfortable. They kept staring at her sullenly but never saying anything, only the Columbian youngster called Otway appeared friendly. They had been sent by Jack's new partner who had men that could be trusted based in Panama; she wasn't so sure they could be trusted and watched them like a hawk. Still it was a reasonable price to pay if they got her to the destination. She checked again the outline of the small snub nosed pistol in her pocket. Ailsa had proved to be more of a liability than an asset constantly worrying about what her errant husband was up to. "So why did you help capture the Chinese girl?" Sandy asked her on the first day of sailing. She had just listened to another familiar monologue, during which she had begun to wonder who this Chinese stranger was and how she fitted into the scene.

"I wasn't happy about it," Ailsa told her. "Douglas was leering all over her on the way back."

"You need to stand up more for what you believe in," Sandy advised her. She intended to make something of her life and would take every opportunity that came her way, possibly this was her big chance. The Latino's leader, a tall Columbian called Moses, only had one arm but it didn't stop him exercising a ruthless command over the crew. He explained how with iron discipline they had sailed from Tahiti to the eastern coast of New Zealand. She would be expected to conform, boss's daughter or not. The drugs had been loaded at night in a remote bay on one of the small Auckland islands well away from the noisy central business district. There was a strong Auckland drug culture and, as a consequence, there were sharp-eyed customs men everywhere.

She had spent a day relaxing in the capital marvelling at the pretty islands and homes to the north-east of the bustling business district and beginning to think it was preferable to Australia. Ailsa had confided to her in a rare un-hysterical moment that she was concerned over Jack's new mysterious business partner and how Duncan had changed following the recent trip. Sandy was young and determined, in a perverse way she found it exciting to be in the big league and sought out Moses at the start of the journey in an effort to understand more about the setup. She only received grunts and was told to mind her own business to which she took exception. She had paid her father's money by bank transfer to take ownership of the cargo so pointed out, it was her business. Still the final payoff would be huge when they sold on to the buyer in Brisbane for distribution across Australia.

The weather was ideal with a strong consistent breeze and sun in abundance so she sauntered onto the deck dressed in the skimpiest of bikinis smiling at the lustful glances from the crew. Although a little on the paunchy side she still had a good figure. Otway was entranced. That night he came to her private cabin and between a fumbled and embarrassing performance did give her interesting insights into what was going on over in Panama. It made her think more deeply about the new business her father was involved in and she resolved to take control of this operation somehow. The next day the wind changed direction and Moses started the engines to keep good time whilst Sandy noticed a hardening of the men's attitudes. He was a man of few words and a frightening temper, with a determination to deliver that bordered on the manic. Consequently he ran the engines at full throttle and ordered full sails at the same time. Sandy gave up trying to relax and then stared at the horizon, noticing with surprise that they had changed direction. "Otway, why are we heading east?" she asked the youngster.

"Moses won't tell me," replied the youngster, "just said there was a change of plan."

"That's not good enough," snapped Sandy getting up.

"You need to speak to him, Sandy, he's going to wreck the boat and kill us all."

"Just how do you propose I do that?"

"I don't know but it's your cargo." he correctly pointed out.

"You're right." she said, "I'll have a word with him." She turned towards the bridge and shouted. "Moses!" there was no reply so she strode onto the bridge. Moses was holding the wheel. "Why are we changing direction?" she asked him.

"Get out of here," ordered the skipper.

"What did you say?"

"If you want to live get below, rich bitch," yelled Moses. "We have company."

"Where?" she looked over her shoulder, a coastguard ship was approaching at speed.

"Now get below before the shooting starts," yelled Moses.

"What are you going to do?"

"Fight," he replied brusquely, "Now get the hell off my deck so I can shoot the bastards without hitting the boss's spoilt daughter."

"You'll get us all killed."

"We're as good as dead anyway if we lose this cargo, now go." He gestured to the men who to Sandy's consternation and horror started to assemble what looked like a machine gun. She couldn't believe it. "Get below unless you want to risk the cross fire. We'll sink their ship, I must stick to the plan."

"I don't recall you having any plans about delivering us to Australia."

"We aren't going to Australia lady and if you had any nautical sense, which you haven't, you'd know we have been heading east for the last day or so. Now for the last time get below and don't try to use the radio equipment, incidentally your mobile has been confiscated."

"I can't believe this," shouted Sandy as the machine gun was tested and there was an ear-splitting roar. She flung herself downstairs to meet a petrified looking Ailsa and Otway.

Jack was in a towering rage, he paced across the room and back again. He paused and turned to the man standing uncomfortably beside him. "What the hell do I pay you politicians for?" he yelled. "My daughter went down to New Zealand to visit friends; she has nothing whatever to do with those coastguards disappearing. What I'd like to know is where she is now. You take our taxes and my backhanders so do something useful, go and find her instead of standing there moralising."

"This could become an international incident for God's sake," retorted Pat Buchan, a Labour representative from Queensland's government in Brisbane. "I can't control this, the media smell something big. It has all the key ingredients, you, your daughter, drugs and the disappearance of a New Zealand coastguard ship. It's too big for me to contain."

"It's your damned job to get them to back off," roared Jack, "it's what I pay you for. Go and find Sandy, she can't just disappear. You'll be telling me next that green men with funny eyes have got her."

"We don't control the media despite what you may think, particularly the current lot of sensationalist right wingers. They've no time for me, indeed it's best I'm not even seen near you. Fact is your daughter was seen getting onto the yacht that was reported to be firing on the coastguard before contact was lost. That means she was complicit in the loss of the coastguard ship whether you like it or not. The view is that since then they've sailed into the Pacific dodging amongst the islands around Tahiti."

"My daughter wouldn't do that."

"Perhaps, but the fact you haven't heard from her means they have either kidnapped her or she is complicit. Unfortunately your own colourful background means the media only see a conspiracy with you at the centre."

"Sort it out fast or I'll ruin your career," threatened Jack. He turned to Duncan as Buchan left the room. "Your wife has disappeared with the bloody drugs, have you heard from her?"

"No and this is the first I've heard of it," replied Duncan. "I thought it was too bloody dangerous, way out of our league."

"You just get back to the reef, damn it, and let me worry about that," snapped Jack slamming the door and striding into his lounge. His mood worsened when he read the paper's leading Article. *Eagles Nest – the outbackers' own dictator in our midst.'* It was an Article speculating that Jack was a secret Nazi.

Annoyed by the Article as he was, the trouble he now faced with the loss of both the consignment and his daughter was by far the greater problem he faced. At a stroke his stupid daughter had lost or taken away his financial base. He had borrowed a lot of money from The Teacher. Now he was totally in the man's power and would have to plead for some more cash. He even wondered whether the new partner had engineered the setback, arranging to steal the drugs to embarrass him and kidnap his own daughter into the bargain.

"I want to know what we do next Jack," muttered Duncan entering the observatory area, Jack's favourite room.

"We do our job faster," Jack told him tersely.

"It's dangerous Jack, he's getting leverage on us."

"I said I'd handle it, now what's happening on the reef?"

"We'll be ready to dive next week," replied Duncan morosely.

"Make it the day after tomorrow," snapped Jack, "the timing has just changed; we must find what he's looking for before he gets here."

"He's coming here?"

"I expect so, that's why we must have the damned items next week."

"But that's impossible; I've no idea of any co-ordinates unless this Chinese girl can help."

"She's invaluable to The Teacher so she must know something; he wanted her brought here for a reason so it's time to find out. Leave her to me and you get the gear ready."

Rose had been held in a small room since her arrival and had so far seen no one but a man called Marc; he hadn't spoken a word to her, just attended to her needs and left the room. Now Jack entered the room and from his expression Rose knew things were about to get difficult for her. "What do you want?" she asked him.

"The Teacher, what do you know about him," snapped Jack. She ignored the question and asked one of her own. "When am I getting out of here? You have no right to keep me here."

"I have every right in my kingdom," he said, then to Marc growled. "Tie her to the chair."

"You will be sorry for this," warned Rose as she resisted the big Australian's efforts to carry out his boss's instruction.

"I want to know about the Artefacts and why the Endeavour Reef is so important to The Teacher."

"I have no idea and if I had I wouldn't tell you."

"Wrong answer," Jack told her, and nodded to Marc who slapped her across the face.

"All I know is there's an Artefact that Captain Cook lost here when his ship was damaged on the reef, anyone with half a brain could work that out."

"There's a call boss," said Marc pointing to the mobile, "it's The Teacher."

"Leave her tied; she can starve for a few days," Jack ordered and left the room wondering what the hell The Teacher wanted, he never called directly.

Chapter 18

Cairns

Jochi and Stefan flew from Vladivostok to Shanghai and then took the direct China Eastern flight down to Cairns on the North Queensland coast of Australia. The sweet feel of success after finding the head of the Battle-axe helped conquer their tiredness as they contemplated their next steps. Jochi had arranged for a translator to decipher the Chinese symbols on the Axe head. They were found to be incomplete and he was beginning to realise the whole Artefact chase was one gigantic jigsaw puzzle. They needed the shaft to give them the complete set of directions to somewhere in northern Asia which he assumed would be Mongolia. The diary told them the shaft was down there on the reef exactly as Cook had left it. Jochi had thought long and hard on the flight, his backers were growing increasingly edgy as he took longer than expected with his quest. He had no doubt that they would be successful and, above all, looked forward to seeing The Teacher's face when he realised the strength of support he actually had. It was all much bigger than even The Teacher thought. He directed his mind to the task ahead. They landed and he sat upright with a jerk.

"The Axe head is heavy," he told Stefan as they came into land.

"What?" Stefan had been dozing.

"The weight of the Axe head. It's like the damned Shield. It's that strange material, extremely heavy and very dense."

"So what does that mean?" asked Stefan trying to gather his senses and stealing a look across at Lorna. She was still under the effect of a mild sedative.

"Cook couldn't carry the shaft after he hit the reef; in fact he needed to empty his ship of ballast so it has to be in the same area. Oddly enough, I know divers went down to that reef decades ago and retrieved items discarded from the original voyage. They found all sorts of stuff even the original keel weights, but they didn't find anything else."

"Perhaps it wasn't jettisoned?"

"I think it was but I'm beginning to think Cook jettisoned it outside the main wreck area and left instructions as to its precise location on the land. After all he had little choice but to lose weight or let the ship go down."

"That would make sense because the co-ordinates in the diary show an island in fresh water inland, not at sea."

"That's what he must have done. Now, where will we find detailed co-ordinates of where it was thrown overboard?" He changed the subject suddenly asking, "How's the girl?"

"Half conscious," replied Stefan pointing to where Lorna was sprawled across the seat.

"Less trouble then," for the umpteenth time Jochi wondered why he had brought her all this way; still she had become far more co-operative since the orphanage. He put it down to Stefan's support which seemed to keep her from causing problems, either that or the simple fact that they had convinced her they had Diane at their mercy.

He felt energized in the warmth of the Australian tropics. Their final quarry was within reach and they alone had the exact details of its location thanks to the diary. Bundling Lorna into the back of their hire car, Stefan drove up Captain Cook highway to the main Port Douglas Marina, crowded with boats taking tourists out to the reefs. They made their way across to the main booking office. The warmth on their faces after the bitter cold of Russia and air-conditioned chill of the planes was gratifying and within an hour they were aboard a substantial Sunseeker cruiser loaded with supplies. They slipped their mooring and headed north to the Danetree National Park calculating they had about four hours of light left. Jochi had identified a good place to moor for the evening as far away from the public eye as possible, they thought.

Jochi examined the diary again, going through the co-ordinates of latitude and longitude numbers and noting a drawing of rocks. According to his charts the island was not located on that reference point and he concluded it must be a small island. This wasn't going to be an easy search and would need a methodical grid system approach. It was much faster to scan the areas with the sonar gear they had on board and he reckoned at best they had a couple of days lead on The Teacher. That was all he would need to find the shaft and get out. Then at last Jochi would be in a position to dictate terms. His intent was to use the

Artefacts to leverage his negotiation. A clear run and he would soon be able to build his own empire that would be far greater than anything The Teacher had been capable of. He had people waiting in Russia for just the right moment, then he would assume control; the culmination of a life's plotting both for him and his father. Working for The Teacher had only ever been a means to an end. He signalled to Stefan as the light faded and indicated a remote bay to anchor in.

They started early the next morning and by the mid-afternoon Jochi was becoming impatient as they made their way slowly up yet another estuary. Finding a specific small island here was like looking for the proverbial needle in a haystack. As he stared at the vast expanse of fresh water, he noted it was prime crocodile country. His clear advantage of having the diary coordinates gave him time in hand, a commodity he mustn't squander. They kept working the broad grid system; methodically working their way up and down looking for a small island shaped liked a lozenge. To help, Lorna had been let out on deck, there was nothing she could do for company… except swim with crocodiles.

Lorna indeed had no plans to do anything yet, her mind was clearer than it had been for some time. The orphanage had given her fresh impetus and now in the warmth of Queensland her mind was focusing onto a future after she had escaped from these men. She had formed a small bond with Stefan. He did seem to be concerned about her welfare, unlike Jochi who would react violently to any further problems; she would have to choose her time carefully. Stefan standing in the prow of the boat, called out. "Up ahead, I see rocks hidden by the undergrowth, it matches the diary description of a lozenge shape and the coordinates are broadly right,"

"Great," smiled Jochi as a small heavily wooded island came into view. His first thought was that it was an impenetrable mass of vegetation, impossible to land on; then he saw a small bay. "Get the tender out of the yacht," he shouted. "Handcuff the girl, then row us ashore, it's got to be here somewhere."

"I've got the fire axe, let me go first," said Stefan as they neared the shore line. He scrambled past Jochi looking with dismay at the thick vegetation. "This is going to be hard work," he said.

"Head for the centre," replied Jochi, "I reckon the island is about twenty metres across, maximum, little more than an outcrop, but of sufficient height in the centre to fit the diagram."

"Hard work," mumbled Stefan but carried on chopping his way through the vegetation. Twenty minutes later he gave a shout and pointed to a flat rock lying partly covered by the undergrowth. "Found it," he yelled triumphantly.

"Well done," Jochi reckoned the stone was at the highest point; it would have been the marker that was referred to in the diary, a stone on the pinnacle of the island. His pulse quickened as Stefan pulled away the moss from the rock and looked closer. There are faint marks here," he shouted exultantly ripping away the surrounding vegetation. "Get digging," said Jochi and grabbed a large knife he had taken from the galley and pitched in beside him. Thirty minutes later the rock finally moved and straining together they managed to move it to one side. A box was exposed very similar in shape and texture to the one in Russia and wrapped in oilskins that had partly decayed. Inside lay a leather parchment. "What does it say," asked Jochi as Stefan read the parchment slowly trying to understand the script and seeing a few words in English. "*It is a great responsibility to ensure that as a fellow mariner, success only comes to those most worthy.* "Must be Cook himself who wrote this. Ah there are a clear set of ocean grid co-ordinates latitude and longitude. Looks to be about three miles south east from here." said Jochi checking the map.

"Endeavour Reef," replied Stefan, "the exact coordinates for the Axe shaft."

"Time to go," snapped Jochi straightening up.

"We need a permit to go on the actual Endeavour Reef; bloody coastguards are very touchy," replied Stefan.

"We'll go at night when there's no one around. If we are quick enough they'll never know we've been there. This is it Stefan, we as good as have the damned thing and the bloody Teacher won't be far behind."

They headed back to the tender. Suddenly Stefan stopped, his face whitening as he saw something moving fast through the water coming towards them. "What the hell is that?" he asked. Jochi knew what it was. "Get into the boat," he yelled as a black mass streaked through the water towards him. He grabbed his gun and fired blindly as his world became blurred by a huge shape that crashed forward propelled by its own momentum.

Jochi vainly tried to get out of the way as the crashing hulk fell on him, and felt indescribable pain as grotesque yellowed teeth sank into his leg. He screamed in agony and fell sideways into the water, trying to avoid being dragged into the depths as the creature thrashed around in its death throes. "Christ almighty!" Stefan stared in horror at his partner's bloodied leg as he dragged him aboard the tender. Together they lay heaving in the rocking boat, "you all right?" he asked him.

"No I'm bloody well not alright," snapped Jochi clenching his teeth. "Find something to stop the bleeding, your shirt, take it off and tie it around my leg tightly… and get us out of here," he snapped. Then gasped as Stefan tightened the makeshift bandage into a tourniquet; he knew it was a bad wound that really needed medical attention urgently.

"You need a doctor, there's a danger of gangrene," said Lorna nearly gagging at the sight. It looked as if the entire leg was just hanging by loose flesh.

"That bastard has taken inches out of my leg; tie it tight, there's no time for doctors." Jochi gritted his teeth and poured whisky onto the wound.

"It needs stitches and professional treatment or you may lose the leg," persisted Lorna.

"Work first then there will be time," snapped Jochi gesturing to Stefan to get them out of the area. "Do as Stefan says or you'll be feeding the crocs next." Stefan headed back to the yacht and made for the Reef.

Chapter 19

Guy and Monty arrived at Cairns Airport jetlagged after their long flight. Guy had used the flying time to read up on Cook's exploits particularly his actions on hitting what was now called the Endeavour Reef. The explorer fascinated him as a leader of men, someone who had set off around the world with no guarantee of returning. To be able to convince hard boiled sailors to risk their lives in such a situation took an amazing feat of leadership. To Guy's delight the police had tracked Rose to the Port Douglas area and Monty's enquiries had revealed the name of a businessman who was suspected of holding her captive; he wondered why he would do so. The police had also recorded Jochi, Stefan and Lorna entering the country under assumed names.

Their diversion to Malawi had been productive and for the first time Guy felt the Elders' support was making a real difference; they were now a joined up unit rather than just Rose and him reacting. He was missing her badly, that cheeky grin, the determination to succeed; he reflected a great deal on all that they had been through together. It was hard to believe she was still in her early twenties; she displayed the maturity of someone much older. He missed the banter, using their names for each other, Bear and Viper. He recalled how they had first met when she and her aunt Beatrice, a formidable dragon of a lady, came to the *Hidalgo* enquiring after him. Since then they had shared many escapades and learnt how each other worked. This was their longest separation since that meeting; he was anxious to see her again and be sure she was alright.

Another concern was the news from Africa. Tapiwa had disappeared. Not for the first time he wondered at the spread of The Teacher's malign influence. He said as much to Monty. "The man has a strong network, of that there's no doubt," reflected the inspector "but he's not all-powerful."

"Perhaps he's only part of a bigger network," surmised Guy.

"That's possible," agreed Monty.

They checked into the luxurious Sheraton Hotel on the town's outskirts and, after settling into their rooms, later went down to the Marina for a meeting with the local coastguards. They had to decide which was more urgent, a visit to the businessman at Eagle's Nest, or to go straight on to the reef. "We must accept what the Coastguards say. They have no reason to conduct a search of any craft out there," said Monty. They spent an hour surveying the area for activity and saw only one craft in the Endeavour Reef area and that had a locally authorised permit. "I suppose so but it's not very helpful," observed Guy.

"Rules are made for a reason, or they waste time and money," counselled Monty. "So we try to get Rose away from this Australian Hitler in his own Berchtesgaden." They got into the car Guy had hired and drove towards the Eagle's Nest. "His name's Jack Hogg, apparently he's been riding his luck with the law for years, bankrolling crooked politicians. He's also in the news because his daughter's disappeared. She was last seen on a yacht just off New Zealand, the same area a coastguard ship disappeared. The police reckon he's up to something." He broke off as his mobile burst into life. He listened intently, thanked the caller and looked excitedly at Guy. "The night watch has just changed at the harbour and one of the new customs men remembers seeing a man fitting the description you gave me of your assailant in St Lucia. He reckons it was the same man who took a Sunseeker craft out to the reef under the local licence."

"That's the one on the Endeavour Reef - it has to be. We have enough to go on now," said Guy, he was beginning think they were making the sort of progress he had hoped for.

"Unfortunately no, Hogg has powerful friends. We need more evidence before the police can act."

"Not Tromso again?"

"Not quite but they have absolutely nothing factual on him to justify overt action."

"Isn't democracy wonderful? So we have to do their dirty work?" said Guy sarcastically.

"Up to us," agreed Monty as they parked below the mansion's ramparts. "Duck, there's someone coming." A car drew up and its sole occupant climbed out.

"That's him! Duncan, the bastard who knocked me out in St Lucia. I owe him a crack over the head; it proves Rose is in there," hissed Guy, "We have to go in now when they least expect it."

"No we need to wait," replied Monty.

"But if Duncan's here with Rose, Lorna could be here also; they could be tortured or hurt."

"The police forbade me making any move without their authority; I'll give them a call."

"Ten minutes, then I'm going in," snapped Guy pacing back and forth beside the car. Fate though had other plans. Seconds after Monty switched off his mobile to await a call back from his police contact, it rang again. He listened for several minutes without making a comment then turned to Guy and said. "Good news Guy, the Harbour Master's been told that the Sunseeker out at Endeavour Reef has a person on deck who matches Stefan's description."

"Do they still have the boat's location?"

"Yes, he's trying to make contact with them as we speak, they're going out to intercept and they've asked if we want to go with them. We'll soon catch them on a powerful coastguard boat." said Monty.

"What about Rose?" said Guy, "we can't be in two places at once." Monty was still talking into his mobile. "She'll be safe enough where she is for the time being. We have to get out there. We'll tackle the Eagle's Nest when we get back. Jochi and Stefan may already have the Artefact." He started the car and they set off at speed to the Harbour.

The sea was choppy as they left the protection of the harbour area and met the swell of the ocean waves. The tide was running against them but the coastguard boat was sturdy and powerful. Fifty minutes later there was a shout from the bridge as the silhouette of a yacht slowly came into focus. "It's them," shouted Guy, looking through his binoculars. "Leave this to the experts," advised Monty above the wind noise. "There are procedures to follow." A loud-hailer told the other craft to heave to and when no response was received the coastguards fired a warning shot across their bow and pulled across preparing to board the yacht. As Guy and Monty followed they heard a shot ring out and rushed to the lower deck looking around anxiously. In a corner of the lower saloon stood Lorna and Stefan, the latter looking crestfallen as the police disarmed him. "Lorna," shouted Guy and ran across to take her in his arms. "Guy, oh my God, you've no idea how glad I am to see you." Lorna hugged him tightly crying with relief.

Jochi lay on a couch covered in blood, his face pale and shivering with cold. "A long time since Valgrind and Helsinki," commented Monty. Then, noting his wounded leg he said. "What's happened to you?"

"Croc attack, it's infected and he needs help." Stefan answered for him.

"You tried to shoot one of the coastguards," replied Monty looking down at Jochi and the bullet hole in the door frame. "You are too late," snapped Jochi lapsing into semi-consciousness, still angry that they had been so close to their goal and had failed because of a crocodile. "Believe me you do not want to get involved in this, it's bigger then you think," he said through gritted teeth. "Go and arrest some fishermen or something for God's sake,"

Lorna was trying to answer all the questions put to her by Monty and Guy. "Earlier they drugged me but I'm OK now," she assured them. "They have the exact co-ordinates for the Axe Artefact. Stefan was about to dive for it when you turned up, that's how you caught them unawares, Jochi is half dead."

"Where are the co-ordinates," asked Monty.

"The parchment," said Lorna pointing to it lying on the table..

"A leather parchment with map co-ordinates?" said Monty looking at the document. "The precise location of the Axe, am I right Stefan?" The lack of any reply told him everything he needed to know.

"They have the Axe head already; they found it in Russia. It's down here in Jochi's cabin," said Lorna.

"Well done," smiled Monty. "Make a detective of you yet. Perhaps at last we have beaten The Teacher to an Artefact, has there been any activity on the Endeavour Reef," he asked the closest coastguard.

"A local salvage ship is licensed for the last few weeks; I've just given them permission to continue for a few more days, they have authority from the government."

"Who are they?" snapped Monty.

"The boat is owned by a man called Hogg, lives up there at the Nest," replied the coastguard after consulting his notes. "His permit is genuine," he confirmed seeing the startled look on Monty's face.

"God almighty," snapped Monty. "Didn't it occur to any of

you that this was a little unusual, we have to catch them up?"

"They won't find anything without the precise co-ordinates," said Stefan.

"Hogg must have some idea," replied Guy, reluctantly releasing Lorna, "even to invest in the search at all."

"You're right," said Lorna. She felt as if she was emerging from a long dark tunnel. "Jochi's racing The Teacher for the third and fourth Artefacts."

"We have an idea where the fourth is," said Guy, and looked closely at the Axe Head Monty had retrieved from Jochi's cabin. "You can see it's made of that special material." Monty agreed. "Now we must find the other half," he said.

"So do we dive now?" asked Guy eagerly, "It's a great chance to get it."

"No, first we must get Jochi to hospital and even the coastguards need permission to go down onto the reef," said Monty.

"So we just do nothing?" said Guy.

"Jochi will be flown to the nearest hospital; his leg is in a serious condition; we have the Axe Head and the coordinates for the rest." Guy contented himself with that thought and all the way back to the harbour puzzled over the problem of finding Rose.

It was a full moon as Guy and Monty walked carefully down the drive to the Eagle's Nest. Lorna was safely tucked up in the Sheraton Hotel under police guard. They were here without formal authority or police support but there was no time to wait, even now they might be too late. The burly bodyguard Mac answered Monty's knock on the front door. "Police, we'd like to see the owner," snapped Monty.

"He's not here," snapped Marc.

"Then we'll wait until he returns."

"I don't know when he's coming back and where's your badge?"

"Here," replied Monty hoping the man wouldn't notice the Bermuda coat of arms.

"You can wait in the hall; I'm not inviting you in until Mr. Hogg says so."

"Very well, then kindly inform him that I have something of great interest to him," Monty told him. They made their way into the cavernous hall, taking note of the layout of the house as they did so. "Worth looking around whilst we're waiting," whispered Monty as Marc left them. "Nosiness comes with the job, all coppers have it."

"You stay here, I'm fitter and can move faster," whispered Guy and he headed off along the main corridor and sharp left down some stairs. He had noticed the servant look anxiously that way when they arrived.

Three rooms lay ahead, the first two were unlocked and empty, but the third was locked. Taking a run he kicked out hard shattering the door, before he could move someone pushed him from behind and he staggered into the room and fell to the floor. As he regained his feet he faced a terrified Rose tied to a chair. "Guy, watch your back," she shouted, but too late someone hit him again and he stumbled backwards. He caught hold of her chair in an effort to remain upright. "Rose, are you OK?" he gasped. "Behind you again," warned Rose."

"A very touching reunion," The voice was familiar and he turned to face whoever had hit him. "You!" snapped Guy looking at Duncan standing beside another man he took to be Jack Hogg. Duncan raised a gun and pointed it at Guy's head, "I thought I'd left you for dead, can't have hit you hard enough last time," he grinned.

"I owe you," grated Guy and he lunged forward. Jack swung his arm knocking Guy down again. "Just as well someone has their wits about them, why do I always have to clean up after you; this bit of business was supposed to be finished in the Caribbean," snarled Jack.

"Go and get his damned partner."

"Stitched him up good with the binoculars; he should be dead," mumbled Duncan.

"You should have killed me when you had the chance," hissed Guy standing up shakily. "You planned it all didn't you?"

"Just had to put up with your boring chat for a week whilst we got the arrangements made, told the coastguards you'd killed Rose in a fit of anger, they should have arrested you if you weren't dead."

"Well they didn't."

"You should have finished them," snapped Jack raising his gun. Marc came into the room. "I've got the copper upstairs," he announced. Guy tried to play for time. "We have the Artefact so it's too late; the police will be here any minute."

"Oh yeah? That's very interesting," replied Jack.

"Leave the girl tied up, my friends will have a little entertainment, Duncan go and prepare the special room."

Jack pointed his gun at them and waved it indicating he wanted them to leave the room with Duncan then became angry as his mobile rang. "As we thought," whispered Guy, "He's up to his neck in it with The Teacher."

"Guy, I'm sorry, I had to give them the coordinates, the bastard was going to throw me in there," said Monty pointing down to the crocodile pool.

"Doesn't matter, we'll stop them before they recover the Artefact," Guy assured him. Duncan forced them into a large room and Guy looked down from a perch high above the sea. "We call this the scenic room, see those beauties down there, they're very hungry today," smiled Duncan and operated a switch beside the door. To their astonishment they felt the whole floor begin to move, retracting in on itself. "We need to move fast or we're dead," snapped Monty. "I'm ready," nodded Guy as the inspector with amazing speed flung himself at the door pushing into a surprised Duncan as he began to close it. The Australian cursed and tried to lift his gun but Monty knocked it away, Guy moved into the fray and flattened Duncan with a hard kick to the groin still struggling to free his hands as he did so. The ropes came loose just as the door opened. "What the hell's going on here?" snarled Jack. Guy hit him hard on the side of the head.

"The door Monty," yelled Guy running forwards as the floor reached half way.

"You idiot," growled Jack picking himself up and glaring at Duncan, conscious that the floor was now almost gone. "You bloody idiot Duncan, get hold of them. Where the hell is Marc?"

"Run," yelled Guy slamming the door shut and pushing Monty down the stairs. "Another minute and we would have been croc food…This way," he yelled, running down the steps to the room where Rose was still held. He kicked open the door and released the cords that held her. There was a shot and Monty stumbled forwards.

"Are you ok?" Guy asked Rose.

"I'm fine," she whispered rubbing her legs as she ran. "Monty what's wrong?"

"I've taken a bullet in the leg," gasped Monty staggering to keep up and in obvious pain.

"We have to keep going, can you move?" asked Guy as they ran into the fresh night air slamming the front door behind them and half carrying Monty into the forest. "I'll have to be for the time being," said Monty gamely.

"Good! and well done Monty you saved our lives."

"Only had one chance," gasped Monty. "That bastard was going to feed us to the crocs."

"Am I glad to get away from those creeps!" panted Rose taking deep breaths of fresh air, "I've spent two bloody weeks in there."

"Did they hurt you?" asked Guy.

"Not physically," she said, "Hogg left me alone but Duncan was about to do something nasty to me, thank God you came."

"He'll pay later," promised Guy recalling his crude remarks back in St Lucia.

"Are you badly hurt, Monty?" asked Rose as they ran on deeper into the forest.

"Winged me in the leg,"

"We need to get you to a hospital," said Guy as they slowed to a fast walk, the vegetation getting thicker. Monty was bleeding from a small hole in his calf muscle.

"I'll last until we get back."

"Let's take a break. They won't follow us, it's too dark. Guess they'll head out to the reef first thing in the morning now they have the co-ordinates. Been on the reef all week," she continued as they heard the howls getting closer. "They've brought in some top divers for tomorrow's action."

"We need to call the police now," said Guy reaching for his phone. "Seven of the ten most deadly snakes in the world are lying around this forest; we need to get out of here."

"That's the real reason no one is following us," replied Monty, "they reckon the snakes will get us."

"I'll carry you to the road," said Guy.

"No need, just heard from the police, I gave them our co-ordinates."

There was a joyous reunion that night at the Sheraton. A late supper boosted everyone's morale and Monty's leg was professionally treated, still they all recognised it was simply a lull in the storm. Next morning Monty and Guy made their way down to the waterside café in the harbour where they ordered cappuccinos and surveyed the seafront. Lorna and Rose were safely with a police guard being debriefed about their separate experiences. Despite stringent protestations, Monty had insisted on coming along to prevent any misunderstandings with the local police and coastguards. They scanned the Marina and Guy spotted a large cruiser making its way slowly out of the small harbour area. "There he is," he said pointing seawards, "I can see Duncan on deck."

"We know the location so it's best to let them go to to the area, then we pounce," said Monty. Then the cruiser began to pick up speed as it left the harbour and was about to pass the narrow entry point. "Too risky Monty, they may have an escape plan. We have no guarantee they don't have a helicopter to lift the Artefact away in front of our eyes, follow me." But Monty didn't follow him. He watched helplessly as Guy ran at a crouch along the quayside partly hidden by the shops, waiting until the ship passed near. The men on board were concentrating on manoeuvring their ship out of the marina and didn't see him jump onto the stern and disappear below deck. He found a small storage room and settled down out of sight as the powerful diesel engines accelerated. Two hours later he heard the unmistakable sound of scuba gear being donned.

Duncan signalled to his two divers as they pinpointed the exact place where Cook had struck the reef over two hundred years ago. Sabine had sent him the co-ordinates so he was sure of success and was diving himself, stung by the harsh criticism from Jack. He had to find the casket immediately, their escape plans depended on it with the helicopter already hovering nearby. He nodded to Mack and Bill, the other divers, and they all fell backwards into the water. Guy heard their splashes as they hit the sea and cautiously made his way up onto the deck. The sailor servicing the diver's equipment saw him and came towards him; Guy was in no mood to argue, he grabbed a harpoon gun lying on a nearby hatch and rammed it hard into the man's midriff driving the air from his body. As he folded double he brought the heavy handle crashing down on his head and the man sank to the floor without a sound. There was no one else around, the ship was his.

Far below, on the beautiful Great Barrier Reef, Duncan smiled to himself when he saw amongst other detritus on the sea bed, the shape he was seeking; he knew that much of the jettisoned cargo from Cook's voyage had been found about half a mile away so Cook had deliberately moved it away from the main site. The casket stood proud though covered in barnacles. He signalled to Mack who helped him fasten the chains and then sent the signal for it to be lifted. Slowly it rose from the sea bed and for an instance looked like it would fall before the chains took the strain. He followed watching with satisfaction as it broke the surface and was swung aboard. He reached the steps, grabbed the rail and as he did so realised something was wrong, very wrong. Staring at him over the rail was the grinning face of Guy Tresanton and anchored nearby was the solid looking form of a Coastguard Cutter. The covering helicopter was nowhere to be seen.

Guy pointed the harpoon gun at Duncan's chest. "Bad news Duncan," he said. "In fact your worst nightmare," he added and pushed Duncan to the floor. "All clear Monty," he yelled as the Inspector emerged from behind the wheelhouse with two coastguards, who ran to the rails and arrested the other two divers as they climbed aboard. Guy pointed to one of them. "Open it," he ordered. Mack didn't move but looked to Duncan for guidance.

"This is trespassing, we are here legally," protested Duncan getting to his feet, desperately trying to think of a way of escape.

"Considering that yesterday you tried to feed me to the crocs that's a bit rich, now open it." Mack shrugged his shoulders, this wasn't his fight. He prized open the casket and whistled at the large metal axe shaft. It was nearly a meter in length and despite years in the sea shone brightly in the fading afternoon light. Guy noted the markings along the side; they would need to record them as soon as possible.

A slight movement caught his eye and he saw Duncan edging towards the ship's side. "Stop him," he yelled but too slowly to stop the man jumping over the side still clad in his diving gear, above them they heard the roar of the helicopter returning. "They did have an escape route, get him from the water." He called out to the coastguards at the same time gesturing to Mack and Bill to sit down. Duncan came to the surface with a splash. The helicopter came closer as if attempting a rescue but thought better of it and turned sharply to pull away. "No honour amongst thieves if they don't deliver," Guy smiled as coastguards picked up the bedraggled Duncan. Monty was interested only in their prize. "For the first time in over two hundred years... reunited," he declared with a flourish, and pushed the two Artefacts together. "Brilliant workmanship," he said as the snug fit made the Chinese text readable. "We need to get a translator before The Teacher can get his hands on it. Jumping aboard like that was brave work Guy, but foolhardy, you could have killed yourself."

"Sometimes you have to take risks like you did in Valgrind."

"Fair point," conceded Monty getting his pipe out for a chew. "What of the crew?"

"Nothing to charge them with as the dive was authorized, but Duncan can be done for the assault last night and removing the Artefact from the Reef. We need to think of a new approach to the Nest though; there are developments there."

"What of Stefan and Jochi?"

"Stefan's under arrest, Jochi's in intensive care and its touch and go for him, even if he survives he won't be up to much. Come on let's take this beauty."

"Shouldn't we leave it with the police?"

"No, we need a bargaining tool."

Later, on a balmy evening, with the sun slowly setting, the four dined at the Sheraton in the open air. Guy and Monty recounted their adventures to the girls and they embraced a brief return to normality. Guy was frustrated by Lorna who didn't seem to want any private time with him; they had so much to discuss, she pointed out. He put a brave face on it knowing they had a long way to go. Rose though was quickly returning to her old ways using the Bear term with him, that was always a promising sign.

"Aren't we making ourselves a direct target by holding the Axe?" asked Lorna. "It's so beautiful," she said looking closely at the exquisite workmanship.

"No doubt made by the Khan's best craftsmen and in the strictest secrecy," Guy told her. Monty answered her question. "That's the plan," he said grimly. "The Nest is a bloody fortress, full of nasty little surprises so we must tease him out."

"So you want Hogg to come after us?" queried Guy.

"Ideally yes, but we need to be ready for all eventualities, continually on guard."

"Why don't we just leave here while The Teacher is elsewhere?" asked Rose.

"Hogg's the only definite lead, catch him and we take a major step forwards," said Monty. "I'll bet he has already been instructed to stop us at whatever cost."

"Our fathers are still held by The Teacher," said Rose, "we can't put them at any more risk."

"There's something I have to tell you all, something I overheard," said Lorna quietly. Jochi was talking about a plan to create a major epidemic; a Contagion."

"A Contagion?" frowned Monty.

"It's the reason why Jochi was concerned to get the Artefacts."

"Makes it all the more necessary to draw The Teacher out, if this Contagion Project is real then the Artefact is just a by-product. I need to interrogate Stefan and Jochi," he continued. "Meanwhile I suggest you get some rest but don't leave the hotel environs, there are police officers everywhere."

"Do you think we'll ever be free?" Lorna asked Guy as they walked in the grounds.

"It's like an albatross around our necks that won't go away until there's closure on so many issues. I'm convinced my father is still alive so it can't end until The Teacher is finished," he told her.

"You mean until he is dead."

"He'll always be a malign influence alive, problem is I've lost my ability to know what he's doing, the Whistler has gone."

"Whistler?"

"A man who used to communicate with me. I haven't heard from him for a month which is very unusual." He looked at her closely and asked, "Have you recovered after all that's happened to you recently?"

"I'm getting there," she said slowly, "It was a mistake to go to Valgrind; I was driven by guilt now I'm just confused."

"Confused?"

"Yes, there must be a reason for them wanting to use me and

I can't figure out what it is. I suspect it has something to do with my father."

"Your father's legacy," said Guy thoughtfully.

"In Russia last week I saw real poverty and suffering, that's what needs to be addressed. I spent time at a children's orphanage; the conditions were awful. That's where the Axe head was located."

"Is that where you heard about this Contagion Plan, what do you think it means?"

"I don't know, but I do know that Jochi was worried about it, said it could shake the core of many countries."

"So we have to stop The Teacher and get the Artefacts."

"Those damned Artefacts; you're just like the rest beguiled by their glitter, the Contagion Plan is real."

Chapter 20

There was no choice; Jack had not been enticed away from his lair, so they would have to go in and get him. The direct approach was best so the front door was forced open and Monty, accompanied by a local police inspector with a warrant, and followed by Guy, stormed in. Police were stationed at every exit. Monty had questioned Stefan further but gleaned little more information except that a site in North Vietnam was becoming the major conduit for the Contagion Plot. It added urgency to their tasks and was the reason they had thrown caution to the winds.

"What the hell is this," yelled Jack angrily barring their way, "Invading my home as well as kidnapping my dive team?"

"Oh it's gone far beyond such petty charges, Hogg," snapped Monty. "You are under arrest for attempted murder and the loss of a coastguard vessel in New Zealand." Jack was shocked and muttered. "I demand my solicitor."

"Of course you do, after all we have enough on you now to put you behind bars for ten years or more, though if you help us things may be different. What I suggest you do is stop blustering and help us find your partner; then I might ask the police to go leniently."

"I don't know what you're talking about," Jack replied and looking across to Guy said, "I demand my lawyer."

"It doesn't work that way anymore Hogg; you broke the rules when you tried to kill us so the game has changed. You're not going to be very popular with your partner when he finds out we have the Artefact, are you? On top of that your cousin is already singing like a canary about your drug runs in New Zealand and elsewhere. They're going to throw the book at you so no one will particularly care if you have a few nasty scars. Also you've brought shame on the Aussie nation; they don't forgive that easily," snapped Monty stroking the blade of a long and very sharp knife.

"This is outrageous." spluttered Jack but he was clearly frightened. He wasn't used to being on the receiving end of such danger. Monty appeared unmoved. "Probably, but I find it gets results and don't think you are going to be protected by The

Teacher, he's notorious for how he treats failures."

"Usually a bullet to the head," said Guy helpfully. "Where's the hulk?"

"Your stupid attempts to threaten me won't work," snapped Jack walking to the main room.

"Your daughter is in big danger if she's not already dead; doesn't that mean anything?" asked Monty.

"Keep her out of it."

"Then perhaps this works best," interrupted Guy raising a gun he'd borrowed from a policeman. That changed Jack's mind. He slumped into a chair and said.

"He has a place in Vietnam; it's a compound of some sort full of doe- eyed followers who think he's going to change the world. There's something big going to happen there."

"I assume you know The Teacher's business."

"All I know is that I contract with ZTW in Bermuda. I've never met this man you call The Teacher, what sort of name is that anyway?"

"Use the gun, Guy." Jack saw the barrel point towards him and again he lost his nerve. "I want legal representation," he whined. Monty was unrelenting. "Are the Artefacts kept in this place in Vietnam?"

"They may have told me they were there, yes."

"For when you deliver the Axe?"

"Perhaps, but I only know of the Axe not of this epidemic you speak about, so don't ask me," snapped Jack.

"And the fourth Artefact?" asked Guy.

"I told you I don't know anything else."

"Why did you kidnap Rose?" asked Monty.

"Zheng told me to; you do what he says, though as I have told you I never met him."

"Even if it means breaking the law?"

"She was brought here to help with our work; now I really don't have any more to say."

"Your daughter has disappeared, doesn't that worry you?"

"Of course it does. You should stop wasting time on me and try and find her," snapped Jack and began moving backwards. He seemed to half stumble to his right and then fell through a nearby door which slammed shut after him; they heard him scramble across the observatory floor.

"That damned room again," cursed Monty as it started to move, "run Guy," he roared as clear water appeared below them. Guy grabbed a light fitting on the side wall and reached for the switch as Monty, hindered by his damaged leg, fell and started to roll towards the gap. "Hold on Monty," yelled Guy and flicked the switch, the floor stopped moving. "Twice in two damned days! I'll have nightmares about this bloody thing and those crocs."

"Well done," said Monty gratefully. "For a minute I thought Fat Albert was going to get his dinner a bit early." Then he cocked his head to one side and asked, "what's that I can hear?"

"A damned helicopter rotor starting up, come on."

"Shit, he's left with his henchman."

"Oh my God! Lorna!" shouted Guy in alarm, "We shouldn't have left the Artefact there."

"They have police protection," Monty reminded him. Guy tried to call Lorna without success.

"My fault," Monty repeated several times as they drove at breakneck speed to the Sheraton. They ran down the corridor past startled guests. He groaned as he saw a slumped policeman in the corner of Lorna's room, "I should have put more men on duty."

"She's still there," breathed Guy, relieved to see her lying on the floor, "Lorna are you alright?"

"I think my rib might be damaged, that big brute Marc hit me hard," she gasped as Guy removed her gag.

"Wait until I get my hands on the bastard," promised Guy. Then he noticed Monty was limping very badly again and asked if he was OK. "Opened the damned wound when the floor went," Monty explained. "But the doc says the wound will heal quickly." Guy nodded relieved that his friend had suffered no lasting damage, then asked. "Where's Rose?"

"I'm here," came a familiar voice from the door. "I was down on the beach when I heard the chopper. I ran as fast as I could but didn't make it, at least I stopped them from taking Lorna. I wonder why they are so keen to get her. I guess the Artefact has gone, hasn't it?"

"Afraid so," replied Monty. "It was my fault."

"No one's blaming anyone, Monty. Hogg will head for Vietnam; we need to get after him as quickly as possible to stop the Axe being delivered," Guy said urgently.

"The only good news is that we can track him through the police network, plus we have detailed photos of the Axe but I agree we need to chase him," said Monty.

"Guy, looks like it's you and me. We're the only fit ones left," said Rose.

"I'd like to come too," said Lorna, "I owe them one."

"You're not mobile enough, Lorna; this could well get very rough," Rose advised her and shot a warning glance to Guy.

"She's right Lorna, I can't risk it, going after Hogg is going to be extremely dangerous and it seems you are important to them, so we need to protect you."

"I'm sick of being wrapped in cotton wool."

"You mentioned your father; there must be something you have that they want."

"Only the cruiser and that's in debt."

"Is it under your ownership?"

"Yes but it's just a cruiser."

"Specially adapted by your father if I recall," mused Guy. "There's something they want, so you are our most valuable asset now the Artefact has gone."

"An asset, am I?" she sounded offended. Guy grinned at her apologetically. "Sorry, but the point is we need to look after you and besides your rib needs looking at." Lorna looked from one to another of her friends and saw agreement in their eyes. She realised there was no point in arguing further and subsided into silence…for the time being.

Tay Ninh

The Teacher stared balefully across his office at Jack who was relaxing on a wide sofa under a window. "Unconventional, I'll grant you that but under the circumstances you did well; were you followed?"

"No I made sure of that, my assistant covered my tracks; now I'm a fugitive from my own country," Jack assured him.

"Comes with the rewards, Jack. You knew the risks when you signed up." Jack nodded. He'd already written off the past week's activities as unimportant.

"Did you have anything to do with my daughter's disappearance?" he asked.

"That's not the sort of question I expect from a valued partner. I'm as concerned as you are with what has happened. We both lost a great deal of money."

"So who took her and where have they gone?" The Teacher waved a hand at him. "We will find them, now relax there is much work to do here."

"If you're sure," conceded Jack. He felt like he was in the headmaster's study.

"You will have wealth far beyond your wildest dreams. Soon you'll be one of the richest men in Asia, certainly the richest in Australia. There's a lot changing here Jack. Once this was a unit with sixty followers now but we only have thirty as they prepare for the great campaign."

"The Contagion Project?"

"So you know about that; guess I shouldn't be surprised. Now, I have someone I want you to meet."

"Hello Jack, you're now one of the valued members of my team," purred Sabine entering the room wearing a black suit. "The Axe is brilliant and you did very well, so well in fact that you deserve special treatment. Roxanne here will see to your every need, then you will be refreshed and ready for the next steps." She stepped aside to introduce another of her team and said. "Roxanne, see our guest is well looked after. Jack is part of the team now and must be treated as such." A dazzling young blonde woman walked languidly across the room and took Jack's arm. "Come with me," she whispered. "You've had a long journey and must be very tired."

Jack at that precise moment didn't feel the least bit tired but stood and followed her from the room anyway. As the door closed Sabine said, "So what now?"

"Is Shaka ready?"

"Yes but we need to watch him. I'm to pay him a visit when I leave here."

"It's time to activate the final phase now we have the three Artefacts. I take it they have been moved?"

"Yes, to a place where no one will ever find them," smiled Sabine.

"Then you are clear about what you need to do. It's the culmination of all our hard work, Sabine. The compound has had its day; the followers have spread their message and done their

job, even the dear old Caodaists, so it's time for our reward."
Sabine felt a glow of expectation flow over her. The future
looked so very promising for her and all The Teacher's followers.

Chapter 21

Mongolia
Ulaanbaatar

After being selected for special 'sleeper' training at The Teacher's academy in Vietnam, Shaka Khan, a tall, imposing man in his early forties, returned to his homeland with his bodyguards to be the Presidential nominee for the People's Party, presenting himself as a man from the Steppes and of the people. The Khalkha people of Outer Mongolia had declared their independence following the Xinhai revolution in 1911. It had been a false start as their more powerful Russian and Chinese neighbours bartered over the fledgling state. Then in 1945, as the invading Japanese forces were finally swept back, Mongolia once again achieved formal independence that was recognised around the world.

Shaka wasn't going to risk losing this election. He had a straight fight against the ruling Democratic Party and the powerful incumbent Geyut. He had gained momentum helped by The Teacher's money and a direct appeal to the newly enfranchised youth of the country. With his western ways and easy, outgoing manner he felt the tide was turning in his favour. The ruling party was increasingly portrayed as being out of touch. The only issue was the amount of time he had left to make an impact; the elections were to be held in three weeks' time. Mongolia was blessed with huge deposits of various minerals ranging from coal to gold and beyond; he wanted to be the one to exploit that natural wealth. His People's Party predecessor had been dismissed on trumped up corruption charges fabricated by The Teacher's organisation and Shaka had stormed to the leadership on a heady mix of messages from what was essentially a third world country with advanced world potential.

His messages were simple; dramatic changes were needed to bring Mongolia kicking and screaming into the new century and he, the new Khan, was the man to do it. He had learnt to write in Uighur, the official language of the Khan's and that used in writing the '*Secret history of the Mongols.*' He even claimed to be a direct descendant of Genghis himself which was not that difficult as most Mongolians could claim some DNA links to him due to the great man's proclivities with the opposite sex. Genghis's grandson, Kublai, impressed him more. It was Kublai who had built on the Chinese Empire's learning and organisational skills. That, combined with their inherent fighting ability, was the potent force Shaka intended to replicate. His country was going to be an industrial powerhouse and it needed a strong leader, someone with close links and influence with the Chinese but that also had its own independent strength.

He'd started life as a shepherd boy from the Steppes but now, indoctrinated with psychological training from Doctors Tresanton and Ling, he was working to a simple agenda, to make Greater Mongolia able to stand up to its powerful neighbours, particularly the Chinese. They held Inner Mongolia where the citadel of Xanadu, the historical centre of Kublai Khan's Empire was located. He had also to keep the Russians at bay; a difficult balancing act as both China and Russia had always viewed his country as a potential acquisition, never more so than now with the vast wealth being discovered under its surface. As he made his way back to his office in Ulaanbaatar, his mobile bleeped, telling him that he had a visitor. Shaka cursed; he didn't like surprises and the sudden nature of the visit was never a good sign. The Teacher should trust him. He entered his campaign offices on the main street and acknowledged his visitor, a slight frown on his face. "Sabine, good to see you and what a surprise, you should have told me you were coming."

"I always travel to my own timetable," replied Sabine silkily, "It's easier to find out what's really happening. How's the campaign going?"

"Good, we are approaching the final stage and the latest opinion polls are in my favour."

"I'm pleased to hear it, but it's tight in the short time we have available to us."

"I'll take my chances."

"Chances aren't good enough Shaka, there can be no mistakes on this and we have to move faster because of developments with the traitor Jochi."

"I was put in here to win democratically so don't change the rules," replied Shaka coldly.

"We are not changing the rules; you will be President by

whatever means it takes because we need the concessions immediately."

"Even if I am President I can't sign them immediately."

"Yes you can Shaka. We see you as our brightest prospect but we have to move fast."

"I'll do my best."

"I'm sure you will," replied Sabine feeling the man's hungry eyes on her. He had made advances to her once before but she had rejected them. Shaka was the key to their success, the other sleepers had lost focus as the going got tough and had in the end proved unreliable. Despite the assurances of the Doctor that Shaka's mind programming was strong, she had little belief in the two quacks. The whole concept of changing people's minds bothered her so she was going to watch Shaka like a hawk.

Chapter 22

Vietnam
Ho Chi Minh

The Singapore Airlines Airbus taxied across the tarmac and stopped at the impressive new airport building. The passengers streamed into the arrivals lounge. Guy had slept deeply, no longer suffering strange dreams but still awakening with an innate sense that his nemesis, The Teacher, was close by. "Into the lion's den," he smiled across to Rose as they cleared immigration. "Good to have you back, Viper; you did well to remember the old compass plate on *"Hidalgo."*

"How could I forget? I didn't have time to write anything before we got into the helicopter other than 'Teacher'. That bitch Ailsa tied my arms."

"Yes, you've been through a hell of a lot recently," Guy acknowledged her ordeal and wondered what was yet to come. Both their fathers were still held by their enemy and Guy had heard nothing about his mother either for some time. Rose became contemplative. "Yes, but I've recovered quickly. I saw my father last year in Shanghai. He seemed fine then, I hope he still is." she went on to refer to her meeting with Beatrice and Blackie. "Despite our initial disbelief, Beatrice and Blackie seem to be getting on well, arguing all the time in fact. At least we haven't got to worry about them." Guy grinned. "Mother couldn't stand Blackie after she was denied her due inheritance. The old sot is surely dead by now, his liver must have given up the fight long ago."

"Apparently not," she disagreed. "Have you not heard anything about your mother yet?"

"No, both parents have gone off the radar screen," admitted Guy. "I haven't had time to give it much thought but hopefully my father will be here. Fortunately the Elders are funding all the travel costs now; my air travel bill alone will have gone through the roof."

"I'm just pleased they are more proactive; I'd really like to meet this Jade," said Rose.

"You will. We just didn't make it to the monastery when we

last went to La Gomera; next time you can see the place for yourself." Guy promised.

Rose was conscious that this was their best chance to find their respective fathers, if they were still alive. Monty had confirmed that Jack had passed through a day earlier on his way to Tay Ninh. Their plan such as it was, consisted of no more than taking the fight directly to him as he would undoubtedly know they had arrived; it was time to finally confront him. Their only back up was Monty's somewhat tenuous connections with the police, but the question was whether they could be relied upon. All in all a highly dangerous strategy, but there wasn't much choice, time was against them, particularly as nothing had been heard from Tapiwa.

Jade had furnished them with information on the location and layout of the compound at Tay Ninh. "At last we can help our fathers," Rose said. Guy nodded. "I hope so, Rose, I really do but don't get your hopes up." He was pleased at how well Rose and he had slotted together again as partners, unlike the new awkwardness between him and Lorna.

They hired a driver who promised to look after them, Guy grimaced as they entered the antiquated road system. Rose leaned back into her seat and again thought of her father. Was he still alive? She refused to believe he wasn't. He had described his secret role in The Teacher's organisation and how he was trying to help. He had warned her to keep away, it was too dangerous for her to be involved, but she had rejected the advice much more actively than Guy during their six months of self-imposed leave. For Guy it had been two years since he'd heard from his father and one year from his mother.

As they headed towards Tay Ninh Guy recalled the proud history of the country. Like the Balkans and Afghanistan, Vietnam had a successful history of resisting invasion going all the way back to the earliest days of their Hung Kings. "I was wrong back in St Lucia, Rose; there is no avoiding this conflict," he said suddenly. Rose smiled at him, "I went along with the sabbatical too, remember? Now let's just focus on getting out safely. Is there any other way of approaching this place apart from just walking in and taking our chances?"

"The local police are the only route but, as Monty says, it's high risk after our experience in Norway."

"Why would they help?"

"The greater good of law and order I suppose, and of course that's what they are supposed to do. Unfortunately it often depends on how desperate they are for money; still we have the Elders actively helping us now."

"The Whisperer?" asked Rose hopefully, "He's always been there for us." Guy shook his head. "He's gone Rose, I can sense it." She absorbed the news and sat quietly trying to think of another way to get into the complex. Guy took his mobile from his pocket and read the text. "Monty has confirmed Jack Hogg is at the camp," he told her.

"So we have them," said Rose as they pulled to a halt on the side of a valley.

"You go there now," said their driver, a man called Ngoc, pointing to the compound in the distance. "It's a religious place."

"Religious?" asked Rose

"Both religion and language are unique to us," continued Ngoc. "Religion here is a customized thing, many disparate elements, and here we have the strangest in Caodaists. They believe in the reincarnation of famous people like Mao Tse Tung; maybe you are a famous person."

"Hardly, we need a small hotel and a good rest, any ideas?"

"Yes I can take you to a good local hotel; it's owned by a cousin of mine."

"We also need to meet with the local police chief," said Guy. "Can you fix that?"

"Of course, I can fix most things," he told them. "I know Captain Tsieu, I will arrange."

He was as good as his word. Soon after they arrived at the hotel the local police chief, a small wiry man came to see them. His handshake was firm, his English poor as Guy explained about their intent. "It's a religious site, very important, they must be left in peace."

"That's what the owner wants, don't you see?" replied Guy.

"We cannot help unless there is a crime," he insisted.

"There is a man called Hogg in there; he's wanted for a crime in another country," continued Guy with a mounting feeling of disappointment.

"Very well we will come with you to enquire about this man Hogg."

Next morning Ngoc drove them to the site with Captain Tsieu following. At the gates a solitary monk looked down at them before seeing the police badge and gesturing them inside to a visitors' room. A robed monk entered and looked serenely at Guy and Rose before talking in rapid Vietnamese to Captain Tsieu, who translated for them. "He says there is no Mr. Hogg here, this compound does not condone violence and would not support criminals; they cannot help, I'm afraid you have had a wasted visit."

"No! you mustn't go," pleaded Guy as Tsieu strode to the door, "Behind this façade is an evil organisation."

"I don't have to do anything, Mr. Tresanton, and may I remind you that you are a guest in my country; do not abuse that privilege. This is the complete site and you have been misinformed. I recommend you leave immediately, good day." He strode back to his car and drove away without another word.

"Damn!" said Guy as they were left alone in the room with the smiling monk.

"We need to get out of here, Guy, this is dangerous," Monty said nervously.

"Agreed, let's go."

"Going somewhere?" Enquired a familiar voice, "Fancy saving me the trouble of finding you both," Jack Hogg entered the room and smiled at them. "Search them," he snapped to the guard. "No crocs here but I'm sure I can find something equally interesting."

"You took the Axe illegally," Rose challenged him.

"Didn't know you owned it, anyway it's mine now."

"I want to see The Teacher and our fathers," Guy said, changing the subject. The argument over the Axe could come later. Jack shook his head. "You're out of luck mate. He has more important things to do. He's already left the camp and your old man's gone with him. Now that's a real shame; you only missed them by a couple of hours; it would have been such a touching reunion."

"Were both our fathers here?" asked Rose.

"Yeah, course they were; they're key components of his strategy, indispensable I've heard."

"They would never betray us," snapped Rose.

"I couldn't care less about what you believe lady; you're both as good as dead already. I don't know what you thought to achieve by walking in here as bold as brass expecting the local police to help. Still I will enjoy discovering what little information you may both have." He called the guard back into the room and said. "Put them in the interrogation room; I'll start on the girl first, something I've been looking forward to since she arrived in Oz. Our sturdy female commander, Yen Lai, specializes in torturing females; she will look forward to seeing you."

They were bundled away separately by fierce looking guards and Rose noticed a small number of uniformed men and women in green and yellow staring at her as she was escorted across the compound. She also noticed a queue of monks heading towards the main gates and wondered where they were going. She was flung into a cell with a disgusting smell and in complete darkness. "Let me out," she yelled hammering on the door angrily. She cursed as her fists started to bleed and sat down wondering what to do next. The door swung open and the woman Yen Lai smiling grimly strode in, followed by another woman with a hard looking face. "I have a little job to do, a job that I will so enjoy as I did with the mute man."

"The mute man, why what happened to him?"

"He didn't make much noise, wasn't much fun, whereas you will sing like a baby."

"The Whistler, oh my God," said Rose looking around desperately.

"You'll be singing your life story in a few moments," smiled Ye Lai."

"You bitch," shouted Rose and backed away, Yen Lai advanced. The other woman moved forward, grabbed her and dragged her into a small padded room where they both strapped her onto a table. "Now I want you to tell me all you know about this group called the Elders, I will know if you are telling the truth," said Ye Lai.

"I don't know anything about them," snapped Rose screaming as the woman assistant grabbed her shirt and ripped it off snapping her bra in the process before grabbing her right breast and twisting it viciously. "Wrong answer my dear," said Yen grinning. "Think carefully, now about the fourth Artefact and what you know about it."

"For Christ's sake I don't know anything about any

Artefacts," Rose screamed as a hand was thrust into her hair and again when an electrode was attached to her hands and switched on; she felt the current begin to flow and knew she was about to suffer a great deal.

Rose had been gone some time before Guy was roughly pushed out of his cell and across the compound towards the central office. He saw Jack standing next to a form slumped on the ground in front of him and was horrified to see it was Rose. "What the hell have you done to her?" he yelled breaking loose and running to her. He lifted her gently into his arms but she slid slowly to the floor again. A blind rage consumed Guy's mind, he blindly spun around with all his might landed a tremendous punch on Jack's jaw. The Australian went down as if pole axed. Guy was grabbed from behind by two attendants. The woman Yen Lai rushed forwards as Jack picked himself off the ground. "You've just signed your own death warrant," he snarled and hit Guy hard in the stomach. Guy fell to the floor next to Rose winded. He groaned and tried to rise seeing pure hatred in his assailant's eyes. He knew then the man wasn't going to stop. If he was about to die he'd do so on his feet fighting. He staggered upright stood there swaying expecting to take the final blow. But it didn't come, an unusual movement caught his eye and realisation dawned. He voluntarily fell to his feet and rolled over to face Rose. "For God's sake stay down," he shouted and flung himself on top of her as out of nowhere a tongue of flame enveloped his vision followed by a huge bang as the world turned into a flash of orange and then darkness.

———————————————

Kit looked down at the compound, a broad smile showing his pleasure at the carnage he and his sister Kat had created before they quickly closed the top of their converted van. The mortar bomb had obliterated the two main cabins whilst behind the Caodoist's quarters he could see the remnants of another bloc. His instructions had been clear and unequivocal; to obliterate the place. They had no interest in knowing the place was used by a group that could only be described as earnest student types. They didn't care who or what the target was, it was just a job to them. Emotion never came into their reckoning. Their escape route would be similarly well planned and they were now keen to get out of the country as soon as possible. "Won't be many survivors Sis, if any," Kit said using his binoculars to survey the scene. "Better get moving in case there are any."

"We've done a hell of a lot of damage but the main block's still standing; our orders were to wipe the place out," replied Kat.

"There's no time, Kat, it's too risky, we'll claim that we blew the whole place up. It's not our job to look for survivors."

"We should make sure," persisted Kat looking around.

"It's too dangerous," snapped Kit getting into the driving seat. "Come on we need to move."

The lone man smiled with satisfaction as he stood looking out of his window at the tranquil scene across his private island. Holding his mobile phone close to his ear he listened intently to the report from Alfonse. It was a particularly pleasing message and marked the start of his direct engagement. Alfonse had also reported that all except the fourth Artefact were now in his possession; the acquisition of that one was in hand. He thought about the explosion, the Caodaists had been easy to bribe and the local police chief, Tsieu, had also succumbed to the vast amounts of cash on offer. He was particularly pleased to hear that the interfering amateurs Tresanton and the girl, people The Teacher seemed incapable of removing from the scene, were now eradicated and would trouble him no more. The final piece in the jigsaw was Lorna Oleson, then he would be ready.

Hong Kong
Peninsular Hotel

Zheng Wan flew into a towering rage when he was told of the destruction of the complex at Tay Ninh. "This is absolutely monstrous, Sabine," he ranted. "What the hell is going on? Not only is the camp ruined, the Artefacts have gone too?" he knew the answer.

"I'll find out what happened and who did this." Sabine tried to calm him with assurances she wasn't entirely sure she could deliver. All thoughts of the erotic night she had planned at the hotel gone from her mind; work first - this was serious. Zheng held up his hand.

"No, stick to the original plan, Sabine, we have copies of the inscriptions on the Artefacts."

"At least we have the consolation of knowing Tresanton was there with his friends so that problem is sorted, as is Jack Hogg." She reminded him. Sabine saw logical thought returning to her master.

"True," replied Zheng, "I need to tie up a few loose ends in Australia; you proceed as planned," he knew he would have to move fast.

"Whoever has done this would have known we were there yesterday; is it a veiled threat or an attempt to kill us?" asked Sabine.

"It's a warning and a mistake because they have shown their hand."

"You don't think it was the authorities."

"No, the Vietnamese are depending on us. I'll handle this, the plan goes ahead," replied Zheng staring out of the window. "We have less time than I thought."

"I'll go tonight." She headed for her room to pack a few things to take with her.

"Take the private jet," said Zheng wondering how, at the climax of his plans, this calamity had happened. The base had been his heritage, a place with many fond memories and many dedicated followers. He picked up his mobile and called ZTW headquarters in Bermuda. This called for a major rethink. He had to get his hands on the fourth Artefact… or was there another way? He thought back to his father, Zhou Wan, and what he would have done in these circumstances. He had been a wise man, had set the groundwork for Zheng and spent his life infiltrating the Elders. Zheng wondered again what his father would do here and now. He stared out across the Hong Kong skyline in reflective mood.

Chapter 23

Mongolia
North of Ulaanbaatar
Gorkhi Terej National Park

Shaka Khan scanned the cold desolate Mongolian steppes as he planned his next move to achieve power. He knew his position was dangerous, he'd known from day one that the 'mind treatment' could be resisted; the western doctors had encouraged it. Jochi had befriended him at the complex in Vietnam, showing him how to discreetly hide the pills they were given and play along with the regime. Like Jochi he had been selected as a prime candidate to be an ambassador, unlike Jochi he had been selected as a sleeper. That had been a year ago and since then he had worked closely with the Russian, well aware of his plans. He was convinced he'd hoodwinked The Teacher so it had come as a huge shock when Stefan had told him Jochi was dead. Murdered in his hospital bed by an unknown assassin after being savaged by a crocodile and losing a leg in the struggle.

He went outside and ordered his favourite horse to be saddled; riding always cleared his mind and allowed him time to think clearly. He stared across the green steppes in front of him almost believing he was Genghis Khan's descendant. He had visited every town, investing heavily in social and mass media advertising. Targeting the young and idealistic had paid dividends in a country only just awakening from its long slumber, and heading into the future in the fast lane using its vast mineral wealth. He would get control of that wealth through investments made by the ZTW group. He knew he had taken a risk by secretly allying with Jochi, a risk that was now exposed. Still he had his own private army to defend him and it would officially be his kingdom after the election. He resolved to take extra precautions and work further on his image with the people. A plan for the next step started to form in his mind; an ambitious step. Still the call from Stefan had worried him. "It will be you next, so take precautions; I have gone into hiding and at the moment it's every man for himself," Stefan had told him. He knew he must be doubly careful in future.

On his return he was surprised to see Sabine waiting to greet him. "Great to see you again, Sabine, I wasn't expecting you until after the election." She had arrived late the evening before but had gone straight to her room. Her interference was intolerable, but forcing a smile he jumped off his horse and walked quickly towards her, right hand outstretched in a sign of welcome and friendship. "Change of plans, how are you feeling?" asked Sabine sitting down on a rocky outcrop. "Never better, my dear," he lied watching her carefully. Wearing a yellow blouse and with red hair and green eyes she was one sexy lady but his instinct for self-preservation told him to go carefully. "I'm pleased to hear that you have acclimatised well," she said.

"This is my homeland; I'm living the natural way before it's ripped up for minerals."

"Progress, Shaka, and you are the new Genghis; with the mining deal you will have the power needed to build a true empire."

"I haven't won the election yet and what about the Vietnam problem?"

"What problem?"

"I heard it was blown up."

"Who told you?"

"I have my contacts."

"Concentrate on the election, Shaka; you have the looks, the energy, the birthright and the passion." She didn't want to go into the details of the disaster in Vietnam.

"Perhaps you should be on my PR team," smiled Shaka, sensing the latent energy in the girl. He found himself beginning to think of her sexually but stopped himself before getting too interested; he didn't mix business with pleasure. "We should go back to Ulaanbaatar now as the fight is far from over and the opposition is mobilizing," he told her.

"Never take an election for granted unless it's been rigged," replied Sabine. "I see the opposition is claiming you are more interested in the trappings of power than helping people. How are you handling that?"

"In my speech tonight I'll prove the People's Party will look after everyone's best interests."

"They all say that. Hakim is a strong opponent so concentrate on selling yourself."

"And you'll do the dirty stuff?"

"We need those concessions, Shaka. Losing is not an option so call it an insurance policy. We have won similar elections before against the odds in Spain and Aruba."

"Only I understand my people. They will not take kindly to perceived external interference; I can win this the proper way"

"As I said, you concentrate on what you do and leave me to what I do. You only have two days left for campaigning.

The two days passed in whirl of activity for Shaka; he visited as many towns and villages as possible and met and shook so many hands that his own hands began to ache. Election Day proved to be long and hard and he was totally exhausted as the polls closed. During the last few days he had felt a growing sense of optimism but, despite the opinion polls giving him a narrow lead, he was nervous as he sat in his room awaiting the result. He glanced fearfully at the television. The presenter was saying that the outcome depended on the people of the Karakorum province; ironically, this had been the home of Genghis Khan. To calm his nerves he was trying to read a book when the door flew open and Sabine swept into the room.

"Congratulations Mr. President," she said with a smile.

"Too early, another two hours they say, but thanks for the thought," he said.

"I have it on good authority that you will win Karakorum."

"Really? They're still counting."

"Shaka, trust me when I say I have it on good authority; deals have been done."

"Damn it Sabine, I wanted it fair and equitable, not underhand stuff; the international election observers must be satisfied."

"It's all above board; just certain precautions have been taken," smiled Sabine turning to the screen as an excited announcer took centre stage. "We can now confidently predict that the winner in Karakorum is the People's Party," he said. "That means they have won the National Election too." Shaka leapt to his feet in delight and did a quick dance around the room.

"Now, Mr President, remember your part of the deal."

"That can wait, Sabine; I have to meet the people, so much to do."

"I'm afraid it cannot wait," a man's voice said from the doorway. They all looked towards him with surprise. None of them had expected him to be there in person.

"Teacher! You weren't expected so soon." Shaka stood and offered his hand; The Teacher didn't accept it. He just looked at them and finally said, "Well done Shaka, a great result."

"Thank you, I must make my speech of acceptance."

"Of course you must. But you must wait for Hakim to concede victory to you. As soon as he does you will automatically have Presidential Authority and power will formally transfer to your office. That will enable you to sign these contracts to mine mineral rights as a reward to ZTW. In your victory speech you will announce the building of a magnificent centre of homage to Genghis Khan in the north of the country, paid for by us; it will go down well and be seen to be honouring the most famous man this country has ever produced."

"After which you are going to dig it all up."

"All part of the plan as you well know," agreed Zheng silkily. "Along with your generous concession of the historic Khan's lands; time is of the essence. Incidentally I also think it would be a smart move to announce that you consider it time Xanadu was returned to Mongolia. That will serve to keep the Chinese on their toes and will be a populist measure."

Shaka nodded slowly. "The Khan's lands are yours for three years," he said, his plan crystalizing in his mind.

Three days later Zheng led a small party of Land Rovers and trucks to a deserted area north of Karakorum, cordoned off by Shaka's men who stood guard with guns. Though the legal rights had been signed over to him, Zheng knew that realistically it wouldn't be long before there was a national outcry about foreigners gaining access to heritage lands, particularly as they had been extended for nearly one hundred miles around this point. He expected Shaka to change his benevolent attitude once the euphoria of victory and the heady brew of power took hold, no matter how well the mind programming had worked, so he needed to act fast to get to the Khan's Prophecy. The third Artefact, the Axe, had given a precise location here in Mongolia near to the place Genghis had called home. Zheng had studied the Khan's words carefully realising that Kublai was the real visionary who tapped into the potential of the Chinese and who had understood the complexities of politics. Genghis had been a leader of men, Kublai the real empire maker. "The Artefacts we decoded confirm this is the area where the cavern lies and where we are the owners," he told Sabine with satisfaction.

They were now near the ultimate secret, so close it was tangible; it was still a gamble without the fourth and final Artefact but timing was against him. His team of experts had de-coded the three Artefacts relating the fascinating story of how Kublai had conceived the 'grand puzzle' ensuring that it would not resurrect itself for a thousand Mongol years. They told how Kublai alone had seen the Prophecy for himself and determined that it would be given to whoever could earn it. For that alone, Zheng deserved to be the real beneficiary of Kublai's grand puzzle; no one else had the vision or the right; he was Kublai's true successor. Like Kublai, he'd built his own empire, a modern corporation built on the work of his grandfather and, later, his father's work, just like Kublai. He cast his mind back to Shaka; he had decided he must be disposed of. There would be no repeat of the mistakes made in Spain or the volatile Latin American politics that had lost them their position in Aruba. His reverie was disturbed by Sabine. "We don't have the exact co-ordinates and we're struggling to get a correct fix," she told him. "The men don't know what they are looking for."

"They'll know when they find it," replied Zheng, listening to a voice message that was causing his brow to furrow. "There is less time than I thought. We will use the explosives."

"That could destroy everything and how can you be so certain it's here?"

"Because the cavern is over there and time is running out."

"We can't find the Prophecy without the fourth Artefact. Zheng, it's there for a reason; a key clue is missing," she insisted. Zheng waved her away. "The Axe inscription is quite clear; there is a hidden cavern."

"But it could be anywhere."

"There are clues," Zheng insisted. "My only concern is that Kublai may have designed pitfalls deliberately. We have an area of fifty kilometres over which there can only be five or six possible caverns and it's not difficult to explore all of them. The sonar imaging equipment will identify the metals we seek, so get on with it and stop finding excuses." He poured over the complex series of Chinese symbols and charts. The best scholars, the best scientists had explained how to understand the complexities of the clues. Sabine shrugged her shoulders; there was no point in arguing with him when he was in this sort of mood. She called the leader of the group to her and gave the order to use the explosives.

The explosion was deafening in the confined space of the fourth possible cavern. Sabine examined the newly disturbed ground not sure what she was looking for. She was tired of the continual blasting, trying to find some sign of previous human presence and rich metals. She shivered, hating the climate which as a sun worshipper was purgatory for her. Her favourite location was the hot tropics where she could shed her clothes and revel in the stares at her myriad of body piercings on her supine figure. Instead here she was covered in layers of heavy clothing feeling instinctively that they were in the wrong place. Indeed she genuinely believed they were in the wrong area altogether; the subject of an elaborate trick set out by the Khan centuries ago. She would be better employed finding the fourth Artefact in Africa. She determined this would be her last day here; she looked down at the newly disturbed earth. There she noticed a slight glint in the soil. "Over her," she called out.

"Where, what have you found?" asked Zheng hurrying over.

"Unusual metal, down amongst the stones in the blast area," she told him.

"Get it out quickly." It was here, Zheng could sense it, the Khan's lost tomb. No one since the thirteenth century had ever found the resting place of the great Genghis Khan. Everyone had always assumed that the Khan had been buried out in the wild grasslands, where he had fallen ill with disease, and after his death a thousand horses had trampled his remains into the earth. Zheng knew differently, and now as Kublai had written on the Artefacts, the last great secret of the Mongols, the tomb of Genghis Khan, was here and not at the fabled northern retreat of Xanadu in Inner Mongolia.

Xanadu had been reclaimed by Mother Nature long ago, only nondescript grassy knolls, miles from anywhere, gave any clue it had ever existed. This was different. His mind went over how Kublai had taken the decision to entrust the great Khan's secret to the Chinese Emperor, Zhu Dis, sending him the Artefacts with the vital clues for Admiral Zheng He to scatter around the world. It still niggled him that there was a wild card, the man from the Pope as Kublai had called Marco Polo. An itinerant traveller who had somehow gained the full trust of Kublai and had first revealed the existence of the secret Artefacts in the Elders' files. Marco Polo's name sent shivers down his spine. "We have it," he smiled as he saw an inscribed stone appear out of the soil. Finding it hard to contain his excitement, he watched as the men lifted it out and an interpreter started to read the inscription. "What is it?" asked Zheng.

"It says *trust in the ambassador*," replied the scholar nervously.

"Marco Polo!" his fears were justified. Zheng pushed his way through the group surrounding the shallow hole and looked down. Apart from an old parchment all he could see was what looked suspiciously like animal bones. Then he saw the original piece of metal Sabine had spotted; it was a large gleaming metal box. "Get it out," he yelled and pointed to it kneeling down to get a better view as the men broke open the box and stared inside. They saw metal coins, more bones and a scroll. "What does it say?" Zheng asked. "*Only the most diligent.*" The scholar translated. "I don't believe it," snapped Zheng looking down in horror. Kublai the damned trickster had insured that only the most diligent would succeed. He's entrusted the final Artefact to that damned charlatan, Marco Polo."

He'd always believed that Genghis wasn't interested in material things. His was the joy of leading men into battle; he wasn't interested in building cities.

He turned away from the dig bitterly disappointed with the day's discovery. As he did so he saw standing in front of him a stranger in a long black cloak. "You speak of my ancestor. He most certainly was not a charlatan but rather the man who will have the final say. You have failed." The stranger said harshly. "He entrusted everything to Marco because he couldn't trust those who worked for him; does that sound familiar, Zheng? Kublai had to kill his own brother to take power; he knew those who would follow him, his own offspring could not be trusted."

"It's here, I'm convinced of it," said Zheng defensively turning back towards the dig.

"No, you have failed," said the foreign sounding voice.

"Our agreement," protested Zheng," we had an agreement."

"The agreement is broken because you have failed Zheng; the time has come."

"I have the first three Artefacts," Zheng blustered desperately.

"No, you do not have them; they are in my custody now Zheng. You have outlived your usefulness to me."

"No," screamed Zheng looking at the figure in disbelief.

Chapter 24

Northern Mongolia
Khan Khentii

For the first time in his life Zheng was frightened. "What's the meaning of this?" he whispered and stared at his partner as if hypnotized. Almost unable to believe he could be staring down the barrel of the snub nosed automatic pistol pointing at him. "The Khan's prophecy is not here. I would have thought that obvious; instead you press on blindly. Your compound in Vietnam was a security threat; do I need to go on?"

"You agreed to keep in the background," snapped Zheng, incandescent rage replacing his fear.

"You have failed me, and I have broken my golden rule; for years keeping out of the spotlight, now through your sheer incompetence I must take charge. What's more I disapprove of the Islamic nature of your work. Religion is your weakness; it dulls the mind. Just like Tamerlane, he was a descendant of Genghis but a Muslim; he lost his direction because of faith unlike Genghis who stuck to pragmatism."

"I wasn't aware that Kublai could be so duplicitous," replied Zheng angrily. "I will get you the Prophecy but put down the gun first. The choice is simple, a long hunt to find the fourth Artefact or find the answer here."

"Without the Confucius Staff?"

"My experts tell me the long lost grave of Genghis is narrowed down to two sites; you have to give me time. Officially he was buried in the Kentei Mountains. That's only a rumour, as was the report he was left on the grasslands to die and so was the grave where he was supposed to be buried with forty of the most beautiful Mongol girls. My point is that there is more to this than you see."

"Very well, against my better judgment you have one day, Zheng," replied the man coldly his menacing voice accentuated by his long flowing garment in the half light of the evening. "Don't threaten me," warned Zheng,

He was whispering so others couldn't hear. "We are close to Operation Contagion and must stay focused."

"And you think I don't know that; it's precisely the reason I am here, and by the way don't even think of calling on those around you for help. They are all loyal only to me."

"You know I am loyal, Professor, after all these years our conglomerate would not have succeeded without trust and loyalty."

"You would do well to remember Zheng, it is my family's legacy and my company, ZTW, that funds all of this, your empire, your compounds, your foibles. Look what happened with the Elders! I had to join the group to save your mismanagement from damaging our cause."

"I didn't fail," snapped Zheng angrily. "I have dedicated my life to this cause and done everything necessary to find the Artefacts and I've taken all the personal risks."

"Real success and power lies in the backroom, out of sight of the baying masses and media. The Calvi's achieved this in Venice and even the British did it in Egypt in the nineteenth century by running the country as a protectorate. Visible leaders are vulnerable to the masses which is eventually their downfall, if they don't get corrupted by their own power first. Sometimes they lose their self-control and become dictators believing that everything they do is correct. The Hitler effect where no one tells them they are making mistakes, so they keep on making bigger ones, becoming detached from reality. Is that you Zheng? I hope not, you have one day."

Zheng returned to the requisitioned house he was using as his headquarters and thought hard over the next few hours before summoning Sabine to join him. The sun was setting as they went over the details of what to do next. "There is still time," he announced. "Time for what?" asked Sabine. She was confused and feeling the tension rising. "Who was that man you wouldn't let me speak to?"

"It doesn't matter."

"Yes Zheng, it matters to me. I have served you since I arrived from Texas, and that was a long time ago now. I have carried out your orders without question, but I don't understand what you are doing now." She had used her boss's first name for the first time and he didn't seem to object.

"He calls himself the Professor."

"An apt name, so he's your boss?"

"Yes, but I see him very rarely. No one else sees him at all. Now you don't need to know any more, I have never let you down before, and we have time to find this Prophecy." Sabine was satisfied…for the time being. "Very well Zheng," she said. The stranger intrigued her. She had watched him dominate the conversation by the very force of his personality. He exuded power and authority and the genesis of a plan started to form in her mind. She found it seductive. His every whispered word dripping with menace, his deep penetrating eyes the only visible part of him beneath the robe. Normally she could manage men either by engaging in intellectual debate or letting her body do the work. She knew neither would work here as she had seen The Teacher shrink before her eyes. As if reading her thoughts, he turned around angrily. "We have to go north now, there is still time."

"But we don't know where the Prophecy lies."

"Trust me, Sabine, My experts tell me that they have decoded something in the Artefacts that indicates there is only one place where the Prophesy could be. It's about fifty kilometres north of here. They say Kublai's remains were taken along with all his earthly possessions to the same area as Genghis, not that far from Burkham Khaldum, the sacred mountain. Sabine looked doubtful. "Zheng, this Professor won't take prisoners." She warned.

"Have you heard of the metal rhodium?" Zheng asked her. "No."

"Well it's the rare metal the Artefacts are made of; it can only be found in a few places in the world; it's part of the platinum family but more precious. My men know where the sole mine in this hemisphere lies; it's just two hours from here, the tombs of the Khans lie in the same place.

"Legend has it they were buried in the grasslands here."

"Caverns, Sabine, the Coleridge poem if you recall, talks about Xanadu and mentions *through caverns measureless to man*', large grave sites cut into the hillside by armies of men and all their most valuable possessions including their favourite wives entombed with them."

"And the prophecy lies there?"

"When have I ever let you down? Now get packed. We need to leave immediately."

"But we need to be certain."

"We are meeting someone there who can help; don't forget we are in a very dangerous area of the world. We are literally on the edge of the world's two strongest nations, Russia and China. Do you think that when they realize what lies here they will let it stay that way? Time is of the essence."

"The fourth Artefact wasn't with Zheng He was it?"

"No, Kublai gave it to Marco Polo. God alone knows where it is so we need to take a short cut."

"It's in Africa, Zheng; it just needs hunting down, and I would advise…."

"Sabine, my word is final; I have a plan and that is the end of the matter."

"A plan to do what, exactly?"

"You have never questioned me before! Your attitude has changed recently, and it's beginning to concern me. Now, get in the vehicle and read this," snapped Zheng thrusting a sheet in front of her, "it's the Coleridge poem."

> *'In Xanadu did Kublai Khan*
> *A stately pleasure home decree*
> *Where Alph the sacred river ran*
> *Through caverns measureless to man*
> *Down to a sunless sea.'*

Sabine read it through several times then looked at Zheng and said. "I don't get it." She was beginning to wonder if the pressure was getting to him. His decisions seemed to be getting wilder, causing her to have grave reservations about this project. "The man wrote it when he was high on drugs but he researched ancient texts. Don't you see the clue lies in the poem not Xanadu but the cavern? Not Kublai's Xanadu but further north of here a place where the country's largest river runs through an enormous cavern before heading to the sunless Caspian or Dead Sea. The *'measureless to man'* is the value of the metal rhodium."

"Are you sure?" She was still unconvinced.

"Of course I am, with this measureless amount of metal we will find the Prophecy; one is the clue to the other. They couldn't carry rhodium far because of its weight and the geologists have confirmed that rhodium is more plentiful here than anywhere else in the Mongol Kingdom. As that kingdom stretched all the way to Turkey and Poland in the west and Tibet in the south, that is reason enough to cut away from the final Artefact. We need to drive about three hours north across the Steppes; there is no other way."

"And the alternative?"

"There isn't one," replied Zheng grimly, "there are no other options left."

"None at all?" she queried.

"No, we only have tonight to find this precious metal."

Zheng leaned back and closed his eyes, settling into a semi trance as they travelled north in the Land Rover. The weather was cold and the deep winter was about to arrive though that wouldn't stop the mining activities from transforming Mongolia's sweeping grasslands and jagged hills into a lunar landscape.

The light was gone and the cold biting as they finally pulled to a halt and the driver indicated a path across a field, their torches lighting the way. Zheng pointed to the distance "Over there are the caverns," he said and lapsed into silence. Sabine was feeling distinctly uncomfortable. She hated cold weather and couldn't remember ever feeling so chilled. To make things worse she had no idea which part in this remote area of Mongolia they were in, with nothing but grass and sky for company.

"This will be the equivalent of the American wild west," said Zheng suddenly. His voice startled her. "Except it's all minerals not just gold like in their great gold rush. Ironic that a country that dominated the world before will now do so again but as an economic powerhouse because of the very ground the Mongols ignored." He stopped as he saw the first of the caverns in the distance. "What do you mean ignored?" asked Sabine shivering again.

"Their life was nomadic; they never settled in one place and despised those who did."

"But that changed?"

"Kublai changed them or it would not have been a sustainable empire; they needed to raise taxes not conquer then move on." He pointed to a dim light ahead. "Ah, here we are. Do you see the light by the cavern."

"A light?"

"Yes, it's our protection."

"Protection from whom?"

"Who do you think," snapped Zheng signalling ahead and then breathing a sigh of relief as his light was answered. "Ah, there you are my friend," he shouted as a large bearded man came slowly into view.

"Who is with you?" boomed a heavily accented voice.

"My closest adviser," replied Zheng, and turning to Sabine continued.

"Sabine meet Sergei Rostov, our Russian member of the Elders, someone who has always been loyal."

The Russian seemed unimpressed with the flattery and said gruffly. "Zheng, why this unusual request to meet? It's not easy to get over the Mongolian border, all hell would break loose if a man in my position was found here illegally; especially now, with the strained relations between the two countries."

"It won't, no one knows we're here, so thanks for coming." Then he said to Sabine by way of explanation. "Sergei heads Roscroft Mining in Vladivostok; one of the world's most successful companies. Unlike some of his compatriots he returns his profits to the Russian people." Again the Russian seemed not to notice the glowing commendation from Zheng.

"Why am I here, Zheng; we're not that close you know that?"

"The chance of a lifetime Sergei," Zheng replied

"You've been promising me that for years; then you went cold on me."

"A misunderstanding my friend," replied Zheng switching to the Russian tongue much to Sabine's annoyance, "today I will present you with the biggest opportunity of your life."

"And what would that be?"

"Exclusive rights to the largest metals mine in the world with a third of all the proceeds as an investing partner."

"I'm sure that doesn't come for free Zheng; what's the price? Knowing you it will not be insignificant."

"Protect my interests here as a joint partner to stop others from muscling in. After all this is the nearest metal mine to Russia without actually being in the territory and a potential competitive threat."

"I heard you had internal plans with the new President."

"This is a contingency plan and we need to spread the opportunity by building a good relationship with the Russians."

"I don't get it Zheng; in return for muscle you give me a

fortune.”

“There is one other small thing.”

“Ah now we have it. What does the new Khan want?”

“He came to power as a nationalist and will make a big deal out of rebuilding this area.”

“Yes I’d heard about the idea to resurrect memorials to Genghis.”

“I knew you would see things that way.”

“So what exactly is it you want?”

“The new President wants Russian help to protect him from possible Chinese interference in his country. He needs to know that he can tackle the Chinese without worrying about his back door so to speak.”

“In other words he wants to avoid a battle on two fronts.”

“Exactly, I thought you would see it.”

“And just how would I do that?”

“Come, Sergei, I know you have huge influence with the Russian government; they will go with your recommendation and exert the appropriate pressure on the Chinese.”

“How?”

“Tell them China is planning to retake Upper Mongolia. That’s partly true as there is a long-standing desire by the Beijing rulers to take what they consider is rightfully theirs; the reward for you is millions of dollars.”

“Indeed a huge prize,” replied Sergei. “What are you going to do with the Elders?”

“You can be the President. I still have enough significant influence to make that happen,” replied Zheng.

“What of your disciple Jochi?”

He was a traitor and paid the ultimate penalty,” snapped Zheng. “Now do we have a deal Sergei?”

“Leave me for an hour, I have some calls to make to see whether this can be done; it is a great deal you ask. My colleagues in Moscow will want to know what could be worth so much that they should exert such pressure on the Chinese.”

“Very well, my assistant and I are going over to the caverns; join us when you are ready.”

Sabine had stood quietly listening during the exchanges between Zheng and Sergie. She didn’t speak Russian and was highly suspicious of Zheng’s choice to use that language. What was he up to that she shouldn't know about? "What were you discussing Zheng? It was all in Russian," she asked as Sergei walked off into the gloom. "You'll see," replied Zheng enigmatically. They had reached the cavern by now and Zheng looked for his attendants. "This is the exact cavern according to my scientists," he paused and then said irritably. "Where the hell are they? I told them to join us here." They walked across to what looked like a burial ground. "This is definitely the place the co-ordinates say," said Zheng walking to the entrance.

"We can't trust Shaka," said Sabine, "he's too ambitious, and has access to files he hasn't turned over. That makes him dangerous too."

"He knows who is in charge," smiled Zheng coldly. "Look at these stones, the inscription on the Axe talks about a cavern hemmed by such multi-coloured stones."

"It's too easy Zheng, something is not right, I'm convinced we need to be north of the Selenge Gol river."

"No, you're wrong," Zheng pointed to the uneven turf. "That equates exactly to the front row of one of the Khan's tumens." He gave her a superior look and explained. "A tumen was an army unit of 10,000 soldiers. His fighting force would comprise a hundred men who would attack in a line and their length was as here. Also it's a northerly direction as the Khan worshipped the northern star."

"But there are many here like this."

"Look at the slight discoloration and also the mound we are standing on. It's a burial mound."

"Perhaps," said Sabine. She was unconvinced and looked around her, the torch picking out eerie shapes. Oddly she was now perspiring in the cold as she bent down and held up a dull metallic object next to a line of bones; something was wrong. Suddenly her finely-tuned instincts made her fling herself down into a nearby indentation without knowing why, then she heard an ominous metallic click to her right. She screamed inadvertently as the peace was shattered by the death rattle of a sub machine gun and she pushed herself further into the turf hearing a grunt as The Teacher was hit. Powerful lights scanned the area as she pushed her body harder against the earth and rolled to the side of the cave.

"One thing you forgot Zheng," hollered Sergei's voice, "an

eye for an eye."

"You were my ally," screamed Zheng trying to push himself up as more bullets hit him and made him reel in agony. "He was a traitor."

"He was a loyal Russian," yelled Sergei. "Introduced into your organisation years ago to ensure we knew what was going on. It's over, Zheng, your days of manipulation are at an end; you have outlived your usefulness."

"I will double the amount if you get me out of here," gasped Zheng writhing in agony.

"I don't control these men. I think your President is exercising his power; sorry to say it but I must go."

"No," pleaded Zheng as Sabine heard the machine gun erupt again, "he's dead for God's sake," she screamed.

"You have done your work."

"Come out with your hands over your head," a rough voice ordered. Sabine thought she recognized as one of Shaka's guards.

"What guarantees do I have? I'm on your side, ask Shaka. The Professor and I are working closely together?"

"You can make this easy for us and come out now," shouted the man, "If we have to come for you it will be slow and painful."

"Shit," Sabine grunted wondering what the hell to do as she started to move around the area, her hand clasping a sharp stone, it wasn't much but it would have to do. Either they weren't working for the Professor or didn't believe her. She had to make the first move or she would be joining Zheng.

She waited silently as she heard one of the men move closer in the dark his torch forming odd patterns in the sky, one on his own, there was just a chance. "I'm here," she whispered quickly to the man who was close undoing her coat and working on her buttons and shivering as she did so. It was her standard trick and she hoped to God the man wasn't gay. She breathed a sigh of relief as she recognized the familiar looming shape of Shaka's bodyguard who had been ogling her before at the palace. "I'm so glad it's you," she breathed huskily, "come here and tell your mate that you will be a few minutes. See if you can find all my body piercings and believe me they are all in interesting positions."

"Pretty woman," whispered the burly guard his eyes widening as he saw Sabine in the torch light smiling and beckoning. "I'll be a few minutes, "he snapped into the phone. "That feels good," whispered Sabine as the man thrust his hand inside her bra grabbing her nipple rings. With a superhuman effort she avoided screaming at the pain as he tugged clumsily and then reached for her trouser buckle. She made sure he was totally distracted and then she struck. With all her strength she rammed the sharp metal hard into his neck. The man screamed in agony as the stone split his skin and bit deeply into his neck. Blood sprayed out and she pushed herself away scrambling to the side and hastily fastening her clothes, still shivering violently. The man was in convulsions and would die a painful and deserved death as his lifeblood drained. Sabine grabbed his automatic gun as she heard the other man approaching; they would have been told to finish her off; Shaka would pay for this. There was shouting in the distance and gunfire erupted. Sabine dropped quickly as dirt sprayed around her, one dead, one to go.

She used the man's writhing body as cover and stared around; the odds were even now though the other man knew where she was. Hardly daring to breathe she tried to sense any movement and held her breath, listening for the slightest noise. It came with a sudden rush of air, just as she had been ready to move; she swung instinctively towards the danger managing to duck to the side as a volley of bullets slammed into the dead body. Footsteps sounded to her side as the man loomed, silhouetted in the dark his gun pointing directly at her. Instinctively she rolled to her left and fired, the bullets lighting up the darkness. She heard a grunt and then a thump. She rolled across ground grabbed a torch and flashed it around her, both attackers lay in crumpled heaps. Making sure there were no more guards looking for her; she scrambled up and ran across to their vehicle. Running warmed her and her blood was pounding by the time she reached the large vehicle. No one was inside it, even better the keys were in the ignition and it started at the first attempt. She slammed it into gear, reversed onto the track and roared away to the trunk road. She turned south and relaxed as she felt the engine's warmth spread through her frozen limbs. Reaching into the glove box she smiled as she saw a bottle of vodka and took a large swig.

Shaka finally answered his mobile, what he heard didn't please him. "You left me for dead," Sabine hissed at him. "The Teacher was killed and I only just survived, you bastard."

"You chose your side Sabine," replied Shaka. He was surprised and somewhat shaken she was still alive; he had thought the plan foolproof, Sergio had assured him all had gone smoothly. The damned woman had done it again.

"I didn't choose anything Shaka; you're in big trouble with the Professor."

"I had nothing to do with the attack and you're bluffing; he doesn't even know who you are Sabine," he lied.

"Call him yourself and find out," snapped Sabine. "And whilst you're at it remind him that only I know where the fourth Artefact is, which is key to the Prophecy. The Teacher was wrong; the cavern he seeks isn't here."

"I don't know what you are talking about," mumbled Shaka.

"Just remember this," Sabine said coldly. "The Prophecy is here and only I know exactly where. I don't suppose that bothers you, but this should. I have never failed to kill anyone who crosses me and your friend Jochi was the last example of that. Difference is that for him and old times' sake I made it quick; for you it will be slow and painful. If you don't help me now then you will die that way."

"Don't you threaten me, Sabine, you forget where you are. I can have an army after you in minutes."

"If you do, they will go the same way as the last two idiots you sent, but you forget Shaka it was me who put you where you are. A couple of phone calls revealing the huge amounts of money used to pay off specific officials and you will be finished. I have it all documented and if anything should happen to me, my solicitor has clear instructions what to with them. I am a pragmatist, The Teacher's time has come but the Professor will hunt you down if you lose this chance to get the Prophecy." Her warning seemed to have some effect; after a couple of seconds he said. "Very well, what do you want from me?"

"Call the Professor and arrange for me to meet him alone. I will give you the location details when I get closer."

"I thought you were in contact?"

"Look, I am not stupid; I need your protection, so do it Shaka." He made the call and the arrangement for her to meet the Professor.

She chose a remote café in the middle of a busy market and arrived early to ensure Shaka hadn't sent servants to kill her before the meeting, and sat coolly in the darkest corner drinking Turkish coffee. The Professor materialised out of the gloom and greeted her with a faint smile. She invited him to sit down and pushed the coffee pot across the table towards him. "It takes guts to do what you did," murmured his cold voice as he filled the small cup with steaming hot coffee. "Now, tell me why I shouldn't just shoot you here and now."

"Because I'm a survivor, Professor," replied Sabine coldly. "I called you before you came to Mongolia, gave you my concerns and yet you hung me out to dry."

"You were too close to him."

"That's as maybe but I reckon you owe me."

"Really, why?"

"Without my information you wouldn't have known where The Teacher was going to be, but more importantly I can give you the one item you seek."

"Which is?"

"The fourth Artefact and I can also activate the Contagion Project; without me you are relying on untried camp volunteers who don't know you."

"And how do I trust you?"

"You saw that I was loyal to The Teacher; he's gone, you have taken his place. Now you are the boss and I respect power and authority."

"Very well, I can see you and I will get along just fine; we think the same way and have the same needs," replied the Professor with a smile.

"Good, a deal then," Sabine lifted her hand from the small gun she had been cradling in her pocket.

"I have a place for loyal soldiers; you have my authority in Asia and there is much to do, so put away the gun, Sabine. I could have had you riddled with bullets as you came in."

"I thought I was here first," she said. The Professor shrugged his shoulders. "Just proper planning, which was beyond Zheng. I will not tolerate maverick behaviour. Now that I have assumed direct control there is a need to reshape our forces, away from the outdated alliances that Zheng made. There is one person in particular who I need to play a key role in the final stages of my plan."

"Who is that?"

"You will be told in due course; it's your first task to prove your loyalty."

"There is one favour I would ask of you before we begin," Sabine said.

"Which is?"

"Control over Shaka." He nodded his head, "I expected you to say that, he said with a smile, "and I'll grant you that, but more importantly you have a job to do in Africa. If you think that you can manage Shaka as well, then do it."

"I am sure I can live up to your expectations with him and deliver the Prophecy."

"Excellent, then we have a deal."

"One more thing."

"Don't try my patience," a note of irritation crept into his voice.

"If we are to be real partners, I want to know who you really are."

"You'll know that once I see a clear demonstration of loyalty," smiled the Professor. "All you need to know for now is that the plans you were working to with Zheng are my plans. I was always in control but behind the scenes; we've simply removed the middle man. The only difference is how I will achieve my objectives. I always intended to take control of events at some point, but the failures in Mongolia have made it necessary to bring the plans forward."

"Zheng found you three Artefacts and the rhodium."

"The Khan's Prophecy is not here; Zheng should have known that and not tried to make deals behind my back. He sought to betray me at the end, and that's unacceptable. He never intended to find the fourth Artefact. The real tomb of Genghis is not at the cavern you saw; it is much further north of here beyond even Burkham Khaldum."

"Zheng assured me this was the only source of rhodium and was the key to the Artefacts."

"The rhodium here is in its pure form, a white silvery substance, whereas the rhodium Artefacts are a colour between silver and gold that is only found to the north. Zheng chose not to understand that and panicked by going for the closer mine."

"You blew up the compound in Vietnam?"

"Yes, it was necessary I'm afraid. The Caodaists are not

without influence and the authorities were receiving complaints. In addition there was a murder there, someone was hanged and they reported it. The police were about to move in and close the place down and find all the evidence of what we were doing. I couldn't allow that to happen."

"But many died," said Sabine choosing not to reveal it was she who had been responsible for the hanging.

"Causalities of war and not needed for the next phase."

"Jack Hogg? Where does he fit in?"

"Ah yes, Mr. Hogg. His dear daughter has caused chaos in Latin America. We will take care of it but you will find, my dear, that I don't forgive failure; Zheng and Hogg failed. The Prophecy will never be found without the fourth Artefact. Kublai planned it that way."

"The fourth Artefact. You seem to know a great deal about it."

"It's what started all this," smiled the Professor.

"Can I see your face?" Sabine's curiosity overcame her detached attitude. She simply had to know who she was dealing with.

"Very well," said the man dropping his hood. "The fourth Artefact. You know where part of it is?"

"I know where all of it is. Just leave all that to me but I'm puzzled when you say that's where it all started."

"Another story, my dear; now I suggest I leave first. You will go to Ulaanbaatar and see Shaka. Incidentally ZTW ownership is now mine so the company will own the mineral rights here. You need to make sure that Shaka sticks to his pledge or the consequences will be grim."

"Indeed I will," she smiled and thought it was indeed an ill wind that didn't blow some good; one had just delivered.

"We head south west in three days' time; make sure you are ready."

"Absolutely," smiled Sabine watching the Professor stand up to leave. Events had definitely taken a turn for the better. No one would stand in her way now. Change had been inevitable and Zheng had become dated; now all she had to do was find the fourth Artefact.

The following day she confronted Shaka again. Her meeting with the Professor had restored her confidence and it was clear that the news of her reconciliation had already reached him. "The Teacher did everything for you, Shaka, and this is how you repay him," she chided him. He was unmoved. "You can prove nothing and here my rule is law," he snapped looking up from his desk.

"No doubt you could have your guards turn on me now but you know I enjoy the Professor's patronage. He wants me to tell you that in future you will be reporting to me." His face contorted with fury. "Get out of here," he snarled. But Sabine would leave when she decided. "The exclusive rights will remain, instructions for your next task will be sent in good time. Oh yes, I think you'd be a lousy lover; I'd eat you for breakfast."

"How dare you talk to me, the President, like that!" Shaka blushed with embarrassment.

"You do exactly as I order and you will live, if not you will die slowly and beg me to kill you. As I said earlier Jochi had a fast death, you won't. So I suggest you listen well. There's plenty of time to achieve everything we set out to do, only now the players have changed." She smiled as she left the President and made her way to the door. "I'm going for a hot bath," she said and flounced out of the room. An assassin she might be but she was still a woman and revenge was sweet.

Shaka kicked his desk in anger; the bloody woman had outsmarted him again. He stalked angrily around the room. He would have the last laugh on her; there were one or two tricks up his sleeve yet. Sergei had been heaven sent when Jochi had introduced the two of them as he lay incapacitated in hospital. That The Teacher would head for Sergei was to be expected and they had been ready. Well that battle was over; the problem now was the Professor. He was a totally different kettle of fish, a much tougher customer; he looked down at the note Sabine had left him and cursed. He would have to take more care with that bloody woman.

Chapter 25

Jade looked carefully at the gathering, Zheng, the Russian, Sergei Rostov and the Italian Fabrizio were missing but she had expected that and they still had a quorum. "This extraordinary meeting has been called because we have important new developments to discuss," she told the assembled group. "Recent events require all our awareness and action. I note that our former President has not graced us with his presence, therefore under our Articles I formally declare that his term of office is over and will ask Doctor Oboto to take the lead to discuss our next steps."

"Thank you," replied Oboto standing up. "As you all know Zheng Wan left us in a predicament. The Artefacts have not been returned so we find ourselves severely compromised. Worse, I have heard that the man called Jochi known to some of you is seriously ill, maybe even dead by now, as a direct result of his actions. I also have to tell you that our Italian colleague, Fabrizio, which incidentally is not his real name, is aligned directly with Zheng and we believe goes under the title of the Professor."

"What of Sergei Rostov?" asked Dufresne, the French delegate.

"Sergei has not been in contact but unlike the others we have no reason to suspect he is involved in any plotting; in fact he is actively helping us and therefore putting himself at considerable personal risk. All in all a grim story but we must be decisive, I am sure you will agree."

"Are you sure of all your facts?" asked Stanton, the American, quizzically, "Seems we are proposing strong prescriptive actions."

"As sure as we can be," replied Oboto. "Fabrizio has been linked to Zheng's plans by documents in our possession, so to protect our integrity we have to act. I need your support; we are, to put it plainly, at war." He looked around as the Chair returned a unanimous vote. "Thank you, now to the good news; there is still time to avert disaster. We have knowledge of the fourth Artefact, called the Confucius Staff, which is the key to finding the Khan's Prophecy, our heritage."

"You know where it is?" asked Stanton, his voice booming across the ancient auditorium.

"We think so," Oboto told him. "What I am about to say to you is not to be minuted as it could compromise actions on the ground, but it is appropriate to share this information with you. For some time now our people in the field have been without direct support; we have corrected this by sending an agent into the field to help. Indeed, I have been involved myself and can tell you we are making progress towards the fourth Artefact currently located in Africa."

"These people, who are they?" asked Dufresne.

"Guy Tresanton and his partner, Rose Ling. They are being supported by my African fighter, Tapiwa. Make no mistake our very existence is under threat and this direct action is necessary."

"It is in direct contravention of our charter," said the Canadian woman Brandy, "it sets a dangerous precedent."

"A precedent we have to make," Oboto insisted.

"What exactly have you discovered since the last meeting?" asked Stanton.

"A great deal of data rests here at the monastery, beneath your feet in the cellars. That's where we made our main discovery, and there's more out in the Garonjay valley," said Jade. "It may help if I explain some of the history of all this. It goes back to the thirteenth century and the legendary traveller, Marco Polo."

"Marco Polo here?" asked Stanton.

"Yes, he's part of Admiral Zheng He's legacy. According to the records that's the direct link between him and the fourth Artefact; he had a role in hiding another, though we can't prove that conclusively. We also found the record of a visit by a German Count von Steppenhof; he came here from Zanzibar and left clear evidence that the Artefact was in Kenya. We believe this was Marco's own work as he travelled home down the Old Silk Road from China via Africa. He left his secrets here in the valley and actually my grandfather, Jack Silver, and The Teacher's grandfather, Zhou Wang, were responsible for finding them. They were then brought into the cellars here."

"It sounds like a lot of suppositions to me," said Dufresne.

"Maybe, but it's detailed in the manuscripts we've just found in the cellars. They are written statements by past Chairmen. One of the manuscripts led us to believe The Teacher was controlled by someone called Giovanni.

"Can you prove any of this?" asked Stanton.

"Not conclusively," admitted Jade, "The facts we have appear convincing but so far our attempts to confirm them have got us nowhere. Someone powerful is suppressing information."

"I doubt The Teacher is managed by anyone anymore," said Stanton. "I reckon he's dead."

"Why do you say that?" Jade was shocked to hear the comment.

"Because he would have been here."

"That's conjecture," chided Jade. "Anyway even if that's true, there's no doubt the time has come for us to be active in finding more information as well as the fourth Artefact."

"What's so special about it, that particular Artefact?" asked Stanton

"It's the last link in the jigsaw. Without it I believe the Prophecy cannot be found and it's enshrined at the heart of our own mission."

"Not a mission I signed up for," snapped Stanton.

"I took the precaution of checking our original Articles of formation," replied Jade calmly. "I have a copy here that talks about the thousand year quest for the prophecy, sometimes called the Khan's Prophecy."

"A thousand years from when?"

"By our calendar the thousand years of the Mongol calendar, when Genghis Khan had a vision alone on the Steppes, has passed; it's the equivalent of eight hundred years of our calendar. It means the vision is imminent. The only document from that era, '*The Secret History*', records the Genghis legacy in Mongolia as being the centre of the universe. It is also likely, though not definite, that the Prophecy shares the same location with the burial ground of both Khans. Unfortunately they have never been found," concluded Jade.

"So as to this Artefact, do we know exactly where it is?" asked Stanton. Doctor Oboto intervened in the discussion. "As I reported, we have people on the ground in Africa, in particular my own trusted agent Tapiwa who has already been attacked by The Teacher's men. Those particular men will trouble us no more but it appears The Teacher does have a lead on us. We need your help now." He said.

"Very well, what can we do to support this action?" asked Stanton.

"In Africa we have a saying that to kill predators you must stop the hand that feeds them. Both the Professor and The Teacher rely for funding on ZTW Corporation; we have to stop them in their tracks."

"How?" asked Stanton.

"By creating a run on that company's share price. Get it reduced to junk status and put them out of business. It's listed on the New York stock exchange and registered in Bermuda. All it requires is a coordinated attack to bring it down," said Jade.

"The Duke of Wellington claimed he defeated Napoleon by working his way around the Peninsula, always ensuring he had strong supply lines; he even retreated after a victory because of the stretched supply situation," said Oboto.

"Exactly, their money supply is critical; cut that off and we have them," continued Jade.

"I have a confession to make," said Stanton. I foresaw the need to choke off the supply of funds to the Zheng Corporation some while back. I had words with a number of friends on the exchanges, and they started a few rumours. The effect of that action is already being felt as a glance at their share price will confirm. Perhaps I should have obtained permission from the council first and for that I apologise," said Stanton confidently.

"Perhaps you should," said Jade, "but you have saved us a lot of time so no one will be offended by your action I'm sure."

"In the meanwhile I have been working on ground activities," advised Oboto. "Ladies and gentlemen, you've heard of the Star Wars movies *'The Empire Strikes Back'*. Well this is the time for the Elders to strike back. Make no mistake we are in a fight for our very survival."

Oboto sat down and smiled at Jade; they had done what they could, and it now depended on Guy, Rose and Tapiwa wherever they were.

Tay Ninh Camp

Guy and Rose stood looking at the devastation, shell shocked. Their lives had been saved by Guy's quick thinking and the huge concrete block in front of them. All around them lay dead bodies including Jack Hogg's. It looked as though the whole place had been bombed or sabotaged by The Teacher, dramatically deciding in his own fashion to move on. Guy went across to the only building still standing and saw over twenty bodies sprawled around with some crying and others screaming in horror. Something metallic illuminated by a shaft of the sun's rays attracted his eye. His eyes slowly focused through the glare and, some way away from the compound, he eventually made out the form of a tell-tale pipe sticking out the back of a truck. "Damn it! A mortar," he muttered. He was more concerned by the loud groaning of people needing help. The youngsters attracted to the compound by promises of excitement and adventure lay dying. "Damned mortar attack from over there," he shouted at Rose as he saw the vehicle move. "Doesn't make sense for The Teacher to kill his own people," replied Rose dusting herself down and wincing at the pain from the earlier torture. "You saved my life, Guy."

"That's what partners are for, Viper, it's good to have you back."

"But why kill his own people?" Rose could see no sense in the action.

"Passed their use-by date, the ruthless bastard. Perhaps a decoy for something much bigger?" replied Guy thoughtfully. "This word 'Contagion' that keeps cropping up, perhaps it's all to do with that. Something he's about to launch elsewhere but maybe there were clues here so he blew the place up to keep us from finding out more."

"You assume the attack was aimed at us, but I'm not so sure."

"Why?"

"Who would have known we were here at this point, and why use a bomb for God's sake? They could have had us shot; no, there's more to this one. Perhaps he's no longer in control?" continued Rose.

"Who knows, but we have to help these poor people until help gets here. I've called the emergency services."

"Was that wise Rose? We'll be arrested by the police. We need to get out and find Lorna and Monty," said Guy, searching for his mobile and relieved to find it still worked. Rose shook her head. "That's as maybe, but I'm going to help these poor kids first," she told him, and began tending those worst hit. Guy called and explained what had happened while Rose moved from one victim to another helping where she could. "What do you think Monty?" Guy ended his description of the attack with the question. Monty's answer was direct and unequivocal. "I agree with Rose," he said. "This attack had nothing to do with you two."

"Perhaps you're right." Guy could think of no better explanation.

"Has Lorna arrived?" asked Monty.

"Lorna?" said Guy, "she's with you."

"No she isn't. She left as per your instructions," replied Monty.

"My instructions?" yelled Guy in alarm. "I didn't give any instructions."

"You booked her tickets to Hong Kong; first class; she said you wanted her in Hong Kong immediately."

"Oh my God!" yelled Guy in alarm and ran over to Rose.

"We have to get out of here fast; Lorna's in great danger," he told her.

"Running out of here makes us little better than them," she replied while applying a bandage to a young woman's arm. "We must go, we're sitting targets," urged Guy explaining what Monty had told him.

"Guy please listen to me. We have to think this through logically and, in the meantime, help these kids, look at it." He looked around again and saw her point. The devastation was horrendous with body parts strewn haphazardly across the hard ground, blood leaving deep red stains everywhere. They did what they could but it wasn't much.

"What on earth possessed The Teacher to do such a thing? Perhaps he is no longer in control," she wondered aloud as they tried to provide comfort to those they found alive. "The Teacher wouldn't do this to us," gasped one young woman trying to clean her face of blood. "Then who did?" asked Rose gently as the girl looked at her gratefully. "He was a tyrant but he cared for us, gave us hope," she said.

"What is your name?" Rose asked her.

"Anita."

"Anita, you don't need that sort of hope," Rose told her gently. "What's gone on here?"

"He never told us about his plans."

"It's really important you try to remember anything he may have said about where he was going."

"The last sleeper left the camp about two months ago," replied the girl starting to cry on seeing one of her dead friends lying nearby. Rose felt sorry for her but pressed her further. "What do you mean sleeper?" she asked.

"Brain washed, conditioned; it doesn't matter what you call it, it's all over now."

"You mean conditioned into believing they are someone else?"

"Yes, like the Caodaists believing key figures from the past are reincarnated. That's why The Teacher chose to establish his centre of operations here. We all believed the religious messages and followed when he asked us to help with his historic quest in the name of Islam."

"Historic quest to do what?"

"I don't know; it was a great secret but I do know it will have profound consequences."

"The Contagion Project Lorna mentioned," murmured Rose. "Who is the sleeper?"

"Shaka is one; he's the strongest."

"And where did this Shaka go?" asked Rose carefully.

"Mongolia, the home of the great Khan."

"Mongolia," breathed Rose. She called Guy to join them, told him the girl's name and to go easy when questioning her.

"I recognize your face; you remind me of the doctor that took care of us all in the complex," said Anita as Guy sat down next to her.

"What was his name?" asked Guy.

"Dr Tresanton. He was a nice man always keen to help us when things got difficult; he was the originator of the sleeper programme."

"Are you sure?" asked Guy barely able to conceal his angst.

"Yes, he and Dr Ling worked on it together."

"He was my father," acknowledged Rose. "Where are they now?"

"They moved out two days ago. I don't where; they went without even saying goodbye; so unlike them but they were upset over the death of their friend."

"What friend?"

"He never had a name; we called him the mute man. He came and went all the time; he was harmless and yet they hanged him," said Anita shuddering. "It was horrible."

"The Whistler," gasped Guy. "I thought something must have happened to him. He relayed messages about The Teacher from our fathers."

"Why did you come here, Anita?" asked Rose.

"My friend Janine persuaded me, but there was too much emphasis on military training for my liking. It intensified when The Teacher arrived a month ago with his big Contagion plan."

"Did he explain what this plan was?"

"To control the youth of Asia through some dramatic event; he said we all would be part of the new elite."

"It gets worse," said Rose trying to come to terms with the fact that both their fathers had been at this very camp. Her aunt Beatrice who had cared for her during her childhood and teenage years had told her both parents were dead. It was only last year she had discovered this was not the case and had briefly met her father in an emotional Shanghai reunion. "Who did The Teacher say would help him with this?"

"We all helped him but he had his favourites. In particular a despicable girl who did dreadful things. We all hated her as she so was violent," said Anita starting to cry again.

"Who was she?" asked Guy quietly.

"Her name was Sabine; she's a dangerous woman," said Anita quietly. "I didn't dare say anything. She was his favourite and her word was law. We, my friend Janine and I, were planning to run away next week and now she's dead; if only we had left earlier!" She dissolved into a flood of tears again. Rose waited patiently for her grief to subside a little and then asked her. "Please tell us more about the two doctors."

"Nothing much more to tell really; they were both very nice to us but under a lot of pressure to deliver the sleeper programme; they were always watched very closely. Am I in trouble?"

"No of course not, especially if you help us," replied Rose quickly. She would find a way to save the girl from any action by the Vietnamese Authorities. The local police had arrived and she could see them sifting through the ruins looking for survivors. "Anything else, Anita, please? It's very important."

"I can see the resemblance to both your fathers in you two," repeated Anita quietly.

"Was there anything different in the last few days, different behaviour?"

"Not that I noticed. The doctors left to go to the other complex though they did seem unusually agitated."

"What other complex? Do you know where that is?" they both asked the same question at the same time.

"Yes, it's about two hundred kilometres north from here; we weren't told exactly where it was, only that it was for the special ones who moved out. Some of the youngsters were also sent east, I don't know where."

"How many were there here?"

"At its height over sixty, split almost equally between men and women; there were only a handful left today. Now there's even less," sobbed the girl. "Normal followers like us weren't allowed to go, but the doctors went."

"This new complex, was it for this Contagion plan?"

"Yes I think so."

"How do we find this other complex?" asked Guy. So many questions, so much to find out.

"I don't know exactly where it is but Dr Ling secretly gave me his mobile number and asked me to call him yesterday; he was worried about one of the staff members. He wasn't allowed a phone really, but the Whistler smuggled one in for him just before they killed him." She dropped her head, clearly exhausted by the tragic events of the past few hours. In Guy's judgment there was little more she would be able to tell them. Rose reached the same conclusion. "That's great, you've been a terrific help Anita and I'm very sorry about your friend." Rose stood up as the police approached. She recognised Captain Tsieu from the previous night and turned to Guy. "I'll bet the good Captain was in on that damned explosion. We need to move before he sees us or we could be in trouble." Turning again to Anita she said. "We'll make sure you are looked after Anita. I promise, here is my mobile number if you ever need me just ring and I'll always try to help."

Guy took her hand, "Follow me Rose; I saw a car at the other side of the complex. Hope it's still there," and pulled her roughly towards the edge of the compound where they located an old

Mercedes. He heard a shout and groaned as he saw a policeman running towards them. "Jump in Rose the keys are in the ignition."

"You drive while I call this number," shouted Rose jumping into the passenger seat. Guy didn't answer. He took the driver's seat and accelerated down the narrow path towards a minor road about half a mile distant.

Guy nearly lost control of the car when he heard Rose cry into the mobile. "Oh my God, Dad. It really is you. I can't believe it!" She switched to Mandarin, speaking animatedly. When she stopped she turned to face Guy and said. "He's given me the directions." Having said goodbye to her father, she continued, "The main Contagion site is a hundred and fifty kilometres north of here; something is very wrong up there. I can sense it in his voice; we need to hurry."

"Probably take all day on these roads but we'll give it a go," replied Guy grimly. It was great news and he accepted it must take priority over Lorna. He was still very worried about her; he didn't even know where she was or why the opposition wanted her so badly. "The further we get away from this place and the police the better. They'll probably have all the airports watched by now."

Over three hours later and after a number of wrong turns they finally reached their destination. It was well hidden amongst the scenery. The locked gates confirmed they'd reached the right place. "Why two compounds?" Guy wondered aloud as he pulled to a halt exhausted by the drive. "Independent cells, each not knowing the other existed, totally separate and independent. That's how The Teacher operates. I'll bet our fathers didn't know it was here either," Rose suggested.

"Rose, if the name Contagion means something real and isn't just a code word, this place could be contaminated."

"You mean nuclear?"

"Possibly, we need to be very careful, the place looks deserted."

"My father's mobile is ringing but there's no answer. Looks as though something's happened. I can't hang about waiting to find out if it's dangerous or not, I'll risk it," she said and began moving forwards. Guy followed her.

They walked across to the gates nervously wondering what

they would find. To their surprise the gates were not locked so they entered the compound. "We need to check it out step by step, Rose. We can assume it isn't contaminated radioactively." The silence was palpable as they walked carefully around what appeared to be a deserted site; they found nothing even inside the crudely constructed huts. It became evident they had arrived too late; the place was deserted. Guy opened the door of the last hut carefully, gesturing to Rose to stand back as he grabbed a large stone. "No further and put your hands up," snapped a voice out of the gloom. "Father, it's me," shouted Rose, and ran past Guy at the sound of the familiar voice. "My dear Rose," gasped Zichu Ling. "It's been so long since I saw your pretty face in Shanghai. I've so much to tell you," he whispered hugging her close to him. "Just after you rang, those bastards tried to kill me. I stole a gun from one of the guards, escaped and hid over there in the forest. They nearly found me a couple of times but I was too much bother and they knew I had a gun so they fired tear gas at me, hence my cough." He broke off to recover his breathing rhythm.

"Your leg's bleeding," Rose had noticed a nasty gash down the side of his calf muscle.

"Yes, it's not too bad though. I fell out of a tree when the gas canister exploded." He explained. With a tired smile he released her and limped across to Guy. "So you are Jack's lad," he said and handed him the gun. "I've heard a great deal about you." Guy smiled back at him. "Only believe the good bits," he said.

Rose was in a hurry now, she was worried that someone might return to see what had happened to the guards if they were not responding to their mobile calls, or had decided to come back for Rose's father. "What's Contagion, Dad?" she asked.

"It's a programme to distribute drugs. There are ten large truckloads of containers of the worst, most addictive type possible, heading north from here for the Chinese border."

"They're going into China?" said Guy incredulously.

"Yes, they'll be over half way to the border by now; if you want to catch them we need to act fast."

"What sort of drugs are they?" asked Guy.

"All sorts. They're to cause epidemic scale problems with the Chinese; that's all I know."

"Do you know what's happened to my father?" asked Guy dreading the answer.

"Ah of course, I'm sorry. Poor old Jack, he has been very unwell since the loss of the Whisperer. Not himself if you understand me. I'm worried he might have done something stupid."

"Where's he gone?"

"He went with about twenty of them in the trucks; said he was going to finish the job once and for all. I told him not to be a martyr but he didn't listen, just said it had gone far enough."

"One man against twenty," said Guy despairingly. So close and yet so far, would he ever see his father again? It felt like an eternity since he had seen his father in Hong Kong. "There must be some traces of the drugs," said Guy looking around the cavernous warehouse.

"One of them is a mass produced grade of opium, rather like the stuff the Brits brought to China centuries ago," said Zichu. "Jack only had the chance to tell me it was a special cocktail of drugs before they took him away and began to shut the place down."

"The Chinese border and drugs; it has to be a large scale diversion," speculated Guy. "No one in their right mind would take on the Chinese in such a way."

"No one messing about with those classes of drugs is in their right mind. Perhaps they plan to flood the place which will prompt retaliation from the Chinese," Rose suggested.

"Is The Teacher with them?" Guy asked.

"No he's yesterday's news," Zichu shook his head.

"What do you mean?"

"Someone more powerful than him is in charge now; the real mastermind."

"More powerful?"

"Yes by far. The Teacher always deferred to him, though only a few of us even knew he existed."

"The man who mortared the main camp," guessed Guy.

"Ideological act," replied Zichu. "We know him by the code name of the Professor."

"Huh! An insult to the academic profession."

"What were you doing at the other place?" asked Guy.

"Transferring knowledge through an advanced form of psychotherapy; neither of us was happy about doing it but we had little choice; it was that or die, so we sought to at least ensure that no one got seriously hurt. We thought we could control things from the inside and we were wrong."

"This Professor what does he want?"

"Who knows? I would guess he's providing the funds using the resources of ZTW; there's even a rumour he has the Vietnamese government in his pocket."

"That wouldn't surprise me seeing how the local police acted," replied Guy. "Can you help us find him?"

"Of course, we've been helping you for over a year," smiled Zichu. "The Whistler was used to keep you abreast of what was happening. It was the only way we could communicate with you; anything else would have been spotted. Your father knew the Whistler from the past and spent hours learning how to communicate with him."

"That explains how I always seemed to know what The Teacher was doing."

"We fed the Whistler whatever we knew; he was smart enough to know our methods so we taught him our mind control techniques. He told us he had managed to send messages to you in your sleep; a very talented man and such a waste. That vicious woman Sabine killed him last week."

"We were told," said Rose quietly. "Where is The Teacher now?"

"Mongolia, that's where he was going with Shaka, our latest sleeper."

"Mongolia, the home of the Khans?"

"Exactly, Shaka is now President as of a couple of weeks ago; our biggest success yet though I have my doubts whether they can control him."

"Just like the sleepers in Spain and Aruba," said Guy.

"Yes, and that reminds me to thank you for taking such good care of Rose for me. Guy; your fortitude with her has been exemplary."

"She's a very special lady; we looked after each other." said Guy, then changing the subject quickly he said. "It looks like we have little choice here but to head north and try to avert a disaster."

"If by north you mean China, then no," replied Zichu strongly. "There is too little time. They will have almost reached the border by now and there's nothing we can do to stop them;

they are too heavily armed."

"We could alert the Police, couldn't we?"

"And tell them what? That we think there's a major convoy heading over the border? We don't know where or when. It's a big border, believe me. No. We have to strike the snake at the head; that's where the damage is done not by striking the tail."

"But my father!"

"He would agree with me; please do as I say," pleaded Zichu. "It's a long shot but I may be able to influence Shaka. He's our only chance to stop them."

"To Mongolia?" asked Rose

"That's where The Teacher and the Professor intend to strike. The Prophecy, do you know of this?"

"It will be suicidal to go up there," said Guy.

"As I said I know Shaka and hope I can still manipulate him. I programmed him so there is a chance."

Chapter 26

Ulaanbaatar

Sergei was immensely rich due to significant mining concessions in eastern Russia. He had, like many wealthy Russians, made many enemies, but unlike a number of other Russian billionaires, had used his money to help his countrymen. He invested heavily in social care in his home town of Vladivostok and was seen as a benevolent populist. He was also a member of the Elders and had originally supported Zheng until Jochi created the schism; after which he became his most fervent critic and had supported his expulsion from the council. He knew Shaka was no more than a puppet for a much darker and dangerous force that he didn't understand, the Professor. "You are making a big mistake," he said looking across at the new President.

His mass of white hair flopped over his face as he shook his head angrily at the man he had helped earlier. The skirmish had been bloodier than he had expected and ended with the death of The Teacher; something he hadn't planned or wanted. His huge bulk, hardly fitting into the chair, was intimidating as he leaned forward and stared at Shaka. "You need the support of people like me, Shaka, if you are going to survive," he snapped. "You all think yourselves omnipotent because you come to believe your own window dressing, but the real power lies behind the scenes. That's how the Elders work, and that's how all countries, including yours, works." He rose to his feet and said. "Don't let the trappings go to your head; you won't be the first and certainly not the last to come crashing down." The new President was unmoved. "Don't make the mistake of interfering in my country, Sergei, you may be an Elder but you are Russian too and not trusted here. You have an hour to get off Mongolian soil before I have you arrested."

"Idiot," growled Sergei and stormed out of the room. He was leaving a disaster of epic proportions brewing on the doorstep of his beloved Russia. He went to his Embassy and used their secure phone to call a familiar number thousands of miles away.

Lorna made her way through the Hong Kong airport complex marvelling at the huge achievement in reclaiming the land around it and building a mini city. She had no idea why Guy had arranged for the tickets or why he wanted her in Ulaanbaatar but she made her way to the boarding gate to be ushered into first class by the smiling Air China stewardess. The instructions and tickets were explicit down to the exact details of where they would meet. She had been very suspicious at first but, in the absence of direct contact from Guy, she had swung into action. Sick of sitting around wringing her hands, she wanted to be out there doing something. The verbal message said he had found The Teacher and they would be able to finish the job at last. She must join them in Mongolia. She slept on the long flight north and four hours later arrived in the city of Ulaanbaatar, Upper Mongolia. It was like something out of a sci-fi movie as they arrived and she shivered in the cold night air as she made her way through to the main Arrivals area. There she was met by a serious looking woman in a grey uniform with her name on a sign. "Where's Mr. Tresanton? He was to meet me here?" Lorna's suspicions were aroused again. "You come with me," she replied in halting English. "He meets you later."

"Very well," partly placated, Lorna stared at the grim landscape as they left the terminal; a fast changing vista of rapid industrialisation. Consistently unable to contact Guy's mobile that constantly rang out, her trepidation grew as they pulled up at a large white mansion. Guy would never have brought her here. "This way please," gestured her guide. "Where is my colleague?" Lorna demanded. "Sorry don't understand," replied the woman sweetly. "You go please," she said gesturing ahead to the main entrance hall.

Shaka was revelling in the fact he was master of all he surveyed. It had been a relatively simple task for his new intelligence people to patch together a fake recording of Tresanton's voice from an old tape they had been given by Sabine and the girl had fallen for it. This was the last job he would do for his paymasters; then he was going solo. He was the President and had outwitted everyone else; it was all his and would stay that way.

Just this final simple job for the Professor; he smiled as his door opened. "She is here." announced the woman in grey.

"Good," he said. "My dear, please come in, the Professor will be so pleased you have arrived safely," he said.

"The Professor?"

"The King is dead, so long live the King," replied Shaka and waved her to a seat.

"If you are allied to The Teacher; we are sworn enemies, Mr. President," Lorna told him.

"The Teacher is dead. You and I are not enemies; he was my enemy, so in a strange way that makes us allies."

"I have come a long way to meet my friend, Guy Tresanton. Kindly show me where he is."

"A little subterfuge I am afraid; it's amazing what technology can achieve these days."

"The voice call was a fake?"

"I'm afraid so," Shaka said with a grin.

"Then I demand to be taken back to the airport; this is kidnapping."

"Granted the situation is not quite as you expected," said a familiar voice as Sabine emerged from the side door, "but the Professor has great plans for you, my dear."

"Where's Guy?" Lorna said. She was beginning to get very worried; she'd walked into a trap and had no idea why they wanted her here.

"Did you really think that he would be here? Grow up girl. I didn't believe you would fall for the trick but Shaka did. You are an idiot but it seems the Professor values you so my hands are tied. You are bloody naive girl. As for your half-wit lover I have it on good authority he and his interfering partner have been killed in Vietnam. Such a shame but these things happen to interfering amateurs; now you and I have much work to do."

"He can't be dead!"

"As I said the only reason you are still alive is because the Professor has decided to bed you so let's get real, girl. If you play your cards right then you will survive and, if you are lucky, you may get into my bed too."

"You disgust me," spat Lorna.

"Even better," grinned the redhead.

"You have another value of course," interjected Shaka looking across at Sabine, "you own a cruise ship which is sailing south to a predetermined rendezvous as we speak. Instructions are needed from you on the change of direction. The Captain is a stickler for order; we have a secure communications booth next door.

"Sail for where?"

"The Indian Ocean."

"Why should I do what you ask?"

"You know what Mongols do to girls like you. A quaint transition I believe started by the great Khan himself. Believe me you would rather die than be subjected to that," smiled Shaka.

"Why should I believe any of this?"

"You really don't have much choice, my dear; believe me you and I are very similar. We live in a man's world where we have to use what we have to best effect. The only difference is I enjoy all this whilst you are too bloody prim and passive. Get a grip girl." Sabine wanted to assert her authority and felt Shaka was having too much to say.

"Let me tell you and the bloody tinpot dictator here that I am sick and tired of being pushed around," snapped Lorna. She burst into action leaping from her seat and running for the door. She saw an ornamental sword hanging on the wall and grabbed it as she pulled the door open, only to be confronted by a burly bodyguard. She whirled back and headed for Sabine swinging the sword and catching the larger girl by surprise. "For God's sake," snapped Sabine spinning around and grabbing the sharp end before wrenching it from Lorna and throwing it down. Shaka looked on with amusement as Sabine, impervious to the blood on her hands, pushed Lorna to the floor and kicked her.

"Lucky for you my orders are to deliver you alive but there is nothing specific about condition."

"Bitch," yelled Lorna struggling to her feet but feeling pain in her back, she ran straight at Sabine knocking her to the ground and gripping her hair as they both fell to the floor screaming and shouting. "You're lucky that you are useful to the Professor or you would be dead now," hissed Sabine getting to her feet. Lorna stayed curled up in a ball. "Excellent," smiled Shaka, "you've just given me a brilliant idea." He turned and bellowed orders to his guards in the Mongolian tongue smiling as he did so. This was going to be hugely entertaining and a fitting start to his Presidency.

Guy, Rose and Zichu arrived at Ulaanbaatar airport and took a taxi straight to the address that Zichu had been given. "It's a forbidding place," said Rose. She was overjoyed to be working with her father particularly after her recent incarceration; she smiled to Guy knowing he was still worrying about his father and feeling slightly guilty that she had found her own. She shivered in the cold. "It's minus thirty degrees in winter so let's look on the positive side," she observed.

"Not much of a consolation," replied Guy pulling his coat tighter and looking out at the bleak landscape. "The Mongols must have been a hardy nation, no wonder they conquered the world with a homeland like this."

"Apparently it's beautiful in the summer," said Zichu, "so Shaka told me."

"Give me the Caribbean anytime," said Guy staring ahead. He had slept a great deal on the flight. Torn between trying to track down his father and coming here to find Lorna, he had accepted this was the more logical step. From what Zichu said no one knew for sure where his father would be. He was proud to know that all along they had been seeking to subvert The Teacher from the inside. "You're sure Shaka will agree to meet you, Zichu?"

"He told me I had an open invite to visit. Whether that's changed in the light of recent events I don't know, but it's our only chance."

"Monty wondered whether we should contact the police, but it's too risky until we see Shaka; after all he's their boss so they'll do what he wants."

Zichu used Rose's mobile to make a call. "Good news," he said as he handed it back to her. "Shaka's agreed to see me; we're to go straight to his Presidential Villa."

"That's great," commented Rose, "Though it could mean he just wants to arrest us." Their taxi took them to a tree-lined avenue and came to halt in the forecourt of a grand building that dominated the area. "He's wasted no time in acclimatizing to power," smiled Zichu, "the peasant boy has turned leader. I'm sure that story all over the papers will be without his missing years in Vietnam. Who was it said power corrupts and absolute power corrupts absolutely?"

"Lord Acton, one of ours," replied Guy liking the little man more and more as they got to know each other. He saw in him much of the tenaciousness Rose exhibited, dogged and resourceful. On the flight Zichu had explained how both he and his wife had been kidnapped on the streets of Hong Kong; his father had been taken the same way. A woman hurried towards them as they entered the building. "Let me do the talking," said Zichu.

"Mr. Zichu Ling?" she asked politely.

"That's me," he replied.

"Please come this way." They were taken to a lift and waited ten minutes before a surly Mongolian guard escorted them up to the top floor. The door opened to an opulent world with the latest in western furniture and Shaka, now clad in military uniform, looking every inch the President.

"Zichu," boomed Shaka, "it's good to see you again old friend."

"This is my daughter, Rose, and her friend Guy Tresanton."

"Welcome, friends of Zichu are friends of mine," said Shaka gesturing to them to sit down. "How's the camp?" he asked.

"Gone, bombed," replied Zichu bluntly, "Many are dead. It was a sad end; I want you to help me find out what happened and confront The Teacher; it's time he was brought to account."

"I'm afraid that's not possible, Zichu," replied Shaka taking a sip of whisky. "The World has moved on and left you behind."

"What do you mean?"

"Zheng has already been brought to account; he's dead, and there is a new regime."

"The Teacher's dead!" exclaimed Rose "that's hard to believe. How did it happen?"

"He thought he was unbeatable; he tried to double cross me and paid the price."

"So it's ended," said Guy; he felt cheated.

"Far from it, a new leader has emerged. The man behind the scenes all along; the puppet master."

"Who is he?" asked Guy.

"A man they call 'the Professor,' he's the strongman who controlled The Teacher from the start, only we didn't know it."

"I thought you were against them," said Zichu coldly. "You told me you didn't agree with them, remember? We had a pact." Shaka just stared at Zichu. "That's all over now, I am beholden to no one. I'm my own man so don't try your mind games with me."

"I've done with all that Shaka, there has been enough damage caused and it has to end; the innocent followers who trusted The Teacher, what will happen to them?"

"History's winners are those who have the vision and ruthlessness to succeed. Now I have much to do. You came here to stop The Teacher and your task is complete."

"I'm looking for a girl called Lorna," said Guy. "I believe The Teacher brought her here."

"Very well," sighed Shaka, "I was hoping to avoid this but clearly I can't. I know nothing of this girl but perhaps my associate does," he pressed a button and Sabine came into the room. She smiled an unpleasant smile. "Guy Tresanton, the gifted amateur," she said.

"You!" gasped Rose, shocked at seeing her.

"Shaka you will let me handle this now; these two have been a pain in the backside, even outlasting Zheng. Tresanton this is the end of the road for you. Zichu you betrayed the programme."

"Zichu is my friend and under my protection," snapped Shaka.

"That's as maybe but the others aren't; they are old adversaries and I claim the right to deal with them."

"What have you done with Lorna?" demanded Guy." Sabine ignored him and turned instead to the President. "Shaka your loyalty is to the new regime, don't forget our little deal," she snapped.

"And don't you forget who is President here," responded Shaka rising to his full height. Zichu interrupted the exchange. "I saved you from the worst excesses of the mind controls, Shaka," he reminded him.

"That's true," conceded Shaka. He remembered Zichu's help very well; it had often reassured him that he wasn't going mad. Sabine though, wasn't to be quelled so easily.

"There is a new master now; you know the consequences of treachery."

"I could have you all thrown in prison on no charges whatsoever," threatened Shaka.

"But I can ruin you. A word to the right people on how you were elected, and don't think I haven't taken precautions," snapped Sabine angrily, "ZTW have the legal rights to the metal deposits and I demand you hand them over."

"You have no rights here, Sabine. Do I need to remind you of that? You can only trust my goodwill which at the moment is sorely stretched, so it's just as well for you that I have a different proposition," he said, and turned to an aged Mongolian who had just entered the room. He whispered something to him and the old man left to return immediately with three guards. "What is the meaning of this?" snapped Sabine.

"It's the Mongolian way; don't you find that often the old ways are the best?" smiled Shaka, "there will be a tournament and the winner will take all."

"Shaka what is this?" asked Zichu.

"The test of truth. A physical contest to determine who is right and uniquely Mongolian."

"What do you mean?" snapped Sabine.

"Here females fight in times of conflict for the right to have their way. Take Tresanton as he means nothing to me, but my old friend Zichu and his daughter have the right to this trial; they will fight for their freedom," grinned Shaka wolfishly. "Mongolian tradition is that, to avoid male bloodshed, female members fight to prove who has right on their side."

"Shaka, I am warning you," hissed Sabine, "You may think you are in control but the Professor will kill you for this."

"I do things my way and I have absolute authority to act as I see fit, besides what are you worried about? You get the chance to fight the Chinese girl."

"I don't have time for your perverted male desire to see females rip each other to bits," snapped Sabine turning back to the others.

"Then you will all go with Tresanton to prison whereas if you beat Rose you will be free to go and take her with you, along with the other girl. I can't say fairer than that." He gestured to his guard, "You have nothing to fear if you are as good as I have heard and the Chinese girl is scrawny. Now I have work to do, so until the evening."

"This is medieval," shouted Guy as he was grabbed roughly by the guards.

"The Grand Hall," snapped Shaka turning to leave.

"What of the Khan's Prophecy?" Shouted Guy.

"I don't know what you are talking about," replied Sabine.

"I'm guessing that you need the fourth Artefact and we are

ahead of you," shouted Guy.

"I've heard the Mongolian secret police are particularly adroit at getting information out of prisoners before they die," spat Sabine turning away. "Start praying, little girl, you'll soon wish you were dead."

The rest of the day passed in a mixture of dread and anticipation for Rose. At the chosen time, she was collected by the guards who had locked her up and delivered to the Grand Hall. She looked around the small arena with distaste, seeing people in the gallery and knowing she was on show. She walked across to the other side of the arena from Sabine who, like herself, was clad in a one piece leotard with oil on their skins. Sabine stared back at her impassively and started to limber up, confident that she would soon destroy this upstart. Normally she would have enjoyed such an event but this was just an inconvenience.

She stepped into the makeshift ring and looked around, taking in the spectators in the gallery and the guards around the ring. Shaka sat in the centre of the gallery and looked down at the spectacle. Zichu was on one side of him staring ahead and blaming himself for getting her into this mess. On the other side sat Lorna. To Shaka this was what power was about; forcing others to comply with his will. It was an aphrodisiac and he wondered idly whether Sabine would bend to his other wishes later on. He stood up. "The combat rules are quite simple, no gouging, no hair pulling and no weapons," he shouted. "It is a traditional Mongolian test and must be treated with the respect it deserves."

Rose looked around as she psyched herself up. She had no illusions that Sabine was stronger and would fight dirty. She took a deep breath and tried to attract Lorna's attention receiving a slight nod in acknowledgement. "This is barbaric," Zichu said angrily to Shaka.

"Exactly. We are filming it to show our people the true nature of westerners and that they must abide by our rules," said Shaka. He would enjoy his revenge on Sabine. He hoped the Chinese girl would be a real scrapper and would give a good account of herself, whilst he succeeded in building his image with his people. He had no intention of ending up as a pawn of another's ambition when he alone had the keys to the richest prize, the

Prophecy. Zichu was a problem, he knew too much about Shaka's past so was too dangerous to let go free. He would contrive Tresanton's death tomorrow at Zichu's hands then he would have grounds for arrest. He watched the girls move forward and shouted for action.

Rose and Sabine circled one another slowly, their feet making squeaking noises as they shuffled around on the sand underfoot. Rose gritted her teeth as she watched Sabine circle her like a hawk before leaping forward and kicking out catching her a glancing blow on the thigh and then in the groin. She tried to silently suppress the pain; there would be no rules of fair play and she would have to fight dirty. She stumbled momentarily losing her balance and grimacing as the sand stuck to the oil on her hand. She grabbed a handful of the sand as she stood up, and flung the fine grit into Sabine's face momentarily blinding her. "You bitch, you'll pay for that," promised Sabine shaking her head to clear her vision and returning immediately to the attack.

Sabine was fast but Rose was faster and ready this time. She side-stepped the lunge before hitting Sabine hard across the face. Sabine stumbled and fell forwards. Rose hooked her foot behind her opponent's calf muscle and jerked it forward. Sabine fell in a heap and, before she could recover herself, Rose was on top of her. The larger girl writhed in the sand and was too strong for Rose to hold down. She pushed Rose off with a shriek of pain before springing up and hitting Rose hard in the stomach. Rose gasped in agony and fell face down into the sand, Sabine hit her hard in the back and deliberately began to kick the softest parts of her body. Rose curled up into the foetal position trying to evade the barrage of kicks and regain her strength. She wriggled onto her side, grabbed Sabine's left foot and pulled. Sabine again hit the floor hard. They grappled and struggled with each other, each trying desperately to gain an advantage. Rose's mind now was on a different plane as she traded blows ignoring the fierce pain. Sabine realised this was tougher than she expected. Finally they rolled away from each other trying to regain their breath, staggering up and circling each other warily.

"Come on there must be a winner," yelled Shaka feasting his eyes on the heaving bodies."

"Creep," mouthed Sabine as she put her head down and tried to figure out a new approach; it was now or never, like lightening she wrong footed the Chinese girl and pushed her right leg away, shouting in triumph as Rose fell hard to the floor hitting her head as she did so. Sabine was in the ascendancy. Sensing victory, Sabine rushed at Rose and threw sand into her face before kicking her hard in the groin. Rose groaned, writhed away across the floor and again grabbed hold of Sabine's legs and both girls fell to the floor locked together scratching and screaming. Finally Sabine managed to grab Rose by the hair and twisting hard kicked a heavy blow into Rose's midriff. Rose slipped into unconsciousness as Zichu ran down the steps to help his daughter. "I win," snarled Sabine looking up at Shaka, "you've had your thrills."

"Very well, it shall be so," replied Shaka.

"I only want the girl, Lorna, you can finish the others yourself," she promised. "You and I will meet again Shaka."

———————————

The ancient prison stank of decay as he was pushed inside. There was no heating and his gut clenched as he saw the scene ahead where other prisoners were moaning and shouting. Guy listened to the sounds of despair coming from other cells, his spirits slumped as he was pushed into a cell and the door slammed behind him. How the hell was he going to get out of here? He could be left to rot forever? He looked around in the near darkness feeling exhausted and full of despair? He flung himself onto a dirty-looking bench, and at least he had a cell to himself. He had fallen into a fitful sleep when he was awoken by a commotion outside and the rattling of keys. He sat bolt upright, blinded by a light as a man came to the cell. "Tresanton?" he asked. Guy quickly gathered his wits and replied "Yes, that's me. Who are you?"

"A friend come to get you out of here," said the man. Guy still didn't have a clue who he was but if he had come to get him out of here then he was certainly a friend. "Who are you?" he asked again. "I am a representative of the official opposition party; we are dedicated to removing that dictator in the Presidential Palace. Follow me," he ordered, and opened the door wide. "I don't seem to have a lot of choice," murmured Guy to himself reasoning that things couldn't get any worse. He glanced at two fallen bodies before being directed across the road to an old car. No words were spoken as the man pushed him into the back, jumped into the driver's seat and accelerated away into the night.

His rescuer spoke little English and Guy wondered if it was a case of out of the frying pan into the fire. The roads were largely unlit and they appeared to be heading out of town when he saw a larger building ahead. It was a railway station and standing ready to leave was a train. Then he understood. It was painful running away from both Rose and Lorna but he had no choice. They were out of their depth; it was Shaka's country. Entering the station he saw a large figure with white beard and clad in black ambling towards him. "Guy Tresanton?"

"Yes."

"Sergei Rostov, I'm a member of the Elders, we're going to get you out of the country."

"My colleagues, I can't leave them." The very idea made Guy feel sick.

"I will do my best for the rest of them," Rostov promised.

"Why are you helping me?" asked Guy.

"Shaka was undemocratically elected; Jade asked me to get you out, simple as that."

"But the others?" Guy couldn't stop thinking about his friends.

"I said I will try later, you have my word. Now the opposition is helping us, but we have to move fast."

"Where are we going?"

"North to Vladivostok; there will be much fighting and Shaka will lose eventually but your fight lies elsewhere. I hear you have been a bulwark for the Elders for some time and thank you for that; there is much still to be done and Jade wants you in Europe."

"Thank you, this must be a tremendous risk to you," Guy said.

"I owe it to the Elders; now here's a false passport and papers. We will travel together north where there is a flight booked for you. Ah at last," he gestured as a small man approached, "this is Timut, a key leader in the opposition party; you can trust him," he said as the small wiry man approached.

"Our country has been usurped by the big conglomerates, Mr. Tresanton. They have Shaka in their pocket. We need to regain it, that's why I help you. We have the President's home closely watched and will seize a chance to get your friends."

"Thank you," replied Guy; "I thought the north was uninhabited and was only religious grounds for the Mongols."

"No, it's now owned by ZTW mining company. There is a huge expanse of land that would not be allowed in any other country but here," replied Sergei. "They are a competitor to my companies and were given the mineral rights without any tender process. It was all dishonest and basically a front for Zheng, now he's gone and the man they call the Professor is running things."

"I know ZTW, I've come across them before," replied Guy, "why is it so important to them to get the mineral rights?"

"Mineral wealth makes up eighty percent of this country's exports; they've just found a whole mountain called Turquoise Hill in Oyu Tolgoi for example that will be demolished just for its copper," said Timut passionately. "The lands north east of here have even more unique metals. Thanks to the resurgence of coal mining and the metals, we now have the most polluted city in the world. The Mongolians true National Party will overturn the last election results which were a fraud. We have proof of outside interference, but the state intelligence system is stopping us moving forwards. We may have to take drastic action before the country slides into a full dictatorship. I and others are currently wanted by the police on trumped up charges."

"I wish you luck," said Guy keeping to the shadows as they walked across to the train. "So ZTW bought huge quantities of special metals?" he asked Sergei as Timut went ahead to check all was clear.

"Yes unique precious metals and specifically the home of a special metal called rhodium. Perhaps you've seen it? It's what the Artefacts are made of. I know all about them from my work with the Elders. What is more, we also believe it's the location of both Genghis and Kublai's burial tombs. It remains to be seen whether we can isolate the area before the fourth Artefact is found."

"And the Prophecy?"

"Ah, so you know about that also."

"I guess that it's up here."

"We have to isolate the area as there is no doubt that the Prophecy does exist and is located north of here. Whether it is as meaningful as people claim who knows, but we do have a real fight on our hands? This Professor is far more dangerous than The Teacher.

"So we need to get there first."

"That was Zheng's mistake. It's a barren land of steppes and frozen tundra. Precise directions are needed to trace the fourth Artefact; another reason to get you out; your reputation has spread."

"As a gifted amateur?" Guy said with a smile.

"Sometimes that's the most effective way; you're unencumbered by bureaucracy and professional competence or rather incompetence."

"And Zheng's demise. I still can't quite believe he is dead?"

"He lived by the sword and paid the ultimate penalty. I believe passionately in the Elders; it is the only way we can succeed in the long term, fighting the perverted desires of people like Zheng. Come on, the train's waiting; we have private compartments in the first class section; it will attract far less suspicion that way and you don't want to go second class on this train, believe me."

Chapter 27

Hanoi

The Professor was in a hurry as the private jet touched down at Hanoi International Airport. He was immediately driven away by a waiting 'S' Class Mercedes into the centre of the city and taken to the Hanoi Hilton. He noticed many luxurious cars parked outside the hotel and reflected on the changing times in the country as it morphed into an industrial powerhouse. He had encouraged The Teacher to use the country as his base after they established significant influence with the government. "Everything is ready Mr. Ho," he smiled as the Security Minister greeted him in his penthouse suite.

"The payment is arranged?"

"It will transfer to your account as soon as Contagion is launched."

"The price has increased Professor."

"You know better than to play those games with me Ho."

"The Chinese are starting to make noises; they sense something is going on; the stakes have risen." The Minister smiled but it wasn't the smile of a friend and never reached the man's eyes. "They are my problem, Mr. Ho. I'll take care of them," snapped the Professor. "We have to preserve trust in our relationship or we have nothing. Now this is what you are going to do and no more talk of money."

Ten minutes later he left Ho, taking the car to a large building on the outskirts of Hanoi that housed the headquarters of ZTW Worldwide. As they reached their destination his mobile rang; he listened intently and smiled briefly as he climbed out of the car. He was greeted with due deference as he went inside and strode through to the lifts that took him directly to the executive floor where the boardroom was located. He was met there by Else Chan, ZTW's Vice President for Asia and Jacques Savior, the Swiss Finance Director. With Zheng's demise, it was all change.

"Be seated," he snapped. "You are all aware that our colleague Zheng Wan unfortunately died from an accident in Mongolia?"

"We are," replied Else fifty-three years old, she had been a long-term supporter of Zheng but she was also someone who quickly recognised the shifts in power.

"What exactly happened to Zheng?" asked Jacques.

"An accident in an inhospitable land, Jacques; what I am more concerned about is our stock price. It continues to slide."

"It's under control; a temporary blip."

"You think so, it seems worse than that to me."

"I have taken measures to stop the rot," replied Jacques, the financier. "I will say that it has not been helped by Zheng deciding to take us into private ownership. I've had a hell of a job managing that. Fortunately our sales and profit margins are as strong as ever and we have record amounts of cash in the bank and the new fields in Mongolia will be invaluable."

"And yet a number of our larger shareholders have been selling us short; that's hard to fathom." mused the Professor.

"It will change."

"Really?" said the Professor, "Quite clearly you haven't a clue what has happened, so I shall tell you. A group of rich individuals have taken it upon themselves to sell us short and you, Savior, have personally taken advantage of it." Savior reacted as if he had been stung by a wasp. "What! That's slanderous, we are a successful company and you both have put us at risk through your ambitions."

"Do I take it from that outburst that you have lost confidence in my judgment?" queried the Professor calmly.

"No, of course not. You know what I mean; the recent actions have caused the market to take a different view of the company…"

"No, I do not know what you mean and I will not tolerate such insubordination."

"As a senior board member I have voting rights….." The Professor held up his hand and gestured Jacques to be quiet. "You do not have those rights any more because, as of this very minute, ZTW is back into private hands, mine. As we speak my aides are buying out the stock and as of five minutes ago I achieved over fifty percent so the company reverts to my ownership and away from the thieving hands of others. One thing that Zheng did get right only not quick enough."

"You need public goodwill," Jacques protested.

"Not anymore; it has served its purpose having a respectable public company funding our activities but those times have now gone, finished."

"You can't do this without the board vote."

"Oh yes I can and I have, Jacques. My first independent act is to declare that you are surplus to requirements."

"I have put ten years of my life into this company."

"And stolen a fortune from it. You are an inept financier who has leeched this company for too long."

"You have no grounds for making such accusations."

"Don't worry, you will be well recompensed. Now get out of my sight." Jacques recognised his days with ZTW had come to an end and stalked from the room. When the door had closed behind him the Professor said to Else. "He will need taking care of; he knows too much. He has a role to play though not one he will be keen on. All part of your important assignment up north."

"I will see to it," she said quietly and followed her erstwhile colleague out of the Professor's office.

Giovanni, now known as the Professor, relaxed as he was driven back to the airport knowing he had to get possession of the fourth Artefact. A private helicopter took him south from Hanoi to a temporary compound where he made a quick inspection and held a meeting about the Contagion Project. Having established all was well, he flew back to Hanoi. It was time to begin the final countdown to Operation Contagion. Ten hours later he completed his journey to his secret mini-fortress on Ascension Island in the Indian Ocean. On the way, his blackberry flickered and he smiled as he listened to the voice message. "Bring the girl to me when you arrive," he ordered. Later, after taking a shower, he hurried to his private office with its panoramic view of the sea and activated the video link-up with Victor Gonzales in his Panama office.

"Everything ready?" he enquired.

"We have a problem. The men who took the boat to collect the cargo from Australia." Victor sounded nervous.

"What about them?"

"They've disappeared with the goods; we last tracked them to about ten miles from the Panama coast. Then they just disappeared."

"This is preposterous; they can't just disappear," barked Giovanni angrily.

"We can recover the situation, Professor. We believe we know where they are, and it's just a matter of time before we get them."

"You'd better! Is there a ringleader?"

"Yes, the Hogg girl; she must have turned the heads of some of the crew."

"Operation Contagion will not be delayed through incompetence, Victor; the border crossing will proceed to plan."

"It will happen; the Hogg girl will be history before the week is out."

"She'd better be. The whole plan was predicated on getting the cargo across from New Zealand. See to it." He slammed the phone down cursing as he mulled over the various activities that were synchronized; he didn't need anything to go wrong now. His door opened. "I gave strict instructions," he began…

"Sorry boss, but it's urgent," said the fat man coming further into the room.

"It'd better be."

"The bulk carrier support, we need it now. The shipment is ready to make the rendezvous. We have less than five days before the cargo becomes contaminated in this heat."

"We have transport on its way; it won't be late," snapped Giovanni well aware of the criticality.

"Good, then I will be ready."

"Make sure you don't mess up," warned Giovanni. He was beginning to feel tired as he returned to his console. He switched on the island's video surveillance system and for the first time since returning to his retreat smiled as he saw a helicopter land on his helipad; two women jumped from it and headed towards him.

Five minutes later the knock on his office door announced their arrival and Sabine entered half dragging a drugged Lorna into the room. "Welcome to the island, Sabine, you have done well," he greeted her cheerfully. Sabine returned his smile and dumped Lorna into a lounge chair in the corner of the office. "Brought you your merchandise," she said. "The views are stunning here. What a lovely place!"

"Glad you like it," smiled Giovanni and strolled across the room to study the half comatose Lorna. "The daughter of Stig Oleson, my old friend, a very important guest. How are you, my dear?"

"Go to hell," Lorna answered as she struggled to see through a drugged haze.

"You look like you've been in a fight, Sabine."

"That idiotic Mongolian President and I had a little falling out," she replied still feeling her bruises, "thanks to him I lost Tresanton and the Chinese girl. He has his own agenda it seems."

"Of course he has; all the Sleepers did. I never believed in Zheng's magical mind-bending powers. Just look at the other three. I have little faith the one in China will work either."

"That girl's a pain in the backside. Why do you want her?"

"That's my business. Now you have a very critical task with the Artefact and my new recruits. They are a very talented pair who are extremely effective, but in need of a little guidance. After refreshing yourself, you must leave immediately; you'll find some new clothes and travel instructions in the room I've prepared for you. Sabine nodded her understanding and left the room. She was tired after her journey and needed to rest before any further travel."

Lorna had watched the exchange between her captors only half understanding what was going on. She tried to sit up. "What do you want with me?" she moaned.

"You have a cruiser I want to borrow; there are some papers over there you must sign after you give the Captain verbal instructions."

"And if I don't?"

"Oh you will," replied Giovanni coolly. "Your cruiser is heading here already and you need the money. If I don't transfer the money it will be impounded in the nearest port and you will never see it again."

"I am not going to hand it over to someone I don't know."

"You may not know me but I was a good friend of your father's."

"That's an even better reason for not handing it over. Why have you brought me here, you already have the damned ship?"

"You don't remember do you?"

"Should I?"

"Your father brought you here many years ago when you were just eighteen."

"Why would I remember that? He took me to many places?"

"It was a very special visit with an extraordinary outcome, but you are tired so it can wait until tomorrow when you have recovered. I do apologise for the way we brought you here."

"Where exactly am I?"

"You will find out tomorrow. Now tell me about your friends."

"What friends?"

"This Tresanton and the Chinese girl; they seem to be unusually proactive."

"Look, whoever you are, various criminals, no doubt linked to you, have seen fit to kidnap me and drag me half way around the world. That idiot Shaka mentioned your name so I have to assume that you are behind all this so why should I tell you anything? The minute I get the chance I will stop the cruiser."

"Very well, then I will tell you the facts. Firstly you are talking to an extremely prominent man who will soon become immensely rich; secondly you are on a remote island in the Seychelles Archipelago far away from the world you're used to and, thirdly, I suggest you brace yourself and read this." With a smile he passed to her an official looking document. As soon as she looked at it Lorna froze with horror. "No I don't believe it," she screamed.

Chapter 28

Uganda
Kampala

Entebbe Airport was unlike anything Tapiwa had expected. She'd heard stories of the raids there by the Israelis during Idi Amin's reign and half expected a bullet-scarred building stuck out in the middle of nowhere. The scene that greeted her instead was a nondescript building with limited facilities and a whole host of United Nations airplanes standing on the apron loading emergency supplies for a number of African countries. A Ugandan man told her with considerable pride that the airport was now the main UN distribution base for aid and relief supplies to those areas. "It demonstrated his country was coming of age," he said. She passed through passport control conscious that Doctor Red had been quiet since flying ahead of her to Kampala on personal business. They'd agreed that it was best not to be seen together.

She tried again to call him before hiring a taxi to take her on the hour's drive along the northern shores of Lake Victoria into Kampala, but without success. She was reassured by the feel of the ceramic knife strapped to her thigh which had again avoided airport detection; she was as prepared as she could be. Red's directions were straightforward enough. She went over the directions again in her mind. The Doctor had assured her The Fourth Artefact had been buried in a sufficiently remote place in the Northern Uganda forests about three hour's drive north of the city, in Bokora Wildlife Reserve. She half dozed on the drive thinking through the steps she would take after finding it. They had arranged for her to head into town and meet there. She swapped the taxi for a hire car and, ignoring the admiring glances of the car hire administrator, drove a mid-sized Toyota north, reckoning she had about four hours before light faded.

A little over an hour later she found the forest she was looking for and, following Red's directions, made her way to the very end of the road. Leaving the hire car hidden under some thick bushes she set out on foot. She felt she had returned to her natural environment. Her senses adjusted to the surroundings and the hidden noises as she made her way deeper into the dense forest. Red had told her it was well hidden; they had been petrified that Amin's men would track it down. Most people would be uneasy in the deep forest but to her it was less frightening than a city. Soon the closeness of the trees and impenetrable growths of prickly bushes became difficult to penetrate.

After about thirty minutes she arrived at a river bank. For the umpteenth time she surveyed the map co-ordinates from Red and double checked her position using her GPS system, only switching it on for short periods to avoid detection. She had covered what felt like miles when she realised that the co-ordinates had been created in a deliberately misleading way to deter casual hunters. Dr Oboto had told her on her mobile just after landing she was looking for an Artefact shaped like a Staff that had being brought to Africa by Marco Polo himself. After finding the Staff she was to talk to no one and go to an address in Kampala, not even trusting Red. His voice held an urgency she hadn't heard before; her mentor was worried. The Artefact was being sought by others and remembering her own dreadful experience in Malawi it illustrated just how dangerous this task was; if she wasn't careful it could well be her last. Still, she was a hunter and risk was part of her daily existence.

It was almost dark by the time she found the river she was looking for and she stopped beside it with rising excitement. She couldn't help wondering what it must have been like for Red all those years ago. He'd stolen the Artefact and hidden it right under Idi Amin's nose; it was great daring or great stupidity depending on which way you looked at it. She was now relying on her finely honed instincts in the bush as she followed the river's course. Was it a false trail, had Red misled her? He hadn't. She found the point defined by the map and made preparations to camp for the night. She could hardly see the small outcrop of rocks shaped like a horse's head, but there it was, in front of a large boulder roughly shaped like a lion's head. She decided to see if she could find anything using her flashlight. She set to work with a small trowel under the lion's head as Red had instructed. After fifteen minutes she hit something hard, she dug deeper using the flashlight to determine what it could be. Finally with a grunt of satisfaction she saw a long metal casing.

She tried to recall Oboto's advice about the Artefact as she cleared away the earth around it. She had no doubt this was what she had come to find and she set about lifting the casket gingerly from the foot of the boulder. That completed, she filled in the hole, stamped it flat and covered it with leaves. If anyone else came here they would have to make a new search and that would take time. Satisfied with her camouflage, she made her way back into the forest to ensure she was alone. At home in the darkness of the trees, she opened the metal box by smashing the lock between two rocks and studied the item inside. There was no doubt she had found the legendary Confucius Staff. It was about a metre long and exquisitely embossed with Chinese characters. The metal itself was a strange colour that glinted oddly in the light of her torch. She wrapped it in a clean cloth and held it close to her as she slept in her perch in a massive tree.

She slept well feeling that at last she had achieved something significant. She dreamed of the old days and her brother; this was their natural habitat, the one place she felt at peace with herself. If by some miracle she did survive the current adventure, what would she do next? She couldn't keep on running, she was getting older. She needed a new occupation and recent events had served to confirm that thought. She awoke at the crack of dawn and quickly made her way down to the forest floor. As the light got stronger she examined the staff more closely, feeling a thrill that, aside from Doctor Red and his friend, no one had seen the icon since Marco Polo. The name Confucius was etched on the top in English and Chinese in exquisitely crafted words. The unusual metal colour somewhere between silver and gold was exactly what she had been told to expect by Oboto; she called Doctor Red but again got no answer. She left an innocuous message on his answering service and headed back to the Kampala Sheraton Hotel and checked in before luxuriating in a hot bath.

Vienna

Kat was far better at handling pressure than her brother. They had left Vietnam within hours of the mortar attack as was their custom after a major job; to leave fast and lie low well away from the attack. This time they were heading for a vacation in Mexico when she received the message. "Another job for us, Kit," she told him, putting her mobile into her pocket.

"We never do back-to-back jobs," he reminded her.

"The Professor wants us on a straightforward job, very different location. It should only take a day and he's offering us a small fortune, look."

"I thought we were going to get some rest," complained Kit. "Do we have to do this?"

"The money is our pension fund; you can lie around as much as you like afterwards. The flight is already booked for us; we just need to get over to the Austrian Airlines gate."

Nairobi

Dr Walter Oboto was apprehensive as he made his way to the Intercontinental Hotel, Nairobi. It had been a long flight from Madrid and he felt uneasy at getting directly involved. He'd left Jade trawling the archives and had come here because direct action on the fourth Artefact was required. He felt the warmth of the Kenyan heat as he climbed out of the taxi and checked in before making his way to the hotel's main restaurant. Holiday makers packed the pool as he sat down and ordered a beer. He recognised one of the waiters from a previous visit and chose a steak from the menu. Tomorrow he would fly to Uganda. The Elders were showing real solidarity in fighting ZTW; even Sergei Rostov, someone he'd previously regarded as being less than helpful, had contacted them and offered to help in Mongolia and Russia. The body was taking its responsibilities seriously; perhaps Zheng had done them a favour by providing a common enemy. Get the Confucius Staff and they would have the upper hand, though they still needed to find the elusive Professor's headquarters.

He called his deputy, one of the more respected members of the Elders, a woman of Arab origin, called Faustino Asprillo. Based in Qatar she had launched a women's fashion business that had boomed as women gained importance in the region. He'd known her for many years and had personally introduced her to the Elders, regarding her as a brilliantly incisive woman who would be a more than adequate replacement for him when he retired. He left her a short message and returned to his steak. His instincts increasingly told him that Mongolia and the Khans were the keys to the Professor.

A young couple sat down at the next table and nodded to him; the girl reminding him of Faustino, probably because she was clad in the Arab national dress. He chewed absently on the steak checking his mobile from time to time; the more he thought about Mongolia the more it all fitted together. He would have to get to a land line as soon as possible. The steak was good, the trifle better, and he drank his coffee quickly before making to rise, noticing that the Arab woman had disappeared. "I hope you don't mind me asking, but could you give me the directions to the mosque please?" asked her partner, a tall man clad in a white robe. Oboto shook his head. "Sorry, I'm a visitor myself, try the waiter," he suggested.

"Thank you I will," replied the man turning to go and stumbling slightly against Oboto. "I'm so sorry, my apologies."

"No problem," replied Oboto and called the waiter to sign for the meal. He put on his glasses to read the bill and frowned as the writing became blurred, "I can't read this, is it written in a dialect," he said before suddenly gasping in agony and clutching at his chest. He fell forwards crashing to the floor taking the contents of the table with him. "Well done, Kit," said Kat watching from the reception area. "Mission accomplished."

"Not quite finished yet," corrected Kat her black dyed hair falling in front of her face, "we have another assignment which may not be so easy."

<hr>

Tapiwa parked her hire car in the garage of the Sheraton Hotel acutely conscious that the Staff was in the boot, so she decided play safe and move it to her room. She'd been looking for Doctor Red's house and again had failed to find it; she was now really worried that he was in trouble, even Oboto wasn't answering his phone any more. She had tried both numbers continuously, the only response she'd had was from Oboto. It said simply; *'Sheraton Spa two o'clock'*. She frowned, Oboto had never sent her a text before; perhaps he had mastered the new technology? She doubted it but decided to answer the call anyway. An hour later she made her way down to the Spa, a small confined area with separate access to the outside pool area. Two women attendants looked up expectantly. "Are you here for a massage?" asked one of them. "No thank you," Tapiwa replied, "I'm meeting

228

someone," She looked across to the stairs leading out of the basement up to the pool outside. "Is your name Tapiwa?" the second woman enquired. "Why do you ask?" Her suspicions were now fully aroused.

"We've been expecting you, in here please," gestured the younger of the two. She opened the door to a small room and waved her hand as an indication that Tapira should follow her. Before moving she tried again to call Oboto without success. "Can I ask you to step inside and make yourself comfortable, normal procedure is to remove your clothes except pants, the female masseur will be with you in a couple of minutes?"

"I just told you I didn't book a massage," said Tapiwa firmly.

"Doctor Oboto did it for you; he was very insistent that you would enjoy the relaxation and said that he will be with you very soon as he needs to talk to you," replied the African girl.

"Very well," her suspicions partly allayed, she headed into the room and looked around. It was a normal treatment room with two beds side by side. She stripped to her bra and pants getting under the towel and taking care to keep her knife handy. The door opened and a white female masseur entered. "Are you comfortable?" she asked.

"Yes thank you," said Tapiwa.

"Good then I'll begin."

Years of finely honed instinct for survival saved her from death. She reacted quickly but too late to totally avoid the deadly karate chop across the back of her neck. She groaned and stunned by the pain rolled off the bed cursing in anger as she tried to untangle herself from the sheets. "The staff where is it," hissed Kat surprised how fast the black girl had moved after what should have been a fatal blow. It had been meant to look like a natural death now she was in a fight and she slammed her foot into Tapiwa's back as she scrambled for her knife. Keeping the table between them she staggered up reeling from the pain and thrust out the ceramic knife making Kat step back. "I have no idea what you are talking about," she hissed hefting the knife. "The staff," repeated Kat and knocked on a door behind her, then she suddenly jack-knifed forward slamming the bed hard at Tapiwa's midriff. Bent double Tapiwa waited until the Austrian girl came within her reach and aiming carefully slammed her left fist against her assailant's head. Kat fell back stunned and Tapiwa moved in for the kill, as she did so the door swung open and a man charged in with a knife in his hand. Tapiwa groaned and stepped backwards raising her own knife. This was going to be a fight to the death. She steeled herself and catching Kat by surprise knocked her hard against the wall rendering her partly unconscious. She was briefly neutralised. It gave Tapiwa time and she turned to meet the male attacker head on feinting to her right as he lunged forwards. She parried the strike and nicked the man's arm as she did so drawing blood. She sensed Kat stirring behind her and felt vulnerable; she had foolishly left her rear unprotected. She deflected the next blow from the man, who she now realised was identical in looks to the woman.

She saw Kat trying to clear her head and then felt a sudden pain to her groin as Kit kicked out. She fell to the floor and rolled as a vicious kick aimed at her head missed her by inches and struck out blindly catching Kat a vicious blow to her chest and then spinning to confront Kit. "You have no chance, give us the staff and we'll let you go." Kit snapped eyeing the knife. "You can go to hell," snapped Tapiwa springing to her left to avoid a blow from Kit who was trying to rise from the floor and back into the fight. She caught Kat's blow turned it to her advantage and used a judo throw to catch the girl off balance. Kat went down again. Tapiwa tried to preserve her strength. She was starting to tire badly and knew she would be finished if she couldn't end this soon. Kit snarled at seeing his twin on the floor and kicked out again narrowly missing Tapiwa but then rammed the bed at her again knocking her sideways with a painful blow to the stomach. Tapiwa fell to the floor grimly holding onto her knife and knowing she had to do something or face certain death. "You'll soon join the old man," he snapped circling warily then attacking again. She only had one chance left. As she fell forwards in a feint, Kit grinned and raised his knife and started to bring it down in a killing stroke. Tapiwa, having transferred the knife from her usual right-handed grip, spun to her right and lunged upwards with her left arm using all her remaining strength. The move surprised Kit who had prepared to parry a move from the right. He looked down in surprise as Tapiwa's knife buried itself deep in his chest. He reached down to pull it out and Tapiwa realised she had missed his main artery and desperately looked around for something with which to defend herself. She grabbed the treatment tray and pulled it towards her. Kit took hold of the other side and rammed it against her, pushing her hard against the wall.

She felt the air driven out of her lungs and groaned as she saw his knife rising for the fatal thrust when he suddenly stopped in mid-flight, a look of shock spread across his face and he fell to the floor with a groan. The knife wound must have eventually caused severe internal bleeding, causing him to collapse. Kat rose to her feet murder in her eyes and Tapira roused herself to one more effort, but Kat wasn't attacking she was leaving the scene. Tapiwa tried to follow but tripped over Kit's body and was unable to stop her opponent vanishing through a side door. She picked herself up just as an audible click confirmed the door had been locked from the other side. She looked down dispassionately at Kit; she had seen enough death in her time. Thinking of the Staff, she cursed. Kat would have found her room key in her clothes and would have ransacked her room by the time she managed to get out of here. Grabbing the only item she could see, a white coat she kicked at the door until finally a startled attendant opened it.

Tapiwa ran back to her room knowing she must exit this place as soon as possible. She had no doubt the police would arrive soon. She cursed when she saw the state of her room; the staff was gone and she recalled Kit saying they had taken take care of the old man; had she meant Red or Oboto? She looked down at what was left of her bag, they had ripped it to pieces; fortunately the safe had not been tampered with, her passport and money were safe. Where had Kat gone and where the hell were the Doctors?

She ran to the garage, flung herself into the hire car and drove briskly out of the car park; there were no signs of alarm from the hotel staff and she belatedly realised that the texts she had assumed were from Oboto had actually been sent by the twins. She tried to call Oboto's emergency number but there was no reply. She needed help and there was only one source left. She rang a secret number and told Jade all that had happened in the past few hours. "Leave it with me, Tapiwa;" Jade told her, "I'm sure Oboto and Red are there somewhere."

"But I've lost the Staff." Tapiwa felt she had failed Oboto and was distressed by it.

"Abandon the car and mingle in the streets, that way they'll struggle to track you. Keep on the move; I will call you within the hour." She made her way ever deeper into the crowds feeling safer after her ordeal. She found a suitable coffee shop and ordered a latte taking a seat at the back to observe the street before trying Red again; he still didn't answer. Her phone rang, it was Jade. "I'm sorry Tapiwa I know he meant a great deal to you, but a body has been found in the hotel you mentioned. We believe it's Oboto; he's been poisoned; witnesses say that it was a young couple in Arab clothes."

"The same twins who tried to kill me," Tapiwa told her, devastated that her mentor was dead. He had always seemed indestructible to her.

"Please work to me in future; now, we need to get you out of Uganda. The twins were killers, part of something much bigger and they will come back for you; we have a network that can help you."

"I can take care of myself." averred Tapira, and went on to describe the fight in the spa and confirm she had killed one of the twins.

"This is different," said Jade earnestly. "Others will hunt you, not least of which will be the other twin. You must find Doctor Red; he has the clues we need."

"I will, but this is personal with me now; that bitch that killed Oboto will pay for it."

"Concentrate on finding the directions to the Prophecy, Tapiwa please," Jade instructed her. Her next call was one she had hoped she would never need to make, it was to Faustino. She must now get more involved even though she was a strategist not a foot soldier. It was war now and she would have to take extra precautions with her own personnel. The Professor had captured the fourth Artefact and possibly directions to the Prophecy itself.

Tapiwa returned to the Sheraton Hotel's breakfast area keeping her eyes peeled. She needed to hire another car, pick up her stuff from the hotel and try to find Red at the new address Jade had given her. Time was running out. She hoped Red had found the Prophecy directions and avoided Kat. After many years evading Amin's forces and more recently The Teacher's men, surely he could outwit the blond maniac. She recalled Red telling her there was something much bigger than the Artefact, Amin's own Holy Grail that he had sent his personal Doctor, Nicholas Garrigan, a Scotsman, to find.

She gingerly felt her bruises as she tried to follow the new directions. It was early in the day and she risked using the hire car for the privacy it provided and, of course, the speed. She navigated the roads carefully, trying to find Red's house as the sun began warming the deserted streets. She finally found the address and pulled the car onto the driveway in front of a neighbouring house that looked even more empty and uncared for than the address she had been given. She recalled that Red had told her he had relocated his family to Malawi. From the condition of the other houses she concluded he hadn't been the only one to up sticks and move somewhere safer. She looked around for any signs of life, but there were none.

Her nerves were on a razor's edge as she surveyed the garden looking for anything out of the ordinary. She had little stomach for more fighting and took her time. Finally, sure no one was watching she rang the bell. There was no answer, she looked through the windows but lace netting obstructed her view. She decided to try the back door and walked confidently around the house trying to give the impression she was viewing the property with a view to purchasing it. To her surprise the back door was open and after a moment's hesitation she silently made her way inside, drawing her ceramic knife as she did so.

This side of the house was almost in total darkness with heavy curtains drawn; she moved from room to room listening intently for any movement. Her senses reeled as she heard a scuffling noise, then a grunt. Holding her knife tighter she entered the lounge area and saw a figure slumped on the floor by the window. "Red," she whispered and ran to his side, she cradled his head in her arms and checked his pulse, which was very slow and noted that his breathing was very shallow. He was clearly in great pain and near death. "Who did this to you?" she asked trying to stem the flow of blood from a gaping wound in his chest.

"A blonde woman," he gasped.

"When?"

"Hours' ago, the penalty for what I did for you in Malawi, the Prophecy directions, she has taken them… Not complete….you need to find Amin's secret." His rasping voice was getting weaker. She held his head and gently asked again. "What do you mean not complete and where has she gone?"

"Amin was a tyrant," he croaked, finding it hard to get the words out. "You have to beat her to the Prophecy directions." Tapiwa could hardly hear the words now they were so faint,

"Doctor, you have to tell me where she's gone."

"Idi Amin tried to solve it on his own, saw the chance to make a name for himself internationally."

"The Prophecy," repeated Tapiwa anxious he stayed alive.

"I thought I was helping my family," he gasped "It was a great honour to be chosen to find the Prophecy. It was to be Amin's great success then he sent it away with his Scottish Doctor Garrigan somewhere safe. So safe it has never been found."

"Red you're not making any sense; the girl has the directions."

"She only has the parchment clue to the prophecy directions. Amin took the tablet itself that Marco laid down, which has the detailed directions to the Prophecy. I had to give them to him or my wife would have been killed, God rest her soul."

"Where did Amin take them?"

"Tell you later, my friend said we should take the parchment directions for the staff to Malawi but now it's too late," rambled Red, "He said it was special magic."

"Red help me, I don't understand, what exactly has the girl taken?"

"A parchment with instructions as a puzzle."

"A puzzle? Kat had taken a parchment that detailed how to find Amin's tablet. That in turn would lead to the prophecy. I need directions Red."

"Amin never understood it was a complex puzzle; that's why we had to run when he saw he hadn't got the whole tablet. I have stayed alive waiting for you."

"Please Red tell me where this girl has gone with the parchment."

"She told me she worked with the Elders and wanted to help, she was pretty," he murmured, "Always had a weakness for a pretty girl," he gave a weak smile and fell back against her.

"Where has she gone Red? Tell me." Her voice hardened as she became ever more desperate to trace the girl with the vital parchment. It was clear Red was fading fast and, if he didn't give her the information she needed, life was going to become very difficult. Almost as if he too recognized the importance of giving her what she wanted, he made a supreme effort to tell her. "Amin was a very evil man; I gave him the main tablet, the one they call The Golden Piaza. I had to otherwise he would have killed my wife. He hid it a long way away; I kept directions to it hidden for years, now she has most of them."

"But not all, you said part was missing," she tried to encourage him.

"Ah! Yes, we have a chance. We removed some of the words from the bottom of it; she will never find the exact location without a lot more inside information to enable more accurate calculations. Amin's Scottish doctor, Nicholas Garrigan, went away with the tablet."

"Where has she gone?" asked Tapiwa desperately. The man's voice faded again from exhaustion after the effort of talking; he was still losing blood, a lot of blood. "The Scottish Doctor Garrigan," Tapiwa repeated. "Is that significant?" Red seemed not to understand her question and went off at a tangent. "We got him, you know, hunted the bastard down. He was contrite when he learnt that Amin had killed so many, claimed he didn't know about it, but they all say that don't they?"

"You got the tablet?"

"No, he hid it but we recorded the directions; a deal to preserve the legacy," he whispered, now getting weaker still.

"Please Red, you have to tell me where."

"Do you have a tribe?" Red asked so faintly she wasn't sure she had heard correctly.

"A tribe?"

"A Scottish tribe," whispered Red croaking the words out.

"What do you mean? Listen carefully to me Red, I must know where to find it." She knew she should have called for an ambulance but that would also involve the police.

"*Well of Sighs*," murmured Red, then suddenly he convulsed and fell from her arms onto the floor into the pool of his own blood. She would be getting no more information from him.

"Damn it!" cursed Tapiwa looking around the room. All she had to go on was something called the Well of Sighs and an unnamed 'Scottish tribe'. She erased all traces of her having been in the house then called Jade as she left and relayed Red's words to her before driving for the airport. "It's Scotland," said Jade, "Doctor Nicholas Garrigan came from a town called Ballater in the Highlands; he was talking to you of tribes meaning clans, the Highland clans. Garrigan took the tablet up there and hid it; you have a chance as Kat doesn't know about the *Well of Sighs* piece."

Chapter 29

Panama

Sandy Hogg looked disdainfully at the Colombian rain forest and turned back to the truck, rubbing her stiff limbs. The voyage across the Pacific had been torture; it had become clear Moses had never intended to do anything other than head straight to Panama. Her father had been set up. His involvement in the new partnership had encouraged him to invest heavily, but even he hadn't realised the sheer scale of the shipment. It had quickly become evident the yacht was stuffed with high quality heroin, from bow to stern; even the keel; there was enough to pollute a continent. It was a totally different scenario to anything they had expected; she swore she would have her revenge.

After disposing of the coastguards, Moses had taken control of the yacht and confined the women to a single cabin for most of the voyage; he was power-mad and answered to no one. Ailsa had been useless, sitting on her bed all day crying to the point where Sandy had yelled her lungs out to be allowed to go into a different cabin. Her only hope was the love-struck young Columbian Otway who came to her most nights and let her out of her semi prison. She worked on him as they headed further east. Moses meanwhile, became ever more dictatorial. The crunch came the night Moses demanded she sleep in his bed with him. She played her part with disgust and afterwards gave him a drink spiked with the generator's battery acid. It burned his throat and while he staggered around the cabin Otway rushed in, stabbed him and threw his body overboard.

She easily won over the three crewmen by offering to share the proceeds from the drugs when they docked on the South American coast. Unfortunately events had got out of hand. A drunken member of the crew had tried to rape Ailsa and when she resisted him had strangled her. Otway, who had tried to help her by pulling him off her, lost his temper in the ensuing fight and used his knife again to deadly effect. The remaining two crew members demanded retribution against Otway that Sandy refused to grant and the journey across the vast expanse of the Pacific became fraught with danger for them. After another day of heavy drinking, Otway and Sandy had pounced and shot the two drunken sailors. The large yacht was perfectly capable of sailing itself for long distances by using the autopilot and as they neared Columbia the weather improved greatly. So much so that for the first time Sandy actually began to enjoy herself. She came to some momentous conclusions about the future, being the daughter of Jack Hogg was paying a dividend.

Fortunately Otway was an experienced sailor but it was a long voyage to Columbia. Sandy made repeated attempts to contact her father but only on landing learned he had been killed. The drugs were hers now by right. Her father's legacy and no one was going to take them off her. She would start her own crusade to revenge her father's death. Otway was increasingly treating her as his chattel and she decided that once the drugs were delivered she would fix that situation too.

They moored in the dead of night and Otway paid a local lad to help them load the drugs onto a truck. She was amazed at the amount that came out of the various parts of the vessel: it was an absolute fortune. They drove deep into the Columbian jungle and finally found an abandoned warehouse just over the border from Panama, deep in the rain forest. There was no way they could release this amount of heroin onto the market so Sandy called the contact Moses had spoken to a number of times. She knew the type of person she was dealing with having met them often enough at her father's home. Carefully she laid down her terms, hard cash in non-sequential notes to be handed over at a predetermined time. Her father's estate was worthless; all she had left was this cargo to preserve the Eagle's Nest. That night as Otway writhed in her arms she plunged a short handled knife into his heart pushing him away from her in disgust; he'd been just another pawn that would help her grow richer and richer.

Victor Gonzales cursed aloud as he made his way up to the restaurant overlooking the famous Panama Canal. He was in big trouble and had to act fast or not only would the Professor be after him, but so would half the drug warlords in Latin America. That bastard Moses had got greedy; he should never have relied on the half-breed but there had been no time to get anyone else. Recent government crack-downs had drastically reduced drug shipments from established sources, hence the idea to bring them in from Australasia. He had organised the huge heroin shipment for the Latin American phase of Project Contagion, grateful that the monetary risk lay with someone else. Still it was now his responsibility and he knew the certain penalty for failure was death. When the call had come from a woman called Sandy, he had cursed long and hard. She was an unknown quantity and therefore hard to predict. His phone rang again. It was an unknown caller, and he walked over to the window unaware of a small unobtrusive man fiddling with listening apparatus at the door. "When and where," he snapped.

"Meet me alone at the deserted farm on the following coordinates. It's deserted so I will see if you have company a mile off. Bring two million dollars in cash at midnight and you will get the merchandise."

"I need time for that sort of money."

"Midnight or I go elsewhere and the deal is off."

"Shit," snarled Victor to no one in particular as the phone went dead. He clicked his fingers at his assistant to try and get a trace, but his phone rang again. "You are ready to launch?" asked Giovanni.

"Providing we can get the delivery through Mexico."

"Mexico will not be a problem. I take it you have the drugs?"

"As I told you yesterday there's a small problem. The Hogg girl has them but tonight they will be under my control. He tried to sound confident but the situation was far from resolved and he knew it. "Resolve it Victor, don't give me problems," Giovanni's voice remained even. "Too much planning has gone into this operation to mess it up now; so, no problems only solutions Victor. Use the Aruba rebels."

"The distribution routes are all set. I will retrieve the goods using the locals. I can't trust the Arubans too much after our abortive coup."

"Both routes must work Victor. Make sure they do and the Canal will close?"

"The Americans have a large base just across the road from here next to the United Nations building; once we act the Canal will close."

"No more mistakes!" Giovanni slammed the phone down and called Grasshopper on the barge. "Are you in position?"

"In ten hours," replied the ex-policeman sweating in the heat and cursing the lack of air-conditioning on the barge.

"Make sure you take control when they arrive," snapped Giovanni putting down the phone; a couple more calls then he would see to Lorna.

<hr>

Sandy, a changed woman since the killings, looked around at the jungle clearance. She was now on a mission and determined to succeed. The old truck took her to the rendezvous she'd described to Victor. He'd agreed to her terms one of which was that he should be alone when they met, even so she didn't trust him. She was right not to. She could see a car full of armed men waiting for her. She parked the truck, opened the tailgate and a few minutes later climbed back into the driver's seat then drove slowly forward to meet the car. Two men got out and came towards her. "Open the truck," ordered the man nearest her window. "First the money," she demanded. "Here," snapped Victor throwing a briefcase at her feet, "it's in American dollars as you stipulated, now the merchandise."

"Help yourself," replied Sandy calmly, taking the case. Victor vanished behind the truck and she heard him whistle in amazement at the sheer bulk of the consignment. She grabbed the case and ran off into the forest along a pre-determined escape route, praying no one would come after her and that she hadn't mistimed it. She ran on hoping to God the motorbike she had hidden was still where she'd left it. What on earth was taking so long with the explosion? Had she made a mistake? She groaned as a man shouted, then just as he raised his rifle the world exploded and she was thrown down by the force of the blast. Picking herself up she looked at the scene and smiled grimly; she had done it, bodies were scattered everywhere. She had enough to start a new life and offered a silent prayer to the skies before finding the motorcycle and riding off towards a new life; old Hogg would have been proud of her.

Chapter 30

All the populated islands of the Seychelles lay a few degrees south of the Equator rising from shallow banks as huge granite rocks. The small rugged island of Ascension rises steeply out of the water with little or no beach. As a consequence it has rarely been inhabited. Lying a little to the south of Cap Temoy off the Port Launey Marine Park, it covers an area of sixty hectares and lies within easy reach of the Island of Mahe, the largest in the Archipelago. Its inaccessible nature was exactly suited to Giovanni's needs. He chuckled as he thought of the Elders still trying to find Fabrizio; his assumed name and one around which he had laid a complex web. There was another more profound reason why his headquarters were here. His illustrious ancestor had hidden his greatest secret on this island. Peaceful and deserted with only the occasional bird watcher looking for a rare species called the Seychelles 'White Eye;' it was a haven of tranquillity.

The island could be accessed from the sea via a small, lower level promontory but Giovanni had effectively camouflaged it; only the local people knew of it. He had long ago made an arrangement with the Seychelles Government that ensured his presence on the island was a secret in return for substantial donations to local charities; some of which also went into private bank balances. It was an arrangement that suited all parties on an island relying heavily on tourism for its revenues. A potential problem for Giovanni had been the newly developed major tourist resort of Constance Ephelia on the mainland, but again planning restrictions had ensured that no one could overlook his island. Indeed the only people that could see his home were those perched in exclusive private villas, the richest of the rich and they had little interest in the comings and goings of others. The only outward signs of his presence were the central buildings. They occasionally showed through the tree canopy when the wind blew in a certain direction and lifted the covering of natural foliage.

Secrecy was precious to him as it had always been with the

Calvi's and until The Teacher had fouled up in Mongolia he had prided himself on being known to very few. It was a significant achievement and he delighted in being able to join groups like the Elders under an assumed name without arousing suspicion. Unfortunately that had now changed due to his emergence to oversee the final stages of his lifelong plan, soon to explode onto the world stage. He gazed through the darkened glass window of his private room above the main lounge; it gave almost three hundred degree visibility of the sea beyond the roof of his mansion, a building covered in thatch making it extremely hard to spot by passing planes or helicopters. A secret underground tunnel took him down to the waterfront through password controlled gates, guarded day and night. The single helicopter landing pad was hidden by trees that were torqued outward by steel cables on winches to reveal a small landing area that reverted to upright once the helicopter was in its hidden parking area. In the inlet area a small lift took visitors up to his mansion in total secrecy. Constance Ephelia caused problems when they introduced their own helicopter service for wealthy guests but appropriate words in the right places ensured they never flew over the island.

Ascension Island was one of the most westerly in the Seychelles chain. He had considered colonising the most westerly - Conception Island, but discounted it as being too visible. His was far better hidden and, of all one hundred and twenty five islands, the one Marco Polo had chosen. He'd spent decades researching the *'Marco legacy'* as he called it and the more he discovered, the more excited he became. He set out to make a fortune through drugs and arms deals in Africa in order that he could pursue their Prophecy. It had become both his obsession and his life's work. It had led him to La Gomera and the discovery that a German Count, Von Steppenhof, had found a reference to something Marco had hidden in Africa. It linked to documents he had found here on the island and convinced him that what he sought was truly significant. Marco had talked about it with great reverence but even he hadn't known its true nature.

To execute his plan he had recruited Zheng Wan, ironically at an Elders' gathering. He had recognised a fellow visionary and from there the big plot had begun. He used his Elders' role to allow him to understand their legacy and power whilst linking closely with The Teacher. Always staying in the background, he recalled vividly the day the two of them had clandestinely hatched their plot, scheming to get the Artefacts, peeling away the layers of the onion to find the Prophecy. Even after recruiting Stig Oleson, Lorna's father, he had continued to play a remote role, cells within cells. He had created the ZTW conglomerate using Zheng's own initial in its title to deflect attention from the real puppet master. Now the time had arrived. The final plan was ready including the Contagion Project; it was so close he could almost feel it. All he needed was the fourth Artefact and he had just been told even that was now in sight.

From his window he observed the daily tourist fishing trips. It amused him to think of the tourists relaxing on their holidays totally unaware that under their very noses significant events were being masterminded. From his main viewing platform he could often see the stars unhindered by man's artificial light and he could easily believe that he was master of all he surveyed. He employed a small permanent staff. Two old servants, his new henchman an ex-policeman, and a bodyguard bruiser. Unmarried he would occasionally acquire one of the rich unattached tourists or pay for a professional courtesan to travel from Europe. Now there would be no quarter given as he entered the final stages of his master plan. He looked at the documents in his hand and smiled, imagining the consternation in the capitals of the two most powerful countries outside America. With what would undoubtedly be the greatest secret the modern world would ever know almost in his hands, and the Chinese and Russian governments already making noises of concern, he was feeding the diplomatic channels with Mongolian proclamations.

His plan was simple. Steady pressure and events that would confuse and distract the attention of both nations from his real ambition. He knew how they worked, cumbersome autocracies that moved like large, aged elephants whilst he darted around them and pulled off the most audacious of coups. Both governments had been informed that Shaka wished to renegotiate common boundaries based on historical precedent. Predictably the Chinese had dismissed the whole thing as a hoax but they would soon realise what a ghastly error they had made, whilst the Russians would need different treatment. He picked up the latest draft communique.

'Mongolia calls upon the Russian and Chinese authorities to recognise Mongolia's historic and rightful claims to lands currently under their administration. The Khan's holy lands in the north east and the historic city of Xanadu, home of the great Khan Kublai, full recompense will be made for the value of the lands for the rightful return of ethnic Mongolians to their homeland.'

There was no doubt it would cause serious consternation when released to the world's media. There was a risk in playing for such high stakes but he believed world opinion would side as it always did with the underdog, in this case Mongolia. It didn't really matter. Shaka was expendable and Giovanni would be long gone by the time the subterfuge was discovered. He smiled to himself and told his bodyguard to send the message to Shaka, There came a knock on the door,

"Come in." he said.

"You called for me," the fat ex-policeman was sweating profusely as he entered and waddled across in his ill-fitting guard's uniform. "The bulk carrier is near at hand; it's time to head down to the capital with the cargo on the barge."

"Good! Just do it, Pollard."

"I won't let you down," replied the man; those who knew him called Grasshopper, Guy's old adversary. He'd been at death's door for many weeks after being shot and left for dead in the Caribbean, but he had slowly recovered from the three bullet wounds. He was a man on a mission and during his recovery had much time to plan his revenge on Guy Tresanton. He'd been after him since the arrogant bastard had seduced his daughter. The chase had eventually culminated in him being shot by Jem, niece of Chief Inspector Monty, Guy's colleague. Recuperating, he had regained his full strength by languishing in various dives in Aruba until contacted by Stig Oleson who offered him a new opportunity. Here he had an absolute fortune and enjoyed every minute; his revenge would be so sweet. The Professor had given him a new start and a job that played to his organisational strengths. He had been part of the original plot to kidnap Rose and had done his best with his Caribbean contacts to incarcerate Tresanton; unfortunately the man had escaped, but not the next time. He, Grasshopper, would make damn sure of that.

He clicked his tongue in anticipation as he thought of the exact nature of the torture he would inflict on Tresanton; that clicking had spawned his nickname as a rookie cop. Tresanton would die only one way, slowly and at his hands; it was his destiny. He flew across the island he called home and boarded the large industrial barge owned by ZTW and registered in Angola. On this voyage it didn't carry the usual cargo of metals but a huge collection of drugs. Now, thanks to that bastard Tresanton he was running drugs on a scale far surpassing anything he'd ever seen. He grinned to himself as he looked around the old barge, a wreck that had been used to carry silt deposits away from the newly built millionaire's marina next to Seychelles International Airport. When the Professor's plans came to fruition he'd be able to afford one of those places. He checked the sailing times and called his assistants to tell them to prepare for payday.

Chapter 31

China
Yunnan Province

Zie Lao received his final instructions in silence and signalled the trucks to pull out. Since helping the Austrian twins with the destruction of the holding compound, he'd been on a high. He was proud to be part of this great venture despite Zheng's demise. He was annoyed at been unable to finish off Zichu Ling but Jack Tresanton would have to do. The best of the original compound's followers were with him, the rest little more than naive kids and were disposable fodder. His close friendship with Else at ZTW had alerted him to the switch in power and, like her, he was a survivor, switching sides effortlessly to oversee the movement of the components for Project Contagion to the Chinese border.

"All is ready Professor," he reported smugly.

"Good," replied Giovanni repeating the instructions he had just given to Victor. "Zie, this work will be recognised and I want you to work especially closely with Else on a major new assignment."

"Glad to serve you, Professor. Do you have the destination coordinates for me?"

"Take note," said Giovanni reeling off a set of numbers.

"I will not let you down," said Zie moving back to the trucks. He was totally committed to the programme for a very special reason; the fourth sleeper was his only son, Charles Lao. He was a strong-willed boy who was ready to start his role as transport head of the local Communist Party in Yunnan province in the town of Kunming. The post had been bought for him after a lot of favours had been called in. The area was remote from the central Chinese Communist Party hierarchy and therefore easier to manipulate. Once in position he would authorize the rapid movement of the drugs deeper into China. He'd been assured in an earlier conversation his son was ready for the assignment and that meant Jack Tresanton's usefulness was over.

Jack almost felt sorry for the young man and was suffering mental turmoil as he'd prepared his next steps time and again.

The youngster was a fanatic with a burning will to succeed that made him dangerous. He was Jack's most successful sleeper, learning from the mistakes of the others. "I just need to spend a last few minutes with him before we proceed," Jack told Zie and gestured to Charles to come with him into the school house he'd seen earlier. Jack saw the young man's excited face and recalled the extensive rehearsals that had gone into the role he had been given as a naturalised Chinese. It was on the surface convincing but not sufficient to stand a great deal of scrutiny. Tonight Charles would take control of the local party transport division with authority over all shipments across the State, ready to give the necessary commands. It was a masterpiece of planning and Jack had tried desperately to avoid doing what he had to do now, but there was no alternative. Instead he concentrated his mind on the thousands of kids whose lives could be ruined by what they carried in those trucks.

Mongol Province
Daguurin

As the train rattled on into the night heading south east towards Vladivostok, Guy tried to relax. It wasn't easy as Sergei was on edge, constantly scanning their fellow passengers and not his usual garrulous self. Timut was also agitated and his fears were justified when the train began to slow down. "We shouldn't be slowing here," whispered Sergei looking out of the window. "What's the problem?" he called out to a passing guard.

"Problem on the line, we'll clear it soon."

"We need to get to the border quickly, so make sure you do," growled Sergei, Timut stood up.

"Where are you going?" Sergei asked him.

"To make sure it's what he says it is; I don't like it."

"Very well," agreed Sergei, he leaned back into his seat and lit a cigar. Ten minutes later soldiers appeared and headed straight for Guy and Sergei.

"You come with us please," said their leader.

"I'm a Russian national, I have immunity," snapped Sergei. The soldier was unimpressed with Sergei's credentials. "Come," he repeated and raised his gun. They had no option but to do as they were ordered and followed their captors from the train to a car waiting by the trackside. Already in the front seat was a frightened looking Timut; they were ushered into the back and told to be quiet. Two minutes later the door opened again and the familiar figure of Shaka mocked them. "You're totally naive if you think I would let you go, Rostov, there's far too much at stake for that."

"This is not a sensible move, Shaka, you should know me better than to think you can get away with this sort of action; you will regret making it. Most would have heeded the veiled threat in Sergei's tone but not Shaka.

"I don't think so," he replied confidently. "It's my country and my train set and you are helping a convicted man to escape. What more reason do I need to arrest you? Now I have something to show you."

"I'm, not interested in anything you have to show me; I am a Russian citizen and I demand my rights," snapped Sergei. "In my land you have no rights," Shaka told him. He ordered the driver to move off and the other guard to tape their mouths and handcuff them. Guy looked around in despair, so near and yet so far. They drove for nearly an hour into increasingly hilly and mountainous country and finally onto a dirt track where they stopped. It looked like a one-way ticket to nowhere. "Get out," ordered Shaka. They did so and were led across a field to a hill they were told was called Burkham Khaldum. "This was the Great Khan's favourite place," Shaka said whilst gesturing to the guard to remove their gags and handcuffs. "We are north of his homeland, the place he grew up and in my opinion, where he is buried. I'll show you what Zheng Wan found…this way." They skirted the hill and entered a small valley, at the end of which was a cavern; the moon giving enough light to reveal a ghostly outline.

Guy was unable to contain his patience any longer. "Where are you taking us?" he demanded. "You won't get away with kidnapping; this is the twenty-first century for God's sake." He spoke with more confidence than he actually felt. Again Shaka gave a wide grin.

"You underestimate me," he said. "The report will say you all just disappeared whilst on a walking tour in Mongolia; tragic but these things happen. Your blonde friend has gone with Sabine and an even worse fate is waiting for her. She fought valiantly but lost; she is now my possession."

The news was so devastating that they all were stunned into silence; it seemed they were all to perish as a result of this ill-fated quest. "Into the cavern please," said Shaka, "He was clearly enjoying their discomfort. You can see the seams of rhodium. See how it gets steadily more yellow as it goes deeper in. The metallurgists say it is unique for rhodium to be so yellow."

"Is this the place where the Artefacts were made and the Prophecy lies?" asked Guy.

"That was Zheng's mistake. He underestimated Kublai's cunning just as you foreigners underestimate the ability of us Mongolians. Kublai knew this place would be found and made no attempt to hide it. A deliberately misleading trail that Zheng thought contained the tomb. What you have here is a very valuable piece of real estate with the world's largest quantities of this precious metal; that's all though. No question of a tomb."

"Then why have you brought us here?" asked Sergei.

"It's your personal legacy; you will join Zheng in a never-ending quest for the truth and no one will ever find you. All very apt and tidy I think."

"In other words you're going to kill us in cold blood," snapped Sergei.

"No of course not, that would be too obvious. In any case, I don't need to do anything to you; the cave will do the job for me once the mouth is sealed; don't worry you will get a great obituary in the paper, Sergei, amidst the warnings about the dangers of coming out here without the appropriate guides. I want it to act as a deterrent to others. No one but us knows this place exists so you will never be found. Poetic justice to be buried with Zheng, don't you think?"

"You're a madman," interrupted Timut his eyes blazing with fury.

"I had forgotten about you; we have a different end in mind in your case, you get special treatment," replied Shaka. "The metal lodes at the front of the cavern are invaluable so in time we will extract them but the rest of the cavern will be sealed off. So gentlemen, it's time for you to be left to your own Gods. Zheng's body is over there. If you do come out my men will shoot you in the stomach; that will give you a long slow death." He turned and gestured to the guards to follow him.

Guy looked at Sergei. "We're really in trouble," he grated.

"Doesn't look too good I must confess," replied the Russian. "Still we have to try something - what the hell...." His face widened in shock as a distant rumble became a roar and the whole world seemed to explode about them, the blast blowing them off their feet. "What's this?" yelled Shaka, now covered in blood. The front of the cave had collapsed. "Guards get me out of here," he shouted. There was pandemonium as his guards switched on their torches and ran towards what had been the mouth of the cave; they were greeted by a wall of rock and debris that blocked the entire entrance. "Looks like you've been out-maneuvered," said Sergei coldly.

"Guards shoot them," yelled Shaka hysterically, pointing to Guy and Sergei. As the soldier raised his gun a new sound erupted around them and Guy saw Shaka collapse in a hail of bullets. "Get down," he yelled. "They're bloody machine guns," he fell to the ground and through the gloom saw Timut fall. Covered in dust and grime he crawled across the floor trying to find cover before ending up next to Sergei. There was no way out, they were pinned down in a cul-de-sac with machine guns systematically raking the area, bullets ricocheted off the walls. Guy looked up and saw a maniacal figure standing on the top of the rubble indiscriminately spraying the area with bullets. Was he about to die in this Godforsaken place? He crouched behind a large boulder and hoped, but not for long. He felt the impact of something heavy hit the back of his head and everything went black.

He opened his eyes slowly, unsure how long he'd been unconscious, he tried to raise his head. He was in his own version of hell with bodies all around and a feeling of being unable to move. He tried hard to breathe normally but at first choked and then began retching violently; feeling pain in every part of his body. He shouted loudly but there was no response. He couldn't see anything and fumbled around for the torch he recalled Shaka had carried. It took him a while but eventually his fingers found it and he switched it on, trying to ignore Shaka's body. He looked around; he could see nothing but dead bodies. He felt a slight movement beside him. "Sergei wake up," he urged trying to wake the Russian. After a few minutes Sergei opened his eyes. "My bloody head, what the hell happened?"

"It was a trap that Shaka didn't reckon on and we got caught as well." Guy pointed to the President's dead body next to Timut. "The fact they made sure those two were dead and didn't get us makes me think it was them not us they were looking for; their dead bodies saved us, ironic I guess."

"Shaka would not see the irony," observed Sergei standing with difficulty.

"We need to get out of here in case they come back."

"You're right," mumbled Sergei wobbling a little. "I need to get a mobile signal and call some of my men."

"The machine gun fire came after the explosion so there must be a way through over the rubble," said Guy pointing to the huge pile of rocks. "Are you hurt?"

"Not as far as I can tell," replied Sergei. He picked up his mobile and brushed the dust from it.

"Come on then, we must get out quickly; it'll be a tough climb over the rubble but I reckon we can do it," said Guy.

They scrambled out on hands and knees dreading to hear the click of a machine gun but the place was empty. They saw chunks of Rhodium in the dust as they climbed. "Look up there," said Guy as they reached the summit. "See the cartridges; this is where they sprayed the place from."

"We were lucky," observed Sergei.

"We were," agreed Guy "The fact we were furthest in probably helped." He peered through what was left of the entrance and called over his shoulder. "I can see enough space even for you to get through and there's no sign of anyone so let's go."

"Easy for you to say," grumbled Sergei trying to force his vast bulk through the gap.

"Come on, I'll pull you through." It was getting light as they finally scrambled through and down the other side looking around warily. "Whoever did this will just open another seam into the cave for the rhodium."

"It has to be the damned Professor," snapped Sergei lifting his mobile and confirming a signal. "No one else knew the cave was there; he sent his people to do the dirty work."

"But why get rid of the President after he signed their leases?" queried Guy.

"Perhaps he was trying to double cross him and Sabine threatened revenge. I wonder also whether this Professor is trying to ingratiate himself with some of my more unscrupulous Russian colleagues; they were concerned about Shaka's plans so it wouldn't surprise me."

"Who is that?" asked Guy pointing to the fallen figure of Jacques Savior.

"Who knows; maybe they'll place all the blame on him," replied Sergei lifting his mobile and trying to shake the dust out of his now not so white beard.

"Can we get to Russia from here?" asked Guy looking around at the wilderness that greeted them; they were well and truly isolated.

"Just spoke to my men. They will be here soon, let's start walking I want to get away from this damned tomb as quickly as possible in case they come back," snapped Sergei striding out northwards.

Else Chan was very pleased as she flew back to Vietnam with Tan Lie, one of her aides at ZTW. She had been disappointed that Zie Lao had disappeared from contact and put it down to the Professor's obsession with separate cells acting independently. Her excursion to Mongolia had succeeded beyond her greatest expectations and they were ready to move to the final stage having dumped Jacques Savior's body at the blast site. She had contacted the media with the story that their Chief Executive had been kidnapped three days ago. She had also seen the Russians on the Mongolian border about access rights, pleasantly surprised that the way had been paved for them. She had planned the cave explosion with the collusion of various disaffected factions that Sabine had nurtured. She found the myriad of Mongolian political parties confusing but no shortage of those willing to do anything for money and the chance to get rid of the President. The temporary President Baku would do as he was told and more importantly turn a blind eye to the events that were unfolding, all part of the Professor's insurance plan triggered by Sabine's return.

She made sure Tan set off back to ZTW headquarters to await instructions for the final assault; all she had to do now was oversee the final arrangements. The only thing concerning her was the loss of contact with Zie, she had never trusted the British Doctor.

"You've done brilliantly, Else; well done to you and the team." Giovanni was generous with his praises. The news from Mongolia reporting the death of a disgruntled former employee, Jacques Savior, who had been trying to destroy ZTW, and the President of Mongolia was the sort of news that pleased him beyond words. At a stroke Else had solved all his problems. Shaka had served his purpose and he, Giovanni, would now present himself to the Russians as the man who stopped the idiotic President Shaka. He had already made contact with Moscow.

The Chinese though, would require a different approach. He rubbed his hands with glee at the news that Sergei Rostov and Guy Tresanton had been in the tunnel at the same time. The way was now clear for ZTW to move into the northernmost areas of Mongolia with Baku, the acting President, a far more malleable character and someone they had groomed for the role of Shaka's successor. Everything now depended on speed and that meant the Prophecy directions which, according to Kat, she had just acquired along with the Confucius Staff. He had all four Artefacts stored in his underground site, their inscriptions decoded, just waiting for the final set of directions to the Prophecy. Survival of the strongest was his motto and that of his illustrious ancestor, Marco Polo; his family destiny was to take back what was rightfully theirs. Marco's legacy was his legacy, only the Elders now stood in the way of his reclaiming his inheritance.

He turned from the window looked at some pictures of the beautiful Artefacts, realising that the last person to have seen all four together would have been Kublai Khan himself, just prior to launching the Great Quest. He marvelled at the thought and planning that had gone into them. To others they were just a row of expensive looking items, to him a subtle message on Kublai's own philosophy of leadership and rule. The Cross and the Shield indicated the defensive foundations of any leadership; a core ability to lead without being defeated meant understanding one's own defences intimately. The Axe symbolized naked power that could not be challenged and finally the Staff which Giovanni knew would be Kublai's own dictum. After all, his grandfather Genghis had ruled by the Axe, and Kublai the Staff, building real foundations behind Genghis's achievements. He also realised the puzzle could only be solved by having all four in sequence; the scientists had explained to him that without the sequence they would not have been able to decipher the codes. Masterful, he was a true messiah and one whose management of the Khan's Legacy would lead to its final elevation in the affairs of men; of that Giovanni was convinced. He rubbed his hands in glee and called to Gerd for a stiff drink.

The last piece of the jigsaw for him was his ultimate need for an heir and he went through to the guest bedroom. On the bed lay the prostrate body of Lorna. He had done a deal with her father; a deal he intended would be honoured. If she didn't like it she would have to get over it. Through him she would achieve much more than her father had ever done; she was a lucky girl whom Stig had bequeathed to him. All perfectly legal, the wedding ceremony had been conducted by a Minister and he smiled as he looked down on his wife; his Empress in the New World. It would lead to heirs that would continue the Marco Polo heritage.

Chapter 32

Ballater, Scotland

Tapiwa arrived at Aberdeen Airport in sleeting rain, shivering as she made her way across the open tarmac to the terminal building. Jade had told her to wait for instructions on her arrival. After a lifetime in the tropics, the north was a shock to the senses. She drew her light jacket closer around her neck still feeling aches and pains from the fight but reassured her ceramic knife was still sheathed and intact. Doctor Red had been trying to tell her something more. She was sure of it and she had spent the flight trying to figure out what it could have been. She passed through passport control and hired a Renault Clio taking the road to Ballater trying to get used to driving on the left hand side of the road. She received a text from Jade and made her way south west down into Royal Deeside. She was beginning to feel very tired and, seeing a small café turned into the car park at the side just as her mobile rang. "We have confirmation that a girl fitting Kat's description hired a car and asked for directions to Craigendarroch Hilton at Ballater. She wasn't alone."

"Who was with her?"

"A man, that's all we know. Tapiwa hang in there, let me know how you get on," Jade rang off and Tapiwa entered the café and ordered a coffee. The rain started to fall heavily restricting visibility as she drove on, an abundance of flowers in the small villages lightening the scene. Finally as the rain eased she took the tight turn up to the hotel and, every nerve alert, entered the reception area not relishing another encounter with Kat. She booked a room at the same time enquiring about a fictitious blond girl friend. Unsurprisingly there was no blonde booked in. She proceeded to check the hotel out carefully starting with the crowded pool area to the right of the hotel reception.

She found nothing of interest, perhaps the Austrian had moved on already. So with time to kill and on the spur of the moment Tapiwa decided to use the Jacuzzi and stripped to her swim suit with the ever present ceramic knife tucked inside. She sank into the warm waters relishing its soothing effect on her aching muscles. For the first time since landing she relaxed and closed her eyes. Seconds later an unseen force forced her under the surface causing all her aches and pains to protest and her senses spin. A hand pressed hard and she fought for air, her survival instinct kicking in. She swivelled her head found a finger and bit down hard feeling the salty taste of blood. The pressure eased and gasping for breath she leaped from the bath turning to meet a heavily built East European man. She screamed to attract attention as the man started towards her. The door opened and a lifeguard came in with a puzzled look on his face as she staggered across still gasping for breath.

"What's the problem?" he asked her.

"That man over there attacked me," she gasped.

"There's no one else here ma'am." He was right, her attacker had vanished.

"Can someone help me back to my room," she gasped donning a robe and feeling all the old aches and pains return.

In a secluded corner of the reception area Kat was questioning a man called Gustav.

"Is the bitch dead?" she demanded to know.

"No, not this time. My bloody finger! She nearly severed it." He waved his damaged hand in the air, a bandage covered in blood showing his distress.

"You failed!" Kat was unsympathetic. "You better leave her to me. You need to get in position before the next surveillance round."

"I want that bitch," he mumbled.

"Forget it, Gustav; you've got a far more important job."

Tapiwa, having been escorted to her room by the attendant from Jacuzzi, was recovering fast. He was concerned for the reputation of the hotel. "Ma'am, we need to report this to the police if you were attacked," he said.

"It's nothing really. I must have slipped and banged my head. I've been struggling with jet lag. Can you get me a bandage," replied Tapiwa not wanting the complication.

"If you're sure," he conceded guiding her carefully to her door. As she passed the main entrance she had spotted Kat arguing with her attacker and was sure she heard the words *special target tomorrow*.

Kat cursed as she drove away: she had to move on. She had been sorely tempted to extract revenge on that bitch Tapiwa for the death of her brother and to hell with the mission, but discipline held her back. She'd left Uganda half crazed with grief but slowly sanity had prevailed. She dispatched the Staff through a UPS delivery to the Professor and was now focused on the big one. Killing the doctor in Uganda had made her feel better, finishing off Tapiwa would be personal. She checked her notes on the directions she had taken from Red having only discovered the day before that the bastard had removed key words at the bottom of the parchment.

Meanwhile, Tapiwa sat in her room, her head aching from a combination of the attacks here and in Uganda. She didn't feel safe here, slowly she pulled on her clothes and grimaced as she walked down the very old circular sweeping staircase to the exit. Looking across to the car park she froze. There was something moving in the trees. Looking closer, her instincts screaming, she saw the unmistakable glint of a rifle barrel…Gustav. He was waiting for her, she was trapped. Her survival instinct again kicked in; reaching the fourth from bottom step she gave a loud groan and fell forward. Her ruse worked, hotel staff rushed to her aid, an ambulance was summoned and she was whisked away from danger in minutes.

"Mild concussion and shock," said the nurse, as her eyes opened, "you've been in the wars."

"Where am I?"

"Aberdeen infirmary."

"I need to make a call on my mobile."

"In the corridor please, we don't allow it in here." Tapiwa went into the corridor and made her report to Jade. "You say she was expecting you?" asked Jade, concern evident in her voice.

"Possibly, I don't know, I overheard them say there's a '*special target tomorrow*,'" replied Tapiwa after explaining how she had escaped.

"Get some rest," advised Jade. She was sure matters were reaching a climax and she needed all the help she could get. She'd even asked Emerald to take leave from her day job. "Hopefully I will have some good news soon," she said and rang off."

Tapiwa took her advice and slept deeply for twelve hours. She was eating Scotch porridge when she was interrupted. "You have a visitor," the hotel waiter told her. "It's six in the morning, I don't want to see anyone," she replied fearfully thinking of

Gustav. "It's your Malawi bodyguard," came a familiar voice and Guy walked into the room. "I gather you've had a bruising time again."

"Guy, thank God you're here, I thought you were in Asia."

"Long story," said Guy sitting down and giving her a brief outline of what had happened with Sergei Rostov in Mongolia and elsewhere. "And I thought I was the only one in the firing line," she said with grin.

"Bring me up to speed, Tapiwa, what's happening here?"

"How did you know I was here?"

"Jade," grinned Guy. "After she got me out of Mongolia she sent me here to help you. It's a bit colder here than in Malawi; thank God you're not underwater."

"I nearly was yesterday but managed to escape on my own this time. You're becoming the veritable white knight in shining armour."

"We need to move on, we're sitting targets here." Guy brought them back to the matter in hand.

"I agree," said Tapiwa explaining she wasn't ill, she'd just feigned illness to get past Gustav. "*Special target tomorrow*," mused Guy as Tapiwa described the conversation she'd overheard. "That means today!"

"Maybe the target is a diversionary attack?"

"He's a killer and you don't bring them in for a side show; got assassin written all over him and I've seen a few in my time."

"Who would be a special target up here?" asked Guy.

"No idea."

"Why employ a professional assassin," reflected Guy, "a demonstration of some sort?"

"But why here?"

"This Professor is taking on two of the world's most powerful nations, Russia and China; perhaps he wants to include Britain, perhaps a link to Hong Kong or opium smuggling?"

"Hong Kong's a long way from Mongolia," observed Tapiwa as they headed to Guy's hire car.

"Perhaps he just wants to humble the British. Anyway, it's time we got on the road to Ballater. I always think better when I'm moving and the adrenalin is kicking in; something might occur to us as we drive." Guy was impatient and wanted to get things moving.

"Jade mentioned to me that the clan's main areas are north of here up towards Inverness."

"They're everywhere Tapiwa, not just one location but north of here too. Tell me again what Red said to you."

"Tribes and Scotland and there was something else, the *Well of Sighs*."

"Could be a place name," reflected Guy.

"Maybe I misheard; his breathing was very faint by that point."

"Clans," said Guy as he took the Deeside road. "The battle at Culloden was their last stand against the English. Bonny Prince Charlie had taken the Highland clans all the way down to Derby to defeat the English and was then forced all the way back here, and perhaps Amin saw that as prophetic."

"And the special target?"

"There's something about this area that's nagging at me," said Guy stopping the car to reset the sat nav.

"The flowers by the road here - are they always out in the villages?" asked Tapiwa.

"What? Flowers?" He thought it was an odd time to be discussing flowers. Perhaps she had suffered a blow on the head or something. "

"I noticed earlier every village down to Ballater has lots of flowers along the roads; it all looks so pretty," she said.

"My God, what an idiot!" shouted Guy, banging the dashboard, "The damned flowers only come out when they have a very special visitor every summer as regular as clockwork."

"Who is it?" asked Tapiwa?

"The Queen, she is the *special target*. Balmoral is just down the road from here. Every August without fail the Queen is here. What could be easier for an assassin than a regular schedule! I need to call Monty." He began tapping the numbers on his mobile furiously.

Monty was alarmed by the news, "I'll notify the Aberdeen police and Special Branch if you're absolutely sure of this," he snapped, "They'll know how to handle it."

"It's too much of a coincidence. We can't take chances and we've little time," Guy insisted.

"Certainly the words *special target* resonate. *The Queen goes to Crathie Church every Sunday morning at eleven o'clock, two hours from now.*

We always have a maximum security regime for that."

"You're joking."

"Afraid not, regular as clockwork, goes every Sunday. It's a security nightmare, not only a very public place but a regular routine that she won't change."

"So they mean to shoot the Queen and then head up north to get the Prophecy. Perhaps the Professor will claim it's a warning to others of what he can do."

"More than likely," agreed Monty becoming increasingly alarmed. "Get down there as quick as you can with Tapiwa; she can identify the assassin."

Guy drove along the Highland road at a maniacal speed and finally screeched to a halt at the church parking area in front of startled spectators. He was quickly surrounded by a small police contingent; the Aberdeen Police did overtime to guard the Queen when she ventured off the Balmoral estate; her own protection officers looked after her on the estate itself. The Aberdeen men looked out of their depth as they heard the news being given them through their closed circuit mobiles, but to Guy's relief he saw a tough-looking professional soldier who seemed to be taking charge. "There's no room here for bloody amateurs," snapped the Major.

"We raised the alarm; my colleague can identify the potential assassin," Guy told him.

"I will vouch for them," came the familiar voice of Monty, "By God that was some journey in the helicopter."

"Right but don't get in my way," snapped Major Tower. "You're both under my orders now. Understand?"

"Of course," replied Tapiwa and Guy together.

"If there is a sniper, he'll be hidden in the undergrowth up there," said Tower pointing to the north behind the church. "That's the only high ground with a suitable line of sight as she comes out of the car and walks across to the church. There's no cover on the south side of the road and most of it is the Balmoral estate anyway."

"Perhaps," mused Guy looking closely at the small peaceful Crathie Church, he pointed at Tapiwa, "This lady has seen the man. Can you get a sketch done?"

"Do it," snapped Tower gesturing to an officer.

"He's possibly been up there all night," said Guy taking

binoculars and scanning the hillside deep in thought. Why on earth was this Professor interested in shooting the British Monarch?"

"What do you think, is he still there?" asked Monty looking anxiously up the slopes.

"Wish I knew; guess I'll be in serious trouble if this is a fake alarm," Guy added ruefully.

"Ways and means, but you'd probably have to disappear outside the Commonwealth for a little while unless you fancy the Tower," smiled Monty looking around and chewing his pipe thoughtfully.

"Can we stop her?"

"Special Services personnel are carefully combing the area as we speak with heat seeking equipment. I'm afraid there is nothing I can do without a red alert to stop or even delay the convoy."

"All for the sake of a church service!" commented Guy disbelievingly.

"It's far more than that. If she bowed to every security alert we get, she'd never go anywhere."

"I can't believe it."

"We can't bow to terrorist's pressure every time or they would win," said Monty grimly.

"What about inside the church?" asked Guy "Is it possible for someone to get in there before everyone else?"

"It's been searched and cordoned off for the ceremony," said Tower.

"This is madness," Guy burst out in frustration.

"Go and check it yourself. We'll start searching the hill with the equipment," said Tower scrambling to the south bank and starting to do a circuit of the area using his military binoculars to sweep across the hillside.

"Where the hell is he?" Guy mused; the church was clear; had he got it totally wrong?

"Just heard on the radio. We have ten minutes," snapped Tower, "See, over there, that's the High Sheriff of Deeside," he pointed to a distinguished looking man in traditional costume standing in the front of the group. Here she comes. That's her Range Rover in the middle of the three."

"Oh my God," shouted Guy suddenly spotting a glint of reflected sunlight in the hill behind the church. "He's up there with a long distance rifle, I can see him," he shouted.

"Stop the cars," snapped Tower galvanized into action and running towards the mountainside yelling into his radio.

"He's raising his rifle," shouted Guy as he saw the convoy of cars stop just below the church. He heard a popping noise and recognised the spiteful crack of a rifle. He ran towards the stricken Range Rovers, their blacked out windows looking sinister. To his horror he saw the middle vehicle's windscreen was smashed. A police support vehicle screeched to a halt beside it, the door opened and a figure hustled out. Another car screeched across the road blocking general access as sightseers looked on, wondering what on earth was happening. Guy thought he saw someone carried into another car and then he saw the blood. He reached the Range Rover and saw Towers covered in blood. Next to him lay the Queen's Lady-in-Waiting. "Poor woman is dead," said Tower, "Shot through the throat at that range; must be a professional."

"He didn't mean to get the Queen at all," said Guy looking thoughtfully around. "But why this lady?"

"Oh my God," shouted Tapiwa as she saw something on the car floor, "her handbag, inside there a brooch, it says Fortaleza on it."

"What," said Guy, puzzled, then he saw the item.

"The small brooch, I've seen her before at the Elders, this was no accident," said Guy quietly, "This is Jade's right hand lady, Emerald."

"Make way," said Tower directing the ambulance through, his men stewarding the crowds away and explaining that it had been a dry run for the real thing only and that they were to disperse; the last thing they wanted was a rumour getting out that the Queen had been shot. A helicopter swooped down to land next to him. "The official line is that the Queen's driver suffered a seizure during an exercise, got it?" he shouted at Guy. "The Queen is all right and has returned to Balmoral, I am sure you all understand." Guy nodded, "Understood," he replied. He walked away from the scene thinking furiously, ignoring the sightseer's curious gaze. He had a call to make. "Emerald?" said Jade quietly. "My rock and also the Queen's private secretary. How on earth had the Professor discovered her true identity?"

"A leak?" ventured Guy.

"Yes, we have a mole," acknowledged Jade quietly; she was overcome with the news.

"But why shoot her?"

"Because she knew who the mole was. She was leaving the Queen's service next week and told me she knew."

"Kat intended this as a diversion," said Guy understanding suddenly.

"My right hand support gone and a significant diversion to stop us," agreed Jade.

"I need to go," said Guy as Towers came across.

"Who are you talking to?" snapped Tower striding over.

"A friend of the deceased," Guy said sharply.

"Stick to the script."

"Of course, what's happened about the assassin?"

"Disguised as a bloody policeman. We got him and thanks for the warning; shame it never officially happened."

"You killed him?"

"Three shots to the head."

"Anyone else up there?"

"No, just a very dead Russian."

"I'd like to see him."

"Guess you've earned the right. Come on, we'll go in the helicopter."

Gustav was lying face down in the heather with policemen standing guard all around him. Guy and Tapiwa clambered across, both being buffeted by the downdraft from the rotors. "Couldn't take any chances," explained Tower. "Who the hell is he?"

"It's a long story," said Guy as Tapiwa confirmed it was the same man who had assaulted her. "Best that Monty explains. He must have had a call sign to let his controller know that the mission was successful."

Guy looked around in the bracken but there was little to be seen. "Anything on the body?" he asked.

"Nothing at all," Tower said dejectedly.

"So, how did he confirm the kill?"

"I don't know. There's nothing on him to give us a lead. We'll need to properly scan the area; now you'll both need to leave."

"Over there in the heather," Guy had noticed something reflecting the sunlight. Tower took a plastic bag from his pocket and gingerly picked up a mobile phone. He held it at arm's length as if expecting it would bite him. "A mobile, but no battery, must have got rid of it before we shot him. It's dead, and he's deliberately broken it so there's no connection to his controller."

"Guess so," replied Guy looking closer at the mangled device.

"Sir! Over here!" shouted one of the men, "there's a number in ink on his forearm, like a prisoner's number."

"Well done man," said Tower looking down at the number, "16041745. Check it out," he ordered.

Monty and Guy sat on the church wall mulling over events. "Well done Guy," said Monty. "Didn't save Emerald," said Guy sadly.

"Perhaps not but we have a lead."

"It's only a number, Monty?"

"The experts say it's not a dialling code, it goes nowhere and we've tried every combination possible."

"He must have memorized the report call number," said Guy looking puzzled. "What's its significance?" he wondered as Tapiwa suddenly jumped up excitedly. "Of course," she shouted, "it's a date you're both too focused on the phone number when it's simply the long form for a date, 16th April 1745. I'm willing to bet Gustav wrote it down as code; all we need to work out is its connection."

"My God, you may be right," replied Monty.

"Of course," smiled Guy, its right under our noses, "We discussed it earlier, Tapiwa, everyone up here knows the significance of that date, the last major battle on British soil, Culloden."

Chapter 33

Fortaleza Hidalgo

Jade was stunned. First Oboto and now Emerald. She looked up as Amethyst came in with a stiff scotch. "What's going to happen next, Amethyst?" she asked sadly. "We must find the mole; two people have lost their lives already."

"I'll find them," replied Amethyst grimily. "Emerald shared some ideas. I'll piece it together."

"Thank you; looks like it's just the two of us now."

"Can I suggest we use Sergei more; he's reliable?"

"You're right, he saved Guy."

"Can I also suggest it's time to tell Guy the truth?"

"Too early for that; we have to be ready for the future." Emerald bowed her head and left Jade to mourn alone.

Jade gazed across the valley feeling desperately sad that her key friend and ally, Emerald, was dead after helping her unstintingly for over twenty years. As a personal aide to the Queen she had been able to help the Elders in many ways without betraying any confidences, and doing a remarkable job. How on earth had the Professor unearthed her and who the hell was he to have that sort of influence? No one but her innermost circle would have known Emerald's secret identity. She walked along the ancient corridors trying to overcome her grief; she had no choice but to call an extraordinary meeting of the Elders to seek guidance and authority for the battles ahead. It was now far beyond the guerrilla tactics of Guy, Rose and Tapiwa. They were all vulnerable to attack even here in her peaceful haven. She had wondered whether there would ever be an attack on the monastery and dismissed such an idea but now she wasn't so sure. It was absolutely imperative that they found the mole.

She hauled her mind back to immediate problems and prepared herself mentally for the next task. Oboto's Deputy, Faustino Asprillo, had been with them for about five years and had proved a reliable supporter though more passive than Oboto. Always in a hurry, she was no more than someone to provide cover; Emerald would handle the details. Faustino would make sure the board was controlled and that was all she needed while she directed her energies towards finding that damned mole. She strongly suspected it was one of the monks or nuns with access to the archives; the monastery had always been open to all religions as a haven from persecution and had built up a mixed set of nationalities and races. She recognised most of them by sight but knew only Francesco and a few of the nuns well. There was about thirty in total. All had been here for some time which made it unlikely they had been turned against the Elders, but who else was there except cleaning staff and administrators, besides Amethyst and herself.

"Jade, I think you ought to see this," said Amethyst.

"What is it?"

"The committee's notes on the two new members from Spain and Italy who didn't come to the meeting when The Teacher was expelled; the Spaniard checked out okay but the Italian Fabrizio didn't. With help from Sergei and Interpol we finally tracked this elusive man down. He had evaded all our initial checks last year and I can tell you he won't be coming back; his real name is Giovanni Calvi. He disappeared from the face of the earth two years ago."

"Why didn't our initial search team pick this up?"

"Because his credentials passed every check until now. I'm sure Giovanni is this Professor; it all fits with recent events as he was close to Zheng."

"My God, the damage he may have done having access to the monastery," shuddered Jade.

"This Giovanni would have had direct contact here with the mole, as would The Teacher."

"So if we examine CCTV footage we may be able to find something."

"Won't it take a while?"

"No, I found a notebook in Emerald's room; she had narrowed the mole down to four names."

"Tell me," said Jade excitedly.

"Fernandez, a monk called Jansen, and two nuns called Charlotte and Silve. Apparently all four were in the vaults when Zheng and Giovanni were last here. That's when they found out about the German Count."

"I can't believe it's Fernandez; he has ancestors going back centuries here."

"I'll check them all out; Charlotte and Silve always helped me but that means nothing."

"And Jansen?"

"A surly fellow who spends a lot of time on his own; old school monk," said Amethyst.

Jade waited until all the members were seated and then opened the meeting by saying, "Fellow Elders I have sad news. Our former Italian member, Fabrizio, or rather I should call him by his correct name, Giovanni Calvi, has betrayed us. He penetrated our organisation to benefit his own ends and with Zheng, proved to be the ultimate perpetrator of all we have been fighting against. Even sadder, is the loss of Emerald who was killed by an agent of Fabrizio. It is an insight into the dangers we face and I think you may be at personal risk since he knows you all."

"Very disconcerting news. It raises personal security questions for us all," commented Stanton."

"You are not direct targets," interjected Faustino standing up. "I do believe we have a good chance of winning this fight providing we act decisively. However, no one should be under any illusion that we are safe here."

"Seems like we have little choice," said Stanton.

"We are where we are and our mission to find the Khan's prophecy has been compromised as Giovanni has now acquired the fourth Artefact. Only the Prophecy itself remains out of his reach and we have people out there trying to stop him."

"How can we help then?" asked Stanton

"We agreed a while ago to create a meltdown of ZTW stock which occurred until they withdrew from the stock exchange. Giovanni appears to have unlimited private funding."

"But we have stopped the flow of funds to this empire," said Stanton, "ZTW has cash flow issues. I am also aware that their Vice President, a Frenchman, has recently left the group."

"It's a great example of the Elders working together. However it's not enough as Giovanni is planning something bigger."

"What do you mean," asked Stanton.

"We only know it has the working title 'Contagion Project' and that he has staff on three continents."

"Contagion sounds like nuclear or drugs," speculated Stanton.

"Possibly, so you can see how urgent this has become,"

replied Jade.

"Jade is right, said Faustino, "This threatens to damage us all. We have engaged with Interpol but we need every ounce of help we can get."

"We should confront him; spur him into action," said Stanton.

"Admirable thought but we don't know where he is and we have no proof," replied Jade. "Aside from some tenuous links to Zheng's death, we have nothing."

"Your people in the field, are they up to this challenge?" asked Stanton.

"They have proven their worth a number of times and in fact they are all that is keeping us on his tail at present, even if we wanted to engage others we have no time," said Jade looking around the room.

"So we're permanently on the defensive," observed Stanton.

"Perhaps but we have some progress; there was a pivotal event at the end of the previous century when this very island was attacked and the fate of the Elders hung on a challenge football match, of all things. The attendees included a German contingent led by a Count Von Steppenhof from their East African empire in Tanganyika. He knew the Confucius Staff Artefact had been located in Kenya; our agent tracked down the Staff from this lead."

"The one we've lost to this Giovanni?" asked Stanton.

"Unfortunately, yes."

"Where exactly is this Prophecy?" asked Stanton

"We're not sure; it's the big question."

"So what do you want us to do?" asked Stanton.

"I have various tasks," replied Jade seeing the mood change and grateful she would get support.

Deep in the bowels of Fortaleza the two cowled figures made their way into a small room. "It's over, our work is done; it's too dangerous to go on now," said the monk. "We have done our duty and can go in the knowledge we served our ancestors properly."

"Innocent people have died over what we did," said the nun quietly. "I never intended it to be like this."

"Emerald would have exposed us before we were ready; she had to be terminated."

"You may feel that is right but I find it hard to live with the consequences."

"I can understand that," replied the monk, "But we must be strong."

"We have to do the honourable thing," said the nun rising with determination. "My conscience has to be clear, I am going to pray."

Jade received her visitor in the main hall; she had received the news of his arrival with pleasant surprise. "Sergei, good to see you, come on in. You must be tired after the long journey."

"I'm not as young as I once was. My recent escapade didn't help much either," replied the avuncular Russian entering the main lounge. "First time I've been here outside of a meeting."

"To what do we owe the pleasure?" she asked and, before he could reply, added, "Thanks for saving Guy?"

"He probably did as much to save me; I came to talk about the Prophecy."

"We need all the information we can get about that," she said with feeling.

"Which is why I am here. We need to find a way of stopping what Giovanni is doing in Mongolia. Huge tracts of land have been bought there by his company, ZTW. I'm sure they launched the attack on us and killed both Zheng and Shaka."

"How can we help?"

"I think I can help you. I've some information that will help you trace those leaks."

"You know who it is?" asked Jade.

"When I worked for Zheng, he gave me a contact place."

"Who was it?"

"Well, it wasn't so much who as where actually. It was down in the monastery. Didn't see their faces because of the cowls, but if you call them all into this room, I might recognise their voices," said Sergei. Jade acted immediately and summoned all the monks and nuns to attend her in her room in groups of four. She watched silently as the last group came into the room, a frightened looking Fernandez, Jansen and the two nuns Charlotte and Silve, all looking petrified. "I am one of the Elders," Sergei began as he had with all the previous groups. "One of you met me with Zheng, about two months ago and gave specific information on a Staff linked to Count Steppenhof. I will recognise the one I met, do I have to point you out or will you declare yourself?"

"Enough," said Jensen stepping forward. "I'm not ashamed to admit that it was me," he said, looking defiant.

"For pity's sake why?" asked Jade, "because of what you have done many people have died or been injured. You were trusted to work here and help us."

"Zheng was our leader, a man of vision, his grandfather a true visionary and you betrayed them," snapped Jensen. "He recruited me to lead his campaign; he was good to me and my family."

"Fact is you've caused countless deaths," snapped Sergei.

"You will not defeat Giovanni. He is blessed by the Venetians; his mission to reclaim what is rightfully his is just and proper . We are his people and believe in him absolutely."

"We?" queried Jade. "There are others too?"

"Yes, I also am part of Giovanni's extended family," said Silve standing up equally defiant. "We are from Venice and are proud of our Medici heritage. You will not stop the Polo and Calvi families from claiming their true destiny."

"My God!" exclaimed Jade. "Both of you planted here and we didn't suspect."

"We have been here for over a decade; our devotion gave Zheng the idea for his own sleeper programme. We are proud of it."

"And Emerald, why kill her?"

"She was going to expose us and our families in Venice. That couldn't be allowed," said Jansen. "We were placed here to succeed; no one person's life matters."

"To achieve what," asked Jade.

"The success of our heritage. We don't expect you to understand."

"Are there others?" asked Jade watching them closely.

"No there's just us," said Silve.

"What do we do with you?"

"No one can do anything with us; we are outside your control."

"You're wrong there," thundered Sergei, "I think at the present moment you are very much under our control."

"Only we control our true destiny," snapped Jansen. "That time has come. You will never defeat Giovanni."

"Oh yes we will; we know he's in the Seychelles," replied Jade.

"No one knows where he lives," said Jensen coldly though the slight frown on his face told Jade what she wanted to know. "The time has come for us." With surprising speed the two rushed across to the panoramic window, pushed the side section wide open and before anyone could comprehend what was happening and with an expression of serenity on their faces, they both leaped through the gaping space they had created to fall hundreds of feet to their deaths.

Chapter 34

Culloden

The light was fading on a bleak and drizzly day as Guy and Tapiwa drove the direct route north from Balmoral, a hair-raising drive through the Cairngorm Highlands on single track roads. Two and a half hours later they joined the faster A9 and headed directly to Inverness. Despite aches from her injuries, Tapiwa marvelled at the dramatic mountain scenery. The Culloden clue was a long shot, but all they had to go on. Monty had stayed behind at Balmoral to tie up the loose ends. Guy had been warned not to take precipitate action but felt he didn't have the luxury of due process; there would be time for explanations later. They drove in silence towards the Highland town and stopped at a small café on the outskirts of Inverness with the Culloden Battlefield signposted ten minutes away through a housing estate. To their right lay the dramatic Moray Firth. "Any more thoughts on Kat?" asked Guy as he guided the car along the difficult roads.

"A psychopath pure and simple. Incidentally the Staff I saw had Chinese characters on it like map references."

"Map references of a location in Mongolia I would guess," said Guy thoughtfully. "Best I go first; she won't recognise me, blond-haired you say?"

"She was blond when I first saw her but brunette at Ballater so she's likely to have changed her appearance again. Some place for a battlefield, the views are astounding," murmured Tapiwa looking around and feeling the bitter chill in the air as they drove up onto the moor.

"Stay in the car and keep in contact through the mobiles," said Guy as he parked in the Visitors' Centre.

"Why is Culloden so special?" asked Tapiwa.

"It was the end of the Jacobite rebellion and Catholic claims to Britain. As for the battle, like most iconic events it was little more than a series of confusing and violent clashes, total confusion and horrendous mistakes. Both commanders were in their early forties. Cumberland commanding the English forces had celebrated his birthday the night before and the Highlanders, led by Bonnie Prince Charlie, thought to strike at the English camp that evening whilst their enemy was celebrating. Good idea in principle but they got lost on the moors and arrived back at the battlefield with no sleep or food, begging the Prince for a day to recover. He ignored them, insisting he was invincible, and decided to charge across the boggy ground. The superior English forces stopped the Highland charge with a disciplined rifle volley. Their battalions lined up in three ranks and as there was no protection on the field it broke their resistance on the left flank. When the English cavalry came through the stone walls that had been dismantled by sappers, it turned into a rout and the Prince fled with the help of one Flora Macdonald, end of history lesson."

"How very romantic," enthused Tapiwa.

"She disguised him as a woman to get across the northern lochs to an escape ship. Hardly romantic, but it depends on your viewpoint." Tapiwa grinned, "Hell of a way to run a revolution," she said, then added, "It's an eerie place, this," and shivered, though not with cold.

"You can almost sense the ghosts," agreed Guy. "Now stay here and watch my back while I check it out." He made his way into the impressive Visitor's Centre, where names dedicated to people who had contributed financially to the site, stared down at him from the ceiling. He looked around carefully at the few visitors remaining noting that closing time would be in half an hour. He went through to the display area, intrigued by the moving image display of the battle. From the first Scottish attack, the resulting skirmishes and the entire battle had only lasted an hour. One hour that had left a legacy and everlasting effect on the Highlands. The brutal land clearances that followed were carried out by the man who had won the battle, the Duke of Cumberland, the King's son.

Guy searched diligently for a young woman fitting Tapiwa's description but found no trace of her. Either she was exploring the huge battlefield or had already been there and gone. He refused to accept the latter and hoped to God he was in the right place as he wracked his brains as to where the Prophecy might be located.

Clans and a phrase '*Well of Sighs*' was all they had. He recalled the Jacobean rebellion had been all about uniting the clans, though there were more Scots on the English side than on their own; the clan system split the country, being seen as more important than country of birth. It was the same with the tribes in Africa. The Mongols too originally grew from tribes. It all had a poetic resonance to it and he wondered if there was a master somewhere pulling the strings on the thousand year picture. He went over to the long list of clans on the wall and on the way called Tapiwa on his mobile phone. "Which clan did Amin's doctor belong to, the one who brought the tablet here?" he asked her.

"No idea but I saw clan books on Red's floor, as I told you," she replied.

"Think Tapiwa, which one is it; it's important?"

"Something about a coat, Macintosh!"

"Macintosh, that's what all this is about. Garrigan brought the Prophecy here, as his gift."

"Surely Amin wouldn't have allowed him to do that?"

"Probably didn't know or had other things to worry about by then. Did you see the film, 'Last King of Scotland?'"

"No."

"I'm sure of it; the Macintosh clan comes from this region, and I saw it on the wall. Garrigan brought the tablet, possibly for sentimental reasons, Red got the directions from him, so it must be here. I've got to get out to the field; the Macintosh clan had their own area in the attack, one of the wings."

Guy grabbed a handset so he could appear as innocuous as possible and feigned interest in the taped voice while his eyes searched the field trying to identify anything unusual. The lines of fluttering flags denoting the formation of the two armies and showing their exact positions at engagement created a very weird atmosphere in the fading light, as he listened to the guide. The hairs on his neck stood up as he heard the heroic but ill-fated Highland Charge on the damp morning of the battle. Suddenly his phone startled him out of his reverie with a text message from Tapiwa. *'Garrigan Clan Chatten.'*

As he gazed at the text the voice on the machine informed him that Clan Chatten, a member of the Macintosh Clan, had originated locally and led the ill-fated left wing charge across the boggy land. Of all the clans they had suffered the worst losses as their left flank was obliterated by ranks of red coated riflemen. Quickly he made his way across the field and found the very area in which they'd fallen. It was marked by stones and memorials. If his supposition was correct, the Prophecy lay in this area, but where? He saw a large stone marked with words that said a Macintosh clan leader had been killed there, a place of clan mourning. What better place to hide the prophecy than under sacrosanct grave stones? He also saw an imitation stone well nearby, the *Well of Sighs*, what did it mean?

He stood in front of the large headstone with the Mackintosh name on it shuddering in the cold as doubt assailed him. Was he leading everyone on a wild goose chase? So far he had seen nothing to indicate anything untoward and no sign of Kat. Was he letting his imagination perform flights of fantasy? Perhaps the whole Culloden idea was wrong? A wild goose chase while both Lorna and Rose were in trouble needing help? He drove the thoughts from his head and looked desperately for anything resembling a clue, a sign. He was now on his own as the last of the visitors had gone. He wondered if someone would come to look for him; it wouldn't be difficult for him to hide out here in the undulating landscape. He stared hard at the headstone imagining how the man must have fought desperately as he saw his entire clan being wiped out.

His heart leaped as he saw some recently disturbed earth. Bingo! He looked around; Kat had been here either last night or early morning and must have run out of time as the park reopened. That meant she was here somewhere waiting until the place closed. Even better she hadn't found what she was looking for, the real *Well of Sighs*. Instinctively he ducked down and surveyed the area carefully, avoiding a warden crossing the heather checking that the place was empty. He looked around in the gloom and nearly fifty feet away he saw it, a well standing proud of the rocks. He scrambled across and almost shouted in triumph, the *Well of Sighs*. It had to be and even better Kat hadn't found it. He noticed the warden peering through the gloom, but it was only a cursory check. Guy ducked out of sight behind the well noting there was only one building in the vicinity, a semi-derelict cottage about twenty metres away. A light drizzle started as he scanned the scene. Where the hell was she? The dying sun sent a ray of sunshine across the field and then he saw it, just for a millisecond, a metallic glint in the dying afternoon sun. He fell to the ground and crawled forwards very carefully. He could now see a rifle protruding from the window. Had she seen him? The building was undergoing renovation; it had scaffolding all around it like a second skin. There was a way to surprise her.

He again felt the eeriness of the place, as if a thousand ghosts were moving around observing his every move. He wondered where Kat had parked her transport, and then saw a movement by the side wall; he shivered and watched, waiting for Kat to show her hand. He was beginning to wonder after five minutes whether he had imagined the whole thing when at last a black-haired girl emerged. He ducked down but it was too late; she had seen him and lifted her gun. "Gustav is dead, give yourself up." he yelled, then dropped to the ground and rolled away from the well, grateful for the protection of the boulders around him. He flinched as a shot rang out kicking up dirt a little way away from him. She clearly had an idea of his position. "There are police surrounding the site, so give yourself up," he shouted but received no reply. He cursed as shots came closer and he scrambled backwards as yet another rang out; he was a sitting duck and he cursed himself for lack of preparation. She would hunt him down when she discovered he wasn't armed. He had to move fast. He took a chance after the next shot and scrambled up running to the field as fast as he could. He reached the stone wall before diving over as splinters of stone flew up. Two more shots followed but he had survived for now and he skirted the edge of the field confident she wasn't following him. He made his way back to Tapiwa. "Guy what's going on, I heard shots?"

"That bitch is here alright, hair dyed, she has a rifle."

"We should call the police; you haven't a chance out there."

"Call Monty, let him know what's going on." Then added, "she's close to the wall; it's actually a real stone *Well of Sighs* about a metre high. As soon as Kat spots it, she's found the Prophecy. We need to move fast. Besides how on earth could we explain all this? He thought through the situation. "She will be trying to find the Prophecy so will be distracted, and I'm pretty sure she is on her own. I know where the well is and she doesn't so that's another reason to go back."

"Guy she's got a bloody high-powered rifle and you have nothing except an injured back-up woman."

"I have the advantage of surprise and the fact I know exactly where she will be digging; I can catch her out."

"She's a trained killer, I need to help you."

"Get Monty and ask him to get support here as fast as possible. I need to make sure she doesn't get away. It bothers me how she plans to get away, probably in a helicopter."

"You need me out there Guy."

"No you're not fit enough to start rushing around yet." said Guy climbing out of the car and heading back out onto the lonely moor.

He felt as if he was walking in the footsteps of the young English soldiers who had trudged that way two hundred years before. They were facing an unbeaten army of frightening reputation that had wreaked havoc across the North of England and Scotland before retreating back here to their stronghold. He gave a wide berth to the field on his left and approached from the north, the very point where he now knew the Macintosh Clan's doomed left wing had fallen to the English volleys. It had been the end of a dream for the Highlanders, and if he wasn't careful the end of his own dreams too. He was alone on a killing field against a high powered rifle in the hands of a trained assassin. It was getting colder and he shivered involuntarily, imagining the ghosts of over a thousand Highlanders who had lost their lives here. He hoped his name wouldn't be added to the casualties. Crouching behind a low stone wall he shone a small flashlight and scanned his guidebook; the disturbed memorial was about thirty metres to his left as he made his way carefully forwards to the '*Well of Sighs*'. Kat was digging in the wrong place.

It was now almost pitch black and he could see lights sparkling off the Moray Firth. He shivered again as a biting, cold wind swept across the field. Keeping his head down, he shuffled carefully towards the *Well of Sighs*'. It was slow, laborious work and he cursed the all-pervading Scottish dampness that penetrated his clothing. Moving slowly he saw the Well and a natural hiding place to its side behind a pile of rocks. He crouched down rubbing his hands to keep them warm. He'd decided to surprise Kat; he couldn't risk starting to dig on his own. He lay down pulling his coat tighter to his neck and hoping that Tapiwa would realise what he was doing. He received a text from her saying that reinforcements were on their way. All he had to do was keep Kat pinned down.

The wind howled as it passed through the headstones and

whistled around his ears as he pulled the coat tighter to his neck. He had never been so cold; his very bones were chilled in the bitter wind. He must have dozed slightly when a noise startled him and he heard a grunt and the sound of a spade hitting the earth. She was here at the '*Well of Sighs*' the right location. Kat had clearly realised her error and found it quicker than he had expected. The Well, at nearly three feet high, was no more than an ornament so she wouldn't have far to dig. He kept his head down until he was certain it was Kat then raised himself out of the indentation. A brief shaft of moonlight between passing clouds showed her silhouette. It was his only chance, shuffling forwards in the wet grass he saw her busily digging to the side of the well her rifle lay to one side. Could he risk grabbing for it? He discounted the idea; he wouldn't get five paces before she detected him.

Rain now started to fall compounding his misery but at least it would drown any noise he made, whilst Kat would find it harder to dig. He saw her stop digging and shine a powerful light into the hole then, quite suddenly, panned it in his direction. Guy pushed himself down into the turf and watched as Kat reached down into the well. He had to do something. He moved forwards unable to breathe as she started to dig again squeezing herself into the narrow space inside the well. Guy was transfixed wondering if the object they had scoured the globe for lay here. He noticed a powerful communications handset on the grass next to Kat, undoubtedly for summoning back up. He thought about risking a charge, the rifle his target and tensed ready to jump into action when he heard a metallic clang followed by a grunt of satisfaction. With Kat engrossed in the find, Guy jumped to his feet and ran forwards. The moonlight was sufficient to show an opened metal box and a parchment of old leather in Kat's hands.

He lunged for the rifle as Kat swung around at incredible speed, Guy cried out in pain his left hand nicked by a bullet. She was holding a small Walther PPK pistol. "Kick the rifle over," she snapped raising her phone. "You know; I give you credit for perseverance, I thought the mortar had got you."

"No! You only killed some innocent youngsters." She noted the contempt in his voice.

"Yes, that was regrettable but it was a business transaction; these things happen."

"The Prophecy, have you found it?" asked Guy desperately trying to think of a way to escape.

"Yes, it was simply a process of elimination; the Macintosh site, that fool in Uganda missed off the Well." Guy tried another way to keep her talking. "Gustav is dead," he told her. She seemed unmoved. "As planned," she answered laconically. Guy tried again. "Why the attack?" he asked. She reacted irritably. "You know the answer to that damn fool question. Tresanton, don't think I will fall for your delaying tactics, a chopper will be here in five minutes."

"Where are you going?"

"No business of yours."

"The Prophecy is just a set of directions?"

"You will never know. Just another death on a battlefield," snapped Kat grabbing the rifle. "Always have back up, first rule of combat." She stood squarely in front of him and took aim at his head.

"The Professor is using you," he said, desperately trying to divert her attention.

"Of course he is; it's a business transaction, no more no less, five minutes and I will be on my way out of this Godforsaken place. It reminds me too much of Austria on a bad day. I hope you won't take this personally," she said and smiled. Guy couldn't think of anything more personal than someone shooting him. He looked up grimly realizing that he was going to die on this bleak moor. As if in slow motion he saw the rifle and braced himself; his damaged left hand was already screaming in pain. His eyes closed and then opened to see Kat with a surprised look on her face slowly collapse forwards with a knife protruding from her chest. Guy fell backwards and lay flat, relieved and delighted to feel the rain on his face. He was still alive!

A slight figure emerged from behind one of the larger gravestones. "Good job I ignored your advice," said Tapiwa grimly and checked that Kat was dead.

"Thank God you did," breathed Guy looking up her.

"Her or you; it was a simple choice," replied Tapiwa looking dispassionately at the dead girl. "She looks so bloody innocent in death, yet she killed Oboto and Red. Is the Prophecy here?"

"It's in the metal box. I saw her reading a parchment," said Guy. He rose rather unsteadily to his feet and walked over to the well, reached inside it and lifted the old leather parchment gingerly from the metal box in which it had lain for so long. "Just think how many people have died and suffered to possess this piece of history," he said sadly.

"Yes but we need to get out of here before the chopper arrives or we'll be joining them."

"What about the body?"

"She's got good company; she can spend eternity walking with the dead on Britain's last major battle field," she said without the slightest trace of remorse.

"Monty's only about ten minutes away by car now," she added.

Guy was studying the parchment. "We already have the tablet Kat stole from Red and now we have these parchments. Both are almost impossible to decipher; looks like a map of a large cavern with different coloured metals inside." He looked at them again. At last they had the very thing that would stop the Professor in his tracks. It contained many strange words probably in Mongolian Uighur script. The diagram had numbers that could be dimensions and, in the centre, the words 'Great Khan' in English.

"It has to be the tomb of Genghis Khan," said Guy. "He would have been buried along with valuable jewels; the script on the bottom is different."

"Doesn't look much like it, though it's very well preserved."

"Amin must have realised its importance; a key to untold riches and power," said Guy, "both the Mongol riches and the location of the Khan's sacred tomb."

"How do the Artefacts fit into this?" asked Tapiwa.

"They're the entry tickets to the game. It's like a jigsaw. All four are needed. Notice on the parchment right at the bottom. It's as if words have been deliberately removed, not a phrase like Red did with the other parchment; a set of words."

"The final lines to deter all but the most determined."

"More little twists."

"Kublai Khan, how does he fit in?" asked Tapiwa stretching her legs in the car. Guy had the engine running to warm them both as they sat there on the moor feeling like the only people on the planet. "I can only assume he devised this great puzzle to avoid years of Mongol infighting over what was the ultimate legacy."

"And Admiral Zheng He, what part did he play? Oboto told me he was one of the founders of the Elders."

"I don't know for certain, but assume he was instructed to hide the Artefacts. That way, Kublai would reason, his great secret was protected from falling into one person's hand."

"This Teacher and the Professor, how did they find out?" Tapiwa was finding the whole story fascinating and couldn't stop shooting question after question at Guy in the hope of discovering more. He shrugged his shoulders. "Lot of questions and most of them I can't answer, but I intend to find out," replied Guy. "At last we have something the Professor wants. I'm sure he has the Staff and the other three Artefacts by now."

"Why don't we just go direct to Mongolia with this?"

"The story is incomplete. We would have no idea where to start, that's why the whole package is so important, and all we have here is a cavern somewhere in the remote Mongolian steppes miles from anywhere…Where the hell is Monty?"

"He'll be here soon, what's the significance of the cavern?"

"They are thought to be caverns of gold. In Coleridge's poem about Xanadu he writes of possibly the biggest gold deposits known to man."

"Gold and other metals?"

"Possibly other metals more valuable than gold, after all the intrinsic value of any item is only what people will pay for it. But I'm guessing it all comes down to scarcity. For instance to put it in perspective, they say that all the world's discovered gold would fill no more than twenty Olympic sized swimming pools. Perhaps this cavern will add a few more swimming pools but I think the Artefacts are comprised of a different precious metal."

"So what do we do now?" asked Tapiwa.

"Negotiate, we have something to bargain with now, but let's get away from here, it's beginning to give me the creeps. Thought I could hear something over there," said Guy turning in his seat, "Shit, it's the damned helicopter coming for Kat; we need to get out of here." He engaged the gears and turned the car around as an intense light from above approached them at speed. "We can't outrun him," groaned Guy. "We'll make a run for it," he shouted and stabbed his foot onto the accelerator.

The car hurtled off down the approach track. "Keep your head down," He advised Tapiwa. "Guy, they'll shoot us, he's coming down," gasped Tapiwa as the helicopter banked and a figure holding a gun jumped out onto the road in front of them. Guy slammed on the brakes and went into a spinning reverse as bullets sprayed around the car. "Keep your head down," yelled Guy. The car's tyres screamed in protest as the gunman ran back to the chopper and with incredible speed it started to lift away, a machine gun poking out of the cockpit. "On the floor," he yelled as bullets again raked the car but fortunately narrowly missing them. Guy breathed a sigh of relief as two police cars sped up behind them lights blazing. Seeing them, the helicopter rapidly increased torque and lifted into the air as the police cars screeched to a halt.

"You arrived just in time as always," gasped Guy as Monty joined them.

"Got here as quick as I could, damn slow roads. Did you get the Prophecy?"

"Not quite but we have final directions to it and Kat is dead," replied Guy climbing out of the car. "We spent so long looking at the damned thing the chopper nearly got us."

"The bitch deserved what she got; left a trail of bodies across Europe and Vietnam so she'll not be missed and the helicopter will be intercepted."

"Do you know where this Professor is?"

"No, but we're making progress; Jade has deciphered a document in the cellars from a Count Von Steppenhof. His document was the one that originally told us about the Confucius Staff being in Kenya."

"So what does it mean?" asked Tapiwa.

"Jade thinks the Professor and Marco Polo are linked."

"Marco Polo was with Kublai Khan, wasn't he?" said Tapiwa.

"Yes, the Von Steppenhof document indicates East Africa is the key and specifically identifies a location he believes Marco Polo visited."

"Where's that?" asked Guy expectantly.

"It's one of a hundred and twenty islands in a group called the Seychelles Archipelago."

"Seychelles," smiled Tapiwa, "Close to Kenya and the Confucius Staff.

———————————

The tall, strongly built man stared hard as the cars left the tourist centre and put his binoculars back into their holder. So it was over. He walked to his Range Rover and climbed in activating the hands free system of his mobile as he did so. "Step down, Kenneth; we will have to wait a little longer."

"But the plans," protested Kenneth.

"Cancel them. Our time will come; now do as I say," snapped Shaw Farquharson, the head of Clan Chattan and Chief of the Macintosh clan. A proud and determined man, his face set into a hard stare as drove back to his ancestral home, Moy Hall, some nine miles south east of Inverness. A descendant of the original Clan Chattan, he was fond of recounting the infamous battle for supremacy between the Cameron and Macintosh clans. In 1396 Robert the Bruce issued an order for the two clans to provide thirty men for a fight to the finish. It resulted in the deaths of the Camerons and the supremacy of his own clan. He was immensely proud of his heritage and the fact that, at Culloden, only the Macintosh banner hadn't being captured by the English. Their dead had been piled five foot high but the banner had survived and still lay hidden at Moy Hall, from where his direct ancestor, Lady Anne of Moy, had supported the Jacobite rebellion.

Those days were long gone but his own ambitions to revenge the defiling of the Macintosh graves at Culloden was not. He had been promised great riches for supplying Kat with equipment, but he had wanted the target to be the Queen not her Lady-in-waiting. He had also arranged the helicopter and realised now it was time to lie low. There were sufficient false trails to avoid tying him to anything but he needed to be careful. He would have to move to plan B.

Ascension Island

Giovanni was incensed, his assassin had not reported back; the helicopter pilot had been arrested in Aberdeen and the clan uprising had been stopped. The hunt for the Prophecy overrode any other consideration; he must not allow it to fall into the wrong hands. He was at least comforted by the thought that, without all the Artefacts, the parchment was useless and vice versa. They had all now been deciphered and showed clear directions to the location on the intricate map of Mongolia in front of him. Also here was Marco Polo's tomb that included the last instructions Marco himself had taken from the Khan's document. Only he knew that Marco's body had been brought here in great secrecy by Giovanni's father when locating himself to this island. A small mausoleum stood in front of his mansion, a place of homage; he had to move forward.

"Time to move ahead, Grasshopper; what's the latest on our sources at the Elders?"

"I'm afraid I've lost track of them," Grasshopper told him nervously.

"It's not like Jansen," snapped Giovanni.

"Perhaps they have been compromised."

"They may suspect they have a mole after Emerald's death; get me Sabine," snapped Giovanni. Contagion couldn't wait for a lone assassin. If the Prophecy had fallen into alien hands, it was a standoff so he would have to send Sabine to retrieve the Prophecy directions. He had them all together in his private room on top of the mansion in a secure glass case with a vacuum environment so he could gaze at them in wonder. The Confucius staff, Columbus Cross, Drake's Shield and the Dragon Slayer Battle Axe. He'd known Marco Polo and Kublai were key clues since starting his quest a decade ago. His father, Lucio, had intercepted the obnoxious German, Count Von Steppenhof and his wife, and brought them to Ascension Island, a fortress he'd built to continue the Calvi and Polo legacies. Unfortunately, the Count had been killed and Lucio badly injured in a fight during an escape attempt by the Count. He died leaving the task of finding the Staff to his son Giovanni. Inspired by reading Marco Polo's exploits, Giovanni started to build his own empire recruiting Zheng Wan to be the front for his plans. He had acquired the Count's retinue including the German couple, Gerd and Freda, who were still with him and took care of his household.

His task was to fulfil his father's vision so he built up knowledge of the Khans by reading the *Secret History of the Mongols* and discovering more about Marco Polo. He respected the Mongols' fighting ability; they had conquered the known world through meritocracy with no automatic inheritance rights. Everything had to be earned in battle, exactly as his own family had over the centuries in Italy. The Medici's had originally paved the way with the Venetian State ruled secretly first by the Medici then Giovanni's own Calvi family. That was followed by an amalgamation of both the Medici and the Polo families. He learnt from his inheritance that he was a true descendant of Marco Polo and therefore the possible nature of the Prophecy in Mongolia which was rightfully his. He looked up, shaken from his reveries by the sound of his helicopter arriving; minutes later Sabine entered the room. "Has Kat failed?" she asked bluntly.

"She has disappeared, find out what has happened."

"Best to do these things ourselves," admonished Sabine, "I could have done it better."

"Don't you dare to question my judgment," snapped Giovanni. "However, you will take over operations."

"All the operations?" she queried.

"Yes, but under my guidance, of course, go and find the Prophecy."

"I will," she said quickly, "But you ought to know that the Contagion Project also has problems," she stood up preparing to leave.

"What problems?" snapped Giovanni.

"Jack Hogg's daughter, a woman called Sandy; she joined your people taking the drugs to Panama and then wiped them out in the process."

"Why on earth did she do that?"

"She blames The Teacher and therefore you for the death of her father. She knows you were using Hogg to get into the Australian mining boom. She also knows that her father was used as a scapegoat and, God knows what else. She must be stopped. Wherever she is, the drugs will be too."

"She will be taken care of." Giovanni turned on the wide screen video to see two faces on the multiple screens, Victor Gonzalez in Panama and Else Tan in Vietnam.

"What the hell is going on with the Hogg girl Victor?" he asked.

"The bitch has hidden the drugs in the rainforest; I'm on my way to get them." He lacked the nerve to admit that he had already lost the consignment of drugs.

"You have ten hours," snapped Giovanni turning to the other screen. "Else, where the hell is Zie Lao?"

"We have lost radio contact, though this is to be expected as they enter the Yunnan province. If you recall we were concerned that they would get picked up before they got into position."

"And their final reported location?"

"By my calculation they should be there in a couple of hours. Early morning our time, ready to conduct the handover with Charles. I should hear very soon."

"Good," said Giovanni switching the screens off as Sabine made ready to leave.

"This Contagion Project, Giovanni, what is it?" she asked. "I need to know all the details."

"It's a cocktail of toxic drugs, high concentrates that will flood the markets as a decoy to allow us time to carry out the main event." Sabine nodded, then asked, "Who stopped Kat?"

"Tresanton and a fighter called Tapiwa. Now get the Prophecy; I have a little local business to take care of."

Seychelles
Island of Mahe

In the island's capital, Victoria, Ambassador Cheng Wu, drove out of the Chinese Embassy's forecourt and accelerated onto the long winding road into the mountains. A small, dour-faced man he was a party stalwart who had been given this posting as a loyalty reward. He was heading for his own official residence. It was a sign of the importance given to the Chinese in the Seychelles that he be allowed the use of such a property, situated as it was next to the Prime Minister's mansion. Cheng liked to see his posting as a key position between the emerging nations of Africa and India, one that would lead to greater things. In his early fifties he'd hoped for bigger positions but in the meantime concentrated on doing his job as well as he could. His chauffer drove the Mercedes carefully along the narrow winding roads, its width making for tricky navigation. As he reached a corner with coriander trees to his right and a tea plantation to his left, he saw a broken down truck in the middle of the road. He frowned at the delay as his car slowed to a halt. It was not unknown for the locals to stop on the road for a chat or just to pass the time of day. In the rear view mirror just to the left of his driver's ear he saw another car closing up behind him. Cursing to himself and thinking of his wife waiting with his evening drink he urged his driver to press on. Suddenly a large man stepped out of the trees to his right wearing a balaclava. Cheng started to hyperventilate as he always did when nervous. "Get out of the car," snapped the figure gesturing with a gun.

Chapter 35

Ascension Island

Lorna had surveyed the building diligently, desperately seeking a way to escape. Everywhere she looked presented only two options; the helicopter pad or the small bay, both equally difficult. The house itself was a marvel of engineering with vast amounts of glass and steel set into solid rock, which meant there was no way out the back. It was in essence a hi-tech prison.

Her mind returned reluctantly to the devastating news Giovanni had given her. It had turned her whole world upside down. It was hard to decide which was worse, being married to that creep, or her father's betrayal. Forced to think about it and with the benefit of hindsight she did recall the trip. When just eighteen years of age she had imbibed her first serious amount of alcohol and had been violently sick. Betrayed by her father, she couldn't even claim rape since they had been legally married. All she had left was her own determination to escape from the man's clutches. If she didn't get out of here soon there was the great danger she would be stuck here forever, legitimately the wife of a man she hated, a man who made her feel sick at the thought of him forcing himself onto her and the heirs that could come as a result.

She had taken time to explore all the rooms with the help of Gerd and Freda, a homely and friendly couple who lived in their own little world. Aside from her bedroom she spent most of her time in the lounge with the stunning views. Giovanni's office was above the lounge and off limits so she watched the tourists in their hired yachts cruising up and down the strait, oblivious to her dilemma. As time passed her anger steadily grew. She had been passive over the past weeks, dragged around the world like a piece of baggage; the only bright spot had been her visit to the orphanage at Vladivostok. Now, her mind cleared of drugs, learning she was married in the vilest way possible and held here against her will, she was sick and tired of being abused. Now Giovanni had taken the only thing she owned, her cruiser.

The thought of Diane blithely sailing into the lion's den under the false premise that an African head of state wanted the ship, was almost too much to bear. It was crucial she escaped at all costs to warn her friend of the danger ahead of her. Thinking through her options the only advantage was Giovanni's strict regime. He always disappeared into his private office in the morning where he kept the Artefacts. She was also intrigued by the mausoleum in the garden, about which he spoke reverently. He usually went there about one o'clock and stayed for a couple of hours. She'd asked him what was down there but he would only say it was his heritage and that she would find out in good time. Aside from the German couple, there was Mario the bodyguard who usually ignored her. She kept out of the way of the periodic appearances of Sabine and the horrible, odious man he called Grasshopper, who knew of her connection to his mortal enemy Guy Tresanton. Sabine was a different and more serious problem making no secret of the fact she hated Lorna and took every chance to belittle her to Giovanni.

She had belatedly concluded she couldn't get away from here alone and her best and only hope was a local lad called Enrico who came once a day with groceries and couldn't take his eyes off her. It was her only chance and sparked the germ of a plan to escape; all she needed was to summon the courage. The dinner gong went and she sighed at the thought of another stilted conversation with Giovanni. As he joined her at the table, he appeared to be unusually tense. He finally broke the silence by saying. "I've always wanted an heir, someone to carry on the heritage; family is very important to me." He looked up meaningfully. "Really," replied Lorna staring back coldly, her lack of interest very clear.

"Yes…A great family and a tradition that you should be proud to continue. I would like a little more enthusiasm, my dear." Lorna bridled at the remark. "You've had me kidnapped, drugged and flown around the world against my will and now hold me imprisoned, how am I supposed to feel?"

"I will soon be one of the most powerful men on earth as I reclaim my ancestor's lost inheritance then you will understand."

"What inheritance?" asked Lorna.

"The Khan's Prophecy is a legacy of power as well as riches; I am reclaiming it for Marco Polo's ancestors."

"So the violence and scheming is all because you want to reclaim a family heirloom," sneered Lorna.

"You've got your father's spirit in you. I can see that, however it's only thanks to me that you are still alive," retorted Giovanni.

"Thanks, instead you have put me through hell."

"I don't call this hell my dear, quite the opposite; you will be ready to receive me into your bedroom tomorrow night on my return from a short trip." It was news she had been dreading.

"That will be rape," she said.

"No it won't, it will be all legal and proper; the papers are registered in Victoria if you care to check."

"They cannot bear my signature or agreement. I never consented to the marriage."

"You were a signatory and compliant; it was a particularly riotous weekend, as I recall, you were certainly amenable when I was with you."

"Then I must have been either drunk or drugged, you bastard."

"I protected you, even when you were with that outcast Jochi who threatened to ruin everything with his impetuosity. Fortunately I had him contained otherwise he would have raped you."

"Stefan?"

"Don't think he actually liked you. He has been employed by me right from the start."

"I'll see you in hell," spat Lorna.

"Your legal guardian asked for this union. It will be consummated." he insisted.

"It won't if I can prevent it," she said. "I'm not an object, I have my own mind."

"Goodnight, my dear," he said brusquely and left the table having eaten only half his meal, "Until tomorrow."

Lorna didn't sleep that night, she thought of and discarded plan after plan to get away; her time was up. She spent the next morning exploring the grounds as her 'most likely' plan slowly solidified in her mind. The mansion stood in a sizeable clearing fully hidden from general view and surrounded by lush tropical forest. The distance across the sea to the resort was too far to swim, in any case she had no doubt they would pick her up quickly. No, her only chance was Enrico who would arrive at four in the afternoon as he did every day with provisions. He was young and impressionable and brought the things they needed in a contraption much like an ice cream vendor's cart. She prepared herself when she saw the small boat arrive and Enrico climb out, watched him assemble his cart before slowly coming up in the lift to her floor. She opened the door and before he knew what was happening pulled him into a recess and kissed him full on the lips. His eyes opened wide, he breathed heavily and felt himself responding to her warm soft body as she pressed herself against him. "Take me back with you to the mainland," she whispered and his eyes boggled as her hands crept round the back of his neck and ruffled the short hairs then crept slowly over his head and settled on either side covering his ears and gently pulling him towards her. "I couldn't do that," he stammered, "My father would kill me."

"He'll never find out and think of what lies ahead," she whispered seductively and he felt her teeth close gently on the lobe of his ear; one hand took his and placed it on her breast. "I bet all the girls in the village wait for you to call," she said and kissed his neck. "I bet you make love to them all, don't you?" His resolve began to crumble. "They watch me the whole time and search me," he replied hoarsely.

"Put me in the cart, cover me with an old fish on a tray, no one will know." She said running her hand down his thigh.

"But it's dangerous," he choked; this whole experience was so sudden it had completely disorientated him. She pressed her advantage. "Tonight could be an unforgettable experience for you," she told him in a whisper, thinking of what was planned for her if she stayed and knowing Enrico's mind was wavering. He surrendered; the promise of a night with the most beautiful woman he'd ever seen was too much for him. He did as she asked.

She groaned as the cart swayed violently over the jetty boardwalk; she lay inside clad in tee shirt and shorts, her money and passport in a watertight bag around her waist. She would have been fine in the small enclosed space if Enrico hadn't taken her idea literally and put rotten fish on top which stank and made her want to retch.

"Open up boy," growled Grasshopper at the small jetty side.

"If you want, but it stinks in there, the boss didn't finish it last night," replied Enrico lifting the lid a little. The Grasshopper's nose wrinkled in disgust. "Holy shit, be off with you, if that's the crap you deliver no wonder the boss is in a foul mood today."

The cart slowly went up the specially designed ramp to the boat and Lorna gritted her teeth as Enrico struggled to lift it into the boat. After what seemed like an age the boy revved the engine and they sped across the water towards Mahe. After ten minutes she could stand no more and managed to upend the can and fall out of the cart onto the deck just as they arrived at Constance Ephelia's bay. She fell straight out of the boat into the seawater to clean herself before swimming to the side half hoping Enrico would have forgotten about her, but he was there grinning as she surfaced. "You're all wet," he said ogling her breasts through the wet shirt, "you come to stay at my house," he whispered huskily.

"No I will get a villa here," Lorna replied carefully. "You can join me once your delivery work is complete, "I need to rest." She planned to find a room for the evening and convert her credit card into some cash as soon as possible. It was very tempting to head straight for the airport but it was probably safer to stay in the resort as they would check all exit points from the island. She had to keep an eye on the youngster though and must also call Diane to warn her. One of the Presidential villas overlooking Ascension Island was available and, soon as she closed the door she tried to call Diane but there was no answer, and Guy's number was unobtainable too. She ordered wine, bought some basic clothes from the boutique and then relaxed in the bath while she tried to figure out what to do next. That was answered for her when the doorbell rang and Enrico stood there replete in best suit and tie. This wasn't going to be easy. "Let's go and eat first and it's on me," she smiled not wanting to lose the guy but also not looking forward to having to fend him off later, she couldn't afford to upset him yet. They found the Helios Restaurant full of couples enjoying themselves on holiday. Their presence made her feel more secure, perhaps Giovanni didn't control the whole area though she flinched as a helicopter flew overhead. They would be out searching for her by now. It would only been a matter of time before Giovanni tracked her down. She had to move on soon but needed help, a situation made worse by Enrico who was rapidly succumbing to the heady wine and losing control of himself. Glumly she realised she wouldn't have a chance if Giovanni's men came in here now and looked around in desperation, her eyes fixed on two English tourists behind her who appeared to be friendly. She leaned over and introduced herself. The man responded to her introduction. "Name's Bert ma'am, your partner looks a little worse for wear?" he observed.

"He's not my partner, just an acquaintance," replied Lorna hastily. "I assume you're here on holiday?"

"No, business actually, but in a nice environment."

"What line of business are you in?" asked Lorna anxiously looking at the door as two men came in. She didn't recognise them but remained wary.

"Treasure hunting actually," replied Bert conspiratorially.

"Treasure hunting?"

"Thought that would get your attention, it usually does, pirate gold to be precise; missing for centuries and it's here in the islands. My wife Sherry and I are both experienced divers and reckon we have enough information to find what we seek."

"Find what exactly?" asked Lorna smiling at Sherry. "My companion is the son of a friend, I promised to look after him for the evening. It's embarrassing really," she said conspiratorially. "He's getting a bit randy; I may need a strong arm."

"No problem," grinned Bert. He was well built under the ill-fitting clothes, "What I told you was secret and stops with us," he whispered, "Something like this gets out and everyone wants a piece of the action. Only problem we have is enough investment to get the job done."

"I could be interested," replied Lorna grateful for the opportunity, this could give her the diversion she needed. "What sort of investment?"

"Would need to be cash?"

"How much?" replied Lorna.

"First we need to be able to trust you," replied Bert carefully. "Place is full of French, can't get much worse than that."

"You can trust me, a girl on her own after all," Lorna assured him, the couple could be a very useful conduit for the time being. "I also have to trust you with my money," she added.

"Good point. Very well, for fifty thousand US you get twenty percent, twenty percent of millions."

"Thirty percent for forty thousand," replied Lorna wondering if she could get that sort of money out of her account, it would be tight.

"You drive a hard bargain," Bert said ruefully.

"It's the deal, and also I want to know more about you both."

"My family is descended from Earnest Bickham Sweet Escott who was the Governor of this place back in 1903; hell of a name I know. He took over when the place became a Crown Colony. Don't suppose they even knew where it was and I expect my great ancestor was the last man standing but there you go."

"Spare her the history lesson, Bert," said Sherry coming across to talk more intimately. "Fact is we've put everything we have into this deal, mortgaged the house to the hilt sold everything to find this treasure which Bert claims is rightfully his."

"Quiet," hissed Bert, "Fact is money is tight and it cost more than we thought to hire the boat."

"Well, you have my terms," replied Lorna tensing as the door opened and Mario, Giovanni's bodyguard appeared. She kept her head turned away from him, her body shielded by the other diners.

"OK, it's a deal," replied Bert, puzzled as Lorna tensed and ducked down to pick up an imaginary handkerchief. "Count me in; I'll wire the money to you tonight."

"Thanks that's great," said Bert, his face registered his delight.

"There is a condition," Lorna told him. Bert raised an eyebrow and said. "Which is?"

"My friend here, he's becoming a bit of a liability," she whispered as Enrico tried to down another rum punch. "Youngster's crush, you know? I need to get him away somewhere but he doesn't need to know I'm involved with you guys."

"One of the sun beds down by the shore will suit him," smiled Bert through his misshapen teeth. "By God you've just bought yourself the chance of a lifetime, and in the process helped me out of a jam. I'll be back in a little while; Sherry will tell you more about the treasure." He took hold of Enrico who after a short resistance submitted to his new 'friend' half carrying him from the restaurant, taking him to a secluded part of the beach wrapped in a towel and in a drunken sleep deposited in a deckchair.

As soon as Bert and Enrico were gone, Sherry moved her seat closer to Lorna and began to tell her the story of the treasure.

"The pirate was a Frenchman called Olivier Le Vasseur better known as *La Buse*. He attacked a crippled treasure ship carrying a huge cargo of gold, silver, diamonds and pearls, bound for Reunion. What he didn't realise until too late was that the Portuguese Viceroy and Archbishop of Goa were on board. As a consequence, in addition to a priceless treasure trove he also had an enormous price put on his head. To cut a long story short, La Buse was eventually captured and as he was being hanged in Reunion in July 1730 he flung a scrap of paper in the air. It had cryptic clues to the whereabouts of the hidden treasure written on it. Through Bert's ancestor we have the piece of paper and broad directions to the gold in the region of Bel Ombre."

"How big is the area you are searching?"

"Couple of kilometres but we are closing in on the final target area," she said confidently. Bert returned and took the seat on Lorna's other side. "He'll wake with a hell of a hangover and naked so he'll be otherwise occupied for a while," he smiled. "By then we'll be long gone. We need to be away from here by five o'clock."

"Suits me," replied Lorna.

The morning was bright and breezy as they drove across the island to the south coast where the hired diving boat was harboured. She scrambled into the motor boat; having successfully transferred the money from her now meagre funds but still hadn't been able to contact Diane or Guy, though she had managed to leave a message on Diane's mobile. They had engaged a private solicitor to draw up documents that transferred twenty per cent of the company to her and both parties made wills to ensure that in the event of the other's death the surviving partner would own the salvage company. Bert reported there had been men last night searching the resort in the evening, but he'd sent them to a supposed sighting further north. She relaxed in the sun as they headed out to sea off the south western coast of Mahe and watched Bert and Sherry check over their diving gear. The only other person on the boat was a local Creole called Gerd who said little and smiled a great deal at her in a leering sort of way; she seemed to attract that sort unfortunately. She watched idly as Bert and Sherry finalized their preparations to dive and showed her the grid areas they had covered already. They were over the final area of exploration so it had to be here somewhere.

They both splashed over the side and Lorna stretched out raising her tee shirt top to bare her stomach before sensing a shadow over her - Gerd.

"Very attractive lady," he leered producing a long thin-bladed knife. "We have private time."

"For God's sake," shouted Lorna leaping to her feet ready to defend herself.

"Take your clothes off now," he ordered. The radio burst into life and Lorna grabbed it.

"Lorna my girl we are rich, we've found the beauty," said Bert's voice.

"That's great Bert, fantastic," she stepped back from Gerd shouting, "Get away from me…Bert…help me…No.." She screamed as Gerd closed his hands on her breasts, she fell forwards into the boat trying to evade the sex-crazed man. The bastard was going to rape her if she didn't do something quickly. She looked around desperately for something to protect her from the vicious looking knife. "You do as I say now," he snapped edging closer his eyes leering at her, "Or I cut you with this."

"Of course," she replied lifting her tee-shirt as he bent forwards hoping to God that Bert was on the way back up. She undid her bra and Gerd leaned further forwards ogling her breasts his hands reaching to her groin when suddenly the leer turned to shock as he pitched forward on top of her, blood spurting from his chest. "Oh my God," screamed Lorna, she saw a harpoon sticking into the man's chest. In their struggle they hadn't heard the speedboat which now rammed into their side knocking her off her feet before something hit the back of her head and she tried to scream before blackness enveloped her.

Chapter 36

Shaka was dead, his Presidency the shortest tenure in the country's history. The state media, orchestrated by Baku, were playing dirges on the radio. Baku was a nondescript man who felt uncomfortable with his enforced role but was determined to give it his best shot. He had been Shaka's sop to the right wing traditionalists but a man who was essentially an introvert and tougher than anyone thought. The media had been told that Shaka had died in a horse-riding accident doing what he enjoyed most. Baku's immediate problems were compounded by the disappearance of Timut, one of the opposition leaders and conspiracy theories abounded despite strenuous statements from Baku denying all knowledge of the man's whereabouts.

Despite losing their leader, the opposition was getting stronger by the day, on top of which the woman Else Tan was demanding that he honour the land deals agreed with Shaka. He didn't have a great deal of choice as the country badly needed the money and ZTW had a cast iron contract. Still the whole affair felt wrong to him and he disliked the demanding tones from the company. Just as puzzling was a situation with newly arrested so called guests, Rose and Zichu Ling, who claimed they had been incarcerated illegally. He requested they be brought to him along with Else Tan; he had an idea they were all somehow linked. "Tell me why I shouldn't free them both Else!" said Baku. He recalled earlier conversations with her, someone he regarded as part of the foreign invasion of his country. He had seen with Shaka what happened when you relied on others and was determined to avoid going the same way.

"They are enemies of the state, that's why Shaka held them; I wouldn't be surprised if they were part of the conspiracy over his death."

"If I suspected for one moment that any of you here were behind what happened to Shaka then you would not be leaving here alive. Do I make myself clear?"

"May I speak, Mr President," said Zichu courteously, "I have been held captive by this woman's organisation for years so I have a right to be heard."

"Speak," commanded Baku.

"ZTW are the public front for a dangerous organisation trying to destabilize the world. As their captive I had little choice but to co-operate with them and when I was finally able to stand against them they tried to kill me. It is ZTW who killed Shaka because he was starting to query what they are doing. There is a much bigger plot here that will damage your country."

"Nonsense," snapped Else frowning heavily, "we are helping your country Baku. There is no doubt Mongolia will be the economic powerhouse of the future, a return to the glory of the great Khan himself. ZTW will help you get to that place, so honour the contracts agreed with your predecessor. As for this man and his outrageous and libellous claims, he is a man of suspect character which is why Shaka had him locked up. Have one of your specialists question them closely; you'll find out what happened to Shaka."

"How could I have had anything to do with that? I have been locked up here for the last two weeks," snapped Zichu, "but you've had plenty of opportunity."

"Enough," said Baku looking around at the three of them. "I have rebels in the south of the country threatening to riot who suspect their leader was killed by government forces and you are the least of my problems. Now get out of here before I change my mind, take them all to the airport," he snapped gesturing to the guards. "See to that they are the next flight out of here, doesn't matter where it's going."

"I must protest," shrieked Else.

"I shall be watching you very carefully; there will be another election within the next couple of months so I will need a new mandate. I expect to see you or your people helping me get elected or the rights will be cancelled, you may go." Baku waved them away and turned to one of his aides who was trying to attract his attention. "Yes?" he said irritably.

"A call sir."

"Very well," Baku listened in silence. The voice on the phone described an opportunity not only to help him stay in power but also ensure Mongolia's success in the longer term. He shook his head in amazement at the information he was being given. "So this is why Shaka was killed?" he said.

"Yes, and you have the chance to grab the opportunity left by him."

"You have my interest," said Baku as he replaced the receiver, his mind whirling at the thought of the opportunities just outlined to him.

Chapter 37

The Emirates flight touched down on the reclaimed runway with a discernible thump that jerked Guy awake. Tapiwa had slept most of the journey whilst he had spent the flight puzzling over the Prophecy parchment he was unable to decipher. All it confirmed was a cavern in Mongolia with some co-ordinates that didn't appear to be map references. He suspected that it was the final piece of the jigsaw and carried it in a security belt around his waist. Tapiwa had more or less recovered from her injuries and Guy's hand had been treated by a police doctor. Monty stayed in Scotland to tie up all the loose ends. They had deliberated for a while how to handle the stand-off with the Professor but hadn't reached a conclusion. The good news had been a call Guy received from Rose as they waited for the Air Seychelles flight at Heathrow telling him that she was free and would join them as soon as possible. The bad news was that Lorna had disappeared and was presumed to be under the control of Sabine or the Professor.

As they taxied to Seychelles airport Tapiwa suggested they take the direct route to find the Professor and then confront him. To do that, she reasoned, all they had to do was let it be known that they had the Prophecy co-ordinates. There was a message from Jade waiting for Guy at the Airport Information Desk. It told him she had received a distorted message from Lorna via the Constance Ephelia Hotel. It was a lead, albeit a tenuous one. He tried again to call Lorna's phone but there was no answer. "These temperatures are preferable to those at Culloden, though I still feel chilled to the bone," Tapiwa complained, as they settled into the taxi's comfortable seats. They drove over the mountain range to the west side of the island. Guy was thinking about Rose, Tapiwa was a good companion but he missed Rose's calmness under pressure. They had been through so much together. Apart from the brief meetings in Vietnam and Mongolia he'd hardly seen her, now they were near the enemy's lair he was acutely conscious of their vulnerability.

An hour later they arrived at the Constance Ephelia Hotel. Guy enquired at the desk and was excited to hear that a girl fitting Lorna's description had registered yesterday. Immediately he rang her room but received no answer. He summoned the hotel manager. "Sorry, she's been gone over a day and a half and her bed's not been slept in, we assume she'll be back later."

"Can we have a look?" Guy asked him.

"No, I'm afraid not, you'd need a police warrant for that, but I can tell you there's nothing in there of note, just a few rumpled clothes."

"Its most important we find her," persisted Guy.

"Sorry its hotel rules."

"It's OK," said Tapiwa leading Guy to the side. "You stay here. I'll check it out unofficially, and best you keep away in case I get caught."

"No we'll do it together," replied Guy. "We've come all this way; there must be clues." They walked down the lane and across the central reservation area past the central spa buildings towards the north beach and beside it the Presidential Villas overlooking Ascension Island. "This way," said Tapiwa as they walked up a steep incline. Expertly she picked the lock but as the manager had said, there was nothing but rumpled clothes and Lorna's favourite brand of perfume. The doorbell rang; they looked worriedly at each other. "Leave it to me," said Tapiwa going across and unsheathing her knife.

"Who the hell are you?" asked a rumpled looking Enrico in clothes that didn't fit him.

"I could ask you the same question," retorted Tapiwa.

"I'm Lorna's boyfriend," he said proudly, "I want to see her, and she owes me."

"She's not here I'm afraid, we're looking for her too," said Guy coldly.

"Ah yes, but I'm her special friend," said Enrico his eyes still bloodshot. He'd struggled all day to find clothes and get sober knowing he was in big trouble with his father who would be apoplectic. All that was stopping his father finding out was Mario who had dragged him to the island and roughed him over. "I have a message for her."

"Give it to me, I'll see she gets it," said Guy.

"She's to meet someone who can help her, at the spa, ten o'clock tonight. That's all I know, they told me nothing else, she's got me in a lot of trouble."

"You don't know her at all do you?" said Tapiwa.

"I rescued her from the island over there; she made me many promises."

"Promises," smiled Tapiwa beginning to like the sound of this Lorna. "I take it then that she deserted you after you got her out."

"It's not like that," said Enrico sulkily.

"Oh I think it is," Tapiwa could see what Lorna had done and was totally unsympathetic to the young man. She dismissed him by simply saying "OK, we'll tell her." and closing the door on him. She turned to Guy. "I suggest we make ourselves comfortable in this place as we'll be paying for it. I don't expect Lorna will be returning."

"Why not?" asked Guy.

"Because they have almost certainly recaptured her, why else would the boy come with a message like that? At least we now know for sure the Professor is over there."

Later that evening they made their way across the spa area in the middle of the island to a central block of buildings surrounded by swampland. It appeared deserted as they approached and made their way to the arrivals area.

"I don't like it Guy, it's too quiet," whispered Tapiwa put on edge by a door slamming in the distance.

"You're right," agreed Guy looking around. "This place gives me the creeps particularly with the cicadas in the background and lizards everywhere."

"They're from the swamp, God knows what else is in there," replied Tapiwa entering an area that consisted of a large thatched hut surrounded by many smaller buildings. She felt for her reliable ceramic knife as they walked slowly across to the central pool area. Guy sensed a slight movement to his left and spun around as a rock tumbled into the large pool sending waves of water lapping over the sides. They both turned instinctively in response to a muffled sound that to Guy was all too familiar. "Get down," he yelled to Tapiwa and dived into the pool which was only a meter deep, another shot sounded; it was a trap. He put his head under the water and swam away hoping Tapiwa was doing the same. He rose to the surface at the other side of the pool finding some blood on his wrist and feeling some pain from his damaged hand. The action had reopened its wound, worse was to come. He groaned as he saw Tapiwa floating head down in the pool. "Oh my God no Tapiwa," the words died in his throat as another shot hit the water and he dived down again. He was a sitting duck and had to get out of the pool. Darkness was his only ally as he hurried away from the direction of the gunshots and flung himself over and behind a brick wall. "The Prophecy Tresanton, throw it across and you'll live," came a voice he thought oddly familiar.

"You've killed my partner damn you."

"You're next unless you do exactly as I say."

"Who the hell are you?" Guy asked, with a horrible sense of déjà vu the reality hit him and he groaned inwardly. Surely the man was dead? He asked again "Who are you?" This time there was a reply. "Your worst nightmare."

"Grasshopper!" exclaimed Guy. "I thought you were killed in Aruba."

"Throw the Prophecy out or I'll keep shooting until the whole place is full of holes including you, you have ten seconds."

"What guarantees do I have?"

"None, just do as I say."

There was no mistaking the triumph in his enemy's voice and Guy knew he was a dead man unless he could find a way out. He looked frantically around. There was better cover over by the huts but he had nothing to defend himself with. It was hopeless. "You win," he shouted taking the security belt from around his waist. He threw it into the water and as he did so ran away in the opposite direction towards the huts. He heard a grunting noise and someone in the dark moving forwards. The fat bastard was in the water. If only he had a weapon! He had to do something quickly to try and save Tapiwa. He knelt down and found a rock and moved forwards, the fat man was no match for him physically. If he could get close enough there was a chance. He stepped back into the water seeing Grasshopper in the distance then he was stopped in his tracks as a different voice came out of the gloom again horribly familiar. "Leave this to me and go back to the Professor," snapped Sabine's voice, "Tresanton, we have some unfinished business you and me," she smiled using a strong torch to carefully scan the area. Guy ducked back down behind the pool's wall again as the light flooded the area knowing he now had a real adversary. "You escaped me in Mongolia but you won't again. Incidentally your girl friends are slightly battered," she said goading him. "I had to give them both over to the men, such a waste but never mind there are plenty other fish in the sea."

Guy bit his lip and then heard the sound of water moving as Sabine retrieved the security belt. He edged forwards to the side of the pool trying to surprise her but it was too late as Sabine gave a cry of triumph grasping the belt. "Now we have all the pieces to the puzzle," she shouted as she swept the pool with light illuminating Guy clearly, "now it's your turn Tresanton."

"Stop the shooting," roared a voice as floodlights came on blinding both Guy and Sabine. "Drop the gun Sabine," yelled Monty.

"Monty, watch out!" yelled Guy as Sabine fired and dived in the same motion. Shadows jumped in the dark, two more shots followed reverberating around the arena drawing gasps and moans in the darkness before Guy dared to breathe. "Are you all right Monty?" he called out. "Hit me in the other leg but I'll live," grumbled Monty re-entering the area, where is she?"

"Gone with the Prophecy back to the Professor no doubt. Bloody Grasshopper I can't believe he's still alive."

"Grasshopper? My God he must have used his nine lives. I think I hit her, and there was a grunt.

"Tapiwa is badly hit," said Guy lifting her out of the water, "she's shot in the chest," he checked her pulse, "there's slight movement; we need to get her to the hotel's doctor and quickly. You made it in the nick of time. Monty, I was nearly a goner there."

"Just as well I followed your tracks then," replied the Inspector chewing on his pipe. "We've located the Professor, my bosses at Interpol are delighted, but the problem is we have little to charge him with."

"Where is he?"

"Literally a mile from here over on the island."

"Can't we charge him with attempted murder? He's got everything now including the final directions to the Prophecy. Time is against us, and we have to stop him."

"Did you examine it?"

"Yes, but it's very hard to decipher."

"I saw that from the scanned copy you sent me," replied Monty. "One thing though, there's a bit missing at the bottom.

The boys at Interpol said it's been deliberately removed and it's the bit that will provide the exact location to the cavern's entrance."

"So when he has that last piece he has the lot, the full jigsaw," said Guy.

"Yes we need to move fast, but that's not so easy."

"Why not?"

"We did an aerial survey when I got here earlier. It prompted the Professor whose real name incidentally is Giovanni Calvi to make an official complaint to the government, next thing I know we were incarcerated in the airport until I got Interpol to clear me. He pulls all the strings around here."

"What did you find out?"

"He owns the only house there; it's a fortress with the only entry from a helicopter landing stage. Lorna did well to escape."

"There must be another way in."

"Only thing I can see is a low lying spit of land to the sharp end. We saw a mausoleum next to the mansion."

"Is there any significance in that?"

"It's a mausoleum to Marco Polo; that's what the police told us before the government silenced them. It seems to link together somehow but I'm not sure how. Giovanni has everything he needs to move forwards."

"I thought Marco Polo was buried in Venice," said Guy.

"Maybe his body was moved? There is a direct link between the Calvi family and the Polo's. Wouldn't be surprised if they are related. I'm told by Interpol that there was a strong rumour sixty years ago that Polo's bones had been stolen, though it was never proven."

"I've been thinking Monty, what is it that's so special about the Prophecy?"

"I wish I knew, I'd guess everyone, including this Professor is speculating on what it is. For my part I would guess it's a mixture of valuable objects and perhaps some revelations about the Khan and the lands he conquered. Not sure how relevant they will be to the present day though."

"I reckon it must be very relevant to the present day otherwise why is everyone so keen to find it?" replied Guy. "My guess is that it contains material that's embarrassing to the modern states and perhaps has significance to religion."

"I must get across to the island urgently; we may already be too late, particularly as he has everything including Lorna."

They hurried back to the village after making sure Tapiwa was being taken care of by the resident doctor. She was, they felt, in good hands and had been assured she would live. They traced the unfortunate Enrico and asked him the best way to get to the island. The lad was evasive at first but gradually became more co-operative. Guy asked him bluntly if he would take them there. He shook his head vigorously. "No! It's too dangerous," he moaned.

"I'll make it worth your while; I gather you've lost your job," smiled Guy, "all for the fickleness of a woman."

"So what if I have," snapped a chastened looking Enrico. He'd been berated by his father half an hour ago.

"So, I'll pay you well and help you with your father," replied Guy.

"Perhaps I will take you, but for Lorna's sake as she was recaptured."

"Good, then we leave on your boat as soon as it's dark; I will rescue her."

"Very well but I'm not going ashore," replied Enrico helpful would he be, heroic definitely not.

"OK. You have a deal," agreed Guy.

Chapter 38

Ascension Island

It was midnight when Enrico launched his boat and cautiously headed towards the shore on the other side of the strait, knowing the risk he was taking made him very nervous. His tension rubbed off on Guy and made his damaged hand ache even though it had been professionally bandaged. He still felt shaky after the fight at the spa and wished Monty was with him. Unfortunately his friend was in an even worse condition with both legs damaged. Giovanni held all the aces and, as far as Guy could see, he had little choice but direct action before it would be too late. Enrico cut the engine twenty metres from shore and rowed the rest of the way trying to find the narrow beach. Guy felt increasingly nervous as they closed the gap, unsure of how to get to the main house and knowing sensors could pick him up beforehand. "I can see the inlet," said Enrico nervously, "then I go."

"Move in fast I don't want to get caught by sensors or a helicopter. We're sitting ducks here." Guy wasn't sure about Enrico but the nerves were genuine and it paid to be vigilant. Enrico carefully maneuvered the boat between jagged rocks into a very narrow inlet before gesturing to Guy to follow him. He clambered out, marvelling at the place, totally hidden by undergrowth and invisible from the sea. He steadied himself and started to scramble over the rocks. After fifteen minutes he reached the top of the incline and was relieved to see the lights of the mansion ahead. He stopped to check his bearings. All his senses straining and alert. There was a movement in bushes beside him, something moved through the air; he fell into a black void.

South Indian Ocean

The large cruiser, all 150 thousand tonnes and 300 metres of her, ploughed steadily through the choppy waves of the South Indian Sea. Diane paced the deck for the umpteenth time wondering where Lorna was and who on earth their customer could be. Her doubts about the hire had started early into the voyage when Captain Jenner received instructions to alter course and head for the Seychelles, not Zanzibar. The whole contract had an odd feel about it; they'd been instructed to sail empty and with a skeleton crew. She looked at the distorted message from Lorna on her mobile's screen. Was her friend trying to reach her? The words were so jumbled she couldn't read them. Her position on board was difficult, under Lorna's authority she was technically the owner but Captain Jenner had made it clear from the start that there was only one Captain on board. There was a tiny crew, Rochembach, and herself so they felt like they were on their own. Lorna's idea of converting the ship into a floating health spa was becoming more remote as the bank was becoming increasingly belligerent and not helped by her lack of contact. Diane couldn't understand why the rich benefactor wanted them here at all; surely he had a super yacht somewhere and not this great half-finished hulk. Still it was significant money and Lorna had authorized the trip.

Two days later they reached Victoria Mahe and they docked next to the man-made resort beside the airport. She recalled the millionaire's development had been built on reclaimed land and apparently the cheapest property on the concrete island was worth a million dollars. She was able to confirm to the Captain that the funds had transferred from the client so he could pay the crew. Rochembach met her halfway along the deck; he was clearly excited about something or other. "I've just received a call from Monty," he said, "He's here on the island."

"Here? On this island?" replied Diane in surprise. "What's he doing here?"

"He didn't say, just wants us to meet him in town; he's there now." A taxi rank was nearby so they took the nearest cab and gave the driver the address in the Old Town Monty had given them. As they climbed into the car Diane noticed Jenner chatting animatedly to a fat man but thought nothing of it. The humidity was very high and making Rochembach extremely uncomfortable. He was sweating profusely. She thought again how fortunate she was to have his support, particularly now. He could call upon his network of police colleagues just like Monty. He left her outside the central café and headed down Independence Avenue to the police station. Diane went in for a coffee and waited for him upstairs, she was fascinated by the replica clock called Little Ben, an exact replica of the Big Ben clock in London though in an aluminium coating. The road outside was alive with activity and she let her mind wander as she stared down to the port in the distance. She was surprised to see the cruiser start to move slowly, the damned thing was going without them. She picked up her mobile and called Jenner. "What's happening, I did not give authority for you to move."

"The ship is under my authority now," came an unfamiliar voice.

"Who the hell are you?"

"The man who has rented this heap of junk at an exorbitant price so mind your manners," snapped Grasshopper from the bridge. He was now in control.

"I'll call the police," Diane said the first thing that came into her head.

"We are the police here so forget it, besides we are within our rights under the terms of the hire agreement, if you check the contract."

"Damn it!" cursed Diane as she watched the cruiser slowly move away. All they had left now were the clothes they wore and what little was left in the bank. Their dreams of turning it into a floating spa seemed more remote than ever. She cursed aloud and stamped her foot in fury.

"What's the problem?" asked Rochembach sliding into the seat opposite her. "Damned ship has gone; the hirer's have taken it early. What's the news from Monty?"

"Good news and bad," he replied. "He's been injured in both legs and can only just walk. The good news is that they know where this Professor is located. The bad is that he rules the roost totally and the police are inept."

"So I've found out," snapped Diane.

"Forget the cruiser; they paid to borrow it and that didn't include us. Monty is on his way and has arranged a police vehicle to take us to the other side of the island to a place called Ascension Island. The police are concerned about a missing Chinese Ambassador and they suspect the Professor has something to do with it."

"The Chinese ambassador missing! I bet that's caused a stir?"

"They are very powerful here so yes he's picked the wrong target if he thinks he can take them on."

"Diane," called a familiar figure limping across to join them.

"Monty, how are your legs?" Diane was delighted to see him but worried about his condition.

"Both shot and it hurts like hell; matching wounds in both thighs but it's good to see you again. After Valgrind the extremes of temperature and humidity are wearing me down a bit too. I take it Rochembach has briefed you on the situation?"

"Yes, I gather this Professor is the brains behind the whole thing including killing The Teacher."

"Looks like it and he's got all the pieces of the jigsaw now."

"And Lorna?"

"The Professor or I should say Giovanni has her too; he kidnapped her."

"What are the police doing about it?"

"Very nervous of acting against their paymasters but the Chinese thing has helped. Puts them in an invidious position and turned the eyes of the world on their small country."

"The cruiser has been taken," Diane updated him as she drank the remainder of the coffee.

"By someone I know well," replied Monty bitterly.

"A man called Grasshopper, a renegade cop who has resurrected himself. We thought he died in Aruba."

"What is this Grasshopper using the cruiser for?"

"Transport for something across to Africa. We've picked up a code word 'Contagion. The more immediate problem is that Guy went to the island last night and nothing has been heard of him since."

"We must organize some help then."

"I intend to, but first tell me what you know about the cruiser, and all about your ex-husband's activity here years ago. I need something concrete to get the police onto the island."

"Stig Oleson?"

"Yes, there are links between him and Giovanni that might explain Lorna's predicament."

"I remember just before he left his wife and married me, he took Lorna on a business trip to Africa. I was there as his secretary. One night he left me with some business cronies in Kenya and said he wanted to take his little girl for a treat. They were gone for three days and when he returned he wouldn't say anything. He had his own pilot's licence so he could have gone anywhere."

"Most likely here. What about Lorna?"

"Would never talk about it, a closed shop, but it did create a rift between her and Stig for a while. She would never talk about it to me."

"I'm guessing that Stig brought her here when he came to borrow money for the cruiser from Giovanni; perhaps there was a deal."

"A deal - what sort of deal?"

"I've no idea," replied Monty, "Maybe they agreed on the plan to use the cruiser as a floating hospital."

"A floating brothel more likely," said Diane bitterly,

"There's no need to remind me."

"I'm trying to see how it all links together. Oleson was a dangerous man, but Giovanni was his puppet master as he was with The Teacher. In both cases he pulled the strings and now he has Guy and Lorna."

Chapter 39

The room was spinning and she felt dreadfully sick, hazy memories flooded back, the sensations familiar; too familiar as Lorna slowly came out of a drug-induced stupor and looked around her. Then reality dawned, she was fastened to the bed and wearing nothing but her bra and pants.

"You let me down, wife, and as a result others have died."

"What did you do to Bert and Sherry?"

"They ran out of oxygen, tragic really but that's one of the perils of the sea. You were again saved from being raped; you are a grave disappointment to me, my dear."

"I will never succumb to you."

"Oh you will, everyone does eventually," averred Giovanni, "I believe you have an attachment to Mr. Tresanton, so I thought you might like to watch something," he gestured to a screen that opened up in front of Lorna. "Guy, oh my God," she whispered seeing a fuzzy image of a man in chains laid spread-eagled on the floor. "Strange you should feel an attachment to the man who killed your sister?" he sneered.

"I don't believe you," snapped Lorna.

"I didn't think you would," smiled Giovanni. A heavily built man kicked Guy in the ribs. Lorna bit her lip and looked away. "Oleson told Tresanton to take Leila to Spain on some hair-brained mission that went wrong. She was hit in cross fire during a shoot-out but she shouldn't have been there." Lorna made no comment so he continued. "You really shouldn't have put me to all that trouble; this is not a good start to our marriage." She did react to his last comment. "There is no bloody marriage," she shrieked as she tried to move.

"I trusted you and you betrayed me," snapped Giovanni. "Now I'm afraid I will have to take by force what is mine by right. You should have listened to your father; he was a good man."

"He was like you, an evil bastard," snapped Lorna.

"When you were eighteen, a lovely young thing so innocent; you were my prize for my co-operation."

"What do you mean co-operation?" asked Lorna.

"Your father was bankrupt; he had to do something as he had

a great plan to expand his operations in Norway. The authorities were starting to ask questions; he had a grand vision and needed money to build a cruiser to take his idea around the world."

"His obscene scheme to rejuvenate old people, give them the elixir of youth." Lorna finished his sentence for him, her disgust made obvious by the look on her face as well as her tone of voice.

"That was for the outside world, but really it was a breeding camp, of which you, my dear, are a prime example."

"What do you mean?" said Lorna horrified.

"Oh didn't he tell you? Both you and your dear sister were products of that factory; how remiss of him. I assume he was your father but perhaps not; he was always fairly ambivalent on that point but he did see you both as examples of how to make money. He was going to make millions out of it and use you and Leila as the star-studded face of the enterprise."

"You mean we were born in those camps?" said Lorna, horrified by what she was hearing.

"Of course my dear, you were all commodities to be bought and sold at a price, so that's what I did. I bought you including the marriage certificate; you were the price for my co-operation and the money your father needed to get his floating breeding camp off the ground. So you see you are mine, though I can see that you have had your head turned by others. So now I need to recondition you as I would a horse. You have strayed and now need to be brought back on the straight and narrow just as I did before."

"What did you do to me before?"

"You won't remember a great deal. I even have some photographs of you, so innocent with your developing body."

"You bastard, I won't hear this," screamed Lorna trying to close her ears to the words and straining at the ropes.

"You were mine to take advantage of," replied Giovanni, "A union blessed by your father whilst he enjoyed himself in another part of my house with my own stable of willing girls. I chose not to leave you pregnant last time as it was too early but now the time is right."

"I won't believe all this," replied Lorna coldly. "You are lying to me."

"I have proof if you wish to see it," replied Giovanni. "I have watched you all these years and it has been hard at times seeing the stupid hulks you chose. My men ensured where possible that they were taken care of, all except this Tresanton and his time has now come. Surely you must have wondered why you couldn't hold down a long term relationship; we scared them off."

"You utter bastard," snapped Lorna struggling again with the ropes.

"You are under my control now and I am done with talking; it's time."

"No!" screamed Lorna making desperate efforts to resist the man as he took hold of her.

———————

Grasshopper nodded as Captain Jenner indicated where they could tie up; he had the barge ready and instructed the men to get working immediately. It would take a few hours and the work must be done in daylight. He had in mind a quick trip across the sea to Africa and a night with some dusky maidens to celebrate his achievement. He was amazed by the sheer size of the cruiser. Its 150 thousand tonnes floating very high in the water; it was a monstrosity and more than ample for his needs. "What do you want?" he grunted to the Italian bruiser, Mario. "Are we taking her across the sea?"

"That's the plan, though that smart-arse, Sabine, might muscle in," said Grasshopper, sweating profusely. "She's got the Professor eating out of her damned hand and she worked for his enemy. It can only be one thing and that's between her legs."

"She wants me to help her now," replied Mario gruffly.

"Oh she would, miss high and bloody mighty. She can't do anything wrong now she has the Prophecy," he cursed as he saw the familiar helicopter coming into land. "Talk of the devil," he muttered.

"Is everything in order?" asked Sabine sweetly as she watched the men load the cargo, then observed, "So this is the cruiser the bitch owns."

"It is," replied Grasshopper.

"Good, you'll be pleased to know that Carl has been having fun with Tresanton."

"That's my job, I was promised," said Grasshopper angrily.

"Oh I dare say something will be left for you. Meanwhile you do what I say," replied Sabine stiffly turning up her nose at the disgusting sweaty smells coming from the fat man."

"I am well capable," snapped Grasshopper angry at how she was taking control.

"Good, I am pleased to hear it because I have far more important work to do as the Prophecy and Artefacts have to be moved and final plans made. It's good to know there are people I can trust," she smiled coldly as she stepped off the bridge. "See to it that the Captain and crew get their just reward at the other end and make sure that the cruiser is safely stowed. It's a major asset for the future. Come on Mario." They left together.

"I am more than capable of doing what is asked of me, damn it," snapped Grasshopper turning away almost apoplectic with fury at his treatment and trying to calm himself down. The things he would do to that bitch when he had the chance.

The helicopter flew Mario and Sabine down to the millionaire's village landing on top of a huge Sunseeker power cruiser. It was owned by Giovanni and would be taken around to Ascension Island. Sabine was capitalizing on her surge in popularity with Giovanni after retrieving the Prophecy and the craft was necessary for their final plan. She relaxed as Mario opened up the throttles and they sped around the north of the island. She was on her way below to finalise her plans when she noticed the sight ahead. "Mario what's that wreck of a boat over there? Go closer," she shouted as she saw an old schooner bobbing about with no one on deck. It was one of the fleet that took tourists out, but today wasn't on its usual tack. They pulled alongside and she scanned the deck, there was no one to be seen. "Anyone there?" she shouted, puzzled that the engine was running. "Cover me, Mario," she ordered as she went to the rail and vaulted across to the schooner's deck. "Bet you didn't expect to see me again," came a sombre yet familiar voice. You!" Sabine spun round to be confronted by Rose and her father Zichu. "Yes me," replied Rose grimly and moved towards her with a knife held in front of her. "Mongolia sends its regards though I'm afraid Shaka is dead."

"You really are most tiresome," snapped Sabine, "This time there will be no rules or perverts watching us. I should have finished you before," she raised her pistol. "Hold it," shouted Zichu from the front of the old schooner pointing a gun. "Your time is up, drop the gun."

"Most tiresome," said Sabine again, but she dropped her gun. Having done so and felt the tension slacken, she suddenly dived forward, catching Rose unawares. Mario simultaneously rammed the throttle forward, snapping the mooring lines and making the schooner jerk crazily; the action hurled Rose to the deck. Zichu fired, Mario stumbled as the Sunseeker abruptly lost power, staggered to the rail and fell overboard. Sabine cursed and grabbed Rose in a vice like grip, squeezing her throat and dragging her towards the side of the boat. "This time it's death for you," she snarled, forcing Rose backwards and out over the water. Zichu, prevented from reaching his daughter by the door between upper and lower decks, desperately tried to force it open. Rose summoned all her strength, her lungs bursting in agony as she tried to breathe, her world spinning. With a last desperate lunge she rammed her elbow into Sabine's stomach. The larger girl staggered back the wind driven from her lungs. Rose gasping for breath tried to open the door for her father but it was jammed.

Sabine struggled to her feet and saw the Sunseeker drifting closer; she contemplated jumping back on board. "Where the hell are you, Mario," she yelled, and turned to see if Zichu had broken through the door yet. There was no answer and she again looked at the door that was now showing splinters all down one side. He would be through it in minutes. She had to act fast. She turned to face Rose who by now had recovered her breath and stood ready for her. Grabbing her emergency knife from her boot, she resolved to finish her once and for all. "Time's up, sister," she snarled bracing herself as the Sunseeker hit the side of the old schooner. She concentrated on the girl in front of her. "It's over Sabine," spat Rose, staring back at her. "Your mistake," hissed Sabine lunging forward, the knife caught Rose's arm causing her intense pain. "You'll need to do better than that," she said through gritted teeth. Her eyes narrowed in concentration as she kicked out catching Sabine who stumbled but regained her balance as the Sunseeker continued to bump against the schooner.

Sabine came in for the kill, Rose, her arm bleeding freely now tried to dodge the next blow but the knife thrust caught her in the side of the stomach, her shirt ripping as the knife was withdrawn. She fell to her knees as Zichu who had finally broken through the obstinate door, shouted in alarm and looked on in horror as his daughter stumbled. Rose fell onto her back feeling herself drift as Sabine, poised above snarled, "Time to go," and the knife arched downwards. Rose summoned all her fading strength as Sabine's face filled her vision like an obscene gargoyle and groaned again as she felt the knife rip at her shoulder. Then she saw the laughing face above her fill with pain as blood trickled from her stomach, Rose's own short knife was embedded there. Sabine fell backwards, saw another threat coming from her left. She pulled the short knife out of her stomach cursing as she did so. "You!" she grated, trying to turn to the new threat as Rose rolled away still losing blood. Zichu now stood grimly in front of her. "It's you who will die," he said coldly and raised his gun. Something blurred across in front of his eyes and he felt his legs sag uncontrollably. This was followed by an indescribable pain. Sabine extracted her knife from his stomach.

With a roar of pain and rage Zichu pushed himself forward, grimacing through the pain his strength fading rapidly. He hit Sabine with all his remaining strength and clasped her to him in a bear hug. The Schooner bucked violently, hit yet again by the Sunseeker it caused his legs to buckle again. They both lost their balance and staggered across to the side. Zichu knew he had only one course of action left and with all his remaining strength grabbed the thrusting knife with his hand wincing as the blade cut through his hand muscles and with an animal-like roar used his momentum to propel them both over the side.

Sabine saw Zichu's intention too late, and snarled in anger as they fell into the sea in a death-like embrace, each bleeding badly. Rose screamed at the sight as she managed to lift herself up on the deck and desperately tried to find a rope to throw to her father. She saw both bodies rise to the surface and her father holding grimly onto the woman as they sank below the waves for the final time. She was sure her father smiled at her as he went down and she held her head in her hands in horror at the scene; she'd only just started to get to know him and now he was gone.

Chapter 40

Yunnan Province – China

Jack stood looking on, silently wrestling with his conscience; he hoped his son would remember him favourably and judge his actions fairly. His mind moved fondly to his dear wife whom he had never ceased to love despite their long separation. They had been apart for so long and he wouldn't have the luxury of a last few moments with her. It was his biggest regret. Tonnes of cargo were currently being loaded into the cavernous bodies of the twenty trucks that would lay a trail of waste in the form of a lethal Contagion of drugs, from Yunnan Province deep into the Chinese western hinterland as far as Tibet. He couldn't see any other way to intervene apart from the action he was about to take. "Make it quick," Zie told all within earshot. "We cross the border in two hours. It'll be dark and the border guards will nod us through." Zie's son, Charles, had always looked older than his years and was a consummate actor in his Communist Party uniform. Jack knew their plan would work well. Now here he was with Zie in charge of one of the biggest strikes into Chinese soil since the Japanese invasion in WWII, and the irony of it was that it was probably the largest drugs shipment to enter the Chinese mainland since the British poured opium into the country during the previous century through what had been their new port of Hong Kong, and taken tea in payment.

No one was around as Jack drank a stiff whisky. He knew he would only get one chance to bring his plan to fruition. He casually made his way to the trucks and went into the rear of each of them. By the time he'd finished he was sweating profusely. His task completed, he strolled back to the main office where Zie was enjoying his early morning green tea. Taking a deep breath he entered the outer room where Charles sat looking at some papers; he clutched a concealed switch in his hand. He abhorred violence but sometimes the end justified the means. Zie checked some last minute paperwork and lit a cigarette. He frowned, Tresanton should have returned by now. He strode aggressively out of his room into the outer office slamming the door as he did so. He gave a cry of agony at the sight that met his eyes. Charles, his son, lay on the floor with his throat cut, blood pooling around his supine body. "No!" yelled Zie and rushed forward, only to discover that he too was in trouble. "It's over, Zie," Jack told him, holding a gun in his right hand and pressing the button on the remote control in his left. Zie's mouth fell open with astonishment as the peace of the morning was shattered by a series of ear-splitting explosions as each truck detonated and then caught fire. In minutes the entire warehouse was surrounded by a conflagration. "No!" yelled Zie again and snatching his gun from the holster on his hip fired it. His target, Jack, fired back pleased to see that no one could get near the fires. He'd achieved his objective.

He turned back sadly to Charles who, still losing blood, stared wide-eyed at his father. "I'm sorry Charles, you didn't deserve this but you have to die," he fired twice and saw the young man jerk twice as the bullets struck. He did the same to Zie as the fire ball enveloped them all. His last thought was of his dear wife. He was sure she would have approved of his actions. "I know very well what is at stake, have known it for years," he said to no one in particular.

Ascension Island

Guy awoke and looked around him. He vaguely recalled the beating he had received, the evidence of it still with him in the form of a pain like a stabbing thrust to his heart. Then it came flooding back. He remembered seeing Lorna strapped to a bed with Giovanni leering over her and calling her his wife. Guy had tried to call out to her before the beating started, after which he had been trying to shield himself from the blows and minimize the pain. It had got steadily worse until mercifully, he passed out. As he lost consciousness he was sure he'd seen Stefan in the background. Had the man being working for Giovanni all along? It had to be the only explanation or perhaps he'd switched sides after Jochi had been murdered. It didn't really matter anymore. He had little hope left as he lay there wondering what would come next. To have been through so much only to die here on the floor of a madman's house was galling. What on earth had he been thinking to come here on his own? He faded away, convinced he would never open his eyes again.

But he did…sensing he'd been out for a long time. He'd had

intermittent nightmares about The Teacher. There was no Whistler now to tell him the latest developments but there was no need; he was in the lion's den. As he awoke he felt the shackles holding him to the floor and his aching muscles brought him back to a living nightmare. He strained to look around the room but could see very little except a panoramic window looking down into the bay. He was startled by a voice out of the gloom. "Welcome to my private world, Tresanton, the best room in the house and off limits to the living," intoned the disembodied voice. "You are a fool, you and your interfering friends dabbling in ancestral issues that don't concern you and are way above your understanding." Guy shook his head and wondered what the hell the voice was on about. "Ancestral issues?" he mumbled.

"Yes, Marco Polo, my great ancestor and the only man trusted by Kublai Khan. He gave Marco a Golden Piaza and made him his trusted ambassador. His task was to safeguard the Khan's greatest legacy, his Prophecy, and now I, as his direct descendant, will do just that. Even as we speak my people are using the coordinates from the Artefacts and the tablet of directions you so kindly delivered to us to find the Prophecy."

"You will never get it," muttered Guy trying to turn his head but finding his neck restrained. "Part of the directions was missing."

"You know what, Tresanton; it amazes me that after all you have done you expect to have a sensible discussion with me."

"Perhaps you can't handle the truth?"

"Very well, despite having more important things to do I will humour you for a while before Contagion starts. As we speak Else Tan is heading towards the sacred cave with those details. Must be galling for you after all your sacrifices but you should have left well alone." He turned irritably as the door opened. "Ah Stefan, I hear you and Alfonse did a good job subduing Tresanton."

"As ordered," he replied, staring at Guy. "You wanted me, a change of plans or something?"

"I want you to take the helicopter and replace that fool Grasshopper on the cruiser; you know what to do when you get to Africa."

"Yes, but you should know that we cannot contact Latin

America, and we're struggling with Yunnan," replied Stefan. "There are reports of explosions in Panama."

"That idiot Victor! When did you last hear from him?"

"Three hours ago, when he was about to rendezvous."

"Leave it with me; you have more important things to do," snapped Giovanni.

"And Zie Lao? We've heard nothing."

"That's to be expected. I ordered him to maintain radio silence until he was in position; now get to the cruiser." Guy tried again to turn his head and attract Giovanni's attention. "What have you done to Lorna?" he asked.

"My wife is absolutely fine thank you."

"Your wife?" Guy found that difficult to believe.

"Tresanton you and I are similar in many ways; the same taste in women, the same desire for justice, only difference is that I'm a winner and you're a loser. I will grant you that the trick of getting the mute to pass on his plans really upset The Teacher. Very neat, very innovative."

"The police will be here soon," Guy said, but Giovanni dismissed his remark.

"Brilliant, the man's at death's door and still tries to bargain his way out; guess I would do the same but unfortunately for you the police here work for me."

"Are you telling me Marco Polo came here?" Guy said trying another tack.

"Yes I am, Marco was a trusted agent for Kublai Khan and served on his Privy Council as the only non-Chinese or non-Mongolian in the court. On the screen you will see the Artefacts. Notice the quality of the metal. Rhodium one of the earth's rarest metals and almost unique to Mongolia and the cavern we are going to excavate."

"What's so special about it?"

"It's a rare silvery white metal from the platinum group, a so called noble metal meaning it's resistant to corrosion."

"Used in catalytic converters I would guess."

"Yes but rhodium is far more valuable than that."

"So Marco was trusted by Kublai with his greatest secret," encouraged Guy seeing his enemy was obsessed with the story.

"As I said, Marco split the directions to the Prophecy so the tablet you brought back from Scotland was incomplete."

"Leading to what?"

"Genghis Khan's real legacy, his greatest secret, and the one he took to his grave."

"What exactly is it, do you know?" asked Guy.

"We will only know that for sure when we open the tomb. It's shrouded in secrecy at the moment but it contains secrets that will change the known world. Genghis was convinced it would bring the World back under Mongol control but until we see it we don't know how."

"Heady stuff but I can't see how anything in it will have any relevance today."

"What if it changed how people thought of religion? What if it redrew the tribal boundaries based on hitherto unknown facts?" Giovanni's face took on the look of the fanatic.

"So this Prophecy is in the same location as the rhodium?" queried Guy.

"Likely to be in a joint tomb with Kublai Khan and located far to the north away from the duplicitous Chinese and in the very heart of the old Mongol Empire but not the magic mountain. Kublai deliberately drew attention to Xanadu when all the time the real heritage was north. Again we don't know for certain what the Prophecy contains until we get into the cavern." He was getting more and more excited as he developed the story. He really could see himself becoming the most powerful man in the world. Guy bought him back to earth. "You're sure it's in a cavern?" he asked.

"Oh yes, it's a cavern lined with gold and rhodium. Untold wealth is there, plus, I believe, a revolutionary review of religious thinking, an answer to many who even a thousand years ago saw religion as an excuse to fight; the curse of mankind."

"I thought you were a follower of Islam," said Guy.

"I tolerated Zheng's Islamic views but shouldn't have; it's one of the many things you and the Elders got wrong, believing that the schism was caused by Jochi. That was small and irrelevant, merely another case of Zheng losing control. The real reason was Zheng's fundamentalist beliefs that Jochi, I and others disapproved of."

"So that's why Jochi split?"

"Both he and his namesake, Zheng He, the explorer, were Muslims looking to show the Mongols were driven by the belief system championed by Tamerlane. He sought to show the rightful inheritor of the Mongol Empire was Islam. Fortunately he died early and the Mongol Shaman or, as I call it, the Pragmatic Way was re-established as the true way of the Mongols, the way of Genghis and the one to which I subscribe. Needless to say there are many who will fight to stop this Prophecy being discovered."

"So Genghis had a problem with Muslims?"

"No but the Mongols saw religion as no more than the opium of the masses, to be used to whatever end necessary. Genghis believed that he was a God in his own right and it is recorded in the secret History of the Mongols that he ascended to heaven, so he naturally used religion to further his own ends by believing what he thought practical. In the second parchment he talks about a strange experience after one of his feasts where he was transcended into the air and shown the reality of his own existence. That's when he decided to plan for his own second coming through the Prophecy."

"What?" Guy sounded as incredulous as he felt.

"In a different body of course but that's the whole point of what he has done. Genghis believed he would return one day. He saw it in the sky; he was told to document that time and this is his Prophecy written under strict instructions. So now, Tresanton, perhaps at last you see the point. I will be Genghis, a man who controlled an empire twice the size of Rome's."

"You're mad." Guy commented. "Stark staring mad!" Giovanni continued as if Guy hadn't spoken. "Genghis laid down the conditions of his second coming. It would be in exactly a thousand years' time. He would morph into the body of the man who found the Prophecy and his tomb."

"A thousand years?"

"Yes, it's exactly a thousand years since he had his vision on the plains in the early thirteenth century; I plan to be there to be suitably anointed."

"By my calculations it's only eight hundred years since the thirteenth century."

"No, in the Mongolian calendar eight hundred of their years equals a thousand of today's.

"But this has no relevance in the modern world; it's meaningless," Guy insisted.

"I also believe that the Prophecy is something that will give me authority over nations."

"They will never listen to you."

"You have believed enough in everything he has done this far, why don't you believe the final step? It was never about the wealth with him or me; I have enough of that thanks to Count Von Steppenhof and his inheritance."

"You'll never get all this treasure out of Mongolia; the place is a backwater and in turmoil thanks to your people murdering the President."

"Simple economics. Gold normally lies underground at up to four kilometres deep whilst in Mongolia it's on the surface. I grant you Outer Mongolia is the most inhospitable climate made worse by having two super powers on its borders, but its tailor-made. I even had to kidnap the Chinese ambassador to remind the Chinese I mean business. All part of exerting pressure whilst I conclude my arrangements," said Giovanni pressing a button to reveal the struggling Chinese ambassador Cheng on the screen. "How highly do you think the Chinese government will value his life?"

"You've drawn attention to your location by kidnapping him."

"The time for hiding is over; they can do what they like now. You really are most naïve, Tresanton, I expected you to be more like your father." It was the first time Giovanni had mentioned his father and Guy reacted instantly. "My father? Where is he? Is he well?

"He is well and about to play a pivotal role with the launch of the Contagion Project into China."

"What is your real name?" asked Guy desperately trying to keep the man talking whilst he tried to think of a way out of his predicament.

"Giovanni Calvi. I have a direct bloodline to the Venetian Republic and am directly related to Cosimo de Medici who ran Florence as a private fiefdom. My ancestors used the same model in Venice during the renaissance; the same model used as the basis for the Elders."

"The Venetian Republic?"

"Yes, they were world's first and strongest traders. The whole country reliant on its ability to trade without prejudice to friend or foe. They formed the basis of the modern nation state and had no truck with religion, just like Genghis. It's not surprising Marco was so attached to the Mongol way of life. The Medici's became the most successful commercial enterprise in Italy and for 150 years they ran the Renaissance. It all started with the greatest traveller of them all. His body is in the grounds of this house; my father brought him here to honour his legacy. He was a very smart and careful man to have survived for as long as he did; to gain the Khan's trust as a foreigner took great care and planning. So when he worked to build the puzzle, as you have pointed out, he took one final surety, the final part of the Prophecy directions and kept them here for his own ancestors. I owe him a great deal." Giovanni leaned back in his chair and put the tips of his fingers together forming a pyramid. He put his chin on the point and smiled at Guy; a smile of pure satisfaction and contentment. He was absolutely sure that what he was about to unleash was the right thing to do and would make him the most powerful man in the world.

"So you now have everything to get to the Prophecy?" said Guy.

"Absolutely and I bet you can't guess where the second part of the Prophecy was left by my ancestor Marco all those years ago."

"I'm sure I can't," replied Guy wearily wondering how much longer he could keep the man talking and hoping that Monty's arrival was imminent.

"At the monastery at La Gomera. The very heart of the Elders, left there in a hidden cave in the valley and found originally by Zheng Wan's father Zhou Wang. My father visited the island at the time of the 'great challenge match' as they called it and managed to spirit away the document you see here from under their very noses. He then brought Marco's body here and joined the two together in the mausoleum."

"In other words you stole it," said Guy sarcastically.

"Acquired legally. All this was Marco's and is therefore now mine, and here is the final twist," said Giovanni pointing to another smaller scroll.

"What is it?"

"Marco's own last will and testament kept since his death here in my vaults and declaring his family's right to inherit the Kublai treasures. No one legally will be able to argue with my claim."

He seemed to suddenly realise what Guy was trying to do and stood up. "Now I'm not stupid, Tresanton; you are wasting my time with puerile questions so it's time to finish this." He turned in response to a knock on the door and Guy watched as a middle-aged man entered the room; his left hand heavily bandaged. He recognised the man who had helped beat him up. Giovanni seemed pleased to see him. "Come on in Alphonse," he said and turning to Guy added, "Like you, he had a difficult encounter with the assassin Kat." Alphonse didn't seem pleased at the reminder. "I won't thank you for getting rid of that bitch but she deserved what she got. What do I do with him Professor?"

"It's all over for him, but first he can witness my greatest triumph."

"You told me to report for an assignment," said Alfonse.

"I'll speak to you in private," snapped Giovanni and walked to the far end of the room where outside the range of Guy's hearing he spoke rapidly, Alphonse nodded his understanding of whatever he had been told and left the room. "So," said Giovanni returning to Guy, Alfonse has gone to take care of some housekeeping and I see the helicopter has just returned with a special guest."

The 'special guest' proved to be someone who was even less welcome to him than the Professor. "My God, I've dreamt of this day ever since I first had the misfortune to see your ugly face," came a familiar voice, "Fastened to the floor like the vermin you are."

"Grasshopper, I'd recognise your smell anywhere," spat Guy.

"Can I kill him now?" the fat man asked Giovanni.

"I should have known you were part of this," said Guy and grunted in pain as Grasshopper kicked him.

"Everything is ready Professor, Stefan said you want me back here," said Grasshopper. He was annoyed at missing his African ladies but looked forward to finishing off Tresanton.

"Go and find Sabine and make sure you track down Zie Lai. It's time I heard the latest on the Chinese operation." He pointed to Guy and said to the old man "Gerd, watch Tresanton." Guy made another effort to keep him in conversation. "You were telling me about Marco and Venice," he said, anything to delay him. "Ah yes, the great Elders meeting, Marco and Cosimo met

Zheng He at La Gomera, and at their urging Zheng He set up the Elders then and there as a replica of Venice and Florence. The same principles of universal patronage with iron manipulation behind the scenes, the new Renaissance. As accredited heir of both, the Khan's Prophecy and the Elders are mine. I joined them incognito to see for myself what an antiquated organisation they are. That will change under my stewardship."

"You will never get control of the Elders," said Guy trying to massage his hands.

"Really? I have enough from their archives to show that they have acted illegally."

"No one will believe you."

"The world's wealth is stored here and its knowledge is in the huge archives at La Gomera."

"And the cruiser?"

"Transport from Russia. My newly aware wife wants to turn it into a floating orphanage. What better camouflage can there be for a cruiser carrying such a wealthy cargo?"

"Very impressive," conceded Guy still desperately looking around for a way of escape.

"The final twist was buying Lorna's hand. Indeed I bought both sisters but your meddling killed Leila in Andalucía."

"What do you mean bought them?" said Guy.

"They were bred for that purpose, much as you breed a pedigree dog or horse. Same principle, oh has she not told you? How embarrassing. The artificial product of a breeding factory, hence the real future of the cruiser will be to become what Stig always intended, a floating breeding farm for the super race. Isn't that right, my dear?" he smiled and activated the screen again. "You see Tresanton, I know you have old-fashioned feelings of chivalry but unfortunately you have been somewhat misled."

"Lorna!" exclaimed Guy as the screen flickered to life.

"Guy, are you all right?" Lorna's face registered concern at his dishevelled appearance.

"As well as can be expected with this madman," replied Guy, "Please tell me what he says isn't true."

"I'm afraid it is," interjected Giovanni. "Bred at the camp along with her sister Leila who I gather you also had strong feelings for, must be something to do with that particular breeding strain."

"You evil bastard," spat Guy. He saw Lorna's horror on the screen, "You are worse than Hitler; even he didn't go to these lengths."

"You know nothing, so don't pass judgment. My dear wife has agreed to perform her wifely duties; all official since her surrogate father Stig Oleson brought her here."

"Oleson wasn't your real father?" asked Guy trying to understand.

"Apparently not, "replied Lorna dully. "At least that's good news; the rest of what he says makes me sick to my stomach."

"That's no way to talk after our night of passion," replied Giovanni smiling as he deactivated the connection. "Very convenient when you can just switch your wife on and off like that."

"You are inhuman," said Guy quietly.

"I'm not going to take offence that you have been chasing my wife for the last year because you did in a strange way help her. Now I need to get to work so meet your nemesis," said Giovanni producing a metal dagger, "notice anything special about this."

"It's made of rhodium," said Guy.

"Same family as plutonium. Has twice the value of gold, so this dagger alone is worth a fortune," said Giovanni turning the dagger around in front of his eyes.

"You didn't finish the story, at least let me know that," said Guy realising that appealing to the man's vanity and history was all he had left.

"The Venetians were the richest men on earth and conceived the plan with Zheng He to build a world council, the Elders, whilst Zheng He spread the Artefacts to the four corners of the known world."

"Why with explorers? Zheng He could not have known who would find them?"

"Obviously the explorers would be the first to find them in the far flung corners of the world but Zheng He went to some pains with the Italians to ensure that well-known explorers were targeted and given clues as to the whereabouts of the Artefacts."

"But they came a long time after Marco Polo and Zheng He."

"As I said coordinated by the Elders; the fledgling Elders made sure that Columbus, Drake and Cook were all targeted, but they couldn't move them. The Elders made sure that didn't happen."

"Why?"

"The time is now for the Prophecy to be revealed as Genghis decreed. It would be one thousand years from his vision. Marco's descendants knew the explorers would try their best to bring them back, so made sure they couldn't. With Columbus it was sinking the ship, with Drake scaring them off the island and with the Axe ensuring it was split into two and the Staff was hidden without any clues by Marco."

"Then the scene was set," Guy encouraged him to continue.

"Yes…What brought it to a head was the Columbus Cross."

"So the collection is completed. All you have to do is collect the prize but you need a decoy because the terrain and the neighbours China and Russia are too dangerous," guessed Guy, "is that why my father is involved."

"The Contagion Project will ensure the world's puerile media is entertained while I enjoy my moment of glory."

"Drugs to ruin thousands of lives but you wouldn't care about that would you?"

"All being offloaded as we speak with significant amounts being distributed into Latin America, China and Africa, then I will come along and offer to be their saviour by stopping the influx."

"All to regain your inheritance."

"I was left nothing," snapped Giovanni, "Penniless, the Medici's fortune long gone, others saw to that, so it's time to change it all and ensure only the fittest survive."

"Like Hitler," snapped Guy. He realised his end was inevitable and it would be better to die quickly.

"You are becoming tiresome," he said suddenly, his temper flaring…

"What is it?" Giovanni turned in annoyance as a worried looking Grasshopper returned to the room. "We've totally lost contact with both China and Latin America," he stuttered.

"Well get them back," snapped Giovanni as another screen sprang to life. "Ah Else, just a minute," he turned back to Guy. "Adios Tresanton, you were a worthy, if naïve, fighter," he said and turned his attention back to the screen. "Let him see my moment of glory then he's yours," he said over his shoulder to Grasshopper.

Excited voices came across the airwaves, though the video stream was blurring badly.

"Giovanni we have reached the cavern, Yen Lai and myself," came Else's voice.

"Well done Else," replied Giovanni staring hard at the screen. "I assume you followed the Artefact coordinates?"

"Precisely, to the exact letter on both longitude and latitude, the two geologists with us have verified this is the cavern. Without the detailed co-ordinates we would never have found it. From a distance it's undulating grassland, amazing camouflage."

"The view has always been that Genghis was buried in Burkhan Haldun or 'God's hill' in the Khentii range but now you know different. What is the nature of the cavern?"

"It goes slightly downwards at a fifteen degree angle; the sides are made of the rhodium material."

"What of Baku?"

"He's being supportive; he sent some men. There is no sign of the Russians. In fact the place is deserted. It's dark now and we've cordoned the whole area off with ZTW signs and plan to go in at first light."

"No you must go in now. You have the equipment and it makes no difference underground," snapped Giovanni excitedly watching the live video feed.

"Very well but it could be dangerous leaving no one outside."

"You have the best equipment; there is no time," replied Giovanni gasping in awe as he saw the light reflect off the significant deposits of rhodium. He smiled as he reflected that they were well over one hundred miles north of where Zheng had erroneously placed the site. The screen flickered, "what's happening?" he asked.

"We will have to go on voice only, the equipment is struggling because of the thick walls."

"Very well but keep in voice contact. I want you to look for the tombs first.

"Is the transport route cleared?"

"Yes, that's taken care of. Trucks will be arriving tomorrow from Russia courtesy of Stefan, and the sea carrier within ten days."

"Can we trust Baku?"

"He will not be a problem," replied Giovanni. "Now get

moving," he sat back listening to their breathing as the party of four made their way into the cave. He became impatient, "What's happening, Else?"

"We're in a large cavernous area and in front of me through a side cavern are two large rectangular boxes made of rhodium."

"That's it," shouted Giovanni his excitement rising and even Guy looked intrigued despite his predicament. "Go to the larger tomb that will be Genghis and the Prophecy will be in there."

"I'm trying to lift the lid…help me," he heard Else say to someone. There was a grating noise; then she said,

"It's got the name Temujin on it."

"That's his original Mongolian name; open it quickly," instructed Giovanni.

"It looks as if it has been disturbed."

"That's impossible, no one has been there."

"Perhaps age has made the lid move slightly; ah there is a large leather manuscript with words in Uighur."

"Read it," ordered Giovanni, "It's the Prophecy; we have it after all this time."

"Oh my God what's that!" screamed Else, "There was a bang outside the cave, the whole place shook."

"A bang? What sort of bang? What's happening there?" snapped Giovanni barely able to contain himself.

"An explosion, I'll have to call you back; the others are signalling."

"No stay on the line," ordered Giovanni and waited in silence; the tension getting to him.

"There was an explosion, a long way from here but we can't contact our back-up team,"

"Stay on the damned line, Else," Giovanni repeated frantically as the voice faded again and then went dead.

"Even you can't control everything," whispered Guy. Giovanni turned on him, rage and frustration distorting his face. "That was your death song, Tresanton," and looking impatiently at Grasshopper said. "Finish him off."

"An absolute pleasure," snapped Grasshopper.

"Let my dear wife see his spectacular end," snapped Giovanni, "Alfonse get me the connection back and where the hell is Sabine when I need her?"

Guy squirmed as Grasshopper came towards him the

rhodium knife held out in front of him; there seemed no way out of this dilemma. "No, please don't," gasped Lorna, on the screen, looking on in horror. "I'll do anything, don't do this."

"Sorry, my dear, you already have done everything I want," snapped Giovanni.

"I'm afraid it's time to say goodbye and how I've dreamed of this moment," gloated Grasshopper lifting the dagger to strike as Guy desperately tried to move his arms and groaned inwardly as he felt the metal touch his stomach. "This is far better than you deserve, if I'd had my way it would have been rusty scrap iron," snarled Grasshopper thrusting downwards. "This is going to be slow and painful, a lingering death. Guy fainted as the knife entered his body.

"Take him away," snapped Giovanni, "I don't want the carpet ruined."

"You killed him, you bastard," shouted Lorna hysterically. Giovanni ignored her and leaned forward to switch off the screen. "Why the hell can't you get me back into contact," he growled at Alfonse. "I need to speak to Else urgently and where is Sabine?" His voice was beginning to sound deranged.

"She's disappeared from the Sunseeker and no one can trace her or Mario," replied Grasshopper; he hardly cared where they were at this moment, his ambition was fulfilled. "I've tried to call Else several times," said Alfonse returning and looking very worried. "She's out of contact, so is the entire back-up team. There's been a catastrophic communications failure."

"The most expensive bloody equipment and this is what I get! Find Zie in China; why haven't I heard from him?" snapped Giovanni checking the modules on the consol. "He's supposed to be in place by now."

"There is something coming through now," replied Alfonse reading a text message. "It's from Jack Tresanton."

"Well what does it say, man."

"History repeats itself in the pearl delta, goodbye."

"What the hell is that supposed to mean?" snapped Giovanni.

"I fear it means only one thing," replied Alfonse grimly. "The British opium was burnt in a large bonfire in exactly the same area centuries ago; we're picking up images of a large fire in the area from the satellite."

"Get hold of Zie," snapped Giovanni angrily.

"I'm very much afraid that both Jack and Zie are dead, the report says no survivors have been found," said Alfonse quietly.

"Who the hell is that in the helicopter," snapped Giovanni as he saw the machine start to move without his authorisation.

"Stefan came back to pick something up, told me not to bother you as the cruiser is heading east and he will call you when he joins it."

"What did he come back for?"

"The authorisation from your wife that Captain Jenner needed."

"Jenner will do what he is bloody well told. Stefan has to get to Vladivostok in ten days," roared Giovanni flinging his drink down in frustration. "I'm surrounded by idiots; you all have clear instructions, get me Else."

"I'm trying my best sir. We're contacting Baku for his help; there appears to be outside interference on the signals."

"Contagion is a disaster, Victor and Zie have failed me, only Africa is left at least the main strike is on target. Else, where the hell are you, talk to me woman?" Giovanni was raging and pacing back and forth across the room his face contorted, his arms waving like a madman.

"There's a call coming in from a mobile unit in the Indian Ocean," said Alfonse.

"Very well."

"Mr. Calvi?"

"Who is this?"

"Interpol, we boarded your cruiser and found it full of illegal drugs; according to the Captain you are the owner. We are impounding the vessel and will want to talk to you about it in the next day or so." Giovanni's face went a darker shade of red. "That's private property in international waters, you have no right and will hear from my solicitor," he rasped and slammed the phone down. What the hell was Stefan doing? He must have known the cruiser was under surveillance. An awful thought suddenly struck. "I'm going to see my wife," he snapped running across to take the lift to the bedrooms and calling for Gerd and Freda. "Where the hell is she, that German bastard has betrayed me?" he screamed to no one in particular and ran back to the control centre. He turned to Grasshopper. "We need to activate our own contingency plan; get after Stefan you idiot," he yelled at him. Alphonse re-entered the room and Giovanni, now almost apoplectic with rage shouted,

"What is it Alfonse?"

"I have Baku on the console," replied Alfonse quietly,

"I think you might want to take this yourself."

<hr>

"What do you mean you can't take me there?" snapped Monty staring at the island's inspector who was very uncomfortable at having to deliver the message. "Permission has been revoked from the highest level."

"The highest level?" echoed Monty.

"The President's office," replied Police Inspector Hortha. "I have just received the order and it is quite explicit. I'm sorry but there's nothing we can do."

"I suppose it will take a murder to get you there!" snapped Monty. "Right I'll go alone."

"My orders are that no one must go there; now you must excuse me, I have a boating accident to investigate nearby."

"Nearby?"

"Yes, two boats have collided and someone has drowned."

"Who reported the accident?" asked Monty.

"A woman. I wasn't given a name simply that she was very distressed."

"Where was all this happening exactly?"

"Right next to the island," replied Hortha, "You are welcome to join us if you wish."

"Come on," Monty whispered to Rochembach as he climbed into the police helicopter. "I have a plan."

"What plan?" asked Rochembach settling into the seat beside him.

"I've just heard from Jade; she's unearthed something really exciting."

"What is it?"

"Let's just say it could well turn the tables on Giovanni Calvi or whatever he calls himself; the vaults at Fortaleza have revealed their own gold dust."

Chapter 41

Daguurin Mongol Province

After losing contact Else and Zie made their way further into the cavern, amazed by the sheer beauty of the metal's colours reflecting off their flashlight beams as they traversed the walls. They had lost contact with their back-up so reasoned it was better to move forwards away from the explosion. Zie, keep trying to get Giovanni," said Else anxiously. Everywhere she looked there was rhodium coating the walls and ceilings. The Genghis tomb was huge and impressive but looked as if it had been tampered with. Who on earth could have been here before them unless in her heightened state she was imagining things? "It will take about a week to get what we need out of the cave."

"We have ten days according to Giovanni," replied Zie. "Do you think we have a major problem?"

"I don't know Zie; all we can do is proceed as planned."

"The radio is useless, there is nothing but static as if someone was jamming the system."

"Jamming, you don't mean deliberately?"

"Possibly, I don't feel too well Else, my head hurts."

"Come on Zie, we have to keep going. We either hide or head back now taking the Prophecy with us."

"Let's go back Else, we can try again tomorrow."

"Very well, come on let's get the Prophecy," Else agreed and began retracing her steps. She hadn't gone far before finding part of her back up team. The scientists were lying on the floor unconscious. She jabbed one of them in the ribs with her foot. "What's wrong with you both, get up," she shouted to them. Neither moved. She was about to speak again when she felt an awful pain in her mouth. "The air, what the hell is happening to the air?" She fell forwards bumping into Zie who screamed uncontrollably until they both fell next to the two geologists.

———————

Giovanni picked up his mobile and listened intently. "Mr. Calvi, this is President Baku," he heard. "Baku, what the hell is happening over there? We have lost all communications with our site," Giovanni told him.

"Yes…I have some bad news for you, I'm afraid there has been a dreadful accident."

"Accident? What the hell do you mean?"

"Your people wandered into the middle of a government test area; they should have had permission and no one knew they were there."

"Government test area! What the hell do you mean? It was a ZTW field area," yelled Giovanni his blood pressure rising even higher.

"They made a mistake with the co-ordinates," continued Baku smoothly. "We detonated a large thermo nuclear test device there about an hour ago. There will be no survivors."

"You bastard," yelled Giovanni, "don't play games with me."

"That's no way to speak to a head of state, Calvi; I have done you the great courtesy of informing you of an event personally, even though your personnel transgressed onto government property, goodbye." The line went dead.

———————————

"Grasshopper get Sabine!" screamed Giovanni. He couldn't believe so many things could go wrong with a plan he had personally devised and regarded as foolproof. He began preparing himself for the ultimate contingency. "We need to review the situation and get out now."

"It's over, Giovanni," came a stern authoritative voice. Monty and Kurt Rochembach entered the room both carrying guns.

"How the hell did you get in here, you have no right?"

"Interpol! And we have every right. Your country is a signatory and you are under arrest."

"I own the bloody police."

"Not Interpol, at least no one has told me," said Monty drily, "We are here courtesy of the Elders, and it's all over for you."

"Like hell it is," snapped Giovanni. He snatched up a gun from a nearby table and fired, hitting Rochembach in the stomach. The policeman groaned and went down. Monty didn't hesitate; he fired at Giovanni hitting the Italian in the left chest. The force of the bullet sent him crumpling into the console trying vainly to grab hold of something and at the same time telling Grasshopper to activate the emergency escape. The fat man tried to respond and raced across the room dodging a hail of bullets as he did so. He reached for his gun and pointed it at Monty but before he could pull the trigger Monty fired two bullets into him and he too crumpled to the floor screaming in agony. "How the hell did you get in here?" groaned Giovanni again trying to raise his gun.

"I told you, courtesy of the Elders," replied Monty grimly. "Blueprints for all this were at the monastery in La Gomera. Most thoughtful of your ancestor Marco Polo, particularly the secret tunnel."

"No one can get in here. Marco wouldn't have done that; it's not possible," groaned Giovanni trying to move but fading fast.

Monty spotted Guy's prostrate body for the first time and left Giovanni to attend to him. "Guy?" He quickly realised Guy was badly hurt and shouted down the corridor, "It's safe to come out now; we need help here." Guy was drifting in and out of consciousness; he heard strange words in the distance and felt himself slowly heading down the corridor of death. It was an incredibly peaceful feeling and flooded his thoughts with deceptive warmth before reality flooded in and he heard a fusillade of shots and shouting. He felt strangely detached from it all; then Monty came into view. "Monty stop him," he gasped weakly. "Contingency plan," he grated through clenched teeth the pain almost unbearable.

Monty swung his attention back to Giovanni as Diane and others took care of Guy. "Lift your hands off the console, Giovanni, or I'll shoot you down," he warned him grimly.

"You're a policeman; I'm unarmed you won't shoot me in cold blood," sneered Giovanni trying desperately to get hold of the escape lever. Finally he managed to grab it. "I will be back," he promised and waited expectantly for the hatch to activate, "I never thought I would need this." he mused. Monty saw the hatch opening, realised Giovanni was about to escape and fired twice. Both shots found their mark in Giovanni's chest and he fell to the floor convulsing frantically. "I told you to stop, you idiot," Monty said dispassionately.

Diane called across the room from where she had been trying to stem the flow of blood from both Guy and Rochembach. "We need an air ambulance here, fast," she said. He took in the seriousness of the situation with a practised eye and told Alfonse to summon the island's emergency services. "I remember him from Kenya," said Diane looking down at the Italian, "He took Lorna and would have taken Leila too. Can't believe he was behind all this."

"Well he's not any more. We've stopped him and his organisation." replied Monty through gritted teeth as he surveyed the scene. "We've bought the whole damned empire to its knees." But they hadn't! A familiar figure sprang into the room and said. "Not quite!" Two shots rang out and Monty was hit in the hip. He gasped in pain and turned to face his new assailant. "You!" he gasped. "You were dead in the water."

"Take more than a knife wound to stop me," snapped Sabine her green eyes flashing with hate as she moved towards them with cat-like steps. Despite her bravado she had blood seeping from wounds and looked dreadful. She glanced disdainfully at Rochembach's body then across to Guy before seeing Diane trying to revive him. "This man needs urgent care; I have to get him to a helicopter, he is dying." Diane told her.

"Really, so Tresanton is nearly dead; he's not even worth a further bullet. Shame about dear Giovanni but he was just too ambitious, took too much on," she checked Giovanni's pulse, "faint and slowing but just to make sure, she calmly raised the gun and shot him between the eyes. "Looks like housekeeping is needed. The way I see it this is all mine providing there are no survivors, particularly you my fat slob," she snapped, and fired into Grasshopper's convulsing body.

"Alfonse, can I trust you?"

"Of course," stammered the older man standing at the edge of the room.

"You two start packing," she gestured across to the terrified old couple Gerd and Freda. "I want to be ready to leave with the Artefacts in the Sunseeker in half an hour; see to it. I need to catch that traitor, Stefan."

"People need doctors," mumbled Diane realising with horror what Sabine was about to do.

"Shut up," snapped Sabine checking the console; she lifted her favourite gun, a Walther PPK.

"For God's sake woman, they need help," snapped Diane angrily.

"They won't need any help where you're all going."

Her words triggered a violent reaction from Diane. "Have you no compassion? She screeched and springing up grabbed Sabine around the waist and jerked her off her feet. Her action took the fighter by surprise and knocked her to the floor splitting open her old wounds. "Shit," grimaced Sabine nearly fainting with the pain as Diane kicked her. Summoning reserves of strength Sabine managed to hit Diane hard on the head with the gun and stagger to her feet. Diane fell groaning to the floor bracing herself as the gun was cocked and fired the bullet narrowly missing her as she curled into a ball. She fell backwards as Sabine walked stiffly to the console and Giovanni's escape route, her strength starting to fade. Hopefully by now the Artefacts would be in the Sunseeker she had managed to bring alongside the jetty after dragging herself from the sea. She smiled grimly as she reached for the lever to open the chute then groaned in agony as something hit her in the back; she felt like she'd been kicked by a mule. "You," she gasped as she turned around with her senses swimming.

"Yes me, your worst nightmare," said the new voice; then calling out, "Diane are you alright?" Diane looked up from tending to Guy, saw Rose and beyond her Sabine. "Yes thanks I'm fine but, look out…She's getting away," shouted Diane pointing to where Sabine had been. Rose was unconcerned. "She won't get far, I followed her here and disabled the Sunseeker," she said and looked around the room in horror, bodies were everywhere. It resembled a blood bath. She yelled into her phone for an air ambulance. Rose took Diane into her arms and hugged her, "Thank God you're here," Diane cried and collapsed in tears. "How's Guy, is he dead?" asked Rose.

"There's a faint pulse, but we must be quick with him and Monty too, but dear old Rochembach is dead," Diane replied. Rose felt Guy's neck. "You're right, there's still a faint pulse," she said. Taking a deep breath she turned her attention to Monty. "Take more than a bullet in the leg to finish this old soldier off," she smiled, and applied a wad of white cloth to Monty's hip wound. She looked across to the Artefacts in their impressive cabinet, "So, these are the cause of all this mayhem and violence; it was all for them!" She said and moved to be close to Guy as he was lifted onto a stretcher. "Stay with us, Bear," she whispered to him.

Alfonse operated the winches that controlled the trees as the helicopter come into land with the Paramedics on board.

"We need to find out what happened to his people in Mongolia," Monty whispered; his hip was getting more painful by the minute.

"You're badly hurt, Monty, forget it. We'll deal with it," Rose assured him.

"Others first, I'll live. I must attend to Mongolia, "gasped Monty trying to overcome the pain. "Jade gave me a number."

"Let me do it," said Rose. She activated the speakerphone; then dialled the number.

"Sergei Rostov of the Elders," a strong sounding voice answered. "Who am I speaking to?"

"Rose Ling on behalf of Monty." she replied and moved Monty closer to the phone.

"What happened, Sergei?" whispered Monty.

"Baku did a deal with the Chinese; the nuclear explosion was a test firing but has spread radioactivity across the area of the cavern; it'll be poisoned for decades."

"How do you know?" asked Rose.

"He told us just before it was announced on Mongolia State Television; he assured Russia it was a test only. You have to remember, in Russia we are sensitive to such things after Chernobyl. Baku effectively killed two birds with one stone; getting the Chinese back on side after their Ambassador was kidnapped and also shutting down the Prophecy threat. An ingenious solution, I think."

"One I assume you helped with."

"Couldn't possibly comment on that," replied the Russian.

"Exactly what it was designed to do I believe," replied Monty wheezing badly. "Sergei many thanks, God knows what was in the tombs but I've a feeling you've kept the Elders in business."

Later, sitting in Giovanni's lounge Rose handed over control of operations to an officious looking Inspector Hortha. Monty had recovered slightly and refused to be treated until Guy was stabilized. The news was good; he was in hospital badly hurt but would live. It had taken Monty some time to pacify Hortha with an explanation as to why he had stormed the island against express instructions not to. They had found the Chinese Ambassador alive and well and so were able to claim a great success; the President was pleased.

"Did you know all along?" Rose asked Hortha. He shifted uncomfortably in his seat.

"Know what?" he said evasively

"About the Professor?"

"We had suspicions but there was little we could do; he cleverly kept in the background."

"You could have told us more Monty," Rose gently chided her friend.

"No, I couldn't. It had to be kept secret; if the Prophecy had become public knowledge terrorist groups would have tried to get involved.

"Well the Professor's dead now," replied Rose firmly. He got what he deserved as they all did; now we have to concentrate on those still living. My father died here this afternoon and the bitch who killed him escaped."

"She won't survive the severity of her wounds," Monty assured her.

"And the rest of them here?"

"Alfonse is talking fast about everything; the old German couple are both totally confused; there's only one person I'm still worried about and that's Lorna."

"I thought she was imprisoned here."

"Alfonse says she escaped with Stefan's help, to her cruiser of all places."

"They must have left on the chopper I saw fly off as I was coming up from the jetty," said Rose.

"Giovanni sent Stefan to run the cruiser, the one you told Giovanni you had impounded?" Alfonse said quizzically.

"An elaborate ruse to make him panic; didn't work very well. He didn't take the bait," confessed Monty.

"It will be heading east," continued the older man,

"It's a safe bet Stefan and Lorna will be on it with Captain Jenner; its destination is Vladivostok."

"Stefan might still be trying to do that," said Rose angrily. "This isn't over yet and Lorna is still at grave risk; we need to stop them."

"Let me check with Interpol," Monty said, dialling a familiar number. He listened intently to the person at the other end of the call, cut off and said. "They are on the cruiser, just arrived. Stefan has apparently given himself up to Captain Jenner, and Lorna is safe on board."

"I need to talk to her," said Diane. "After what she's been through, the news that Giovanni is dead might help."

"Not possible I'm afraid, they tell us she has locked herself in her cabin," said Monty.

"Then we must go there. In her frame of mind she might harm herself," said Diane.

"We'll get a helicopter immediately," whispered Monty but started to cough badly.

"You're not fit to go anywhere," replied Rose, "Diane and I will go. Get the helicopter ordered and then you are going to hospital. I assume the Contagion Project is finished?"

"Yes, the cruiser docked in Zanzibar and it's been impounded. Alfonse tells me that the biggest drugs haul in China cost Guy's father his life; he not only burnt the lot, he also eliminated the fourth sleeper. Panama was stopped by a renegade."

"And Mongolia?" asked Rose.

"Baku will survive as President, a real dark horse that one, but someone who has stabilized the situation albeit with a power play. His deal with the Chinese was a clever move; he now has a strong pro-Chinese platform on which to win the election and can also claim to have stopped ZTW's evil capitalism."

"Surely he had help?"

"From Sergei," said Monty pointing to the video monitor. The garrulous Russian was still there his white beard almost filling the screen. "I assume that's correct, Sergei?"

"Didn't hear that too well," smiled the Russian. "No one tries to kill me and gets away with it, so I worked with our new Chinese member of the Elders Hsing Lau. Baku jumped at the proposal for his way out of the mess even though it meant detonating a nuclear device on Mongolian soil."

"And of course it protects the Prophecy for the foreseeable future."

"Yes, the whole area will remain under military protection. The Genghis tomb lies bang in the middle of the major radiation area."

"That's why Giovanni looked so defeated at the end. He spent his entire life waiting to see the Prophecy and failed to do so. Now no one will ever know what's in it; you could almost feel sorry for him… but I don't," said Monty, "the Khan's secret stays lost forever."

"The exact co-ordinates that Giovanni used have been given to the Elders so I think it's fair to say that the secret will remain safe. Some things are best left alone and I think on balance this is one of them," said Sergei sitting back as the video screen flickered off.

"I'll go with Diane," said Rose getting up as the chopper landed. "You're not fit to go anywhere," she told Monty.

"You are not police officers and it's too dangerous," gasped Monty, coughing blood again.

It looked like a stalemate, Monty would insist on carrying on despite his injuries and Rose was equally determined that he was going to hospital for treatment.

"Perhaps I can help?" came a familiar voice.

"My God Jem, it's good to see you, I thought you were on a long holiday," said Monty, surprised but delighted to see her.

"All a smoke screen. I've been behind the scenes working with Interpol to keep you alive, almost impossible at times, particularly having to explain why I helped Guy escape from the Bahamas. We were monitoring the traffic over the last few days; unfortunately my arrival was a little late."

"Doesn't matter, its damned good to see you again," smiled Monty giving his niece a hug."

"So you broke all the rules again, coming in here without any authority," she scolded.

"Technically yes."

"You're going directly to hospital," Jem insisted.

"I have to stop that cruiser."

"No! That's now my job," she said firmly.

"And I'm coming with you," said Diane, "She trusts me."

"Very well, Rose can I suggest you head over with Monty? There's someone there who needs you badly," said Jem.

Guy was back in the tunnel with no light at the end; it just went on and on then something he couldn't discern; it was a rustle, a chink of light, nothing more. He lay there slowly opening his eyes to be surrounded by whiteness. He tried to look around but couldn't, he tried to speak but couldn't, so he lay there and peace returned until a persistent voice kept repeating itself over and over, becoming louder and finally it became real. "We beat them partner, the Viper and the Bear won."

"Thank God," whispered Guy through cracked lips.

<hr>

The cruiser was at full speed heading eastwards towards Singapore and pitching violently in the swell as Jem, Diane and two Interpol officers, Raul and Ade descended by harness onto the deck, trussed together like chickens. Jem took the strain as they landed and helped Diane to her feet. This was a new sensation for Diane but one that she was determined to complete. On wobbly legs they made their way across the sloping deck and down into the gangway to the living quarters to be met by Captain Jenner. "This is most irregular," snapped Jenner, "I could have you arrested for illegal boarding."

"You can try but there are three officers from Interpol here and more on the way if needed," snapped Jem.

"Most irregular."

"And you, sir, are under arrest," Jem informed him as Raul and Ade came behind her.

"What for and on whose authority?"

"A number of issues and on my authority. You are confined to your cabin as of now, I am taking control."

"This is outrageous," protested Jenner.

"So is consorting with a known criminal, and endangering the lives of your passengers plus carrying tonnes of illegal drugs to Africa," snapped Jem displaying her Interpol badge as she summoned the warrant officer, a shrew-like man called Parkinson.

"Officer, take this man below; you will assume control with the two officers here. I want you to turn this vessel around and head for the nearest port."

"Very well," replied Parkinson eyeing Jenner balefully.

"The German, Stefan, where is he?" snapped Jem raising her gun.

"Let me save you the bother. I can't fight three of you," replied the German emerging from a nearby cabin with his hands up."

"I'm arresting you on charges of kidnapping and attempted murder," snapped Jem.

"Don't worry Parkinson, it's all above board," smiled Diane, following Jem and talking earnestly to the officer. "This is what I want arranged immediately; where's Lorna?"

"In the main stateroom; she won't see anyone."

"Leave it to me," said Diane heading down the gangway. The stateroom door was locked. "Lorna, its Diane, you have to listen to me." There was no answer so she shouted up to Jem. "They tell me she's been in there for four days, why hasn't any one tried to get in?" There was no answer so she put her shoulder to the door and rattled the lock in an effort open it. Raul arrived and stood beside her. She pointed to the door. "Break it down," she ordered and stood back as he smashed the lock with a tremendous kick. Lorna was lying comatose on her bed. Diane checked her friend's pulse. "She's still alive but only just, get a doctor quickly," she told Raul. "She's taken an overdose of sleeping pills." Raul returned with the ship's doctor, an old man called Smethers, who examined Lorna's inert figure. "How serious is it?" she asked him. "Her breathing is getting stronger, but I need to get the pills out of her," he said.

Together they carried Lorna across to the toilet where they induced retching. "Leave me with her, I'll see to you later," Diane said watching her friend struggling with her inner demons. What on earth was she going through?

"Lorna, talk to me, please," said Diane.

"Go away, you were one of them," murmured Lorna her eyes opening slightly.

"I knew nothing of it Lorna please believe me."

"You were with my father."

"Yes, but I was young and dazzled by his wealth and power."

"You knew I wasn't his daughter."

"I had my suspicions, but no, I didn't ever envisage that, when I asked him such questions he would dismiss them. In the end as you know he got rid of me anyway."

"You must have known something."

"He told me you had been with someone that night, that was all, and forbade me to ever mention anything about it again. He was a danger to women, that's why your natural mother, Jacqui, left him; she couldn't stand the deceit."

"Natural mother? I doubt it, I'm an obscene creation. You should have left me to die."

"She was your natural mother; you look more like her every

day. Now that vile creature is dead and Guy has survived, so the ordeal is over.”

“You will never understand.”

“Perhaps not but I have someone here who might, someone who cares deeply for you, one of the *Huldra Twelve* you may recall you pledged with me to save,” she picked up the telephone set.

“Hello Lorna,” came a voice she thought she would never hear again.

“Soraya, oh! my God, I thought you had perished in Finland. Where are you?”

“At home in Norway thanks to your help, I’ve recovered from the Helsinki experience. I should never have left you there.”

“What happened to you?”

“It’s not important; you and I are both survivors, Lorna, from the same place, the same horrors. I too have had to live with that, so together we can fight this and win.”

“You’ve no idea how good it is to hear you again. I wish it was so simple.”

“In time it is Lorna, let’s meet up soon.”

“I have no money Diane, everything has gone; the last of it on a stupid venture in the Seychelles.”

“Actually that’s not strictly true,” said Diane smiling. “As we left I heard about a small diving company in the Seychelles run by a couple called Bert and Sherry.”

“They were killed just as they stumbled upon a treasure.”

“All yours, millions of dollars’ worth I’m told,” said Diane smiling. “Money entirely of your own making and I know someone who can manage its retrieval.”

“Wow, it’s all hard to take in,” said Lorna sitting up. “What about Stefan?”

“One right doesn’t make up for two wrongs.”

“He saved my life twice, first from a savage attack by Jochi in Siberia and getting me out of Giovanni’s lair.”

“Either way he will face a lengthy prison term.” Jem could see no other alternative.

“There is one other who cares deeply. What about Guy?” asked Diane.

“I saw him die.” Lorna said sadly.

“He’s not dead; he’s recovering in hospital,” smiled Diane. “You at least owe him an explanation of all this.”

"I guess I do but I am no good for him; he deserves better."

"I doubt if he will agree with that."

"My future is here," said Lorna determinedly, "you are sitting in it. The cruiser which I am renaming the *Huldra Twelve*."

"A spa?"

"No, what I really want to do is in Vladivostok."

"Vladivostok?" repeated Diane in surprise.

"A children's orphanage. I'll use the money to properly adapt the cruiser and run special cruises for poor children from orphanages. Are you interested?"

"Of course I am," smiled Diane.

———————————

Guy was feeling stronger as he made his way down the hospital corridor in Victoria to make his daily visit to see Tapiwa who was slowly recovering from her wounds after being unconscious for nearly a week. "You're looking much better, Tapiwa." he said.

"Thanks, I lost a lot of blood and won't be able to fight anymore; still I have some other interests in mind here actually. Time to stop wandering around; did they ever find the bitch that did this to me?"

"No sign of her but she was badly injured and the escape route she took was basically a chute straight down into the water near the jetty. The physical impact of that on her would have finished her off."

"Did they find a body?"

"Nothing, but there's sharks all around there and nothing had been found."

"That woman is capable of anything," snapped Tapiwa, "I've seen her type before."

"Perhaps but my bet is she lies at the bottom of the sea where she belongs; she had horrendous injuries."

"And the bodyguard Mario?"

"He's certainly dead; his body was washed up alongside Zichu, Rose's father. Funny thing, the kid Enrico who had a crush on Lorna has also disappeared; I expect that's all about starting a new life away from his father."

"So what now?"

"They're sending a private jet for us all to go to the Elders at La Gomera."

"I shall enjoy seeing the ultimate power base," replied Tapiwa leaning back on her pillows.

"So shall I," smiled Guy. He wished her well and headed slowly back to his bed, conscious of the stitches in his stomach wound. They had won and yet he felt there was something missing; he grinned as he saw his partner approaching him. "There's a private call for you," said Rose quietly, "I'll be back in a minute." Guy took the phone and put it to his ear.

"Guy, I never thought I would hear your voice again."

"Lorna! Where are you," he said, his pulse racing,

"A long way from the Seychelles and getting further by the minute."

"Lorna, what Giovanni said I understand it all; it makes no difference to me."

"What he told you was true. I was married to him."

"But you didn't know it."

"Perhaps not but I'm not fit for you Guy. I'm the result of an obscene experiment that went wrong, just like my sister. You see her in me Guy, that's all it is and it can never work between us; we are too different. I am not Leila."

"Lorna, you can't mean that."

"Yes I do Guy, there is someone who really does love you and I think you have always known it."

"Lorna please don't be hasty, let's discuss this." He could feel her slipping away from him.

"I couldn't do that Guy. I'm sorry, goodbye," she said tearfully.

"You are mistaken…"

The line went dead and Guy stared at the handset, finding it difficult to accept the import of the conversation he'd just had with Lorna. The door opened and Rose walked in and when she smiled at him he felt as if the entire room lit up. Then he knew. It hit him like a hammer blow and he grasped the bed to steady himself. "Are you alright, Guy?" she asked.

"Never better Rose, never better. I have been such a fool; time for a new beginning, Viper, and this time it's for real with my eyes open."

"You haven't noticed?"

"Typical man I guess but no I haven't. What a fool and you so patient."

"Not that patient. Bear, but my eyes have been opened too; sometimes you don't see what's in front of you until too late."

"More than a partnership from now on then?"

"More than a partnership," agreed Guy. He took her hand and lay back onto the soft pillows and drifted off into a deep refreshing sleep confident in his newly found relationship with Rose. It had been her all along; he just hadn't realised it.

Chapter 42

La Gomera

Jade couldn't stop smiling as she surveyed her small group of friends gathered at the monastery nearly a month after the climactic events on Ascension Island. She looked fondly around the place she had called home for most of her life, grateful it had not been destroyed; but it had been a close run thing. She was desperately saddened by the loss of her friends, Oboto and Emerald, losses compounded by the death of Jack Tresanton and Zichu Ling. The loss of Jack was most keenly felt by the person next to her. She turned to Amethyst. "It is time, Elizabeth," she said.

"It's going to be very emotional," replied Amethyst keeping in the shadows."

"Welcome friends," smiled Jade looking across at Monty, Jem, Guy, Rose and Tapiwa with Faustino the acting President in the background. "It's been a difficult road to travel but thanks to you all and to those who paid the ultimate price, we made it successfully. I feel like I know you intimately and yet have only just met a few of you face-to-face. Indeed none of you have been here before." Guy raised his hand, "Excuse me," he said, "Rose and I came to the island chasing the mad Spaniard. We didn't make it to the monastery, he stopped us as I recall." He ended smiling at Rose. "It certainly reeks of history and tradition."

"Looks nothing like what I expected," acknowledged Monty looking down through the Garonjay valley from the sheer sides of the monastery.

"The Elders and I shall be forever in your debt," continued Jade. "Thanks to you all we will be stronger than ever and it goes without saying that you have key roles to play in our future should you so choose."

"A handsome offer ma'am but I'm destined for the fishing world and finally lighting my pipe," said Monty. "I thoroughly enjoyed going to Interpol Headquarters in Lyon again and personally handing in my resignation. I have recommended you, Jem, as my replacement."

"You did what Uncle?" exclaimed Jem.

"You can tell us all now my dear. You didn't take a holiday, and it was you that coordinated the whole scheme from Lyon after getting Guy out of the Caribbean."

"Thanks Uncle, I was sworn to secrecy."

"You are amongst friends here, my dear," smiled Monty finally getting this pipe to emit smoke.

"We all have our little secrets," smiled Jade, "Now there is much to discuss but first Guy, my assistant, Amethyst is going to join us." She turned and beckoned Amethyst to join them.

"Oh my God, you are my mother! Why on earth didn't you tell me?" said Guy looking across at the familiar figure. "I've been trying to find you for ages, why?"

"I'm so sorry Guy. It's a long story but I had to avoid placing you in greater danger."

"Don't you think I've had enough of danger? I don't see how it could have been any greater," Guy commented still astonished.

"Perhaps I can help explain," continued Jade seeing raw emotion on Guy's face. "Both Zheng and Giovanni had penetrated the Elders with what we now know were two informers here at Fortaleza, aside from that they had support from some Elder council members."

"They had your father also, Guy," explained Amethyst "He had a use for them whereas if they had got their hands on me they would have used it to get to you and I couldn't allow that to happen. The Teacher was trying to capture me as he had with Rose's father and mother. Jack didn't want that at any cost so persuaded me to come here for protection."

"You could have told me."

"And put you in even greater risk? It was too dangerous, plus Jade needed help and we knew the Whistler was communicating with you. The last thing you needed was anything else to worry about."

Jade lifted both hands and pointed to the vacant chairs. "Please sit down," she said. "I'm sorry for all the subterfuge, Guy, but your father agreed. We couldn't risk Rose and you being compromised as you were all we had in the field; unfortunately the risks got greater as The Teacher and Professor infiltrated the Elders' council." Guy wasn't entirely convinced. "You could still have contacted me, a coded message at least, just to confirm you were alive."

"The problem was the leak from here. We didn't know who to trust and if they got wind I was here they would draw you in."

"You must have met them though."

"They didn't know who I was then and in the chamber all faces except the Chair and President are in shadow, so no."

"Guy, your father was a brave man," said Jade with feeling. "It was dreadful for him as a prisoner in Vietnam not knowing how long he would survive and the way he wiped out the Contagion Project in Yunnan was unbelievable. Even the Chinese state, unofficially of course, has acknowledged the diabolical nature of the drug shipments going into those regions. I'm sorry but I couldn't risk compromising you or your father."

"My father gave his life but why us?" continued Guy.

"It's time you were told," acknowledged Jade. "Two years ago your father was chosen to be our new Chair to replace me and was being groomed to take over, but The Teacher found out and had him kidnapped."

"Why wasn't I told my father had been chosen?"

"His decision; he wanted you to have a normal life. You were in your independent phase."

"Again, why our family?" persisted, Guy.

"The answer is simple; we are related that's why your family was chosen. We all descend from the Silvers as you know from your Uncle Blackie, whom your mother still can't stand. In fact you are directly descended from Jack Silver and his wife Victoria."

"I thought that's what the Elders stood for, meritocracy, not exclusive families," observed Guy looking across at Rose and Tapiwa.

"It's a mix," replied Jade carefully. "What we prize above all is loyalty and often that is a family's greatest strength. The gift of leading the Elders is a great one and your father was chosen through an extensive process, as was Amethyst or I should say Elizabeth Tresanton."

"One that I should have been told about."

"It was his decision. What's done is done though I believe he was about to tell you when he was kidnapped two years ago."

"He was not a leader."

"Perhaps not initially, but he saw it as an evolutionary thing and was growing into a fine inspirational figure as the best ones do. Now there is one of your family who is a real leader," continued Jade. "You!"

"Me? Never." said Guy firmly.

"Jack was holding the role for you. Think about it. There are few who would have had the resilience to achieve what you have; you were chosen years ago but when Giovanni stepped up the pressure we had to move faster. As the threat grew, a different strategy emerged."

"You mean when it was discovered that Giovanni's father had stolen part of the Prophecy right here under your noses?" said Guy.

"To lose the Prophecy directions was a major embarrassment; it confirmed Zhou Wang was not to be trusted. As I have admitted, we made a number of mistakes but we have come through."

"You're right I wasn't ready two years ago," agreed Guy, "I was more interested in the Caribbean Charter business," he said.

"Timing wasn't right," continued Jade. "Not only had The Teacher started to radically change the Elders but we realised there was something far more sinister going on. We arranged other actions. The first was dear Rose and it's great that you two are now an item; we were taking bets on that for months," smiled Jade.

"You arranged for Rose and me to meet?" asked Guy; that revelation surprised him.

"It was arranged through your Uncle Blackie and Rose's guardian, Beatrice, in a way though they were the ones who ended up together. We made sure Rose was looked after in her formative years, and when her parents were captured we arranged her mother's escape. It was our first covert success with the dear Whistler. Fortunately both Zichu and Jack had skills that were invaluable to The Teacher," continued Jade, "We made sure they had as much knowledge as possible on the latest mind control techniques. All we had to do then was arrange a communications channel and your strange dreams; the dear Whistler was a Godsend."

"Where did he come from?" asked Rose.

"He was from here; Silbo is a local skill to communicate across the valleys; invaluable and not needing modern communications. We pioneered it with the Elders, a great way of communicating in code and a skill that is sadly dying out here in the valleys."

"He saved my life many times," said Guy. "How did he communicate with me in my sleep?"

"He used the signals the brain receives when you sleep, pioneering stuff that got Zheng paranoid; that's why he snatched Rose and tried to get you arrested."

"Why couldn't the Whistler just give me notes?"

"The risk was too great so we sent all his messages by computer in code as a series of whistle sounds."

"So my father learnt how to communicate this way."

"Exactly. There was no other way to get messages out of The Teacher's camp; they were strictly monitored except the computed codes that were sent overnight as a download."

"Well it answers a lot of questions but if you'd told me this up front it would have saved me a lot of aggravation."

"You wouldn't have done it. That was our dilemma. Our safe controlled world was falling apart and about to get worse, but I know you must feel betrayed," said Elizabeth quietly.

"I wouldn't say that…perhaps just a bit used," said Guy. "No hard feelings though, you did what you felt was right, but it's not just about me, Rose suffered as much if not more; she lost both parents."

"Ah! That reminds me, there is one other joining us who I believe has just arrived," smiled Jade standing and turning to the entrance. "Mrs. Xian Ling you are very welcome."

"Mother," screamed Rose.

"Yolandi," smiled Xian Ling spreading her arms to receive Rose. "My dear Yat Sen gave his life for us all; Jade got a message to me it was safe to come out of hiding in China. I came here at once."

"I've not been called Yolandi since dear Jiao and Xia called me that in Shanghai last year."

"It was a very difficult time," said Xian, "I saw you in the distance in Shanghai; that was the hardest time for me but dear Yat Sen was so scared for me."

"Yat Sen?" queried Jade.

"His preferred Chinese name after the great doctor and leader Sun Yat Sen. Zichu, suited him better but he will always be Yat Sen to me."

"He saved me from certain death," commented Rose.

"And this is my future son-in-law?" smiled Xian looking across at Guy.

Their conversation was interrupted by the whirring blades of a helicopter landing below them. "Actually there is one other visitor," said Jade, "I wasn't sure he would be able to make it; someone who we also have to thank a great deal… welcome Sergei."

"Good to see you all," said the large avuncular Russian, "better circumstances than last time eh?"

"It was a tough time, but my God it's good to see you again," said Guy.

"And you my boy."

"So Sergei how is Russia and Mongolia after all the recent events?" asked Jade."

"A lot better than it was but it isn't finished yet I'm afraid," replied Sergei accepting a drink. "There's considerable turmoil in Mongolia, though Baku is successfully fighting to hold on to power, trying to explain why he agreed to the Chinese using Mongolia's back yard as a nuclear testing site. Reality is he won some major concessions from the Chinese in return which he will use as the election approaches, but I'm sorry ma'am this is boring detail and not for now."

"Is the Genghis tomb secure?" asked Jade.

"Anyone who goes within twenty kilometres of it for the next ten years will die of radiation sickness. Even with protective suits it's pretty dangerous and the cavern itself has been totally closed by the explosion. It's now a specially protected area overseen by a triumvirate of Mongolia, China and Russia; a pretty tough combination to crack if you ask me."

"So this Prophecy is safe?"

"As safe as it can be under the circumstances."

"That's good to hear," commented Guy. Suddenly he felt a chill wind sweeping through his mind as a distant memory was dredged up, something from his hallucinations. Though it was as clear as day to him now, he reeled at the implications. He was sure he had heard either Giovanni or Else say that the tomb had been opened. He kept his thoughts to himself; perhaps he'd dreamed the whole thing.

"I'd even store my own money there if I had the chance,"

continued Sergei. "Now, I have some other news for you. My shipyards in Vladivostok are overseeing the conversion work on Lorna's cruiser which I believe she is re-naming *Huldra Twelve* in recognition of the twelve girls originally taken by Stig Oleson."

"Where is she now?" asked Guy feeling a familiar pang.

"Working in the orphanage there and loving it."

"We owe you a great deal, Sergei, without you goodness knows what would have happened in Mongolia. I am pleased to confirm that as Faustino intends to stand down, your nomination as our new President will be a formality at the next Elders' meeting."

"I am honoured Jade, and proud to be part of rebuilding this great institution."

"It's an institution that will grow now we have a new President and hopefully a new Chair," said Jade proudly.

"I haven't agreed yet," replied Guy looking across to Rose. "My new wife and I need to discuss whether to rekindle our charter business; incidentally what will happen to Giovanni's island?"

"I'll answer that," said Monty. "Ascension Island is now under the control of a government department. The old couple are ensuring they will look after it until a buyer is found, then they will be pensioned off; it's hard to bring charges against them. Alfonse has been jailed for five years. Eventually ownership will pass to Giovanni's descendants."

"He had family?" asked Guy.

"Ironically only Lorna. It makes her on paper extremely wealthy aside from the treasure she found, though as you can imagine there are a number of claims on the estate particularly from the relatives of the dead followers in Vietnam. She has wisely waived all rights to the estate."

"So she is taking nothing?" asked Guy.

"Doesn't need to, she has the treasure which I believe is worth a great deal even after the government has taken its extortionate share," Monty concluded.

"Enough to fund the *Huldra Twelve*?" asked Guy.

"After two dives myself, I can confirm it's extremely valuable. A small fortune," said Tapiwa. "My fighting days are over, diving is my new passion. After my horrific water experience at the spa I thought I needed to get more adept with water. A new career is opening up for me as a diver."

"There's still one missing person," said Monty.

"Who?" asked Jade.

"Sabine the green-eyed body pierced monster. We've had neither sight nor sound of her; she just disappeared into thin air. When she went down the escape chute she had knife and gunshot wounds so I don't see how she could have survived," he recalled. "We have put a search out through the Interpol network but nothing has turned up. I think you can safely say that she perished down the escape chute and the sharks ate her."

"A fitting end," said Guy vehemently, "But I wouldn't like to bet on it, not with her."

"Jade, out of curiosity, what is happening to the Artefacts?" asked Monty.

"They are stored below where you now sit; it's best for all that no one knows exactly where they are except the Chair; the monks will take care of that."

"If they're below here we all know," smiled Monty.

"Except there are a labyrinth of tunnels and excavations which go back to the time of Zheng He. Anyone would get lost in them; each tunnel has a separate door with unique access codes with a system of passwords known only to one person. Like the nuclear codes even he or she will not be able to activate them without at least two other Elders."

Sergei decided to change the subject. "Now my boy, what's this about you being the new Chair?" he boomed. "They need determined leadership here and you are as determined as they get; now I suggest we all owe Jade a vote of thanks and has anyone got any decent vodka here?"

"Thanks Sergei," smiled Jade, "Guy, what do you say?"

"Just one more question, did you know about Marco Polo and his links to Zheng He?"

"No, we realised it belatedly as Giovanni was ready to expose us. I discovered a secret cellar in the basement; in fact it's more than that, and it's a way out in the valley. In it was a chest hidden by Zhou Wang, Zheng's father. It contained documents that confirmed Marco Polo came here in his last years and left his secrets. Fortunately we discovered them plus blueprints to Giovanni's lair just in time."

"Come on, Guy, it's a great fit," interrupted Monty. "You can count on the full support of Interpol and the Bermudian police, can't he Jem?"

"As long as it's above the law," replied Jem thinking of the escapade in the Bahamas.

"I see." Guy looked across at Rose who smiled warmly with a slight inclination of the head.

"It's what you want Guy and it's a key part of our lives; we can bring the yachts over."

"You and my mother, where will you go?"

"A little house over the other side of the valley, far enough away but there if you want us. We won't need a phone; we have the whistling," smiled Jade.

"Very well then, I agree."

Sergei Rostock smiled and looked down from the monastery's highest point across Mount Garanjonay National Park thinking about his son. He'd left home to go and train with a new organisation at Tay Ninh. He had been the top student so proud in his green uniform. He raised his glass, 'your mentor Zheng is dead but you will live on, my dear Jochi."

Epilogue

Eagles Nest – One month later

The hot Queensland sun bore down on the lone figure approaching the mansion; it was hers now with no father ranting and raving and making her feel inferior as he stalked the long corridors. It seemed empty without his larger-than-life presence and, for a brief second, she missed the old bull. Sandy smiled as her newly re-hired bodyguard Marc entered the room; he had survived Jack Hogg's ill-feted time in Vietnam by leaving the camp well before the mortar attack. She had sent him ahead to open up the rooms. They would rattle around in the place a bit but she had no inclination to sell; there were too many memories and she would miss her pets Fat Albert and Scarface who she was delighted to see were still there protecting their respective fiefdoms. Perhaps they had it right all along, the survival of the fittest was the strict law down there and she had proved she was one of them.

She had made it back from Panama with the help of a mysterious benefactor called Santos who had called her the day after the momentous explosion and explained how he had trailed Victor and helped with the explosion. The call had come out of the blue and directed her to an airport locker containing false papers and tickets that had got her out of the country. There was also a message explaining she was now on the drug cartel's hit list. She had left immediately. Santos, it seemed, assumed she couldn't run her own life and it had made her angry, but she took the gift. The man had said there was more to her father's partnership with The Teacher than she had been told.

She opened the blinds to her favourite room with the false floor and her pet crocodiles beneath. She reflected on the fact there was only her left after her father's death. Duncan was serving time for kidnapping and poor Ailsa dead and buried at sea. She poured herself a brandy and nearly dropped the glass as a strange figure appeared out of the adjoining room. "Hello my dear," he said.

"Who the hell are you and what are you doing in my house?" gasped Sandy trying to steady her nerves and where is Marc?"

"Being taken care of by Santos, the man who got you out of Panama and blew up the truck for you," he smiled coming forwards and sitting down his bulk spreading out on the sofa. "I like this room with the floor that drops away, someone told me about this and how they escaped from it, very Machiavellian."

"Didn't work then did it, mister whoever you are, if indeed it was you, then thanks for getting me out but I arranged the explosion on my own."

"The charges planted by your boyfriend Otway were too short and would have killed you instead. We had to reset them. We also helped you with Victor in Panama when you gave away your location; we covered your tracks so he was misled and ensured he didn't have more back up when you did the handover."

"Why are you here?"

"To help protect you against some nasty people who want to find you, my dear."

"Why?"

"I think you know the answer to that. You killed some of their gang members in the explosion and took their drugs; that's a big deal in Latin America. I wouldn't give more than ten percent for your chances and forget the beefcake he's useless, an amateur."

"What do you want in return?"

"Just need a place to rest my head for a few days whilst I recover something valuable."

"Recover what?"

"That's my little secret."

"And if I say no."

"Your prerogative but Queensland isn't a remote place anymore; they will get you sooner than you think. I can arrange protection."

"This thing you seek is here?"

"A little further south in Kuranda National Park to be precise, place where my countrymen built the *Skyrail* ride, over the rainforest near Kuranda."

"Countrymen?

"Russians, they used Kamov helicopters to place the large pylons into the rain forest in 1995. When they did that it created the opportunity to hide something particularly valuable."

"Why there?"

"The National Park is a protected area so no one is allowed in and secondly it's full of the world's deadliest snakes and spiders to say nothing of the crocodiles in the Meleleuca wetlands. There are no roads to the pylons so the only way through is by helicopter and that is monitored."

"Must be a very special secret."

"Oh it is my dear, the most special secret of all."

"It's a deal then," said Sandy raising her glass.

"A deal," smiled Sergei Rostov looking down at Fat Albert then turning to his mobile and sending a text.

Venice

Number 26 Rio Terra S. Leonardo is well off the main tourist thoroughfare. The gondoliers rarely pass and the inhabitants are not often seen in public spaces. From the outside, the houses are nondescript and attract little if any attention. Inside however many of them were opulent hideaways for the rich and very rich, craving one thing above all else, anonymity. Number twenty six was no different and indeed was the most secretive of all, where few casual passersby could ever recall seeing anyone. Inside was a veritable palace, resplendent with the latest designer furniture the rooms straight out of the pages of a fashion magazine. Only the best and most expensive products were good enough for the owner and she prided herself on being ahead of the latest fashion trends.

Lucrezia Calvi, a middle aged spinster whose own appearance was as immaculate as her furnishings revelled in her first name. It tended to attract people's attention through the similarity to that of the renaissance figure Lucrezia Borgia. Unlike her blond namesake, Lucrezia Calvi was tall, slim and dark with an air of regal dominance about her that demanded respect. She was extremely wealthy and, all things considered, led a contented life. Today was not a happy occasion as she ruminated on the loss of her recently deceased brother. Not because she had any affection for Giovanni; the opposite was true, but that he had failed by committing the cardinal sin of breaking the Calvi's golden rule. It had been drummed into them by their father to never lose their anonymity – that alone was their passport to success as it had been for their relatives going back to Cosimo Medici. Even the two hidden sleepers in La Gomera had kept their secret for over a decade. Giovanni had given in to temptation in his insane quest to find the *'Khan's Prophecy'*. Lucrezia had warned him to take care but he was above listening to a mere woman and now she would have to show them all who was the real Calvi. Just as Giovanni had for decades been the hidden power behind ZTW, she had been the hidden power behind him, but he never knew it. She had lived her entire life in Venice staying true to the Calvi family roots whilst Giovanni had made the mistake of living at Ascension Island, that accursed place. Her father had never intended it as anything other than a monument and certainly not a place to be so visible, but Giovanni had chosen to forget or ignore that.

She lifted the high-tech satellite communications device and spoke briefly to the man at the other end of the video link assuring Kenneth Macquarie, the leader of Clan Chatten, that he would not be implicated in the investigation into the origin of the rifle used in the Balmoral assassination. He would be a key part of her future plan and she needed to massage his ego; he was going to be useful to her in the long run. She replaced the handset deep in thought and went to feed her two cats, Genghis and Kublai; their names amusing her and giving events a sense of perspective.

Two years junior to Giovanni she had lived in her elder brother's shadow for most of her life but, unlike him, had preferred to remain incognito, known only amongst her tried and trusted friends in their homeland. She had vehemently opposed his moving Marco Polo's remains to Ascension Island and all that had followed but to no avail. It was an ill wind that brought no advantage however and now it was all hers, the so-called wife of Giovanni had waived all claims to his estate so she no longer posed any sort of obstacle. The company ZTW though, that would need a new name, the various hidden monies and, above all, the bones of Giovanni's network that required a strong leader to bring it to life. She would succeed where they had failed.

She smiled grimly to herself brushing back her long dark hair and looking at her reflection in the mirror beaming at what she saw. Despite her middle age she had few signs of old age and knew that her slim figure attracted attention whenever she chose to place herself in the public spotlight which wasn't often. She would take over the empire resurrecting all Giovanni's links and the Calvi's ultimate destiny would be fulfilled.

The difference was whereas Giovanni's scheming had been *subservient to history, she would create history* and in the process destroy those in her path without them even realising who it was. She walked to the window and looked down on the canal in the light rain. Venice would return to its days of global dominance, the days when the *Doge* of Venice as she now was officially titled, on the condition that it wasn't public knowledge, would again rule in secret as they had done in the times of Cosimo Medici and the glories of the Venetian Empire at the very forefront of the Renaissance.

Thank you for reading
Khan's Legacy
The final novel in the History Detective Trilogy

Watch this space for the
History Creator Trilogy

- coming soon

Historical Facts

Though liberties have been taken with historical characters and events, there are a number of facts worth highlighting to help complete enjoyment of the story.

New Zealand

Between 1410 and 1490 New Zealand South Island was devastated by fires and a tsunami. The island lies on a fault line so it could have been caused by a seismic event. There is also speculation that a comet hit Zheng's fleet some two days sailing south of Auckland. Eighty Chinese wrecks have been discovered in three principal locations, the Caitlin's on New Zealand's south coast, further north towards Moroak and north again around the Banks Peninsula. The comet impact is recorded by a number of geological events including the crater Mahaika approximately 20 kilometres wide and at least 123 metres deep on the New Zealand continental shelf. It is also interesting that the travels of Zheng He gave relevance to many claims that the original peoples of many nations came from those voyages. "The point is very simple that the indigenous people of New Zealand came from China. DNA evidence is irrefutable" *Gavin Menzies '1421'*

The Mongols

Ogetae, crowned following the death of Genghis Khan was unexpected. It threw into turmoil Tsubodai's plans to conquer Europe. In the meantime much of European royalty was sufficiently alarmed to act together in a bid to stop the Mongol hordes. Kublai himself assumed command and grew the empire to the largest ever land size of one nation including all of modern day China and Tibet. The actual birthplace of Genghis Khan remains a mystery but is largely viewed as being in the Burkham Khaldum region where rumour has it he wanted to be buried in a place no one would ever find. It is recorded that Marco Polo obtained gold tablets, *Piaza,* from Kublai Khan allowing him to travel unmolested around China and he did travel to Zanzibar, East Africa on his way home to Venice.

On December 29th 1911, the Khalkha people of Outer Mongolia declared their independence from the collapsing

Chinese Empire following the Zinhai revolution. The land is indeed blessed with abundant coal and precious minerals, amongst which is rhodium. The country is going through an unprecedented industrial revolution of the same scale as China and continues to look carefully at its Russian and Chinese neighbours, both of whom are investing heavily in the country.

Culloden

The battle took place as described and lasted just an hour. It remains a devastating battle from the Highlanders' perspective though more Scots fought on the English side than on the Highlanders, whose army included Frenchmen and Italians. The Clan Chatten or Macintosh did indeed suffer the heaviest and their last stand was around the place where the *'Well of Sighs'* now stands. To this day the field of the battle lies undisturbed apart from the lines of flags as described in the novel, and walking across its field remains a most eerie experience. There are over 1,000 graves of the clans and the visitor centre is exceptional with a four minute 360 degree film of the battle.

Seychelles

Ascension Island exists next to the resort described in the novel and is currently uninhabited. The treasure of Olivier Le Vasseur or *La Buse* as he was popularly known has never been found and consisted of chests of gold, sparkling diamonds, silks and pearls. There is still great speculation that the treasure trove is indeed located somewhere near the Bel Ombre region of Mahe Island as portrayed in the novel.

Australia

The Sky rail was built in 1995 using Russian Kamov helicopters to transport and fix the pre-assembled pylons into place, due to the protected status of the rain forests and the almost impenetrable terrain.

Venetian Republic

The Medici's were the prominent Signor family in Florence during the Renaissance in the Fifteenth Century. Their family produced four Popes but they were better known for their iron control of Florence. The Medici Bank gave the World the double entry bookkeeping system.

The Venetian empire grew on the back of trade, the merchants of the city were prepared to trade with anyone irrespective of religion, cultures etc. In addition, the Venetian shipbuilders were the most prominent in the world and furnished the crusaders with their entire fleet. The leader or *Doge* was the elected head of state and resided in the Doge's Palace, the Palazzo Ducale located on the present site of St Mark's Square. The Venetian Republic ended in 1797 when it was annexed by the rising power of Napoleon Bonaparte.

About the Author

David J Andrews is a leading writer of adventure thrillers. His novels are published on three continents. In South-East Asia, a major Chinese publisher and a significant distribution chain support his work. Currently the leader of a multinational organisation, he uses his insider knowledge of the corporate business world and his extensive travels overseas to ensure authenticity in his writing. Originating from Yorkshire, he is married and lives in rural Lincolnshire, England, where he pursues his passions for sailing and history.